PONZI
&
PICASSO

Rochelle Ohrstrom

SB
Seismic Behest Publishing

PONZI and PICASSO. Copyright © 2013 by Rochelle Ohrstrom. All rights are reserved. Printed in the United States of America. No part of this book may be used or reproduced in any manner whatsoever without written permission except in the case of brief quotations embodied in critical articles and reviews. For information contact www. Ponzi and Picasso.com
Library of Congress Cataloging-in Publication Data has been applied for.
ISBN 978-0-989155571

To Grant and Lysandra with love,

Without your inspiration and challenge,
this book would have remained in my imagination.

"Art washes away the dust of everyday life."
Pablo Picasso

Table of Contents

Prologue

A fter an hour and a half at the 2008 VIP preview for the Whitney Biennial, Henry Classico had seen enough cutting-edge art to take a pair of scissors and cut it from his memory. Having just greeted three hundred of his closest friends and viewed three floors of work by promising new artists in an exhibit loosely grouped by a narrative of "green and sustainable, his head spun from art-overload.

"Goodnight," he said to the guard at the double glass doors who tried to maintain some formation to the four-person-deep line that snaked from Madison Avenue east onto Seventy-Fifth Street. On the curb just outside the museum, Classico noticed another "green" installation that reiterated the indoor theme. Broken chairs, ripped cartons, plastic bottles, tin cans, and sheets of balled up bubble-wrap lay piled into a heap. It addressed the consumerist culture with a metaphor that he supposed referenced recycling. In the *Deep Deliberations Department* of high art, even garbage was transformed into significant topics of discussion.

He circled the sidewalk sculpture looking for the artist's name. "How clever to extend the work onto the street to consider its fugitive existence," he said to the guard who rolled his eyes. "It could be hauled away at any time," Classico tried to explain. Just then, a robust young man wired to a cell phone hurried by and flung his empty Coke bottle onto the assemblage. Before Classico realized there was no signature, a dog on a leash barked, sniffed at the pile and lifted his leg.

"Well, it could have been art," Classico said. "It posits the same premise as the installations inside the museum, but without the Whitney's branding, it will remain collectable only by the garbage trucks."

The fifty-two year old owner of Classico Gallery on Fifth Avenue and Seventy-Ninth Street attributed his reputation as a branding master and modernist connoisseur to his well-trained eye. Receiving his endorsement was the equivalent of moving from a Myrtle Beach summer rental to a Southampton Gin Lane manse via stealth bomber.

In 2007, art had become the fastest growing asset class. It was sexier than a stock certificate, more prestigious than a Ferrari, and more inspiring than gold bullion. Art collecting diversified a hedge-fund portfolio, and simply would not lose. The trick, however, was to identify the winners, and Henry Classico was the alchemist who turned canvas into gold.

PONZI
&
PICASSO

Chapter 1

Inflationary Multiverses

T he music ramped to a high volume, and Yale's Green Hall smelled of luscious fresh paint, sending Alouisha Jones's creative urges into high gear. The twenty-three year old had streaked her hair blue and lined her lashes florescent green to match her eyes. Her paint-splattered jeans, ripped and shredded at the knees, mapped the various experimental paths she had taken to complete her thesis. Whenever she walked or moved, every part of her five-foot eleven frame flowed like willows in the field.

Standing inside the closed glass doors, she watched the art dealers and collectors clamoring for a first-entry position into the gallery. She twirled and scrunched her spray-painted curls, while glancing at Dean Robert Storr for a signal to let them in. To keep her hands from shaking, she tucked them into her pockets and felt the last of her scholarship checks folded for safekeeping. She would try not to cash it too soon. "Stretch it out; make it last," she told herself.

"Almost ready," she said flashing her megawatt smile. Across the room, standing in front of his paintings, Jason Biggs caught the illumination and boomeranged it right back. Answering the siren's call, he went to her side, slid his hand in hers and locked tightly this pivotal moment that would transition them from students to professional artists. Alouisha's entire future depended on the next hour. She looked at Jason sideways through her lowered eyes. "All I need is a little luck for my work to interest one of the gallery owners; maybe they'd include me in a group show," she said. "Then I could afford to move to New York to live near you in the epicenter of the art world."

"Baby, they are going to love you and your work," he assured her with a hug and squeeze that swelled his well-defined arms.

Maestro Dean Storr turned down the music; the silence halted all movement.

"Everyone, to his place," he said, blasting the sound. Bob Marley's optimism bounced off the high ceilings.

The crowd gathered at the Yale School of Art, as Henry Classico's driver maneuvered the Bentley curbside to cut through the line of traffic. More than a hundred art dealers and collectors had endured the sluggardly parking-lot highway for the three-hour journey north from Manhattan on I-95 to discover the next, "latest-greatest," artists from the Master of Fine Arts class of 2008.

Yale was the country's preeminent art school, affectionately known as the "puppy mill for art stars." Not unlike those certain private nursery schools on New York's Upper East Side, the Yale School of Art shared the same whispered nickname, Feeder School, having launched many familiar names in art royalty such as Gregory Crewdson, Chuck Close, and Matthew Barney. Alumna Alouisha Jones was confident she had a good chance to become a branded artist. After all, wasn't selling art all about relationships, and with famous graduates feeling indebted to their alma mater, she felt certain one of them would help guide her to a mainstream gallery.

The June day was hot and Classico, along with his colleagues, a group that never waited for anything, stood outside the closed doors of Green Hall for the MFA exhibition to begin. Today marked the culmination of the student's two-year visual investigations. The invitation read: "Deconstructing Art Ideologies and Reconstructing Them into a New Visual Syntax." Although the idea intrigued Classico, he knew that art conjecture alone could not make a mediocre painting great. He glanced at his Breitling watch; at 5:05 p.m., they were already late. His collar felt tight, and he was beginning to sweat. A quick tug at the points of his vest straightened the fabric and his shoulders.

Each year Classico searched Yale for artistic talent invariably returning from his pilgrimage with a treasured canvas or two, although the hunt itself was half the fun. Irresistibly lured by freshly painted ideas, he could not stay away. It was as if his life had one single purpose—to discover a new visual vocabulary. Nothing satisfied him more than to feel a dormant part of his brain begin to percolate from an infusion of brilliance when he looked at a possible masterpiece. He remembered that moment of recognition when he first saw a Picasso painting, and a new universe for communicating cracked his world wide open; his skin prickled, his breath shortened. He was yanked from a three-dimensional world-view into awareness that all living things were sewn from one cosmic fabric attached to infinity. Ever since then, he was unrelenting in his quest for artists whose work triggered the same response. Finding them was rare; he had done it before—he could do it again.

Classico was deep inside his laser-focused thoughts when someone pushed up against him, jolting him back into real time.

"Oh excuse me," the woman said before she realized it was Classico.

"Darling, it is so good to see you," he said to the assistant from Gagosian Gallery as she edged closer to the door. Standing a head taller than she, his gaze descended to the activity at her cleavage. She was fiddling and twisting the miniature pendant that hung around her neck, the same one Picasso had made for his lover Dora Maar. Extricating his stare from her fleshy ravine, he kissed her just lightly on the corner of her mouth.

"Henry, how have you been?" she said raising her face to receive his breathy kiss. "I've heard this class is outstanding."

"We'll soon find out," he said.

Scanning the group for familiar faces, he took note of all the women's jewelry, which bore no precious stones, but instead was crafted from metals and ceramics and boasted signatures of famous artists. Six or seven collectors wore circus-figure brooches sculpted from wire by Alexander Calder. Gallery owner Mary Boone had a rare Salvador Dalí medallion fastened to her lapel that commemorated the Wagner opera, *Tristan and Isolde.* Sunglasses protected them all from the glare of the bling and the dazzling cerulean sky, the same color Georgia O'Keeffe had used in her painting *Music, Pink and Blue.*

Classico peered through the glass doors and watched as the students scurried about the gallery, attending to last-minute details: whiting out smudged walls, straightening pictures, and adjusting the lighting. Many had stayed up all night confronting the artist's eternal dilemma: when is a painting finished; which brushstroke should be the last? Any minute now, the invited guests enjoying their exclusive access would enter Green Hall and might just push a promising graduate onto the celebrity conveyor belt headed for art-world adoration.

"Here we go," Alouisha said, her feet keeping pace to the reggae rhythm and her rapidly beating heart. Bubbling up like simmering broth, she took a breath, puckered her lips and exhaled slowly. Time seemed to stop, but only seconds passed. Then she opened the door with gusto, and her smile poured onto the hopefuls like a radiant bath of sunlight.

A cool wind blew into the room along with a frenzied mass of collectors, dealers, curators, and art critics. Pushing her aside, they squeezed through the entrance, intent on identifying a new art form.

Classico strolled the gallery, navigating through the scores of onlookers. Some recognized him and stepped back, allowing him to pass. If he raised one bushy eyebrow, it could signal his imprimatur possibly shifting the direction of the New York art world for the coming season. The prices began at $4,000. Henry Classico straightened his bow tie and pasted a small red dot on the wall. Today was the art world's Black Friday.

Classico walked the scene strategically, not intending to miss any work or a potential new client. Along the way, he spotted someone with whom he wanted to cultivate a deeper friendship. Although Isadora Brioche had a serious job as hedge fund mogul Steve Cohen's assistant, she still enjoyed wielding her lithe, sexual power over men. When she flipped her hair and tossed her head to one side, she allowed a man's stare to linger, unimpeded by a return gaze. Dashed with an attitude of superiority, she qualified for the position of consummate gallerina.

Years ago, Classico sold Cohen a Lichtenstein that recently tripled in value when it resold at the fall auction. Cohen, no longer requiring a dealer's advice, now dealt directly with the museums and auction houses.

In 2004, Charles Saatchi, director of the White Cube Gallery in London, sold Cohen Damien Hirst's "Shark" for $12 million. It supposedly represented an investigation into the meaning of life and death. The art world thought it laughable until Cohen agreed to lend it to the Metropolitan Museum of Art for six years, during which time the museum's branding magic would triple the shark's value. Residing in a formaldehyde-filled fish tank, the ferocious-looking shark proved immensely popular with the busloads of high-school students who visited it each day—to deepen their understanding of contemporary art.

Making his way toward Isadora, Classico noticed her talking to a tall young woman whose effervescence could span the length of the Great Hall at the Met. Her paint-covered jeans and peculiar hair underscored her creative energy. He marveled at her delicate facial features, beautifully sculpted by genetic ancestry, and wondered where she was from. *She would be stunning if she wore some proper clothing,* he thought.

"Hello, Isadora. It's good to see you again," Classico said, leaning over to give the young, blonde beauty a faint kiss on the cheek.

"Henry, so nice to see you," she replied. "I'd like to introduce you to Alouisha Jones and these are her paintings. Don't you think they're fabulous?"

Classico's left eyebrow rose as he extended his hand to Alouisha; he then turned back to the paintings that demanded his attention. The landscapes burst in vivid palettes of color—clear as the daylight after a hurricane. Sensual female figures, resembling bas-relief sculptures, languished and undulated throughout the fertile terrain. Womb-like grassy foliage enveloped the nudes and offered both protection and nurturing. Organically and seamlessly, they commingled their primal, physical, and spiritual responses to the elements.

Alouisha held her breath and waited for him to comment. She could not read his expression. His blank face cordoned off his thoughts. He moved closer to the surface of the painting. Six inches separated his nose and the translucent halftones. With microscopic attention to detail, his gaze strolled slowly across the canvas, as he examined Alouisha's paint application and searched for intimacy. Then, he stepped back to view the entire painting from a wide-angle-lens perspective, gleaning a broader understanding of the work. Crossing his arms over his chest and widening his stance, he pondered the female figures that evoked sensual deities. They oscillated between the foreground and background, embracing the trees, the ocean, and clouds, as if woven into the landscape that transmuted them into great Mother Earth.

Delighted that Classico was taking so much time with her work, Alouisha could barely keep from jumping. Unable to contain her excitement for another second, she blurted out, "Do you like them, Mr. Classico?"

"They are compelling, indeed. This is what it must mean to be at one with nature," Classico said. He read the title: *Body Landscape*[1].

Body Landscape   oil on canvas 3'x4'

"What is your mission statement?" he asked.

"Well, I call this *Sentient Art*. Quantum physics describes parallel universes using equations. I am processing information from my five senses through a lens of sentient awareness to access the same dimensions. By letting go of cerebral boundaries, I can explore my feminine connection with nature. The paintings are a sensual, intuitive response to our multi-verse cosmology," she said. I can give you a copy of my dissertation. It will explain *Sentient Art* completely."

"Thank you, Alouisha. I'd like that."

Alouisha watched with rapt attention, not wanting to make a sound as Classico studied her work further. To give Classico a clear line of sight, she stood several feet away from the paintings and leaned against the

1.To view Alouisha's paintings in color, go to www.RochelleOhrstrom.com

wall. She barely breathed. *Please buy one—please buy one or two,* she desperately wanted to shout out, so she could afford to move to New York City. *I have worked so hard juggling random jobs and schoolwork to cover expenses, unlike the other students whose families have given them everything.* She bit her lower lip. *I deserve this,* she thought and stamped her foot.

Classico moved to the next canvas; an image of a young man and woman collided horizontally and embraced each other in a cloud-filled sky. Other voluptuous, partially visible figures appeared to be floating or flying as if they represented aspects of our divided selves. Two headless female statues in the garden referenced ancient Greek sculpture. The energy in her brushstrokes reminded Classico of the English artist William Turner. He pasted a little red dot next to:

The Ascent of Love with Two Woman that Lost their Heads
oil on canvas 28"x36"

2. To view Alouisha's paintings in color, go to www.RochelleOhrstrom.com

"Thank you, Mr. Classico; thank you so much. It is a discourse on astral flying," Alouisha explained.

"And this one?" he asked, referring to a three-by-four-foot painting depicting a full back view of a naked woman stepping into the ocean. Waves and trees passed through the cutouts in her body, and as her long hair blew in the ocean breeze, she ultimately merged with the sea and sky.

It is about releasing sadness, finding renewal, and becoming cleansed by connecting to natural sources," she said, eagerly spilling out her words.

Classico's chin jolted upward slightly, and his eyebrows followed. "I see," he said in his most earnest voice, nodding in agreement. He was sure it represented an orgasm.

"Alouisha, I need another red dot for: *Self-Portrait Past and Future.*[3]"

Self-Portrait Past and Future[3]   oil on canvas 26"x36"

3.To view Alouisha's paintings in color, go to www.RochelleOhrstrom.com

9

"Thank you, Mr. Classico; thank you so much," Alouisha said again. Unable to contain her joy, she ran across the room into Jason's arms. He picked her up and swung her around until they were both laughing.

Jason and Alouisha had been together for two years, since beginning the MFA program. They were inseparable as lovers and roommates. Jason was six-feet-four inches tall and Photoshop handsome. He made the earth and air crackle as he passed through it exuding a force field of testosterone. Standing on her toes barefoot, Alouisha could reach his lips. Classico chuckled at the enthusiasm they had for art and each other, as they lit up the room like a detonating chemistry experiment.

Meanwhile, Isadora scrutinized Classico's every move, and when he placed the red dots on the wall, she moved in closer as if she had a secret to share. He could feel her breath on his face, and she spoke in her softest, deepest, air-filled voice, like Marilyn Monroe singing happy birthday to President Kennedy.

"Henry, I love your choices; I suspect we will soon have a new Cindy Sherman on our hands. Alouisha is part of the new generation of feminist artists investigating woman's physical relationship with the environment, unimpeded by cultural objectification. Where as Cindy's *Film Series* photographs deconstructed feminine role-models imposed by society, Alouisha's paintings are . . . well, you might call them reconstructivist. You are simply brilliant to buy her work. You must help me choose one or two," she said, remembering that his early artist selections now sold into the high six figures.

He listened to Isadora, engrossed by the scent of her hair and perfume. Often when Classico bought art, the stimulation was more than intellectual. The afternoon sun streamed through the windows, highlighting her blond waves with the colors of firelights and embers. An occasional breeze wafted through the open doors toward him. The perfumed envoy engulfed his senses as a few tendrils of her hair brushed his lips. He wanted to be consumed by her. He wanted to step into her ocean.

"I think she is expressing a woman's sensuality from her point of view, rather than the more commonly objectified male perception of female sexuality," Isadora continued, speaking slowly, saturating every syllable with innuendo. Her clear-blue eyes, devoid of guile, softened and stayed close to his.

Clearing his throat, "Of course, you are right," he said, smiling as he leaned in closer to inhale her sweet essence.

"Her work shows promise, and it is not derivative, but rather completely original. It is as if she lives inside her own head, self-sufficient and undeterred by outside influences. Her painting technique is exceptional," he said.

"It's so rare these days," Isadora replied.

"She is still young, so we will have to wait to see if she can sustain her level of work. So many young artists quickly burn out in today's overheated art climate," Classico said.

"The constant pressure to reinvent themselves can be overwhelming," agreed Isadora.

"And their becoming branded too soon rarely helps. It can stunt creativity if everyone wants to own a trophy piece of the artist's most famous image," he said.

Sitting down on a nearby stool, he placed one hand under his chin and the other on his knee, and again reviewed the paintings. Suddenly, that familiar prickly feeling coursed through his body and tossed inside him like a fistful of jumping jacks. This feeling was his final analysis for deciphering great art. Unfortunately, his viscus never studied art history or earned a college degree, but since there were vast amounts of money involved, he always told the buyers what they wanted to hear: "My connoisseurship is derived from my excellent eye and exemplary skills." No collector would ever understand a decision based on a paroxysm of inspiration.

"Extraordinary," he said, returning from his reverie to Isadora. "And . . . ah . . . how is Mr. Cohen? You must be scouting for him today. Please send him my regards, and ask him to stop by the gallery. I have some extraordinary works from the Walter Annenberg estate, and I am selecting the private collections that can integrate them most effectively. I promised Walter I'd find them an exemplary home with a collector that has the highest standards of scholarship. As you know, a good portion of his collection has been donated to The Metropolitan Museum. His generosity was legendary; he understood that great art belonged to all people. You and Cohen should visit the gallery."

"I'd like that very much," she said.

"Tell him I have an important Picasso that I am sure he'd be interested in. It has quietly come on the market. Of course there are several foreign collectors interested, but as I would prefer to keep it in this country, I will offer it to him first," Classico said.

"I'll let him know. That is very thoughtful of you. I am sure he will be grateful," Isadora Brioche said.

"Well, this has been an outstanding show. I'm glad I came. Can I offer you a lift somewhere, and perhaps we can stop for dinner? My driver is waiting."

He wanted to give her a ride back to the city to find out what Steve Cohen was buying. Then, he would make a few phone calls and find out what was coming to market, who was getting divorced, and who needed to raise capital. The three Ds, death, divorce, and disaster, kept art sales plentiful, supplying the secondary markets with inventory. Afterward, he had only to convince Cohen the painting represented the turning point in the artist's career, and therefore essential to his collection—that would be the easy part.

"That is so kind of you to offer, but Mr. Cohen is expecting me in Greenwich tonight."

"Another time then. I'll walk you to your car," Classico said, taking her arm. Stopping for a moment, he gazed with incredulity when he saw a work positioned on the floor. "Is this a sculpture or an installation? It must be a sculpture," he said.

"Perhaps it is both," Isadora said laughing.

A four-foot-wide and two-foot-high steel rectangle was positioned on the floor. Hovering above it horizontally and suspended by an imperceptible object or force, was a graphite cylinder that measured four-feet long and twelve inches around. It floated in space ten inches above the base in perfect alignment. Classico ran his hand through the empty length of space between the two objects . . . nothing connected them.

"Extraordinary," he said.

Isadora read the label on the nearby wall:

The Human Detritus Of Infinite Broken Hearts Compressed Into Inflationary Multiverses.

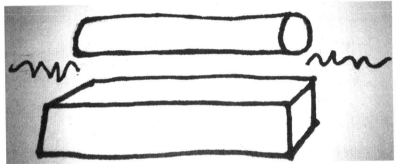

Medium: Neodymium Magnet, Graphite and Wave Particles. Edition 5

Chapter 2

The Artemisian Huntress

"Jason, I'll be down in a minute," she said leaning through the open window that carried an air-blast of fresh-cut lawn. The horn honked again. Jason had the top down and the trunk of the Audi opened. Alouisha beamed like a lighthouse reaching out to sea.

She packed up the last of her art supplies from her student-housing unit, and zippered her plaid suitcase with the corner worn so thin that her purple T-shirt sprouted through the few remaining threads. She took one last glance around the room to embed the memories of all the challenges she had faced during her six years at Yale. Except for the dusty canvas outlines on the walls, which hinted like wispy ghosts of a more colorful time, and the bits and pieces of tape stuck to the crackled walls where her sketches had hung, there was nothing left of her former home.

She bounced the last two bags down the stairs in tandem with her exuberance for her move to New York. The old stone house, covered in ivy, shook and vibrated from her zestful departure.

"Hi, Sweetheart. Got everything?" he asked, taking the luggage from her and flinging it into the back as if it weighed nothing.

"Everything except the nails on the wall," she said.

"Well, let's do it," he said, leaning in for a kiss and revving the engine...

That was three months ago.

"I'm finished," Alouisha said emphatically, putting down her brush and smiling, pleased with her new work. Jason walked to the corner of his loft where Alouisha had set up her easel, and put his arm around her waist. Without speaking, they surveyed the final painted event.

"It's great, isn't it?" she said breaking the silence.

Jason nodded, "It's amazing, your best, yet. What's the title?"

The Floating Heart[4]   oil on canvas 26"x36"

4. To view Alouisha's paintings in color, go to www.RochelleOhrstrom.com

"The Floating Heart, embracing all that is beautiful in life. This is the way you make me feel," she said, wrapping her arms around his waist. "Mr. Classico would love this painting. I don't know why he never returns my calls. I'm going to try one last time."

"Hello, this is Alouisha Jones. May I please speak to Mr. Classico?"

"I'm afraid Mr. Classico is traveling abroad," said Hans with a sharp English accent. "I will tell him you called, and yes I still have your number."

Alouisha slammed the phone and crossed her arms over her chest. "He's never going to call me back. It's been three months since our exhibition, and every time I have tried to contact him, I am told the same thing. Jason, maybe I should just visit the gallery. What do you think? Surely, he wouldn't buy three of my painting to lock them away in a closet. He seemed so enthusiastic," she said.

"Yeah, why don't you visit the guy, refresh his memory," Jason said.

The next day, Alouisha dressed in her finest, took the subway uptown to Classico Gallery. Conjuring up the bravado of an Artemisian Huntress, she reminded herself that this was no time to be timid. The remaining cash from the sale of her paintings was close to zero, and she needed to get her own place. She took a deep breath, and climbed the limestone steps of the historic house. By invoking her rightful destiny, her confidence swelled.

Hans opened the door and, much to her surprise, Mr. Classico was in the entrance foyer, just about to leave when he saw Alouisha. His face lit up, dissolving his serious demeanor. Her profound beauty could make any man smile.

"Alouisha, how have you been?" he asked taking her hand. "I was meaning to call you; it's just that I have been so busy. Please forgive me."

"I understand," she said, and without hesitating, "Mr. Classico, I am preparing for my exhibition, and I hope it will be with the best gallery in New York, Classico Gallery." Her eyes fixed on his with a rare clarity of strength and purpose. Her innocence blended perfectly with her beauty; each quality enhanced the other.

"As you know, I graduated summa cum laude, and I am very hardworking. I will never disappoint you. I'll always be loyal, and you won't have to worry that I will disappear with the next-best offer after you have invested your time and resources in me. You can count on me. When can I expect my work to be shown?" she asked, her eyes rounding, softening, more deeply into Classico's. The intensity of her ingenuous commitment rippled with boldness, and he found her determination irresistible. He could feel the back of his neck prickle.

"Alouisha, I would love to give you a show, but now is not the right moment. I have several obligations that I must take care of first. But perhaps we can plan something for the future. In the meantime, you can create a new body of work and I can mentor you as you proceed. Your work is quite remarkable, and I am anxious to see what you will do next."

"But Sir, I...I..." she stammered, turning pale as the balance in her checkbook loomed before her.

"What is it Alouisha," he asked, noticing her face droop with sadness.

"I'll ... I'll need some income."

"Well, perhaps I can give you a job as my assistant-receptionist."

Immediately, the incandescence in her turquoise eyes was expunged, turning them dark blue. She felt the scorch of her cheeks, as the humiliation welled up inside her. Instead of offering her a show, he offered her—a Yale MFA graduate—a position as a secretary! If he had handed her a mop, it would have had the same effect as his job offer—reinforcing her family's history of constant financial struggles that she had tried so hard to overcome.

"Alouisha, don't look so grim," he said lifting her chin, searching her eyes for the light that defined her happiness. Working in a top New York gallery is tantamount to a condensed submersion course for a PhD in art marketing. You have to be patient. You're time will come."

Her thick lashes fluttered, and with a lowered gaze, she remained silent.

"Well, you can think about my offer. Now, I must take care of some important matters," he said, turning to leave. "It was good to see you Alouisha, and thank you for your visit."

Realizing her opportunity was about to close, "Mr. Classico," she called out. He turned and her eyes rose and tethered to his once again. "Okay, I'll take the job," she said.

Frankly, Classico needed a gorgeous, ivy-league educated, sentry-receptionist to hold the front lines of Classico Gallery. He hired her that day. "Wonderful, Alouisha. You won't regret it," he said.

"You're going to do what?" Jason said, helping her off with her coat when she returned to the loft.

"It won't be for long. Mr. Classico will get my work out there. He said he would mentor me." She glanced at his face; he had that about-to-be-angry look.

"Ali, you don't have to be anyone's secretary. You have a masters degree from an Ivy League University and you have a place to live ... here ... with me."

"But, I have to get my own place. I am perfectly capable of taking care of myself. I can't always be dependent on you. We're twenty-four years old, too young to make a 'forever' decision," she argued.

"Do we have to discuss this again?" he asked. "I thought it was decided that you'd stay here."

"I have got to try it on my own," she said; her fierce pride would not be dissuaded.

"How can you do that to us?" he asked, throwing her coat with a yank onto the chair. Have it your way, but you're making a big career mistake," he said storming away. He bristled from her stubbornness.

Chapter 3

Finding the "True-New" Art Form at Auction

Classico scribbled coded notes in the Conway's auction catalog, while anxiously waiting for the Fall 2008 contemporary evening sale to begin. Flipping through the pages, he noticed with incredulity seventy-five Chinese artists' work with estimates above $1 million. Last year the branding frenzy was scalding hot. A painting by Cai Guo Qiang broke all records and sold for $8.5 million, followed by XU Beihong at $8 million, and Chen Chengbo at $5.5 million. In 2006, the total sales of Chinese contemporary art hovered just below $20 million, but five years ago, he could have bought them for a few hundred thousand dollars apiece, which is just what he did with similar works.

"The sale will be starting any minute now," Classico said to his new assistant Alouisha Jones, who sat next to him eagerly taking it all in. She tugged at her pencil skirt and squirmed, pulling it further down to her knees, too excited to sit still at her first auction. Everything in the room seemed to crackle and spark as if all the people, art, lights, and conversations were combustible. Alouisha had wanted to work on her own paintings tonight, but she could not pass up Mr. Classico's invitation to experience the sale first hand. Her work would have to wait while she immersed herself in this exclusive event, the highlight of the fall art season.

"I hope you get the paintings you want, Sir," she said.

Classico patted her hands that were crossed in her lap with fatherly affection, or so he thought. She pulled her hand away, not too quickly as to acknowledge inappropriateness, but to flick the hair that was sticking to her neck in the hot room. Her face flushed; she turned away so he would not notice.

"Yes, let's hope so," he said, noticing her reserve and exquisite profile. He smiled, thinking how fortunate to have someone so smart and talented working for him.

Although Alouisha's job deviated completely from her plan, taking precious time away from her work, it was not long before the prestige began to assuage any misgivings, and tonight was a jolt of spectacular.

Classico usually sat upstairs behind a one-way glass in a private viewing room reserved for important consignors. Tonight, he preferred to sit in the last row of the auction house where he could exit quickly without engaging in conversation with a third of the attendees, who acted as if they knew him.

His thoughts drifted to the large profits he would receive from having tonight's winning bids. Never were his eyes more vividly blue, dancing and darting from page to people. His heart leapt along with three hundred other potential bidders scrambling to find their seats. Tonight, the overheated art market, infrared with optimism, eagerly anticipated that a Chinese contemporary painting would reach the $8 million benchmark.

Maybe it will be this sale, Classico heard the murmured number on everyone's lips. Low, intoned conversations ratcheted up the excitement, buzzing in a continuous drum roll as the audience speculated on the market predictions and the secret entreaties that determined a lot's outcome. He could feel the air being siphoned from the room as if he were stuffed into a vacuum-sealed container. He straightened the bookmarks in his catalog, and for the last time, reviewed the paintings he intended to buy. Bending down to place the catalog under his chair, he clasped the coolness of the metal tubing, then rested his hands on the textured fabric of the million-dollar cushion he sat upon—the minimum price of a previous purchase needed for seated admission.

He glanced around the room; his bushy eyebrows rose briefly. In the audience, many of the registered art aficionados, dealers, and collectors brandished wooden paddles, while others tuned in by live Internet feed. An unusually attractive, well-heeled army of employees manned the telephones ready to take bids from all parts of the world. They lined the great room on two sides and sat army-straight on elevated stages to emphasize the serious tone of the evening. These solemn harbingers that appeared theatrically trained portended the vast amount of cash that would be spent in the next two hours. The overhead spotlights dramatically highlighted their earnest expressions; staunch and austere, they were ready to performance in the grand money theater.

"Those are Grigory Baronovich's men," Classico said, his eyes flitting in the direction of the bulked up bodyguards standing on the side near the front of the room. "He must be in the house. You've heard of him, the art-loving Russian oligarch? His former spouse Olesya is a performance artist, and before they divorced, she left him with a new hobby—collecting art and donating large sums to museums. Are you familiar with her work?" he asked.

"Yes, we studied her at Yale. I think she is brilliant to investigate relationships between the performance artist and the audience," Alouisha said, tapping her foot on the leg of the chair. "Ultimately, the art was about the audience's reaction to psychologically disturbing, and often violent work."

He slipped his index finger inside of his stiff collar and tugged for air space.

"It's so warm in here. Well, one 'art-coincidence' later," he continued, "The Museum of Contemporary Art has scheduled a retrospective of Olesya's multimedia work in 2010. It's a litany on Serbian suffering and will take up several floors of the museum. I understand that live nude models parody the Roman statues by flanking the entrance. In previous installations, when visitors passed between the naked performers, they unavoidably rubbed up against them. Most of the time, it was unintentional." He glanced at Alouisha's face, his eyes lowered to her breasts and further still, to her legs. "But," he said catching himself, "it garnered a huge amount of press."

"People will do anything for art, stretch any boundary," she said.

"Indeed they will, especially when so much money is involved. Before they married," Classico continued, "Baronovich collected sports cars and soccer teams. Now he has a staggering net worth of $11.2 billion, and I, my dear, am going to curate a world-renowned collection for the oligarch's many palatial estates," he said, conjuring up his optimistic intention.

Alouisha noticed his chest puff up.

"Oh, Mr. Classico, that is so great," she said, her eyes opened wide in amazement. "You certainly deserve it. I hope I can help."

Classico's talent for identifying and curating collections of modern, postwar, and contemporary masterpieces for his gallery, his private-equity fund Apogee Art, and for individual clients kept his reputation circumnavigating the globe. He would continue his zealous art quests and had only to persuade Baronovich on the merits of the Cai Guo Qiang painting that he planned to buy tonight.

"If I buy the Cai Guo Qiang right, not over the high estimate, I can make a sizable commission," he explained to Alouisha. *And that would give me enough cash to pay the balance on the Richard Prince nurse painting that I recently bought for the Apogee Art Fund,* he thought. You see, my dear, buying art and running a gallery requires much shuffling and juggling of both paper and cash." Then, *I'll invent another excuse to delay payment to the Hollywood celebrity who gave me his Picasso on consignment.* Not wanting to part with the masterpiece, Classico had told Hollywood that the painting was traveling abroad in museum exhibitions to augment its provenance and increase its value prior to its sale. Regretfully, he had to sell the Picasso to pay down the endless pile of bills accumulating on his desk. Those however, did not include the profits due to investors in the Apogee Art Fund from previous sales, so he accepted an offer from the Russian oligarch, Grigory Baronovich. There simply was not enough cash to go around, and Baronovich seemed to be the only one with any funds at his disposal. His pen began tapping Morse code on his jouncing knee. His gaze rose upward for inspiration and fell quickly down for a reality check.

Alouisha was happily reading the descriptions of the upcoming lots and taking inventory of the art crowd's rogue fashions, when Classico bent down to retrieve the catalog he had placed under his seat. On his upward thrust, his arm graced Alouisha's bare leg.

"Oh excuse me," he said.

Without thinking, she ran her hand over her leg where he had touched it. He flipped the pages of the catalog like a fan, and a slight breeze reached her hot face.

"Look at this exquisitely nuanced Cai Guo Qiang," he said, leaning a bit toward her, angling the page for her to have a better view.

"He really is the explosive new artist," she said laughing, knowing his medium was gunpowder.

Classico smiled, and like the painting, he too was about to explode. He could feel his adrenalin bubbling up inside his arteries and the moisture collecting around his temples. The great outpouring of cash would start any second now; the spigot would be opened wide gushing limitless liquid resources.

Suddenly, the audience's shrill palaver halted, and from behind a crack in the black velvet curtain, the auctioneer appeared. He walked across the stage mightily empowered, weighted with the confidence of a man about to generate $200 million in two hours. He took his place on the podium behind the lectern. The abrupt silence was palpable, creating vibrating wave particles like the densely filled pause after a symphonic overture. Alouisha felt it too, and nervously fumbled in her purse for a piece of gum, the sound of foil amplified like a jet during takeoff. Sabrina DeMande, sitting in the next row, shot her a searing look of disapproval. Classico pretended not to have noticed.

The silence blanketed all movement in the room except for the spotters who walked the floor like human motion detectors, scrutinizing all activity: every flick, every spin, every tap, every twirl, every wave of every raised paddle, scrupulously recording the bids. Styles of the bidders were as varied as the countries they came from, but the common denominator for exchanging large sums was discretion, prompting many clandestine moments in the business of art. The auctioneers and the spotters were well acquainted with Classico's cryptic signage that changed from paddle to eyebrow. Each time he twirled his thick, bushy eyebrows the hammer fell, sending a message to advance the bidding to the next increment. When he stopped, his index finger rested on his chin, giving the impression that he was deep in thought.

The overflow crowd, including the press, stood five deep behind the velvet ropes along the back and side walls. The hot room was packed to capacity. Alouisha felt claustrophobic and yearned for the cool Caribbean breezes of her childhood in Jamaica. While picking the lint off her black pencil skirt, she read the estimates, provenances, and descriptions of the works in the catalog: "'Property of a Lady—extraordinary diversity of aesthetics—the artist had poignancy and aplomb—derivative from celestial phenomena.' Oh here is a good one," she told Classico. "'Fluidity of reference that implies a global and chronological breadth.' Who believes this stuff? At Yale, we wrote valid interpretations based on historical art syntax. This is cotton-candy art fluff," she whispered closing the catalog with a thump.

"You'll get used to it. They'll say anything to sell art," Classico said smiling.

She watched Classico closely, trying to glean his level of satisfaction with each closing bid. Sometimes his head jolted slightly, sometimes his lips tightened and once or twice they curled inward. Meticulously, he recorded each hammer price, gathering data to predict the future strength of the market. For an older man, she thought he was attractive in his navy blue bespoke suit, but his posture was his most impressive feature—strong and straight as if he were an immutable force.

With each passing second, Classico watched the electronic billboard recalculate each bid into six global currencies. It clattered in rusty metallic grunts, faster than his racing mind. The unstoppable eruption of available cash, displayed by the flipping numbers and decimals, was mind numbing: $100,000 increments, then $200,000; near the end, the bids came in $1 million raises. The overhead lights burned and heated the room to an uncomfortable temperature. Everyone held his breath; the gasps came short and fast.

"Where does all this cash come from?" Alouisha could not fathom the speeding millions. Yesterday she ate box-pasta without sauce for dinner, preferring to spend the little she had on an expensive tube of vermilion paint.

"Mostly oil revenues from the Gulf for their new museums, and the collectors from the ex-Soviet Republics and China spending their newly acquired fortunes. What is a country or a culture without art?" he said.

"Oh, here is the next lot. Let's see if the Chinese contemporary market will hold its value, or is it a bubble about to burst like the equity markets? If only I could foretell the future, and answer the nagging question on the minds of all the art collectors, dealers, and auction specialists who have traveled here from every art-loving country on the planet." *If I gamble correctly, I could get through this financial rough patch, and with my eye for excellence, my profit margins would again surge,* he assured himself.

"I am sure you can, Sir," Alouisha said, having full faith in her employer's judgement.

Classico's credit line with Conway's was currently in arrears. To preserve it, he would have to bid carefully and not be caught up in the maelstrom. For the first time in all the years he conducted business with Conway's, they had limited his financing simply because he had been late with two payments and had another one outstanding. *I cannot believe their impudence,* he thought.

Rivulets of perspiration formed on Classico's forehead as he raised his paddle, yet again, to do battle with the telephone soldiers against the wall. Bidding doubled the high estimate in the glossy four-color catalog. The timbre of the auctioneer's voice took on an urgent plea; the numbers rapidly trilled off his tongue, like a yodeler on a roller coaster. The hammer fell, the bidding stopped, and the telephone soldier's victory was announced. This was the first time a Chinese painting passed the $8 million benchmark, and a new icon was inducted into the Artists' Hall of Fame. The audience applauded wildly, cheering and shouting—thrilled to be a part of a great moment in the history of art.

"Status and prestige are always for sale," Classico whispered to Alouisha. "Okay, five more lots until the Cai Guo Qiang. I love that he draws on canvas using gunpowder. After he ignites it, the line of exploded residue is so beautiful, so ethereal," he said, missing a breath. "The wispy halftones, escape, thrust, and coalesce in smudged shadow patterns, invoking the closest moment to creation and extinction," his eyes glinted. Alouisha listened enrapt by her employer's extraterrestrial experience, her arms comfortably folded on her chest. She did not want to miss one detail of this evening's sale. Smiling contentedly, she reflected on her good fortune to be working for one of the most esteemed gallerists in the world, who was also a kind, elegant man. So far, her plan was on track. One day soon, he would give her a show, and she would wait.

The lots were coming faster now. Each time a work passed its high estimate, the boisterous audience roared. The excitement, the heat and the overhead lights had Alouisha's head spinning, and she began to ascend into her magical dream state. Her shoulders slumped slightly in the chair; the auctioneer's voice disappeared into a cloudy mist. *And now ladies and gentleman, we are offering an original Alouisha Jones . . ., he said. Two white-gloved art handlers carried the painting on stage. The gavel fell, and a bidding war began. Competing buyers telephoned from all over the world. The increments increased ten-thousand dollars every second. The currency calculators flew out of control. Bids came in faster and faster—everyone wanted an Alouisha Jones painting.* Suddenly, her daydream was shattered as the swell of the raucous audience jolted her back to real time. It had taken less than two minutes for the Cai Guo Qiang to sell for double its high estimate—and the winning bid was not Classico's.

"Oh no," he gasped as his face turned white. *How will I make the mortgage this month, the final payment to Conway's for the Richard Prince, and still manage to have them reinstate my credit line?*

"Oh Mr. Classico are you okay?" Alouisha asked upon seeing her employer's face lose all color.

"Yes, I'm okay . . . just disappointed to have lost that painting."

"I am sorry, Sir. It must have meant a lot to you."

"Yes, it did." *Luckily, this isn't eighteenth-century England with a debtor's prison. I'm just temporarily short this month,* he reminded himself. "All the good intentions one may have, at times, can mean very little in the final equation," Classico said wistfully. " You see Alouisha, art investment is like playing a Stradivarius violin, incomparably rewarding and breathtakingly beautiful—as long as one has the cash."

Alouisha thought his sensitivity and gentleness remarkable for such a high-powered man. "But Sir, you were buying art to bring beauty into a world filled with wars, greed, and cruelty."

"My dear, how young you are." He turned, his gaze fixed onto hers. He lingered; he wanted to siphon her innocence and find renewal—find something pure in life from which he could remember—remember what it was like before—before he had all this: the reputation, which he had to uphold, the problems that accompanied every success, the unrelenting cash outlay for gallery expenses, and the countless social obligations. For a moment, he yearned for the simplicity of his childhood, walking home from school through the endless fields of tall grasses and wildflowers in Beatrice, Nebraska. Carrying a stick, he would create his own field music using wallops and whooshes in the tall withies and wheat grasses. The bees buzzed along with the wind composing their own gusty song, and the underfoot crunch, popping like bubble wrap, satisfied his deep-rooted angst—expelling and releasing. The the air was so delicious and crisp that he could not keep from smiling.

"Well, let's collect our things and go home. It has been a long day."

"Is there anything else I can do to help?"Alouisha asked, silently pledging her undying loyalty to her esteemed employer.

"Tomorrow we'll go through the invoices and look for possible discrepancies that can be billed as late fees," he said, standing up as the catalog fell to the floor.

"The catalogs are rather light for this time of year," he said, picking it up.

"You've just torn your coat, Sir."

"Hopefully, Alouisha, that will be easy to repair."

They walked to the front exit. "May I get you a taxi, Sir?" the white-gloved, doorman inquired, taking a deep breath and opening the massive glass and steel door.

"No, thank you. I think we'll walk in the fresh air. Slow down young lady, we are not racing at Ascot."

"Oh sorry," she said as she tried to keep in mind her employer's somber state of mind, although she felt like skipping.

It was 8:30 p.m. when Classico and Alouisha walked west on Seventy-second Street—she toward the subway and he toward Fifth Avenue, each absorbed in his own thoughts. The cool night lifted Classico's spirit, a welcome reprieve from the stuffy rooms filled with crackling egos that needed attention. He raised his coat collar and buried his chin in the fold. With his head bent downward, he searched the mica infused street for answers. She looked upward expecting to see a star, but too much artificial light made that impossible.

Traffic slammed the manhole covers, and jackhammers pulverized the concrete sidewalks. They did not bother Classico. Nor did the pungent assault of street-gyros, steaming from food carts rattle his resolve. He was, however, feeling increasingly overwhelmed by art, debt, colors, and crowds.

Chapter 4

Meeting the Neighbor

Alouisha had spent a long day at the gallery drowning in a sea of paperwork. She climbed the four-flight walk up to her studio apartment on Eleventh Avenue and Forty-ninth Street, impatient to return to her own paintings. The developers had gentrified several blocks in the former area known as Hell's Kitchen and had renamed it Clinton. Her building, however, not having participated in the neighborhood facelift, still resembled Hell and had no kitchen. She used the bottom of her coat to push open the front door to avoid touching the knob. A veritable human petri dish, it carried decades of accumulated bacteria left by generations of resident drug dealers. While heading upstairs, she held her breath to escape the fetor of uncollected garbage, pungent with week-old rotting food. A smoky marijuana haze permeated the hallways like a sickly sweet air freshener, worsening the mix.

Having taken this uphill route several times a day since she began working for Classico six months ago, the shape and tone of her legs rivaled the Aphrodite marble sculpture in the New Greek and Roman wing of the Metropolitan Museum. Her college housing felt like a five-star resort when compared to this apartment building. The maintenance crew at school scrubbed twice a day to override the hygienic malaise, a result of that politically correct invention of the late twentieth century—coed dormitories. The boys' enthusiasm for wet-towel-snapping games and their penchant for eating junk food 24-7 kept the hallways decorated with puddles and wrappers.

Inserting the key, Alouisha sighed as the door to the apartment screeched open. Her heart pounded from the climb, and from the dread of seeing one of her scary-looking, black-leathered S&M neighbors or from running into one of the transgender varieties that frequently appeared in the shadows of the stairwell. Tonight, she needed a decent night's sleep to deal with Classico's increasing emotional demands and her escalating workload. She hoped her upstairs neighbor was not having visitors tonight and entertaining as usual by dragging chains across his floor.

At first, Alouisha had not recognized the leaden, grumbling, basso continuo on the ceiling above her. *Maybe he had a bad dream and was moving his bed in the middle of the night to experience a new feng shui perspective,* she had optimistically rationalized. But one day, Alouisha and her neighbor's paths would cross on the nineteenth-century carved mahogany stairwell.

At the top of the fourth floor landing, she stopped to catch her breath, and gazed up at the stained-glass vaulted ceiling. Its former beauty, partially obscured by one hundred and twenty years of dust and neglect, was still redolent of splendor. The late afternoon sunlight filtered through the aged relic, diffusing warm, glowing hues onto shafts of dust mites. The colors scattered and swirled, spilling kaleidoscope flickers like exploding shrapnel everywhere. Entranced by the colorful motion of changing shadows and light, she barely heard the footsteps approach. Unexpectedly, the nuggets of rainbows splattered onto the neighbor when he reached the fourth floor.

At first glance, the spectral-like figure appeared harmless, lit from behind in a cloudy haze. Alouisha noticed silver glints of popping sparks refracting off his clothes. As he moved past her on the stairwell, she stepped back. There was a burnt, musty smell about him mixed with kerosine. Then she saw them . . . the chains. Instantly, in a synecdochic flash of perfect wisdom, she understood: the smaller part represented a larger more significant whole. The short pieces of chains, maybe fifteen or more, each measuring eight to twelve inches long, dipped and dripped like the maple syrup calligraphy she carefully affixed to her childhood silver-dollar pancakes. At night she could hear the room full of clattering, scraping metal. Her neighbor's shining adhesions fastened with nail heads to various parts of his black leather clothing, hinted at a secret midnight netherworld. Was she living in a mythological Hades? Would he kidnap her like Persephone? Alouisha did not want to wait for an answer. She tucked her head down, and wished she could vaporize that second. She froze instead.

Because their schedules were so different, she had never met the neighbor until now. Looking as if he had just emerged from the underworld, he was an androgynous, skinny, gray-skinned Caucasian. His shaved head was burnished to a high-gloss and shined like the surface of a newly painted car, doubling as a billboard for snake tattoos and metallic piercings. Alouisha gasped, choking uncontrollably on a porridge of dust and bile. Her cover of nonchalance was yanked away. The neighbor ignored her and walked past with a cursory glance.

She managed a muffled "hello," then her gaze fell to the floor. If she looked into the eyes of Chain Man Perpetrator, he would have seen her disapproval, because inadvertently she would be acknowledging his chained delinquencies. She would be unable to hide it. *I am a painter, not an actor.* She would not wait for retribution.

Alouisha slid the heavy bolt across the door. Safely inside her apartment, she dropped her handbag on the floor and lobbed her coat on the hook. Without looking around, she felt the vitality of her paintings charging the space and recharging her focus. Stacked on the floor and hung on the walls, every inch of free space in the twenty-by-twenty foot room with eleven-foot ceilings housed her work in the makeshift gallery-warehouse. The non-residential space, zoned for commercial use only, had been listed under "miscellaneous spaces" in the real estate section of the *New York Times*. Alouisha knew she should not be living there, but it was all that she could afford, and the original pink marble fireplace gave it a dash of history that conjured up a more elegant time.

Closing her eyes for a moment, she ingested the familiar, soothing energy of the paintings and discarded her outdoor layer of emotional protection, which fortified her feelings during the workday. She flipped on her stereo to dim the loud truck traffic. The Stones were singing: "Paint It Black." She danced, jiggled, jumped, and spun around, shaking out the day.

Exhausted, Alouisha flopped in rag-doll mode onto the waiting respite of her pullout bed, which had not been closed up today to resemble a sofa. Fidgeting among the rumpled sheets and covers, she searched for a spot without a protruding coil and grabbed the remote. On every channel, pundits either predicted future economic trends or recounted new financial disasters. Her stomach began to growl, reminding her of more relevant concerns. "Let's see." She got up and opened the two-foot-high portable refrigerator squirreled under a small table beside her easel. Inside, the edges of half of a ham and Swiss cheese sandwich curled upward and an open bottle of coke fizzed flat. She could have cooked eggs on the hot plate and boiled water for tea, but it lacked appeal. She did the math instead. *It's only Monday and I am not paid until Friday, and the rent is due on Wednesday. I should be able to make it if I am careful.*

Rooting around the bottom of her purse, she found a few crumpled bills and some change, but not enough to cover dinner out. Most of her slim paycheck went directly into her bank account to cover the rent. Unwilling to admit defeat, she searched the pockets of her clothing for fugitive loose change. "No, not tonight, I won't be having takeout."

After changing into her colorful speckled jeans, she raced down the four flights of stairs onto the street. "All clear." The light changed and she ran across Eleventh Avenue and entered O'Reilly's Bar and Grill, where she found an empty bar stool in the dimly lit room. Sometimes the bartender gave her a free glass of wine, other times she paid him $4.00, the happy-hour price that included the buffet.

"Hi Nick," she said to the young Irish bartender.

"How ya doing today?" he asked.

"Okay, I guess. Is there anything good for dinner?"

"The usual," he replied, "Hurry while it's hot." She knew if she waited too long the grease would congeal into a soggy morass.

She left her jacket on the bar stool to establish her territorial rights while she investigated the contents of the round-hooded, metal food warmers. Using the metal tongs, she placed six fried chicken wings, two meatballs soaked in cornstarch-thickened gravy, and some fried potato puffy things on a paper plate. The greasy overflow debouched onto the plate, forming lyrically abstracted shapes like Joan Mitchell's gesture paintings. Alouisha smiled from the steamy smells and oleaginous graphics. Both her imagination and appetite were stimulated.

She surveyed the usual cast of characters, hanging around the bar, drinking their happy hour whiskey shots. They were society's leftovers: unemployed laborers, useless men that no one wanted, or alcoholics killing their pain. Filled with sadness, they wore different degrees of unshaven faces in an attempt to cover their failures. She sat on the bar stool and began her dinner and wishing to be invisible, she kept her eyes on her plate.

"Not too bad for $4.00," the old gray Dick sitting next to her said. "So whads a bootifool young goyle like yaself doin hair?"

"I'm getting something to eat before I go back to my painting."

"Oh so yaw a painta, ardist? Ride?"

"Yes, I suppose you can call me that, although I haven't had a show since I graduated school. But that will change soon, everything will change soon. This is only temporary."

"Dat's whad I yoosed ta say. Good luck ta ya kid," he said, downing another shot of cheap whiskey and stumbling toward the food.

Alouisha, picked up the chicken wing and remembered the conversation she and Jason had when she told him she had found her own studio.

"Mr. Classico assured me that he would introduce me to the best gallery to launch my work. And I don't mind taking a low paying job for a while, if I can make the right contacts," she had said. "And, I need to be independent. I have got to do it on my own terms."

"Ali, you need to stay focused on your own work, and not give your precious time away to some pompous gallery owner by answering his phone all day."

" I know my paintings are good—no, they are great! I just need to connect with a gallery that gets my work and wants to represent me," she said.

"So does this mean that you're moving out?"

"It's just for a while," she said trying to put her arms around his neck to console him.

He grabbed her wrists and yanked them from his neck.

Finishing her meal, she wiped the greasy sauce from her hands and face, drank the last sip of house wine, and put on her jacket to leave. She was nearly at the door, when old gray Dick yelled out as loud as he could: "Hey Artzy, if ya need a noode model, I'm abailible." Everyone at the bar turned around and a chorus of "me too's" flushed her face bright red.

"Thanks," she muttered. Leaning with all 110 pounds of body weight, she pushed open the heavy, rotten, wood door and quickly exited before the conversation went any further.

Back upstairs in the safety of her home, Alouisha fastened the bolt and breathed deeply, surrendering to the all-consuming voice of her paintings.

Her gaze settled on the easel propped near the window. It was all there, ready for her to begin. The paint-smeared wooden handles of her brushes pointed upward in the rusty coffee can perched on the windowsill. Two inches of turpentine kept the brushes pliable and smelled as delicious to Alouisha as baking cookies. The late daylight, soft and pink, glossed over the small piles of pigment that she had squeezed onto a wooden pallet.

She stared at the white canvas; her thoughts turned inward as she sought to clarify and access her feelings. After selecting a brush, she dipped the hair into the luscious colors. Sliding and undulating the pigments with a good amount of force, she added the linseed oil, a drop at a time, until the creamy consistency had the texture she felt would glide without obstruction. Then, she took off—transported into another realm—into the world of sentient experience. In her private place of refuge, she would engage freely with colors and feelings, uninhibited by three-dimensional constraints. She could scan the galaxies, become transparent, and take Jason with her to make love.

Chapter 5

Gilded Cartouches

enry Classico held the wrought-iron handrail adorned with gilded cartouches tightly, as he mounted the circular, marble staircase that led to the upper floors of his apartment over the gallery. He looked up at the domed oculus crowning the vestibule and, for a second, vertigo threatened his balance. Instead of taking the small elevator at the end of the foyer, he continued climbing, drawn by the light pooling in circles from the skylight. This might be all the exercise I will have today, he thought as his hand patted his stomach, which was still working on last night's four-star dinner from Daniel restaurant. Not too bad for a fifty-two year old. He ran his hand through his still-thick hair; his eyes twinkled contentedly. Classico flipped open his cordovan leather Asprey appointment book while seated at the French eighteenth-century, Louis XV black lacquered desk in his private library. The gold engraving read: 2009, Henry Classico. Rustling through the gilt-edged pages given to him each Christmas by Goodrich's auction house, he was reminded daily of his valued client status. He lifted the grosgrain ribbon to reveal Wednesday, April 20, and checked the evening's activities.

He could not remember the last time he spent a night at home alone. Merrily, he hummed the tune from the current Broadway revival of *West Side Story* that he recently attended on opening night : "Tonight." *It certainly will be an unusual night,* he told himself, momentarily forgetting his financial problems.

Edwina Mass, celebrating the completion of her newly renovated home, had invited Classico to a dinner party in honor of the legendary interior designer Mark Veneer, who was applauded throughout the world. The self-proclaimed arbiter of good taste had raised the standards of perfection for design. His influence both politically and culturally reshaped the world of furniture and fabrics, giving new meaning to the word chintz. People lined up for access to his decorative strokes and to become part of Mark Veneer's inner-circle—to be privy to his elitist, old money values. Well-versed in the proper etiquette for every situation, Veneer's exquisite manners trademarked all his endeavors.

The newly minted Wall Street financiers competed fiercely for Veneer's services. The contents of their overflowing bank accounts needed to be funneled into prestige and status suitable for the arriviste lifestyle in their newly acquired homes, yachts, and private jets. Having a Mark Veneer-designed home translated into instant social success, but everyone knew only the very select or the very rich would be given that privilege.

Being invited to dinner at Edwina Mass's home, afforded Classico the perfect venue for finding new investors for his Apogee Art Fund, which needed an injection of cash flow. The guests shared a sense of mutual privilege and entitlement, accompanied by an exaggerated sense of trust. Being selected for one another's exclusive alliance gave the distinguished members of these inner sanctums entree to their social and business circles. These "Ultra High Net Worth" (UHNW) individuals conducted business twenty-four hours a day, unable to forget the multimillion-dollar burn in their back pockets.

Classico would persuade Veneer that his art advisory service was an essential element of good design, along with the good commission they would share, and therefore indispensable when choosing expensive works for investment—one that added value, and not simply displayed for its decorative appeal. Tonight, Classico planned to implement his own cachet and forage in the green money forest, and like a wild life preserve, it would be rich with natural resources

Sitting at his desk, Classico scrolled the recent auction results on Artprice.com, when he heard a knock on the door.

"Good Evening, Sir," said Hans, Classico's Dutch butler who towered at six foot six in his working tuxedo. "Can I help you dress? It is 5:45 and you are due at 7:00, Sir."

"Thank you, Hans. I'll just finish up here, and then I'll be right with you, and we'll choose a dinner jacket for tonight."

"Very well, Sir."

Classico checked the hammer price for Picasso's bronze, *Tete de Femme Dora Maar* at the recent Conway's sale in New York. It went for well over its estimate of $26 million. He calculated that Picasso's work, in all mediums, had risen 96 percent in the last decade. "Good work, Pablo. You are still working it from the grave," he chuckled. Turning off his computer, he rose from his desk as his thoughts returned to the important Picasso that hung in his office. The painting would be his "get out of jail card." And since prices for exceptional works were still holding their value in the otherwise terrible financial markets of 2009, he envisioned his financial solvency to be within reach. It would be close, but it might just work. He walked down the dark wood-paneled hallway toward his dressing room feeling ten pounds lighter.

Hans stopped riffling through the rack of dinner jackets when his employer entered the dressing room.

Classico stood in the center of his 20 by 20 foot room and scanned all his clothing at once. Three walls of the room, joined by double-hung solid brass rods, accommodated his suits, blazers, trousers, and shirts. A contiguous section displayed black dinner jackets and white-tie ensembles for more formal receptions. He glimpsed his reflection in the highly polished mahogany drawers and shelving, which was crafted to a level of perfection suitable for the Captain's quarters of the Queen Mary. The fitted cabinetry kept his sweaters and the remainder of his effects neatly organized. Shoes for every purpose, color, and sport shone perfectly and lay shape-preserved with wooded shoe trees from John Lobb, costing upwards of $100 a pair.

"We need to choose something for a very special occasion. Edwina Mass is giving a dinner for Mark Veneer . . . and yes," reading Hans's mind because they had been together for over ten years, "of course, I want him to be a new client."

"Good Luck, Sir."

Classico's looked upward for his inspiring thought to take hold. "I cannot wait to see her two beautiful Agnes Martin paintings," he said. "It is too bad I didn't sell them to her."

"I am sorry, Sir."

"So am I. They are truly poetic and spiritual meditations rendered in breathtaking subtleties of color. What a joy it will be to spend time with them during dinner."

"You are very fortunate Sir," Hans said holding up the first dinner jacket for Classico to consider. Like a proud soldier holding a flag of victory, he repeated the process one hanger at a time.

"After dessert," Classico continued, "we will probably take coffee in the drawing room to be with the two Rothkos. The last Rothko of this caliber sold at Conway's in May for $73 million, three times the former $27 million record. One can only aspire to be in the emotional place the artist imagined—floating in transcendence on subtle layers of color."

"Your descriptions are so beautiful; I wish I could see Mrs. Mass's paintings," Hans said, still holding up a jacket for approval.

"Maybe one day you will. In the meantime, you have so many beautiful works to enjoy downstairs in the gallery."

"That is one of the benefits of working for you, Sir."

Classico fumbled with his garters and abruptly rose from the white tufted divan in the center of the room, shaking a pointed finger toward the jackets.

"That's it," he said running his hand over the beautifully tailored fabric. "Yes, this one, the waistcoat Davies and Sons tailored on my last trip to London. As a going away gift, they gave me an engraved mother of pearl set of collar stiffeners ... so thoughtful. I am not surprised Davies and Sons have been every prime minister's and every celebrity's first choice for bespoke tailoring. Mr. Davies always inquired, 'Sir, on which side do you dress?' And, he accommodates one's preference with proper allowances, whichever side they prefer."

"Very well, Sir." Hans then held up two pairs of evening slippers: one in black velvet with a gold crest embroidered on the top, and the other, a black patent opera pump with a grosgrain bow. "Which will it be?" he asked showing off the bottoms of the slippers, which had polished soles.

"The opera pump, it is more formal. Thank you, Hans," he said. A wistful feeling overcame him. He paused and briefly glanced at all his belongings: the wooden surfaces polished to a mirror shine, the scrupulously clean surroundings, the well-cared for wardrobe, each item hanging perfectly draped and uncreased. Everything refracted in the triple mirror's infinite possibilities. For a fleeting moment, it occurred to him that it could all vanish; he was one, maybe two sales away from financial reprisal. No, it is not possible; he scolded himself for harboring such self-destructive thoughts.

"Oh, Hans," he said looking in the mirror admiringly and checking all angles, while Hans helped him into his clothes. "It is marvelous to be a bachelor in New York City; single heterosexual men are a rare commodity these days. A bit of a bank account, an education, good manners, and a dinner jacket make up the formula for social success with women in this town. They simply spoil me with invitations to dinner parties, weekends at their country homes, gala charitable evenings, and lunches at the Plaza, Twenty-one, or Cipriani's."

"My favorite invitation is from the Central Park Conservancy's spring luncheon held in the park on 110th street when the gardens are fully in bloom. It is so chic; all the women wear divine hats. Sabrina takes a table every year and always sends her driver to fetch me. Why would I ever want to give that up to get married?"

"I cannot think of a reason," Hans said.

"Most importantly, the women love to buy art, and they prefer to buy it from a good looking bachelor," Classico said, trying to convince himself that all would soon be well in the world of Henry Classico.

This evening Classico would be the extra man, which suited him just fine. His single status freed him to pursue business matters without being tethered to a date, obliged to baby-sit her all night with his undivided attention. Unattached men adhered to certain tacit requirements when escorting a woman of high social standing. Good manners were always essential. A gentleman picked her up and returned her home. He walked slowly, remembering she wore high-heels, always taking her arm and coat, and he never allowed her to open a door. His compliments were given generously, most often to reference her beauty, and if she happened to have a sense of humor, he never forgot to laugh at her jokes. However, the most important unspoken rule was discretion: one must never tell.

Hans fastened Classico's diamond studs to his formal pleated shirt, helped him into his dinner jacket, then used a horsehair brush for a final sweep. He stepped back for a full review; his gaze began at his hair sliding slowly to his shoes. He placed his hands on Classico's shoulders, turning him around, repeating the visual journey. "You are perfect, Sir."

"I get better looking each year. Don't you think so, Hans?"

"You are very distinguished, Sir."

Apart from distinct eyebrows and grayed swatches that delineated his pompadour and temples, Classico's features melded generically from his Italian and Austrian ancestry. At five-foot eleven, he differentiated himself with a steely posture and elegant mannerisms that invoked the same spirit in history as his eighteenth-century French furniture from the court of Louis the XV. Classico could often be found bending slightly from the waist when he took the hand of a beautiful woman for a light brush of a kiss, and if she wore white gloves, he would bend more deeply.

Upgrading his demeanor to suit his current lifestyle had taken a bit of concentration, and now there was no turning back. Classico had reinvented himself many times since leaving his dreary hometown of Beatrice, Nebraska, where he was labeled a dork and constantly teased by his classmates for preferring art to sports. They had hijacked his childhood happiness, and now he had no desire to return to his hometown and listen to old high-school jocks recounting stories of their factory-driven, blue-collar lives with weekends spent shopping at Costco—that was another incarnation. Classico chuckled, although he attended a third-tier college, Texas Western, to study Art History, he received a first-tier education in Texas charm. *Nothing like those Texas girls,* he remembered smiling.

Enjoying the crisp winter air, he briskly walked the two blocks to Edwina Mass's Fifth Avenue apartment. The prewar gem built in 1938 by Rosario Candela was intended to evoke the elegance of Renaissance grandeur. The lobby's twenty-foot gilded, coffered ceilings, the elaborate fenestrations, and the hushed tones that echoed through the hallways, imputed exclusivity with each step closer to the elevator.

"I am Mr. Classico; Mrs. Mass is expecting me."

"May I have your coat, Sir?" the doorman asked.

"Yes, thank you," he replied.

"Right this way, Sir."

The private elevator opened into the entrance foyer of the full floor apartment with fifteen-foot ceilings and twilight views of Central Park. The butler in black-tie and white gloves greeted him.

"Good evening, Mr. Classico. Please come in."

Twenty elegant guests in evening costumes, the exact number that could comfortably sit at the dining table, mulled about the drawing room and happily mingled over cocktails. Classico thought he had stepped into a Jean Auguste Dominique Ingres painting. The diffused lighting clung to the silken fabrics of the women's gowns, shimmering as though dipped in a pool of phosphorescence. They had all visited their safes that day to collect their most elaborate jewels. Fastened to their gowns or worn on their arms and necks, their jewelry shone like mini-solar systems capturing and emitting light and contributing to the reflected glory.

"Oh Henry, darling, it is so good to see you," Edwina Mass said air-kissing him lightly, just close enough for Classico to feel her warmth. She was radiant, as if anointed with the blessings of an infinite intelligence.

Edwina's floor-length gown by Madame Gris was a delicious, apple-green confection of draped charmeuse with a matching wrap. Known as the Grande Dame of Haute Couture, Madame Gris, inspired by Roman sculpture, used ideals of classicism to sculpt her Parisian ensembles. Not since Emperor Augustus' reign could anyone configure fabric to undulate so fluidly. A large diamond hatpin held part of her coiffure in place, while a few loose tendrils cascaded gently from her updo, bordering her delicate features like a custom-made frame. To complete her fashion statement, an art deco emerald and diamond pendant necklace from Cartier's, en-suite with matching earrings gilded her long neck. She wore a signed art deco bracelet by Van Cleef and Arpels, also of emeralds and diamonds, which matched only by color and date.

Stepping backward Classico held her at arms length to admire her in full view, "Edwina darling, you are breathtaking, more divine than ever," Classico said.

"You are too kind," she said. "I believe you know Mr. and Mrs. Aristoteil?"

"Of course, how have you been?" Classico asked, distancing himself appropriately as he shook Edward Aristoteil's hand and bowed slightly to kiss Sondra Aristoteil's hand. She shot him a piercing look, warning of caution, before breaking out in her most benignant smile. *Of course, I won't reveal our tryst*, Classico mused silently. *What does she think I am, an idiot? I want her husband's business; why would I jeopardize my opportunity?*

A waiter appeared with a glass of Vintage Dom Perignon, while another arrived with a silver tray of Beluga Caviar served on quarter-sized blinis topped with a dollop of crème fraiche.

Classico worked the room. In the twenty-five minutes before dinner was served, he greeted old acquaintances and still managed new introductions. Although, several of the guests had not been formally introduced, they knew each other from their reputations. Each one had a well-known public persona, having achieved formidable success in his or her field. The evening's mix represented icons in the world of philanthropy, fashion, art, and finance. Because Edwina's guest list always included friends from a variety of fields, they brought disparate perspectives on the latest news and gossip to the dinner conversations; there was never a dull moment at her table.

Edwina slipped her arm in Classico's and led him across the room.

"Henry darling, I want you to meet our guest of honor, Mark Veneer. Mark, this is Henry Classico, whom I have told you about. He has the most divine pictures. We really should visit the gallery one day, soon."

"It is a pleasure to meet you Mark. Congratulations are in order for your brilliant design. I look forward to a tour of the other rooms, and of course, I would be honored if you would visit the gallery."

"Thank you, I have heard so much about your connoisseurship," said the august interior designer. The luster of his highly polished mien shone deep and rich, like the patina of the nearby Townsend and Goddard side table. His blown-dry hair, thick and black, framed his face emphasizing his high cheekbones and square jaw line. Veneer had a slight tan and appeared too well rested for a New Yorker. He projected an inner calm that made one think he had just returned from his yacht. Considering that he was sixty-four years old and had no sagging flesh or wrinkles, Classico thought, *surely he's had some work done. He looks even better in person than in his photographs. I am not surprised the women are so crazy about him. I must have him as a new client.*

"Dinner is served, my Lady," announced the butler who had previously served as Princess Margaret's footman at Kensington Palace. Although Edwina lacked a title, his habit of addressing his female employers as "Lady" continued.

The guests moved into the glittering dining room. Classico listened to the low whispers and soft laughter; the swishing chiffons, puddling charmeuses, and hissing satins created their own polyphonic chorus. Each perfumed woman left an invisible train bearing a distinct fragrance, which Classico passed through, inhaling a trace of their essence. The uncurtained windows beckoned the twilight's dwindling glow into the dining room suffused with candlelight that splayed warm tones on their faces, in their eyes, and in their smiles.

As the end of Classico's game crept closer, he witnessed the beauty of his surroundings intensify with a level of splendor he had not noticed before. Colors were more vivid, reflections became more luminous, the sky and air seemed clearer and more fresh, and his friends appeared more brilliant. He took Edwina's arm and led her to the table.

At each seat, tucked between the flowers and the third red wine glass, a small folded card had the guests' names written in calligraphy. The men stood behind their chairs until Mark Veneer seated his hostess. Classico hoped he would not be placed next to Mrs. Aristotiel and have to endure another episode of her under-the-table groping. *The woman has no boundaries. Just because we had a brief "seal the deal" affair, she is not entitled to my body,* he silently fumed. Luckily, he was seated next to Sabrina DeMande on his left and Suzaahnne Whitetoe on his right.

Like a well-choreographed dance on cue, Classico pulled the chair out for Sabrina DeMande. She had just returned from a trip abroad with her husband, Sinbad. The attractive couple, he in his late fifties and she at least ten years younger, furtively exchanged knowing glances. They sized up one another's dinner partners to evaluate the possible strategic benefits this evening.

Sinbad, the titular chairman of the board of the Apogee Art Fund, and an enormously successful merger and acquisitions man, managed a hedge fund, which returned twenty-five percent or more annually. He, too, always courted new investors.

Thurmond Whitetoe, the former CEO of a large investment-banking firm, sat two seats left of Classico, next to Sabrina DeMande. Now retired, he remained an active board member of several charitable organizations that scouted for major donors. When he married for the fourth time, his friends referred to him as "the eternal optimist." His current spouse, Suzaahnne Whitetoe, was well known for her philanthropy in third-world countries, and for a Victorian bird's nest hairdo that had not changed in the thirty-five years that anyone had known her. Rumor said, her hair was waist-length, but no one would ever be certain—it was only "hairsay."

"Sinbad, how are the credit default swaps doing lately?" Thurmond Whitetoe inquired about Wall Street's latest copywriting endeavor, IDOs (insurance on debt obligations) and mortgages.

"Amazing, buying and selling mortgage packages has been an undreamed of windfall," Sinbad DeMande replied. "The Wall Street marketers grouped the various mortgages together, sub-prime, conforming, non-conforming. Some were good, some were not so good, and some were worthless; it didn't matter to them, no one seemed to care. They simply tied a pink ribbon around the bundle and sold them into the pension funds of banks, insurance companies, corporations like General Motors, Ford, and universities, even Harvard fell prey. The collective greed of Wall Street and Main Street demanding higher returns exacerbated the competition. Investment bankers took higher risks receiving higher returns and invested in worthless paper assets and debts. Everyone bought them. It was the emperor's new clothes," Sinbad explained.

"Extraordinary," Thurmond Whitetoe said. "The business of finance is very creative. The investment bankers hire the smartest kids from the best Ivy League schools and put them to work searching for loopholes in the FTC and SEC rulings. Following their discoveries, they invent financial products that fill the gaps in the legal framework, then the copywriters christen them with a clever name."

"That is one way to see it," Classico said.

"Yes, an interesting point of view," Suzaahnne Whitetoe agreed.

"And they have gotten away with it," Edwina said.

"The rating companies are equally responsible. How they stay in business is a sheer marvel, when it is well known they are paid by the investment houses for their triple-A ratings," Thurmond Whitetoe continued.

"And they were dead wrong. Before AIG crashed, Standard and Poor's and Moody's had rated them triple A," Sinbad said.

"In my opinion," Classico interjected, "all the financial instruments are frivolous when compared with the revenues generated from art collecting. It is by far the fastest growing asset class and a quantifiable triple-A rated—ART—ART—ART," he chuckled to himself. "A rock solid investment. Our Apogee Art Fund has had tremendous success and continues to outperform every other private equity instrument. Of course, we are unable to issue more shares at this time; we are fully committed," Classico said, keeping his eyes lowered to cover his fallacious words.

Ever so slowly, he sipped his wine. Not daring to look up or break the silent pause ripe with future offerings, he allowed the thought to gain gravity—to fester, giving it time to solidify into a viable profit option for the guests. The seconds stretched like bubble gum.

"Oh, that's too bad," Mrs. Whitetoe said breaking the silence.

"Indeed it is," Mr. Whitetoe said. The others murmured in agreement.

Sinbad raised his eyebrows and nodded slightly in Classico's direction, or perhaps it was more like a jerking motion. Sinbad wanted to clear his throat but controlled the impulse. He pulled his stiffened collar instead, and tried to remain focused on the eight-course dinner including the *amuse bouche*.

Classico appeared deep in thought. He placed his knife and fork in resting position on his plate, four and eight o'clock. After seemingly much deliberation, he lifted his gaze to Suzaahnne Whitetoe. "Well, perhaps I can put you on the short list for the new round of investors." He clutched the Baccarat crystal goblet and glanced briefly at the other guests, just long enough for them to understand that he would try to include them as well. He dared not look up again and see their reactions. He held the pause—until...

"We would be so grateful," replied Suzaahnne Whitetoe.

Gotcha! Classico did not flinch. "It would be my pleasure." *I'll call them in a week and tell them something has opened up. Now I can enjoy my dinner.* The hum of conversation resumed with overtones of delight.

Edwina Mass gently clinked her knife against the crystal goblet; instantly, the room became quiet.

"My dear friends, I am so happy to have you all here with me tonight to honor the talented, brilliant, inimitable Mark Veneer and to celebrate the completion of my beautiful home. Thank you, Mark," she said, holding the weighted silence for effect. She gazed into his eyes so deeply as if to access his innermost core; the sacred place where she could promise eternal gratitude.

"Here, here," her guests replied, softly clinking their glasses with their fish forks.

"Mark, can you explain to us some of your design process and intentions?" Classico asked.

"Yes, of course. Edwina's dining room is a contemporary derivative of the Palace of Versailles' Hall of Mirrors," Veneer explained. "I have placed six-foot by five-foot rectangles of six-inch beveled mirrors that are individually framed and recessed with white crown molding around the entire dining room. Each mirror hangs as if it were a painting on the wall. I have created a multilayered, diaphanous experience that works best in candlelight to refract images of the guests into infinite space. They are meant to be like portals into a cyber world," he said.

Classico noted the expressions on the guest's faces. They found Mark to be awe-inspiring.

"Oh I see. We have become the subject of the mirror paintings. Our reflections are embedded into the Central Park view, like a bouquet of trees in a verdant forest," Sabrina DeMande observed.

The crystal glassware and chandeliers tossed blurry images on the table, repeating the deep color pallet of the flowers, and further enhancing the Sevres porcelain service that lay beside the nineteenth century silver Queen Anne flatware, repeating the deep-color pallet of the flowers. The florist had gathered the orchids, peonies, and tuber roses from exotic nurseries around the world, and had them flown in today for arrangement, under advisement, by "Himself," Mr. Veneer.

"Indeed, I can see moving fragments of colors, candlelight, and crystal rainbows commingling and glowing incandescently," Sondra Aristoteil said looking across the table into Classico's eyes, attempting to inspire his memory with art speak metaphors.

Flattery will get you everywhere, thought Classico as he savored the effects of the 1960 vintage Chateau Latour: *soft as a duckling's down, as deep as an ancient cavern, as richly textured as the Empress's brocade, with a nose that inspires transcendence, as if one took passage on the wings of a butterfly,* he thought giving flight to his poetic analysis.

"Have you seen the new art gallery at the Metropolitan Opera? What do you think of it?" Edwina asked her guests, gently brushing away a wanton ringlet.

"The opera house was the last vestige of high art, a pure meritocracy of talent. Why did they pollute it with pornographic art, whose sole purpose is to shock?" Suzaahnne Whitetoe asked.

"Peter Gelb wanted to speak in the vernacular to main street culture. So disappointing," Elizabeth Veneer replied.

"It is always about ticket sales," Sinbad said.

"Who is running the gallery?" Sabrina DeMande inquired.

"It is a disgrace. Why have the beautiful period oil portraits of the Met's greatest stars disappeared? They were hung in the lower level of the house," Elizabeth Veneer said.

"I am afraid they have been replaced with paparazzi photographs," Classico said.

"It is appalling," Edwina said.

"Reprehensible," Suzaahnne Whitetoe agreed.

During the eight-course meal, all appropriate topics for conversation had been exhausted, because politics, religion, and sex were taboo at Edwina's table. Saturated with vintage wines and bubbly, the guests felt no pain and drifted into float-mode, the magic carpet kind. With one more course remaining, their thoughts headed skyward as the waiters served the dessert—steaming trays of mini-cumulus cloud soufflés infused with Grand Mariner appeared before each guest. The aromas struggled to burst forth, impatiently awaiting the spoon to penetrate its billowing crust and to release its precious lava.

Once again, Edwina lifted her glass of champagne. This time she recited Oscar Wilde: "My dear friends, we all must remember, 'Morality like art means drawing the line someplace, and illusion is the first of all pleasures.'"

Everyone laughed, some applauded softly.

"We will take coffee in the library," Edwina said.

The butler helped her from the table, and took her hand gracefully as if they were dancing a Pas de Deux. Dinner was officially over and everyone reconvened to the library. The conversations streamed freely now, with synaptic connections rippling from the bubbly. The staff served ancient ports, liqueurs, tiny petits fours and truffles from Fortnum and Mason of London on engraved, repousse silver trays that glinted in the candlelight. Classico excused himself and went to the powder room. On his way, he paused at the Rothkos, unlocked his iPhone and quickly snapped a photo. He counted the dwindling minutes to the party's end. Never satisfied, he calculated that he had only another half hour to forage in the green money forest.

Chapter 6

The Decision

"Good morning, Classico Gallery. How may I help you?" asked Alouisha.

"Good morning," the far away voice had a Chinese accent that sounded like someone gargling with pebbles in an underground tunnel.

"Is he dere? This Huang Show in Beijing."

"What is this regarding Sir?"

"He know."

"Would you please hold while I see if he is in? Thank you."

Classico sat at his Louis XV ormolu desk feeling quite full of himself, thanks to his success last night. Having hobnobbed with New York's richest and finest social set, he was certain that his full-throttle charm had been well received by both the men and women. He mulled over his witty remarks, chortling to himself with peacock aplomb as he drew his hand through his full-headed coif, another source of great pride. One would never have guessed that Classico used a colorist at Kenneth's Salon at the Waldorf Astoria.

A man can win at Black Jack in Macau, the Point to Point races in Middleburg, the Baccarat tables in Monaco, or the highest bid at auction; but when fate demands a royal flush for luck, those prizes fade when compared to a man who keeps his hair, he thought picking up the phone still grinning.

"Mr Classico, there is a Mr. Show on the line," Alouisha said.

Classico gulped the equivalent of ten lozenges at one time upon hearing the caller's name. In an instant, the wind was vacuumed from both his lungs and his hubris. Last night's largeness that lingered as vividly as an Imax movie, suddenly shrank to the size of a black and white 1960s television.

"Yes ... yes, please put him through."

"I will connect you now, Mr. Show."

"Hello Mr. Show, how nice to hear from you. I hope you and your family are well."

"Yes, thank you. I have painter you looking for. You not be disappointed. Must come soon to Beijing to finish deal. Must bring number one Picasso."

"How long will it take to complete?"

"Not long, maybe one, two weeks."

"Are you certain the artist cannot travel to the United States to work?" Classico implored.

"No possible, no visa, no possible, not from Government. Not this time," he said.

Classico squirmed in his chair and loosened his tie; his body flushed with anxiety. He was roasting in an airless oven. Jumping up, his heart pounded. He was about undertake the worst deal of his life—but he had no other choice.

"Very well, I'll book my ticket right away," he said with grave resignation.

"Good, Mr. Classico. I make reservation at five-star Chinese hotel, Jing Jiang near Tiananmen Square and the Forbidden Palace. You don't want stay at big chain hotel. Too many people you know, too many questions, and too many designer boutiques. You will like it there and feel good. This good hotel. All Chinese diplomats stay here.

"Women come in night and knock on door, 'You want massage?' they ask. Cost 250 RMB, $35 U.S. Chinese massage very good, they work very careful and strong."

The last thing I am concerned about is enjoying myself on this trip. Oh God, this has to work. I have got to raise cash to pay back the investors, he said to himself, digging deep to find his courage.

"Okay, book it. Goodbye," Classico said, slamming the phone with sledgehammer force. He clenched his fists, hit the desk, then turned on the intercom. "Alouisha, please book me a first-class ticket to Beijing for next Sunday and try to use my Sky Miles for an upgrade. Also, send flowers to Mrs. Mass. Call the Plaza Florist and ask for something especially beautiful. Price is no object, but keep it under $500."

"Oh, yes Sir, Mr. Classico, right away."

He had never mentioned a trip to China and Alouisha wondered why he was in such a hurry. *Granted, the Chinese art market was heating up, but plenty of time remained to find excellent art works. He probably wants to buy directly from the artist, since he lost that last painting at auction,* she said to herself.

She went online, ordered his tickets, had the flowers sent to Mrs. Mass and jotted a few notes in her journal, always keeping track of her day's activities.

By this time, Classico, having calmed himself, wiped his glowing face with his Sulka handkerchief, and walked to the front gallery to speak to Alouisha. He had an idea.

She looked up from her desk when she heard Classico clearing his throat to announce his approach down the hallway.

"Alouisha," he said with an upending cadence, as if it were a question. I need you to take charge of the gallery while I am gone, maybe for a week or two. We can talk and email everyday. Do you think you can handle it?"

"Yes, Sir, you can count on me."

"Wonderful, I won't forget this." His instincts had been right when he hired her as his assistant six months ago. She did not disappoint.

"My dear, uh... he cleared his throat again. Since I will be away for a short time in China on important business and you will be running the gallery virtually by yourself, I would like you to dress the part of proprietor and gallery manager. So, I am giving you a clothing stipend. I believe the chicest designer for an art dealer is Prada—something black perhaps. And of course, one must have a Chanel suit for luncheons or daytime appointments with important clients. You will also need a pair of high-heeled Christian Louboutin pumps. You know the type I am referring to, five-inch heels with platforms and red soles. That should do it. Oh, yes, don't forget to buy a Balenciaga handbag. Barney's has all the latest colors."

Classico felt proud that he was well versed with the latest fashion designers. He could flatter his clients by admiring their beauty, their taste, and their clothing. "Darling, you look divine in your new Christian La Croix or Yves Saint Laurent," he told them. Seamlessly, he transposed these accolades into selling paintings at the gallery.

"Oh, Mr. Classico," Alouisha replied, blushing from his generosity. "Thank you, but I'm sorry ... I can't accept your kind gifts; it wouldn't be right. In my world, the way I was raised, I only accept what I've earned."

Alouisha was a demigoddess to her family, and a legend in her Jamaican Parrish of Hopewell. When Yale awarded her a full undergraduate scholarship, she became the community's archetype of hope making anything possible. An exceptional beauty, she inherited the long and lean gene from her hard working relatives. The lilting timbre of her Jamaican voice underscored her ivy-league education with subtle melodic cadences, which gave her sentences a dance step at the end.

Her most striking feature, however, was her light Caribbean sea-colored eyes, which changed continuously from shades of turquoise to coral reef green and then to cerulean blue. Maybe it was not their color as much as their luminosity that made it difficult to unlock one's gaze upon her. She was mesmerizing, and the two drops of African-American ancestral color gave her skin a creaminess and texture that would never wrinkle and fueled her relentless curiosity about who her British, slave-owning, great, great grandfather might have been.

"Your rectitude is impressive, but I can assure you—you will earn it. Consider it a uniform, a requirement for the job. Now, young lady, I will not hear another word about it, and besides, you are helping me tremendously. The owners of both the Prada and Chanel boutiques on Madison Avenue are my friends. I'll call them, and they'll help you choose your ensembles. Not to worry, they'll charge it to the gallery. And here is my credit card for Barney's, you'll probably need to pick up a few things I have forgotten."

"But Mr. Classico, I cannot..."

"Alouisha, remember, you are helping to sell paintings worth millions of dollars, you must dress the part. Now, I will not listen to another word on the subject. The topic is closed. Please tell Hans to pack my bags, and tell him it's still chilly in Beijing this time of year."

Alouisha stared at the floor feeling embarrassed. She was through being a charity case and never accepted gifts from men, particularly something as personal as clothing that always came with strings attached.

Classico could see that she was upset. *Maybe I was too hard on her,* he thought. He took a step closer and lifted her chin gently. Her eyes glistened with softness and vulnerability. He had never been so close to her before, touched her face, or fully noticed the luminosity of her green eyes. He brushed a stray hair away from her cheek, then his lips grazed the spot as lightly as a feather. She flung her hair and stepped back slightly, blushing pink.

"Please cheer up, you are going to look divine in your new outfits."

he smiled. She thought she saw him wink.

Chapter 7

The Chinese Partner

Huang Show hung the phone up, grinning from earlobe to earlobe, like the painting behind his desk. The year of the Ox had brought him great luck and prosperity. His patience, hard work, and fortitude had blessed him with an excellent Picasso deal that would earn him ample amounts of RMB, enough to firmly entrench his political capital in the Organization. Last month, because he was late collecting the full cash payment required to keep "Them" happy and himself protected, they threatened to cut off his fingers. Luckily, his gambling paid off, and winning big at fan-tan covered this month's indemnity on time.

If it were not for the Organization, Huang Show would have remained homeless or starved to death. And, maybe one day, he would find another wife ... if his ancestors would favor it.

Eleven years ago, the police broke down the door of his hutong and wrenched him from his sleep, arresting him for conducting Christian prayer meetings. His wife divorced him while he was in prison; he did not blame her. His ten-year sentence was far too long for her to be alone and hungry, compelling her to remarry. Because of the shortage of women in China, many men pressured her into wedlock. She needed a good provider for herself and her child. During that first year of prison, Huang Show's spouse visited occasionally and brought him an egg or a bit of rice. Having little money, she took the food from their child's portion. After a year or maybe two—it was hard for him to remember, she stopped coming altogether. He heard they were divorced.

Huang Show spent ten years in hard labor, mucking sewers and being beaten regularly by the guards. He shoveled sewage all day, standing barefoot in waist-high excrement and offal. He prayed constantly and managed to endure the ordeal only through "the grace of God." Miraculously, he survived, withstanding the relentless cold, hunger, and disease. When they finally released him, destitute and homeless, he was a broken man. Dumped on the street like discarded trash, he dragged his skeletal body with caul-like skin along the dirt road. He found a rusty rain pipe and drank from it. Unable to continue, he collapsed into a heap on the side of the road. After some time had passed, he did not know how long, a truck stopped and gave him a ride.

Finally, he found his way back to his hometown province of Guizhou where everything had changed. The small cement hutongs had disappeared, replaced by apartment buildings with running water, electricity, and plumbing. People wore western clothing—jeans and collared shirts rather than Mao jackets. Standing in the shadows, Huang Show watched the school children running in spotless white sneakers, which echoed the purity of their intentions—their determination to receive the education they previously had been denied.

Huang Show was a starved, pathetic looking stranger with flesh so thin you could see his bones without an ex-ray. He exuded an unforgettable sadness from his dark, hollow eyes. Knowing he looked frightful, he hid in the shade behind the trunk of an ancient Camphor tree, rather than scare the children. There he searched and prayed, waiting to catch a glimpse of something familiar—some feature he could recognize on the face of a child—his child, whom he had not seen in over ten years. His heart longed for the sight of him. It had been too long; too many years had passed. His son would be a stranger if he were to find him now. A tear rolled down his face as he thought of all the lost years—years that he could never replace; too many years without love. He cursed himself for feeling sentimental, and at that moment, he vowed never to be weak again. All that emotions ever brought him were suffering and poverty. He was through.

A few days later, a former member of his prayer group found him lying crumpled on the dirt road near the local garbage dump, where he had been foraging for scraps of food. He was so thin and his clothing so loose, he looked like a pile of laundry. When the mound moved, the old friend, stepped closer and noticed a vague resemblance to someone he used to know. He felt pity and gave him some rice to eat. That was the only kindness Huang Show received in over ten years.

He could not find a job and was ostracized by everyone for being an ex-con; no one wanted to be guilty by association. He could not blame them. Eventually, a young man asked him for help with a small task in exchange for some food. He simply had to watch the front door of a house for the owners return, while the man entered through the back and took a few household items—a stereo, a television, and a VCR.

The following day, the same man approached him and asked if he would stand watch while he helped himself to a few more items. He was paid 50RMB (about seven dollars), and that was more money than he had ever seen. After a while, he had enough renminbi to rent space in a ramshackle tool shed. At the end of the month, the man asked: "Would you like to have your own job and split the profits with the Organization?

"What organization?" Huang Show asked.

"I will take you to meet them. They are the people who help

the needy people that our government ignores. Think of them as an extended family with a strict father. Once you agree to become part of the family, you must obey the rules or else they become angry and will punish you harshly. They are good for me. I have a good family, a warm home and a big-screen television," said the man.

Huang Show's empty stomach screamed louder than his conscience. His aching bones refused to coalesce with cement floors, or the hay in the shed that offered little respite. Winter was coming soon, and the chill was worse than a thousand icicles stabbing him in a soaking swamp, black with night. He never wanted to be that cold again.

After five years, the jobs became more complex, and the contributions grew larger, as did his responsibilities to the Organization. Soon, Huang Show's complicity forced him to pay unattainable fees. Headquarters threatened him with terrible amputations if he did not produce the money. He had noticed several men in town were missing fingers, and he had assumed they were factory accidents or gangrene—until now. Last month, when the Organization came for their collection, he was a little short. As a warning, they twisted his arms and kicked him hard. Clearly, needing a larger venue, he would persuade the Organization to send him to Beijing.

His new assignment was to transport stolen and forged art through customs. Quickly, he learned the intricacies of the art world, while growing his power base. After a while, he tired of sharing his hard-earned connections and profits with his partners, and preferred to corner the market in Chinese Contemporary art sales by himself. It would be easy if he used a couple of the intimidation techniques the Organization had taught him. Instead of finger amputation, he only threatened to break the artists' hands, unless they signed exclusively with him as their dealer. With that mutual understanding, he opened the Watchtower Gallery in Beijing, and his partner was the Organization.

His business took off when luck finally found him—western demand for Chinese contemporary art synchronistically burgeoned. Huang Show encouraged the artists to work quickly, employ factory assistants for paint application, and to feel free to render any subject they chose. He opened an industrial art colony in an abandoned factory town three hours drive from Beijing in Chengdu. The artists worked without distraction; he paid them a small monthly stipend.

Several Post-Mao artists at the art colony, Tu Hongtao, Zhao Bo, and Han Yajuan, produced hyperbolic versions of Social Realist posters drawn from Communist propaganda. Their paintings parodied the forced utopia of the labor camps and were depicted through exaggerated caricatures of the workers. The highly sought after images inspired the Chinese collective mindset of copying, and as a result, they churned out hundreds of variations. The mass-produced cartoon figures, painted repeatedly by assistants and signed by their artist-employers, garnered shocking price tags when they went to auction. Huang Show displayed many of the artists in his gallery in Beijing.

He finished his phone call with Classico, and stood at the window of the Watchtower Gallery scanning the vast city of Beijing. The building, as its name implied, was a fifteenth century tower built on a hill in downtown Beijing by Emperor Yongle during a civil war in the Ming Dynasty. The vivid swaths of red clay roof tiles cut through the smoggy sky. His thoughts drifted alongside the clouds passing at eye level. Both he and the gallery had persevered through several epic incarnations, and he knew they were not over yet. Hanging on the wall behind his desk was a large cartoon portrait by Yue Minjun. Three pink figures grinned grotesquely, as if fishing hooks pulled up the sides of their mouths. The American dealers spun it into political context: "It represented the forced gaiety the communist party demanded of its workers during the Maoist regime," they had said.

"Americans buy anything," Huang Show said to his assistant Jen, a porcelain-skinned, Mandarin beauty in her twenties who just entered the room.

"Auctioneers know how to make the prices soar. People go crazy, they spend money to look at cartoons."

"It is lucky for us," Jen said.

Huang Show considered this deal with Classico an opportunity sent from the heavens by his ancestral protectors, and he would make certain nothing went wrong.

"I will trade the real Picasso for three perfect copies. Mr. Classico must be in big trouble if he agreed to these terms. Americans not too smart. We will use SoLow, the best copyist in China. No one will ever tell the difference between the real and the fake ones," he said.

"I am sending the messenger now to the industrial art colony to have him prepare," Jen said.

"Good, tell him, we will be there next week."

Turning around, he looked at the three grinning pink faces on the canvas. Who are they laughing at—themselves, an inside joke or me? He did not really care; it would always be his favorite painting. Because when he sold it, he would be laughing exactly the same way. He walked across the room and straightened the painting—just a tad. He wanted everything to be perfect.

Chapter 8

The Arrival

Classico sat in the first-class cabin of China Air trying to focus on the film and relax. He considered turning back and boarding the next plane to the States when he arrived in Beijing. But the voices in his head kept shouting, not giving him a moment's peace ...

If you return without the copies you won't ever look at another painting again without bars in front of it. You'll be off to the slammer, not the Caribbean cruise you have planned.

I can't leave the original in China; it could disappear forever, or for several generations.

It's you or Picasso, one of you is staying out of town, permanently. You choose.

Be quiet, he ordered his dark side. Not wanting to engage further in this internal argument, he turned up the volume on his video monitor to quash the racquet in his head. It offered no reprieve. The grave situation he had gotten himself into would still be waiting upon his return. There must be another way.

With frazzled nerves, his cold, clammy palms clutched the mailing tube containing the original Picasso as tightly as a lifeboat line to safety.

"May I put that in the closet for you, Sir?" the Asian flight attendant asked. Her gentle, sweet voice brought Classico back to the outer world. He was so taken by her delicate beauty, he could not respond to the angelic creature who had entered into his self-induced hell. Instead, he silently lingered in the electricity of her loveliness, allowing its healing effects to ameliorate his anxiety.

"Oh, no, thank you," he replied surfacing from the uncomfortable pause that had lasted too long. "I'll just put it here and try to get some rest." He bent down carefully placing it on the floor in front of him.

He had packed his Ambien in his checked luggage, and three hours later, he still squirmed in the reclining seat that was his bed for the night. "May I bring you something, Sir?" the flight attendant asked.

"Yes, please." The double scotch was his last resort knowing he would regret its lasting effects in the morning.

Finally, fourteen hours later, the plane landed in Beijing. Classico was exhausted and needed a shower. His wrinkled clothing degraded his usual pristine appearance and his subsequent self-regard. Realizing he was the only westerner in sight, he felt disconnected, the same way he felt as an only child growing up in the Great Plains. This familiar feeling triggered all his forgotten insecurities, waffling them back to the surface.

Not now, he told himself. He needed to concentrate and stay on top of his game, if he were to make this deal happen—the right way. *No, I cannot go through with this scheme as planned. I have to think of something...there must be another way.* Fidgeting nervously, he tugged at his tie, hand brushed his jacket, and shifted the weight on each foot to regain the feeling in his numb legs. While he waited for his luggage to appear, everything seemed strangely surreal on the opposite side of the earth. The airport lighting gave off a harsh green cast from an unforgiving florescent source, turning everything cold and one-dimensional.

Classico marveled at the spotless airport, and the exemplary efficiency it maintained as the hub for the multitudes of Pan-Asian people traveling through it each day. *Beijing Airport bore no resemblance to Kennedy Airport in New York,* he thought.

He heard no loud voices, screaming children, or people shouting expletives. He did not see one fast food container thrown on the floor, not one discarded candy wrapper, and the walls were freshly painted, not like New York City's grime gray. People appeared unusually respectful to one another as they waited in an orderly fashion.

Following the crowd through customs, he found the exit and spotted Huang Show's driver holding a name card: Hello Mr. Classico. *Well, that's a relief,* he thought. Feeling comforted by the sight of his name, the alien surroundings demystified slightly and yielded a filmy familiarity. He followed the driver to the waiting car. All eyes were upon him as he walked the Chinese red carpet. He was the only Caucasian there.

He settled into the back seat of a black Buick La Crosse, anticipating a pleasant sightseeing ride to the hotel. Instead, the driver began racing the moment he left the airport, battling his way through the onslaught of traffic. He was thrown side-to-side, bumped up and down and jolted continuously.

"What the hell, I'm not on a bucking bronco at the rodeo," he snapped at the driver.

Beijing's new five-ring highway did not relieve the smog or the congestion. It simply re-routed cars in concentric circles, which did not allow a simple egress when necessary.

"This is crazy," Classico told the driver, knowing he did not understand a word. "A straight, ten-minute as the crow flies route by pedi cab could take an hour going around these circular highways. This makes New York City traffic look pastoral." The driver responded with indistinguishable guttural sounds.

"Are you practicing for NASCAR? Slow down, please," he said to no avail. Classico closed his eyes and gave up; finally, he dozed off.

After two hours of grueling traffic, he arrived at the hotel.

"Good Morning, Sir," said the attendant who opened the car door to find Classico still half asleep.

"Thank goodness someone speaks English," Classico replied groggily. The door attendant leaned into the car to take the mailing tube containing the Picasso. Without thinking Classico recoiled in horror, yanked it away and snapped: "Don't you dare touch that," he said instantly regretting his harsh words. His normally impeccable manners were supplanted by exhaustion. *How déclassé'*, he thought, *to speak to a hotel employee in so vulgar a fashion.* He did not want to leave the doorman with a rude impression, as if he were the ugly American acting superior.

"I am so sorry; it is very fragile," Classico said.

The Chinese man did not acknowledge his remark. His downcast eyes remained fixed on the floor as he continued collecting the remaining luggage.

The spartan hotel boasted thirty-foot ceilings and scrupulously clean unused spaces that gave it a minimalist elegance. The receptionist spoke English with staccato hesitation, registered him promptly and kept his passport.

"It is Chinese law, we keep it until checkout," she said. He recognized the pride she had in her professionalism, and not wanting her efforts wasted on an inconsequential guest, he summoned his remaining ego-strength, straightened his sagging shoulders and tried to appear more distinguished.

"Thank you very much." Exhausted, he headed towards his room, but could not decide what to do first—take a nap or a shower.

The adequately furnished room closely resembled a western bedroom. He sat on the bed with a small testing bounce. It had no give or snapback. Running his hand over the bed cover fashioned from the finest red shantung silk, he watched the light transform into a limpid sheen, spreading its opalescence on contact. He slid his hand under the length of the mattress and looked under the bed, searching for hidden surveillance devices. After determining it clear, he opened the matching curtains and inspected the pleats and folds for micro wires. He found nothing, but more light entered the room to shadow dance on the silken threads. His breath made a small circle of fog on the window. Remaining motionless, he stared at the site of the Tiananmen Square Massacre of 1989.

Classico remembered the Chinese students being murdered by the government during a political protest. The story was front-page news across the world. He lengthened his gaze across Tiananmen Square, and reconsidered the historical tragedy. Previously, it existed only as words on paper, a remote idea jumbled together in life's closet of misfortunes. Now, he could smell the gunfire, hear the cries, and taste the fear of Communist oppression. *But wait, doesn't this incident have distinct parallels to the Kent State Massacre in Ohio, 1970, when the Ohio National Guard shot and killed four protesting students?* A shudder coursed through him with a wallop of reality, which suspended his feelings in mid-air like the flags in the concrete courtyard. *Well, I have more important things to think about.*

Closing the curtains, he undressed and hung his clothing in the cupboard. The hot shower relaxed his aching muscles, and all he wanted now was some sleep, but then the phone rang.

"Hello Mr. Classico. Welcome to Beijing. Did you bring painting?"

"Yes."

"I be there in one hour; take you to artist's studio." The phone went dead.

Chapter 9

The Art Seduction

"Damn it. I have got to do this," he said exasperated, struggling with his belt. Huang Show would be at the hotel in a few minutes to collect him and the Picasso. A jolt of anxiety lurched through his body causing him to stumble and tear a belt loop. He fell on the bed—"one, two, three, four," he heard himself counting to keep his rising anger at bay.

Much as he searched for his inner resolve, he felt disoriented, unable to find his usual unwavering axis. Surely, he had left it somewhere over the Pacific Ocean, *maybe in the Pitcairn Islands*, he snickered. *This jet lag is too much. I feel like an old sock turned inside out.*

"Get a grip," he told himself. Rustling through his dopp bag, he found a Ritalin and swallowed hard. Classico knew there was no turning back.

You are about to commit the most heinous crime in the history of modern art. But, what else can I do? I couldn't bear to be poor again. If this doesn't work, I'll be going to prison anyway. I never meant this to happen, he bemoaned. *Things just got out of control and I couldn't disappoint everyone who invested in the fund. If they hadn't been so damn greedy, insisting on a 30 percent return, and believing they were entitled to a profit margin that paralleled the auction prices, I would not be in this situation.* Of course, that was impossible—a private dealer could never compete with that buying frenzy. Every hedge-fund manager wanted a trophy art collection and to preside on the board of a museum.

Sitting on the edge of the bed with his elbows on his knees, he waited for the Ritalin to take effect and counteract his jet lag. His interior battle continued, and the crease between his brows carved his dreadful circumstance more deeply into his forehead.

For five years, Appogee Art Fund had offered no transparency. He bought whatever he chose with the board's multimillion-dollar investments. Private equity was hot, and his clients pockets spilled with gratitude. Classico could do no wrong, until that fateful day, during Suzaahnne Whitetoe's last dinner party to celebrate her purchase of the most expensive photograph ever sold, for $2.9 million. After several glasses of champagne, she had lured Classico into the laundry room on the pretense of admiring her new Steichen's *Moonlight* photograph in the entrance foyer. *I am not sure if it was her décolletage drenched with Chanel No.5 or the Steichen itself, but the combination was lethal.* He succumbed, knowing her husband chatted up the guests in the nearby sitting room. Then, when she insisted Classico sell her the Lichtenstein, he was helpless to refuse, although it was previously sold in two half-share increments. She wired the funds to his account that week. Now that he had spent the cash, and could not deliver the painting, it too, must travel in the exhibition abroad.

When Classico outgrew his previous gallery, he moved to the

limestone mansion, convincing himself and his board members that it was for the good of posterity. The renovations and the ballooning adjustable rate mortgage for the Beaux Art gallery put him over the edge, and he no longer could cover his monthly expenses. The collection deserved the finest presentation possible, much like the set of an opera. So, he hired Duane Schuler from the Metropolitan Opera to design the lighting. No expense was spared, only the best in the world—for the best collection.

I was "chosen" to be the caretaker of priceless treasures. I had no choice, I had to over extend myself, he ruminated.

He clenched his fists, and recalled the start of his fiscal avalanche. Sondra Aristoteil had come to the gallery that day to have a little chat.

"Good afternoon, my dear Madame Aristotiel," he had said, kissing her hand with a flourish. "Aren't you absolutely exquisite today in your Christian Dior ensemble and lavender alligator handbag? Isn't that the new Darcy Bag from Asprey's?" he asked, knowing the price tag was fourteen thousand dollars.

"Oh darling, you are so adorable," she said.

"What a pleasure to see you," he said. "And what brings you here today?"

"I would love to see your new paintings," she said, leaning closer, encircling him with her perfumed intentions.

She made sure he had a bird's-eye view of her overflowing cleavage, which oozed mellifluously from the low-cut edge of her bodice.

"Do you think there is a picture that would strengthen the mission statement of my collection?"

"Well, perhaps," he said, trying to look thoughtful while fixating on the orbs of desire that were dangerously close and beckoning.

Classico had spent years helping Sondra Aristoteil put together a world-class modern art collection. He had taught her to understand a painting's significance within its historical context by identifying the arc of the artist's career, by defining the prevailing school of art, and by discerning the artist's syntax of his or her visual investigations.

"You need a painting that will continue to redefine the modern art narrative, while comparing the artist to his contemporaries," he said slowing down his art speak and lowering his tone. His forefinger rested on his chin in contemplation.

"These motifs must all be carefully considered when building your collection, otherwise we will end up having a random group of expensive art works strung together like Christmas lights instead of a scholarly theme," he said.

Sondra listened intently. Her eyes grew wider as the wonderment of his words sunk into her realm of understanding.

"Your collection is curated with intelligence and insight, adding a new perspective to the history of art. History judges artistic genius by measuring the influence an artist has on his colleagues," he explained. "Today, unfortunately, the artist is too often judged by his or her amount of press. Over time, that will be adjusted as it always has been. There are many formerly collected artists, one never hears of again. They fall prey into the waste-bin of excessive branding."

"Oh, Henry darling, I would just love to see your recent acquisition. It's a Picasso, isn't it? I heard you bought it from someone in Hollywood. Aren't you clever to have gotten hold of it, and I want to be the most clever by owning it. After all, you know it will enhance the important historic narrative of my collection," she said.

"You are right of course. I have taught you well my dear," he said, taking both her gloved hands into his. "It is a pivotal work that transitions cubism into Picasso's next phase of modernism."

"Unfortunately, I have promised it to Grigory Baronovich for his palace in Russia," he said, releasing her hands.

"Henry, you cannot say *no* to me," she said, grabbing his hands again with a small jerk to confirm her determination. She looked deeply into his blue gray eyes to remind him of that fateful evening when he co-signed the sexual deed of obligation.

I could not help it, my charm went on autopilot, and I sold her the painting...the wrong painting.

This was not the first time Classico had been seduced by the spouse of some megawealthy hedge-fund CEO, trying to jump the line for access to the best paintings. Classico was convinced the very rich had a unique moral code—always to remain guilt free when dealing with life on their own terms.

From Sondra's perspective, she would do anything to make her husband happy, and when she brought home a coveted piece of art, he was thrilled and ever so grateful.

Rivulets formed on Classico's temples. He knew that if Edward Aristoteil found out about their tryst, he would immediately withdraw his twenty-million dollar investment from the Apogee Fund and Classico would be ruined instantly.

Until now, he had persuaded them to stay invested in the fund and forgo the 2008 round of profit taking to compound the revenues and increase their returns. Since, the subprime mortgage debacle hit and the government bailout was enacted, Classico could not find new investors to pay the angel investors. Previously, he had kept them wait-listed. The banks called in all margin loans, and no one, except the lobbyists in Washington who controlled the tarp money, had any access to cash. All the profits from works that had sold in the past five years paid the gallery's debt, covered entertaining expenses, and the house in Southampton. If one person cashed out, the others would follow.

When Grigory Baronovich offered to pay forty million, the prebubble-bust price, Classico agreed. He had not heard a word from Grigory Baronovich, despite all Classico's efforts to contact him in Russia. *Maybe he won't show up, then I'll be free to sell it elsewhere,* he thought.

"Yes, your collection deserves this painting more than any other." The words flew off his lips, repeating like an old 45 record caught on a scratch.

"Thank you, Henry darling; you are the best."

A smile that knows only pure happiness burst forth on Sondra Aristoteil's flawless, wrinkle-free, dermabrasioned face, as she opened her Darcy bag to retrieve her checkbook.

"Does that include tax, or shall we have it shipped to our home in Newport?

"Of course we'll save the tax, and ship it as usual to Rhode Island," he said, handing her his Mont Blanc fountain pen. She wrote the numbers on the check for the deposit. Each zero was drawn more beautifully than the next— each perfectly rounded circle, more lustrous than south sea pearls, was as exquisite as the Picasso itself—a flush of pleasure rippled through his body.

He cleared his throat. "It may take a few weeks before you receive it because it is tied up in an estate settlement. You know how those attorneys are—always taking too long, stretching out the billable hours. I will let you know when it will be delivered."

I haven't seen Grigory Baronovich for several months. It is unlikely he'll show up at the last minute. But, if he does, I can always sell him another Picasso, Classico thought. *I will simply convince him that the new Picasso is as important as this painting, if not better.*

"Oh, Henry darling, you have made me so happy. I will plan a special dinner at home to celebrate Picasso's arrival. We will invite all the top contemporary art collectors, a few museum directors, and perhaps the curators from the Whitney and the Moma museums. I just adore Barbara Haskell, the Whitney's curator; her talent for providing the scope of a work's historical context is unrivaled," she said.

"Now Sondra, let's just wait until the painting is delivered before you invite anyone," Classico said, loosening his collar, knowing he had to stall the delivery.

"Edward will be thrilled," she rattled on. "He loves inviting his business colleagues to our home to see our art. He cannot very well display stock certificates, or gold bullion portfolios. Our paintings provide a great venue to enjoy our wealth, while engaging our friends in conversations about society and culture. Besides, their envy will justify the cost, when they see what I have. I, uh ... mean, it is good for Edward's business.

Classico walked her to the door and kissed her good bye. It was meant to be a friendly, congratulatory kiss, but he lingered a moment too long and their electric currents connected. Before he knew what was happening, two buttons on his shirt flew to the floor.

"Not here," he said, leading her down the hallway into his office. He closed the door and felt vertiginous from her perfume and proximity. Then he fell onto the sofa, taking her with him.

"Oh, how I have missed you," he groaned, nuzzling her neck while untangling her pantyhose. He had already forgotten that Grigory Baronovich most likely would return for the Picasso.

A black curtain drew across his stage of colorful memories. Even the Ritalin could not keep him awake. He fell into a deep anguished sleep as the dollars, paintings, and pantyhose collided in his fitful dream.

Chapter 10

The Journey

lassico woke abruptly from his sleep-induced coma, half delirious with dreams of remorse, when the phone rang. "Mr. Huang Show is in the lobby waiting to see you." "Thank you, I will be right down."

He rubbed his eyes, threw some water on his face, and quickly dressed. After straightening his bow tie and combing his hair, he stared at himself in the mirror one last time.

"You will do this," he ordered the pathetic looking avatar staring back at him. He clutched the mailing tube with the same protective urgency as a mother rescuing her child from a burning building and left the room.

He took the elevator to the crowded lobby where several groups of identical Chinese suits mulled about. Looking up at the thirty-foot ceilings, he felt dwarfed by the dimensions of the massive room, where surprisingly, no seating was provided. Fastened to the ceiling of the imperious lobby were ten or twenty flag portraits of Chairman Mao that reached almost to the floor. Ironically, Classico felt safer knowing an authoritarian dictator had omniscient power and would be aware of his and Huang Show's whereabouts during the day.

Huang Show couldn't just kill an American, and steal the painting, he rationalized.

Walking toward the front entrance, Classico wondered how he would identify his future business partner. Then, a man appeared wearing an invisible name-tag inscribed: earnest, resolute, and dark. His startling intensity distinguished him from the crowd vividly, as if he were outlined in day-glow paint. Classico approached and extended his hand.

"Mr. Show? How do you do?"

Huang Show was slight, wiry, and dressed in Western fashion: a black double-breasted suit, a blue shirt, and a red dragon on his tie. His greased straight hair shone, but not as brightly as his molten lava eyes. They shook hands briefly, yet completely, including gripped palms. Huang Show's penetrating stare, nuanced with sordid mysteries, bore into Classico. At once, he understood, the man had witnessed other worlds—Stygian worlds that fortunately Classico would never experience.

Huang Show nodded and said nothing; he simply turned and walked toward a waiting car. Classico followed with the solemnity of a last walk to the gallows. The tops of his Sulka socks, damp with sweat, rolled downward and stretched out of shape. They were not made for high-anxiety situations, but rather for the cool confines of his New York clubs—the Knickerbocker or Racquet Clubs.

As Classico reached the black 7 Series BMW, a large pockmarked driver opened the trunk and Huang Show gestured for him to place the painting inside. Classico froze—the bile in his throat rose in full-fledged panic at the thought of the Picasso being removed from his sight.

"Mr. Classico, we go to industrial art colony where artist SoLow live and work. You be happy. Please, you like, put Picasso in trunk. It safe."

"Well, I don't know," Classico, replied.

"Put in trunk, better," Huang Show said, not quite ordering him to do so.

"Yes, I suppose so," Classico said. *If they wanted to kill me or steal it, having the painting in the trunk would make little difference.* He relinquished the painting and slid onto the backseat of the car.

Huang Show sat up front with the driver.

Classico looked out the window at the scenery, but there was nothing to be seen on the damn circular highway, only black smoke erupting from the cars as they crawled around and around the eight-lane route. An hour and a half later, the driver found an exit with an egress heading in the right direction.

Classico sighed with relief. "Are we getting closer?" he asked, trying not to squirm. "What city is this?"

"We still in Beijing," Huang replied.

They passed miles of new high-tech high-rises each one more impressive than the next, as if engaged in vertical competitions. Their slick metallic surfaces captured and deflected light from the sky and from the neighborhoods, splashing virtual kinetic light paintings, coruscating everywhere. And just when Classico thought it impossible for one more shopping center to be absorbed by the city, another mighty commercial center appeared. Classico pressed his face against the window. The cold glass, not the scenery, soothed his mind.

America's infrastructure paled in comparison to China's cutting-edge architecture. New York City's crumbling patina of dirt and grime rivaled any third-world country. Everywhere Classico looked was scrupulously clean and built with the latest technology.

"You can eat off the streets," he exclaimed.

They passed by two hundred construction workers who were doing just that—having their lunch. Squatting in the same position they used for defecating, they ate from large plastic bowls filled with company-supplied rice and a single white steamed bun made from flour and water. The laborers filled the sidewalks, creating a navigational obstacle for the well-dressed, young office workers who zigzagged through the human roadblocks.

"Where are all these people from?" Classico asked.

"Men from countryside. They come make money for families left in small village, far away, where no jobs, schools, or electricity," Huang Show said.

"Do you think one day, they will return to their families with enough money to bring them here?"

"They hope to find job and send children to school," Huang Show said.

"I see. And does the Chinese Government have a mandate to build shopping centers and malls on every intersection?" asked Classico.

"Chinese like shopping."

"It appears that way," he said and leaned back to straighten his legs.

He tried to distract himself from the dastardly deed on which he was about to embark. His cotton Turnbull and Asser undershirt soaked and stuck to the hair on his chest, conjuring memories of his third-grade desk in public school—the sticky underside wadded up with chewed bubblegum. Luckily, his blazer hid the sweat stains and the hairy mess. He pulled out his handkerchief to absorb the seepage of his watering face.

Where are they taking me? This is so uncomfortable. What is keeping them from killing me and taking the painting? Get a grip, he admonished himself. *This business transaction will be completed successfully, and I will return with three new Picassos. He thinks he's keeping the original. But, just maybe, there's another way.*

He took out his iPhone and scrolled to the Rothko painting in Edwina's apartment. "Mr. Show, I'd like you to see this very important painting I own by a very famous American artist, Rothko. It is an excellent investment and I can offer it to you at a good price. It is sure to increase in value." Classico said. Huang Show looked at it and grimaced, not having ever heard of Rothko. "What this is painting? There are no faces, no trees, no mountains. What is there to look at but cloud-spill? No I just take Picasso," he said.

Classico caught glimpses of the city disappearing in the rearview mirror as he watched the paved road turn to dirt. His heart sped faster than the speedometer nearing 175 kilometers. *Maybe, I should have listened to that marine recruiter back in high school and trained for a few years. At least I would know how to defend myself,* he thought as he straightened his polka-dot bow tie and tightened his seat belt.

The driver slalomed through the deserted bumpy road, doing his best to avoid the largest potholes, an effort that made Classico feel carsick. They were now deep in the countryside; an occasional mongrel dog, lost chicken, or feral cat passed by. He looked at his watch; they had left Beijing two and a half hours ago, and he was exhausted. With no other cars in sight, an eerie emptiness prevailed. He had never felt so vulnerable, so dependent, so lacking in control of a situation.

The car heaved to the side of the road narrowly missing a large hole and a stray chicken. Classico lurched against the door and banged his head on the window.

"Hey take it easy," he cried out.

"Sorry, Mr," the driver replied.

Everywhere dust spewed, rocks and pebbles gyrated, road debris flew, and blackened soot slathered the car with grime. The hazardous mix of billowing clouds crashed into the car, rendering it unnoticeable to the outside world and the outside world invisible to Classico.

Why doesn't Huang Show say something? The driver is either drunk or trying to slam me to death in this back seat. I'll never see the Picasso again. What have I done? Classico wiped his forehead with his handkerchief and searched for blood; he found only a bump. He cradled his aching head in his hands to calm his rattling nerves. Was this the end?—killed in this desolate hellhole by a car crash. The driver swerved again, missing another crater-sized pothole. Hung Show, having been quiet until now, turned and said in his best Confucius dictum: "Getting the best, never easy. We almost there."

Chapter 11

The Art Colony

As the car sped closer to its destination, Classico heard a strange white noise rumbling in the distance. Eventually, it telescoped its way through the forsaken landscape and into his focus. The pounding vibrations, now vaguely familiar, grew louder as the relentless beat of earsplitting rap music battled with his nerves for domination. Then, it won and he felt nothing—numbed by sensory overload.

Suddenly, the car careened onto another dirt road at a ninety-degree angle. Classico threw his arms up to protect his face. He looked up as he grabbed the door handle to regain his balance and saw hundreds of Chinese men and women in their twenties dancing and mulling about the town center. An entire village of abandoned cement factories had been repurposed into the new industrial art district.

"We here," Huang Show said.

The driver parked in a narrow dirt alleyway and opened the door for Classico. Huang Show walked away from the car. Classico started for the trunk, but the driver stepped in his way and thrust his chin briefly in Huang Show's direction, indicating that Classico should follow. Classico's eyes darted back to the trunk that sequestered the Picasso. The hood lurched upward, unlocking with a metallic grunt that scraped right through Classico's insides, stilling all cardiovascular movement. He longed to hold the painting close—to feel the texture of the canvas saturated with Picasso's DNA, and to smell the lingering scent of the last coat of Damar varnish, which sealed the great work of art.

"I take," the beefy driver said, lifting it from the trunk.

Classico glanced around, a jolt of panic threatened to dismantle his plan. He scanned the situation for a way out, but his nonexistent options were inflexible as the cement structures. He took a deep breath and followed Huang Show. The three men walked in single-file with the driver in the rear.

Classico could not believe what he was seeing—a Western-style fantasy of punks and rappers getting down to the music. They danced under the cold winter sky atop a plywood makeshift stage, which covered a foundation assembled from alternating layers of dead tree trunks and junkyard tires. The star rapper wore a Che Guevara T-shirt, and belted Mandarin lyrics into the microphone. He held center stage like a chieftain performing a tribal ritual, invoking hypnotic powers over the audience. His bleached hair, dyed bright yellow, stood straight up, electrocution style, zapped and stiff as metal rods. The crowd responded with vigorous gyrations.

Behind him, graffiti-torn drawings and photographs wallpapered the walls and sides of several adjacent buildings that were all scribbled with Chinese calligraphy. Classico tried to keep from stumbling, as the images of political dreamscapes loomed large: half-dragon, half-human portraits, corrupt revolutionaries, indicted politicians, and Hollywood stars. The slippery gravel passageways along with the hammering noise dizzied Classico redirecting his senses, until he longed to be home on the other side of the world.

Huang Show steered Classico through the crush of kids. Pretty girls flaunting frizzy pink hair smiled and waved, while young men with painted faces gave them a high five. Some wore wife-beater T-shirts that advertised political views, favorite musicians, dogs, and action heroes. Their preferred uniform, baggy denim jeans slung low on the hips, teased and threatened to reveal a fleshy terrain.

Classico followed closely behind Huang Show to avoid getting lost in the crowd that imitated every imaginable pop icon—Madonna, Elvis Presley, Michael Jackson, Batman, Superman, and G.I. Joes. Previously censored from the Chinese lexicon, these pop icons morphed into doppelgangers that stepped back allowing the three men to pass.

The dusty village in the middle of nowhere teemed with life and splashed with color; it was home to the contemporary art scene. Like a secret coven inside a magic art moment, the clandestine mix pulsated with ideas and energy. Never could Classico have envisioned a gala opening night such as this. *And not a drop of alcohol or a whiff of pot.*

"Unbelievable," he said, pulling his fingers through his hair.

"You like art galleries?" Huang Show asked. Classico noticed the proud gleam in his eyes.

"Yes, very much, very creative," Classico said, glancing backward to check on the Picasso as they continued walking through the narrow dirt passageways. *Now where is he taking me?*

"Amazing," Classico said, admiring the kids as they enjoyed a newly found freedom. "You have provided the venue for their expression of music, art, and fashion. Well done, Mr. Show. *Maybe he isn't so bad after all,* Classico thought.

The music changed to 80s rock and Classico loosened his bow tie and looked downward to avoid tripping on the scattered rocks. The three unlikely acquaintances that comprised the art trifecta continued winding through the alleyways. The driver stayed three paces behind clutching the Picasso. His occasional guttural pronouncements reassured Classico the painting was nearby, reducing his backward glances.

"Almost there," Huang Show said. They turned a corner and approached the largest of the old factories. The front window displayed Chinese calligraphy painted on six-foot-tall canvases.

"What does it say?" Classico asked, looking at the paintings, trying to find some common ground to initiate a conversation.

"It ancient art," said Huang Show. "Four type of calligraphy: standard, academic, running script, and cursive. All use for different purpose."

Classico leapt at this chance. *Finally, an opening to have an art discussion; a civilized conversation,* he thought. He had to make Huang Show think he was enjoying this exclusive entrée into the art scene. Under any other circumstance, he would be thrilled to be here.

Classico took a deep breath and began rambling off the art-speak jargon that he so comfortably espoused.

"Yes, I see the exquisite brush strokes depicting variations of transparency, opacity, and the rough-edged nuances evoking life's mysteries. It is the energy inherent in the characters themselves. The edges can be smooth as glass or rough as sandpaper, but most important is the relationship and tension between the shapes created by the juxtaposition of the negative and positive spaces," Classico said, speaking confidently although he had no idea what the characters meant. He twirled his eyebrow and snuck a glance at Huang Show to see his reaction, but he could not read him.

The Chinese are never one-dimensional, everything has hidden symbolism and multilayered meaning, all viewed from a perspective almost four thousand years long, Classico reminded himself.

A young man appeared, timidly stepping out from the shadows. "This is artist, Xi Wu," Huang Show said. He and the young man spoke briefly in strident Mandarin, barking their exchange. The artist straightened his posture and looked Classico in the eye.

"I am artist. I breakdown writing characters—most important tool."

"Oh I see," Classico said. "You mean you deconstruct the calligraphy tradition?"

"Yes, this way I breakdown tradition of the Great Criticism," the artist explained.

"That was a terrible time during the Cultural Revolution. I can understand your wanting to make sense of it. The People's Republic of China forced everyone to confess fabricated transgressions to an audience of their peers, who then, publicly humiliated and vilified them," Classico said, his sympathy welling.

"We had to make it up, even if we did nothing," Huang Show said, recalling those shaming sessions. "Classico, we go now."

"Good luck, young man," Classico said.

"You like my new artists' colony?" Huang Show inquired after the young man had left. Before Classico had a chance to answer, Huang Show continued, "I build village for artists to work and not be disturbed. Would you like tour of galleries?"

"Yes, indeed I would," he replied.

"Come, my best artists show tonight. Tonight, first night galleries open."

"Why did you build so far away from the cities?" Classico asked, anxiously.

I wish I were in Beijing. Picasso and I, we could just disappear way out here. No one would ever know what happened to us.

"I don't want anyone copying artist's ideas. Few weeks ago, government issue mandate: 'Innovate, no more copying.' This is country built on principles of collective, no individuals, everyone must copy. This built strong in our nature. It is hard for people to change," Huang Show said.

"Are you saying that all intellectual property is public domain in China?" Classico asked.

"Yes, it is why we copy music and movies, 'pirate,' as you say in West. It is communist way. Now that we do business with West and open doors wide to visitors, we try to accommodate your rule," he explained.

"I see," Classico said, thinking he was making progress by establishing a comfortable rapport and actually having a conversation. In one swift tug, he unfastened his bow tie, stuffed it in his pocket, and followed Huang Show into the first gallery.

A young woman dressed in 1940s high heels, a brimmed felt cloche, draped dress, and painted red lips with a pointy cupid's bow sat at the reception desk sobbing.

"Why is she crying?" Classico asked, feeling heartfelt concern for the Chinese people.

Huang Show said something to her in Chinese. She looked up at him, and a new round of sobbing began.

"She is very sad. Her dog sent to be killed by government. She loves dog very much. The government is killing fifty thousand dogs because they found one case of rabies."

Classico recoiled. "Isn't that a little extreme?"

"Country has one billion people. They not want it spread further. Things done different than America. Nothing she can do."

"Tell her I am so sorry."

"We go now," Hung Show said.

Classico wandered through the next gallery with portraits derivative of the Sichuan school. The theme was the exploration of psychological tensions resulting from personal histories. The works addressed social conformity, China's one-child policy, and the effect those mandates had on family relationships. These haunting images rendered in ghostlike gray tonalities were familiar to Classico from the well-known series "Bloodlines" by the artist Zhang Xiaogang. He worked from black-and-white family photographs, most of which had been destroyed between 1966 and 1976 during the Cultural Revolution. "Families disintegrate, but bloodlines last forever," Xiaogang had said.

Classico went rigid when he saw the unforgettable look of melancholy in the eyes of the family portraits—the lost, empty sadness from their painful past and nonexistent future. The figures, cut off above the waist, gazed straight through the viewer. With implacable earnest and extreme vulnerability, they seemed to ask: "When will it end? Have you no pity?"

"Come with me," Huang Show said. His head jerked like an arrow toward the direction of the next gallery.

Classico thought he had seen everything in the art world and was inured to shock art. A cold current bolted through his body upon entering the next gallery. An entire family hung upside down from the ceiling like taxidermy in review.

Gasping, "Oh my God," was all he could say. Huang Show sniggered. The driver waited out front.

Classico removed his glasses from his breast pocket for a closer inspection. The lifelike sculptures depicted the plight of Chinese migrant workers who lived in limbo with no resources for survival except to scavenge each day.

He turned to Huang Show, who leaned against the wall with his arms folded, a hint of a smirk tilted the line of his mouth. He was enjoying Classico's reaction.

"Can you hear them cry?" asked Huang Show. "Artist make from encaustic."

"They are as brilliant as a Duane Hansen sculpture. Do you know his work? It is only when standing next to his hyper-life-like figures, do you realize they are not breathing. These are equally as realistic. But of course, the subject matter is tough and political, screaming for justice. Duane Hansen's work portrays Middle America in a Norman Rockwell-esque genre," said Classico.

Classico understood that the Chinese artists had broken from the government-sponsored art of *Social Realism*. Having quit idolizing utopian workers depicted in the propaganda posters, they now struggled to reinvent their identities—and a new school of art began.

"Come," Huang Show said. Classico glanced one last time at the work and did as he was told.

In the maze of galleries, Classico saw room after room of cartoon images from the school of *Cynical Realism*, which developed in the aftermath of the 1989 Tiananmen Square protests.

These hilarious caricatures are exaggerated, allowing the artist to contradict serious political issues, while keeping their cynical intentions that mock the establishment hidden, he thought, speculating on an interpretation. "Ah, I see," Classico said in a moment of cognizance.

He laughed when he entered the next gallery and saw the cartoon version of a blond-haired, Chinese Marilyn Monroe in the iconic "subway gusting" pose. She struggled unsuccessfully to hold her dress down, while the air from the grating blew it skyward.

"This last one today," Huang Show said, as they came upon a locked door at the far end of a dirt alleyway. The ascending moonlight dappled the rocks and the small clearing with leafy dark patches. The night crickets harmonized with the underfoot scrunch of dislodging pebbles. *Finally, we'll see the copies,* thought Classico.

Huang Show rummaged through a six-inch, round, metal ring that held at least one hundred skeleton keys. The rusted keyhole and hinges were affixed to the ancient wooden door like decoupage. Huang Show held it open for Classico. It was dark inside. Classico grimaced at the sight of the meandering, cave-like hallway. Cracked cement plastered over clay walls was lit by a single naked light bulb, which dangled from a lone ceiling wire. He could taste and smell the musty earthen structure.

He tried not to slip on the unpaved, potholed path strewn with rocks and branches in the semidarkness.

Damn my shoes are being ruined!

Then a glow of civilization appeared from around the final bend to reveal an open space, where at the far end Huang Show's assistant stood smiling in the doorway.

Classico entered the room, froze, and sucked in his breath—hard and quick. His face went white, all the blood drained from his cheeks. A sudden blast from an ice storm in nearby Mongolia could not have halted his movements more stunningly than seeing this underground museum of subterfuge. There before him, hidden away like excavated treasures from a Pharaoh's tomb, were the modern masterpieces of the twentieth century: Warhol, Lichtenstein, Rosenquist, Braque, and Sergeant—each more perfect than the next. Classico stumbled backward, reeling with disbelief.

Seeing these familiar masterworks displayed in this surreptitious setting, away from their proper museum homes—in this godforsaken corner of the world—was like finding the Hope Diamond in a brown paper bag at a laundromat. He glanced at Huang Show, who leaned against the wall with a strange grin that stretched across the bottom of his face, but failed to reach his lifeless eyes.

"Go," Huang Show said. "Take good look."

Classico removed the gold-chained monocle from his vest pocket and examined each painting with microscopic attention, giving particular scrutiny to the penmanship of line, brush strokes, texture, and half tones.

"I can always spot a fake when a stilted brush stroke interrupts the flow of creative energy and the work becomes static. The truth of identity is in the frozen parts. It is subtle, but distinct, and will never escape my well-trained eye," he told Huang Show.

"You are expert," Huang Show agreed.

Slowly, Classico moved from painting to painting, examining every square inch.

"My connoisseurship is impeccable, and these are perfect. I cannot tell them apart from the originals. Where are all these paintings going?" he asked.

"Some will go to auction in States and Russia, some commissioned by collectors who have to sell real paintings to raise cash, and do not want to part with them. Some just want copy for their second or third home," Huang Show said.

"So, that is the storyline," replied Classico.

"They are so good, they can sell on secondary market in auction as originals," Huang explained.

"You are probably right; with copies this good, no one will ever see the difference, and with copies this good an expert can easily overlook any evidence of a forgery," Classico said.

He knew the drill when dealing with the art history scholars turned authenticator experts. Sixty percent of them could be encouraged to ignore a false attribution with a lovely lunch or dinner accompanied by a bottle of 1959 Chateau Lafite Rothschild. If that proved ineffective, an invitation to a special country weekend at a grand estate often provided enough incentive to validate the owners opinion, regardless of its origins. Eventually they capitulated, and the authentication documents were signed, as the scrim of vintage wines, three-star Michelin restaurants, vacations, and yachts, which were particularly efficacious, softened the acuity of the art historian's vision. It was not exactly a mendacious conclusion, Classico consoled himself; however, one tended to prevaricate on this issue. And because there were so many gray areas to consider, at times, one simply acquiesced to the consensus—like a well-oiled rumor mill, people believed what they heard repeatedly.

Being on the board of the official Rembrandt Research Project, Classico had experienced this often. The experts vetted one thousand Rembrandt paintings and classified only 320 as authentic. The others were either copies or student work declassified into the circle of Rembrandt. Currently, Classico knew of nine-hundred fifty Rembrandts that hung in museums around the world; they all claimed to be original.

"I cannot believe I am surrounded by forged masterpieces, and I am still feeling the same thrill as if they were the real thing," he told Huang Show.

It must be the jet lag making me weak from so many inspiring artists, he thought. He did not blink, but continued staring and pondering the unanswerable questions that plagued every art connoisseur: What makes two identical paintings so different in price? What is that indefinable distinction that compels someone to buy a painting at auction when a similar painting by the same artist is available two blocks away at a private dealer for $500,000 less? Classico struggled to find the answer, but the Ritalin was beginning to wear off, and this was no time to lose his focus. Covertly, he swallowed another pill.

"And now, Classico, I'd like you meet number one copy artist in China, SoLow."

SoLow appeared from behind a tattered burlap curtain that led to his workroom. Gnarled as an old tree trunk, he hobbled toward them, bowing his head. His hands crippled by arthritis, painfully clutched several well-used brushes. Classico thought his hands looked as if they had once been broken. *It must be extremely painful for him to work,* Classico thought.

Each painting in SoLow's life had left a color-stained souvenir in the creases and folds of his palms and fingers. His matted hair, pulled back into a ponytail, had long ago turned gray, not because of his sixty years, but because of his poor diet. His weathered face, deeply etched with emotional scars, which, like gutters, expelled the residue from both a life growing up in the work farms and the endless sadness inherited from his family. His ancestors, like millions of others, had endured the Long March and had survived debilitating disease and hunger.

"Are these all your paintings?" Classico raised his arms shaping an arc to encompass the collection and then pointed at SoLow.

"Yes they are. SoLow very talented. He works for me, only," Huang Show replied with a gloating smile.

SoLow's eyes, fixed on the floor, caught sight of Classico's English, handmade Lobb shoes, which were polished to a mirror shine. He glanced at his own wretched slippers that he found discarded in a back alley near his home during the government demolition of his family's hutong. SoLow did not dare to look at Classico directly.

Earlier that month, the Russians had come and threatened to burn all the paintings if they were not finished in time for the spring auctions in St. Petersburg. Somehow, he had managed to complete them. Huang Show had made sure of that.

"SoLow does not have many painting left in him, but he promised me three more perfect masterpiece before he retire to a life of tai chi in the Summer Palace Park with the rest of the elderly."

SoLow returned to his work on the El Greco that had been

commissioned by a Russian arms dealer. He put his brush to the canvas, and, like a mountain waterfall, tears fell over the craggy terrain of his face. He grimaced with pain.

"Don't mind him," Huang Show said. "He has over-sensitive emotion. It translates into sensitive for colors and art. Give him Picasso, he said to the driver.

Classico took the painting and clutched it to his chest one last time before parting with it. Tears welled up in his eyes but did not fall. He pulled himself together, and gingerly unrolled the painting onto the table with the same delicacy used to touch hand-blown Murano glass, the original Gutenberg Bible, the Magna Carta, or the Preamble. The painting represented the pinnacle of the love life of the twentieth century's greatest artist. The pivotal work transitioned cubism to Picasso's next phase—integrating classicism with surrealism.

Classico's heart and burgeoning headache pounded in unison, creating their own symphonic torment.

"Oh, why can't I be home in my bed reading auction catalogs?" He muttered under his breath. *What am I about to do? This is a tragedy, to give a bona fide world treasure away—to be lost to society forever, never again to know its whereabouts. I am watching it get sucked into the black hole of the underworld.*

A chopped strident voice startled Classico out of his morass of worry. "The guard will stay with Picasso at all times. In one or two week, you have three new copies. No one ever see difference. Let's go," Huang Show said, briskly jerking his head in the direction of the exit.

With a final adoring look, Classico gently caressed the surface of the painting, touching it perhaps for the last time. He turned to leave with a stilled heart and tender remorse flooding his emotions. Wistfully, he remembered: All those years, almost a century, had passed since the great Picasso influenced generations of artists and art lovers alike. Like a beacon beckoning in the night, the painting dared viewers to find their own truth, to find their inner creative source, and to connect with the divine, as Picasso had done. Using his imagination, Picasso validated the universal potential for all possibilities on canvas and in life.

Classico clenched his fists in his pockets, lowered his eyes, and followed Huang Show out into the night. The crowd parted like the Red Sea, but he did not feel deliverance like Moses.

Chapter 12

A Grisaille-Colored Sleep

"We here," Huang Show said at three a.m. as the car lurched and sputtered into the hotel driveway. The long flight and grueling drive back and forth from the art colony had Classico's aching muscles screaming for repose, reminding him that he had not had a good night's sleep in days. He wanted only to rest in his own cosmic universe covered with dapples from the bedspread's silk shantung reflections. Finally alone in his room, he threw his clothes on the chair, put on his pajamas and crawled into bed. He closed his eyes, pulled the covers to his chin and sighed deeply. He was just about to drift off, when a knock on the door startled him. "Who is it?" he asked.

"I give massage. You like now?" said a female voice from the hallway.

"Aha, the famous Chinese massage. Well, why not, I certainly need it," he said.

Opening the door, he saw a beautiful young woman from Thailand, not taller than five feet, smiling at him so sweetly that he forgot about his separation from Picasso—at least for the moment. He motioned her inside and helped her with the massage table. He preferred to have the massage in his bed so he could remain in that pleasant floating zone and ease off to sleep afterward. He pointed to the bed and said in his best broken English, "I get massage here."

"Yes, okay, anything you like," she said. "Do you like China? The art is very good. Don't you think? Is it good as New York?" she chatted inquiringly.

What is she talking about? he wondered.

He peeled off his pajamas, left his shorts on for modesty's sake and lay down, groaning like the foghorn of a steamship. Her technique was partly Swedish deep tissue and partly Thai. She walked on his back, sat on his legs, and pulled and twisted his body, reshaping it like a pipe cleaner. *Crack, creak,* went the floorboards of his aching bones.

"Ooh that feels good; oh yes over there," he moaned.

"You get massage in Central Park?" she asked.

"What?" he said, lifting his head slightly. "Oh never mind. Yes, right there, mmm."

Slowly she massaged the soles of his feet, circling each toe in its own orbit and upon returning to his arches, kneaded the meridians of his connected soul. By this time, he was on his back. Continuing with the same focused intent, she crept up his legs to the forest primeval. His whole body stiffened. Rabid with desire, he tried not to beg.

"How much extra?" he asked.

"It present from Huang Show."

"What the f—?" He jolted to a sitting position.

"No worry, it's okay," she said gently pushing him back down.

"That bastard, now he is in my bedroom." *She is probably his spy.*

"Okay, Okay. Let's get this over with."

Like feathers escaping from a pillow ripped open in the wind, Classico saw hundreds of tiny Picasso paintings fly away into the sky. Then he fell into a dreamless black and white, grisaille-colored sleep. She quietly slipped out of the room with her table. Huang Show had paid her that afternoon.

Chapter 13

Waiting for Picasso

T he next morning he awoke with a laser-sharp pain in his head that forced him back onto the pillow. Looking at the unfamiliar surroundings, which were still out of focus, he recalled his location and the orphaned Picasso. He tried not to panic as his anxiety level and blood pressure soared. He rose from the bed, paced the floor, and opened the curtain to another overcast day, dense with industrial smog from the factories and car emissions. It matched his gloomy mood, which was somewhat comforting providing a visual buffer, distancing him from yesterday's guilty journey. He found some Tylenol in his suitcase, swallowed three, and went back to sleep until his headache disappeared.

An hour later, he woke to his stomach growling. Feeling much better after he showered, shaved and dressed, he took the elevator to the lobby for breakfast.

Having nothing to do but wait a week until the paintings were ready, Classico planned to visit the Forbidden City and more of Beijing's art galleries. The concierge gave him directions for the short walk. He headed west, passing large community square parks with ancient trees and shrubs that bordered reflecting ponds. For centuries, they had been a source of beauty and pleasure for all who passed through them. He imagined the Empress Wu Zeitan and her ladies in waiting, spending long summer days delighting in their reflections. Walking through Tiananmen Square, he stopped to buy a watch with a Chairman Mao face for twenty-one RMB, or about three dollars. *These will make amusing gifts,* he chuckled and decided to buy five more. *Alouisha would surely like to have one.*

After walking thirty minutes, he arrived at the Palace of the Forbidden City at the Gate of the Heavenly Peace, the former home to twenty-four emperors and the hub of all significant historic intrigues in China. The 178-acre city had ninety palaces and lines of tourists long enough to wrap the entire periphery and fill the Heavenly Palaces.

Of course, it's mobbed with thousands of Chinese tourists, he scolded himself for not being smarter about his day's plans. *Where else can they go?* He remembered the government made it difficult and expensive for the Chinese to acquire visas to leave their country. As a result, the Chinese people spent their holidays visiting domestically.

Feeling tired and his headache rebooting, he stopped when a man selling pirated DVDs approached him. He flipped through the selection, and came upon The Last Emperor filmed entirely in the Forbidden City.

"Great," he exclaimed. *I'll watch the movie on my computer and have a close up view of the interiors, not just the rooms opened to tourists.* He gave the man a bill for ten RMB. "Keep the change. Sheh sheh," he said, thanking him in Chinese.

Leaving the palace grounds, he looked for a restaurant with those ubiquitous plastic-coated menus, which were translated into English and illustrated with photos. He settled on a hotpot restaurant and followed the maître d' to a table near the window overlooking the gardens. Classico admired the familiar foliage that the Chinese had rendered on scrolls for thousands of years. The flowing, leafy drawings had the same grace and energy inherent in calligraphy. Mountains and waterfalls depicted in transparent, delicate halftones filled the edges of the landscapes. They symbolized ancient Chinese lore, often interpreting *The Kingdom of Heaven's* philosophy of rule by divine right.

Except for the dog and boiled bullfrog, the menu looked tasty. The server brought him a cauldron of steaming broth and placed it over a lighted flame that recessed into the center of the table.

"What you want cook in pot?" he asked and pointed to the pictures on the glossy menu.

"I'll have the chicken, shrimp, string beans, bok choy, and carrots please," Classico replied, thinking this was an Asian version of a Swiss Fondue, poaching and simmering the flavor into a glorious broth finale.

As he waited for his lunch to arrive, he reached for his favorite amusement, his iPhone. He loved having access to an entire media galaxy through the lightweight command center. He rooted around in his pockets, gently at first, then wrenching the lining of his pockets, as if he were unearthing an active landmine with ten seconds to detonation. "Damn it, that son of a bitch, stole my iPhone." Classico jumped up from the table, threw his napkin on the chair, and ran out of the restaurant back to the Forbidden City.

"Waiter, I'll be back."

Flushed and out of breath, he arrived back at the Palace, but the DVD counterfeiter had disappeared. He pushed through the crowds, peered over bushes and around corners, searching the streets for the thief. He was gone, replaced by a dozen new DVD salesmen.

"Where the hell is that black-market bastard?"

"Damn, just what I needed—to lose my iPhone, with all my information, all my business contacts, everything," Classico muttered, kicking a fallen tree branch out of his way.

While walking back to the restaurant, he stopped at a newspaper kiosk to buy the English–language China Daily. He glanced at the front page, the headline read: "Chinese hospital gives internet addicts shock therapy."

The article explained that an iPhone to an Internet addict was like heroin to a junkie: They killed for them. Because the disease was so prevalent among the children and young adults in China, Internet addiction clinics had become widespread. Their preferred treatment was electric-shock therapy. The parents of the patients were assured no torture or pain was involved. But Classico, scanning the story, read that three medical practitioners were sentenced to capital punishment after they kicked a child to death during a difficult withdrawal session. He winced from the severity of the child's treatment. *Well, losing my iPhone is not such a big deal,* he reassured himself.

Back at the restaurant, he intended to relax and enjoy his lunch, but when he turned to the second page of the newspaper he winced again. "Ouch," he said, reading a headline quoted from the Guardian: "American financial crisis unmatched since the great depression."

"Damn it! It's getting worse. I'll never be able to sell paintings in this economy."

Greenspan had assured Americans that the economy was stable and healthy. Why did he continuously insist that the numbers were on track? "His circumlocutions were impossible to disambiguate and intentionally confusing!" Why did he speak in such obtuse, convoluted sentences, whenever he gave a speech on television? Was he covering up the truth? And why had he granted Wall Street immunity from having any responsibility to the American consumer? *He and Paulson, what a pair!*

His eyes grew rounder; the whites on top of his pupils became more visible. He raked his hand through his hair and scanned the article for news about the credit markets drying up. He tugged at his collar, which tightened around his neck. *I'll never be able to sell anything now...or raise any cash.* Infuriated, he crumpled the newspaper and threw it along with two hundred RMBs on the table, where it landed on top of the plastic-laminated menu with color photos of the daily specials. Classico left the restaurant steaming more hotly than his hot-pot lunch.

"There must be a way; there has to be a solution," he mumbled repeatedly. He walked the streets for hours trying to regain some clarity, searching his mind for a new strategy. The pollution in the twilight sky formed pink sheaths of low sun reflections, which glowed on the windows of the buildings.

Realizing it was getting late, he looked for a taxi to take him back to the hotel, but all he could find was a pedi-cab. The three-wheeled bicycle attached to a cart with a plastic seat inside would have to be sufficient. He gave the driver the hotel card with the address written in Chinese on one side and English on the other side. The leathery old man, bilingual in financial phrases, took the card, uttered a huff-grunt, and said, "Twendy dollar." His clothing looked as worn out as his face. Classico climbed in with trepidation, fearing the old man would over-exert himself from his load-bearing haul. The driver would take the shortest and easiest route, requiring the least effort; Classico could be certain of that.

Relaxing onto the plastic covered seat, Classico watched the changing architectural landscape. Each new building rivaled the next with an innovative design that seemingly defied geometry. Unimpeded by code restrictions, Chinese postmodern architecture reached creative heights unattainable in the U.S.

Passing by the Olympic Stadium, "The Birds Nest," Classico was awed by its enormity and its intricately woven branches of steel. *Its creative genius is unsurpassed*, thought Classico. *The Chinese have given us post-neo pop architecture: Instead of Andy Warhol's soup cans, their lexicon is a bird's nest!*

He pulled his collar up and hunched away from the wind.

Tomorrow, I'll go to the new CCTV station, he thought, flipping through his guide-book. "A twenty-first century Chinese gem, the CCTV headquarters is the largest office building in the world. Designed to reinvent human interaction, it contains five million square feet of office space and television production studios. Integrating the latest green technologies within a light-drenched environment, CCTV is the paradigm of innovation, creating a new symbiotic relationship between work and life," it read.

Classico thought the new CCTV building resembled a parallelogram with a donut square cut out of the center. It tilted to one side—a salute to the leaning tower of Pisa. It gave the impression that an enormous pair of hands had descended from the skies, twisted it slightly, and pushed the entire structure until it almost toppled. Remarkable, he thought.

Continuing on his way, Classico noted the well-landscaped park settings of Beijing functioned as stage sets for each architectural marvel's imposing presence. The steps to the entrance of many of Beijing's properties reached to one-hundred feet. Imperious and foreboding, these architectural warriors laid claim to their territorial imperatives. At street level, Classico felt dwarfed by their size, but later amused when the interiors gradually lit up, as if they concealed mysterious inner sanctums that were harvested with LED's. The resplendent colors replaced the waning glow of dusk with breathtaking, full-spectrum colors. Classico imagined the world-renowned conductor, Leon Botstein, creating a musical score that synchronized the lighting.

The driver turned onto a main street filled with hordes of people. A cacophony of unintelligible dialects expressing consumerist urges rattled the Hutong district, as the throngs of people went about their daily routines, hawking and peddling wares to the shops and restaurants. Signs were displayed in every direction, shape and color that advertised the latest imported fashions or restaurants. Astonishingly, the driver kept up his pace only slowing slightly when he turned the corner into another crowded side street. Classico held on tightly when the third wheel left the ground. The confusion of colors, ambient smells, and noises ascended like a mushroom cloud, embalming his senses with overload as they drove right into the thick of it.

Some ancient store frontage remained in the partially renovated streets. Sculpted dragons climbed broken columns that peeled with remnants of gold and red-flaked paint. Plastered birds tried to break free of their caged, carved origins. Gargoyles made of concrete, old wood, and stone jutted from doorways, windows and facades, twisting in anguish like ghosts unable to escape from an ancient cemetery after a violent kill. The store's bland interiors, 1970s version of modern functional replete with vinyl-covered furnishings, contrasted sharply with the riotous exteriors.

They turned the corner, and in every window boiling cauldrons of suspicious, offal-looking soup steamed and sputtered in frothy eruptions. Classico could only surmise the contents; his imagination spurred along by rows of restaurants proudly displaying the catch of the day: snakes, fish, and unnameable sea monsters exhibited their wrenched innards to be savored for an evening's delicacy. Dead fowl hung by their feet from the ceilings of the windows. Their necks stretched like elastic and elongated to unimaginable lengths that distorted their faces into grotesque proportions. Lifeless eyes stared vacantly at the waiting cauldrons, which soon would seal their fate.

Classico felt as though he were passing through a reenactment of Damien Hirst's exhibition of dead animals that hung from the ceilings of the Lever Brothers building on Park Avenue and Fifty-first Street two years ago. Carol Vogel called it "The Noah's ark of road kill." Carnivorous passions prevailed in New York on opening night in the Spring of 2007. People lined up for blocks; Classico could not get near the entrance. *They should see this street,* he thought. *This is the real thing.*

The darkening sky descended and crept slowly, sensuously like active lava. It enveloped the streets with gray and purple crusts of clouds, which lost their color when the sky-ceiling came close enough to touch. The shopkeepers turned off the boiling hot-pots, turned out the lights, and closed the doors until tomorrow in the business district of Beijing.

Classico motioned to the driver to stop the pedi-cab; the old neighborhood, an historic preservationist's dream, inspired further exploration, and maybe he could still find an open restaurant. His empty stomach growled after his walk. The driver held up his hand, and rubbed his thumb back and forth along the other four fingers—the universal signage for "give me the money." Classico paid the man 200 RMB.

He stepped out of the pedi-cab and turned the corner. In the empty, dark side street, a strange quietude descended. Even the food smells had disappeared—shuttered indoors behind the closed storefronts and windows. One by one, a trail of cartoon neon signs that reached the length of two blocks, lit up the street, beckoning the onlookers to follow its path: California Cowboys, Pink Pussy Pussy, Captain Jack will get you High, Heavenly Homebodies, Big John Saloon, Get-yar-Grits, Girls-Nite-In, Nieces and Nurses, Titty–Tatler, Hooters and Booters. The signage continued down the long street into the darkness, configuring a deep perspective, until the furthest sign became a tiny unreadable speck of neon light, like a star that could have fallen from the sky. The transformation from a daytime business district to a nighttime red-light district was complete.

The Americanized slogans rendered in Las Vegas-garish alluded to the late-night activities offered by the young women standing in the doorways. They arranged themselves in groups of twos or threes, posing provocatively as if sitting for a John Currin portrait. They dressed in baby-doll nighties, nurse uniforms, as French maids, geishas, cowgirls, or just strippers. Most of them had acquired short-term work visas and would send their earnings back to their families in Thailand.

It was still early, and the streets were empty except for the girls and a few Western men appraising the evenings' possibilities. Classico walked the street delighting in the nighttime spectacle, inspired by his coincidental luck this evening. *They are all so gorgeous,* he thought. *It is hard to resist.* He twisted the hair of his right eyebrow. *When in China, do as the Chinese do—or do as the tourists do.* As he walked down the street, he wrestled with indecision; no longer *whether* to engage, but the much larger issue—did he need a nurse, a cowgirl, or a baby girl? *Perhaps all three! No, I'm not a pedophile,* he reprimanded himself. *Maybe a hooter-booter or tits and boots; now that sounds like my kind of woman.*

The New York women he slept with would never guess Classico's real cravings. They all wanted to be sex goddesses, revered, placed on a pedestal, then, made love to. Especially Sabrina, who was more worried about tearing her lingerie than letting Classico have fun ripping it off. By the time she had removed and folded it neatly, Classico's thoughts were out the door. He lusted for a down and dirty woman wearing a cheap wet T-shirt and high-heeled boots—one that would not be afraid to rough him up a little. *I get so bored always having to be the elegant, well-mannered lover they expect of me, simply because I happen to have excellent taste in art.*

Just as he was about to come to a decision, he was approached from behind and thrown to the ground.

A Chinese man screamed, and a current of fear seared through Classico's chest as

"What the hell," he yelled. "Help, help!" This only got him a swift kick in his shins. The man dragged Classico by his legs into a garbage filled alleyway. He was too shocked to feel the pain in his leg or his bleeding hand as it scraped along the cobblestone street.

"No, don't kill me," he shouted. "Here take my money." The man searched Classico's pockets, rooting and ripping. Classico screamed. It all happened so fast. He received another hard blow, this time to his side. The pain seared like a blow-torch. He could not breathe—suffocating from fear and the rotting fish smells. The last thing he remembered before passing out, was the sound of screeching cats rattling the metal trashcans and their smoldering, marbled eyes.

Chapter 14

The Garbage Dump

"Wake up, Wake up."

A soft female voice entered the dark corridors of Classico's unconscious as a hand gently slapped his cheeks. The voice came closer and grew louder. The wind whipped his face, or maybe it was the tall stalks of corn in the Nebraska meadows, beating against him as he made his way home from school. Groaning, he opened his eyes to see a milky white décolletage two inches from his nose. Her excessively sweet perfume mixed with rotting fish, stung like a spoonful of tabasco. Feral cats clamored all around him on the overflowing trashcans; their eyes, like narrow-beamed flashlights, pierced the darkness and scared the hell out of him. His head spun as he tried to recall the sequence of events that had brought him to this current state of despair: crumpled on the filthy stone floor of a back alley. Nearby, a rusty metal grating recessed into the floor topped the drainage system, which was the final resting place for the leftover contents from the restaurant's cauldrons. Classico surmised its utility from the fish heads and other refuse, which collected on the drain, too large to fit through the bars. His scraped hand bled and throbbed. He wrapped it in his handkerchief; red blotted through the fine cotton.

Frantically, he searched his pockets to see what was missing: cash and his Breitling watch. Luckily, the hotel had kept his passport—— *Probably for this very reason.* The young woman from Thailand tried to help him up but he fell back down, wincing in pain. Holding his head in his hands, he supported the weight of his misery.

"I must get back to the hotel," he said to the girl.

"Please, can you get me a pedi-cab?" Fumbling in his pocket, he retrieved the crumpled hotel card. "Here, here it is."

Suddenly, from behind, two hefty hands slipped under his arms and pulled him up. He wanted to resist, but had neither the strength nor the grit. His body hurt too much to struggle, and his dented pride had battered his will. With his vision still unfocused, the stranger helped him to the street where a car waited.

"Oh no, I'm not getting in there," he said turning to face the blurred man.

"Get in, Classico. I take you to hotel," the stranger ordered.

First, the pockmarks came into focus, looking like enlarged pixels of excavated pustules through a zoom lens. Then, after a few seconds, they receded into a recognizable full-face formation.

"It's you. Huang Show's driver," he exclaimed, not knowing if he should be relieved or afraid. *How did he get here? Is he following me? Did he steal my wallet?* His head cleared, and the accusatory thoughts raced in his mind. "What are you doing here? Do you know who stole my wallet?"

"Get in," the voice from the back seat of the car ordered. The driver opened the door, and there was Huang Show. Was that a snicker creeping up the corners of his mouth?

"It good thing we look after you. Tomorrow we find thief. You need doctor? Not good, be on streets at night alone," Huang Show said.

Classico dragged his body, which felt like a lumpy bag of rocks, into the car. "No doctor ... hotel." He couldn't think about Huang's complicity, not now. Before the driver closed the door, the girl from Thailand ran over to the car, smiled and handed Classico her card. It read: Hooters and Booters.

"Here you need this," said Huang Show and handed Classico his iPhone.

Chapter 15

The Young Artist

lassico stumbled out of the car when he arrived back at the hotel. The doorman rushed to his side to catch the seemingly drunken guest as he lost his balance and staggered through the door.

"Mr. Classico, are you okay?" the doorman asked, looking shocked at the sight of Classico's soiled clothing and the bloodstained handkerchief wrapped around his hand. The driver, speaking harshly in an agitated Chinese voice relayed the incident.

"They robbed me," Classico said, mumbling, feeling weaker and more disoriented by the moment.

What was Hung Show doing there? How complicit is he? Why would he want my iPhone? Did he have me followed? The questions kept hammering at him in a brittle voice buried inside his head, insisting that he find an answer.

"You want doctor? I call Police?" the hotel attendant asked.

"No, no, please; I'll just go to my room. I think I'm all right," Classico said, though grimacing with pain, he attempted to walk without wobbling. The last thing he needed was to report the robbery and involve the police and the American Embassy. *Then I'd really be screwed,* he thought. *If that happened, they would interrogate me about the purpose of my visit. Of course, I would say it was to buy art. But, if they chose to investigate further* ... his thoughts trailed off. *I have to be more careful in the future.*

"I send up doctor," the doorman insisted.

"No, thank you, it's nothing. I'll just go to bed; tomorrow I should be better. Good night," he said.

"Is there anything I can get you, Sir?" asked the receptionist.

Classico stopped, pausing to think for a moment. "Yes, tomorrow you can get me a translator."

Classico stayed in bed for two days, sleeping, ordering room service, and treating his wounded pride with massive doses of self-pity. Jettisoning back and forth between anger and depression, he waited for his bruises to heal and the Picassos to be completed. By the end of the second day, he felt well enough to learn some Mandarin and called for the translator.

He leaned toward his bedside table for the telephone and noticed the Hooters and Booters card the girl from the alley had given him. He closed his eyes and remembered waking to her beautiful breasts, one inch away from his lips. Sadly, his bruises prevented his having another massage. With nothing else to do, he slipped the second DVD of The Last Emperor into his computer and ate his lunch of steamed dumplings and bok choy.

Feeling incapable of dealing with any further problems, he had avoided calling Alouisha for the past three days. He used all his energy to heal his mental and physical wounds, and, by invoking his childhood version of magical thinking, he hoped the problems would simply disappear. When his tortured conscience would no longer remain sequestered, he placed a collect call to the states to avoid the hotel surcharges.

"Alouisha, answer the phone," he ordered, tapping his foot impatiently.

"Good afternoon, Classico Gallery."

"Will you accept a call from a Mr. Classico from China," the operator asked?

"Yes, of course." There was a pause and then the call connected. "Mr. Classico, how are you?"

"Not so great," he said and continued to tell the story of his assault and robbery, leaving out certain details. He could not very well mention he was roaming around the red light district.

"I'm so sorry about your injuries. Will you be okay?"

"Yes, yes. I am just a little sore. I'm lucky I didn't break anything. Today I feel well enough to go to some art galleries."

"I am so glad you're feeling better. That must have been a frightening ordeal," she said.

"I can assure you, Alouisha, it was not pleasant. How is everything at the gallery?"

Alouisha paused, she had news, but none of it was good. Not wanting to upset him any further, she would let the worst of it wait until he returned home.

"Everything at the gallery is under control, Mr. Classico. Don't worry about a thing. Let me see," she said, flipping the pages of her calendar. "Oh yes, that movie star called and wanted to know when the check for the Picasso will clear, and Sondra Aristoteil wanted a date for delivery of her painting. Sinbad DeMande called to inquire about payments from the art fund, as did Edwina Mass. She also phoned to thank you for the lovely flowers. The mortgage company wanted to know when your refinancing application would be complete. The contractor will paint the last five layers of skim coat on the gallery walls if you pay him the remaining thirty percent of his fee. Goodrich's called and is offering you another Picasso from a private source. Your mother called and wanted you to call her, something about her Medicare. And thank you so much for the beautiful clothing. I certainly do look the like the elegant gallerist. How is the art in China?"

He paused for a moment. "Interesting," he said.

"And of course, you have several invitations to dinner parties and luncheons. And Lisa Grovesnor called inviting you for a weekend in Millbrook; I believe that is on the seventeenth. Would you like me to respond to the other invitations from Isadora Brioche, Steve Cohen, and Sir Jenson and Lady Ellen? I have checked your calendar and you are free those evenings," she said, pulling open the drawers of her desk and rifling through her papers to make sure she did not forget anything. "And, oh, yes, GiGi Townsend bought a fabulous Milton Avery at auction and is dying for you to see it. Mrs. Rosenfeld needs a letter of authentication for her Monet. Also, the Whitney Board of Trustees asked that you kindly submit your annual giving. Other than that, nothing else is new," she said.

Classico sighed deeply, aware that he had been gone less than a week and the pressures were already mounting.

"Thank you, Alouisha, you are doing a great job. I won't forget this. Accept all the invitations and hold off on everything else until I return home. If any of my clients or bankers call, tell them I have gone to China to purchase the latest Chinese sensation, Zhang Xiaogang. Tell them, I had a once in a lifetime opportunity to acquire these works before they went to market. Ask them if they could please be patient until I return in a week's time."

"Yes, Sir."

"Good, I will see you in a week or so, good-bye for now."

He hung up and wiped the moisture from his forehead. Feeling a bit more cheerful because there was no immediate crisis at home, and Alouisha seemed to be keeping everyone calm, Classico pulled himself together and changed out of his pajamas for the first time in two days. Automatically, he reached for his Breitling watch, having forgotten that it was stolen. "That bastard, I'd like to strangle him." Stepping into his trousers, "ouch" he said flinching, when the bruise on his leg rubbed against the fabric. Then he tripped on his pant leg, stumbling and hitting the chair with his ribs. "Ow!" A throbbing ache replaced the dull pain of yesterday.

This is not going well. I have only a short time left in Beijing. I may as well go to a museum as planned, Classico thought.

He tried to enjoy the rare smogless day as he left the hotel and walked in the direction of the contemporary art museum. He ignored any residual physical discomfort by walking faster and concentrating on the sights. The boulevards were wider than Boulevard Haussmann in Paris although not as charming, and the office buildings, lacking human proportion appeared to be built for giants.

"Excuse me, Sir."

A nice looking man, no older than twenty-one, approached Classico.

"Sir, I have just graduated University," he said speaking softly, punctuating each word with extreme sensitivity. "I have spent five years studying painting, and today is the last day of my graduating class's art show. Would you please come and see it? It is just around the corner."

Even though the young man's English was excellent, and his well-honed manners impressive, "No, I don't think so," Classico said, not knowing where he would be taken and not wishing to have any further adventures on his trip.

"Oh Sir, please," the young man implored, sensing Classico's fear. "The exhibit is in a public space; you will not be alone and will feel safe. It would mean so much to me. Five minutes only." He was so earnest and sincere that Classico felt sympathetic.

"Well, okay, but only for five minutes," he said.

Singled out to see the University of Beijing's graduating student's vernissage delighted Classico. It would have a different syntax than the Yale exhibition. He never tired of seeing countries engage in the global art dialogue, and to see how the young have processed their world.

The artist led Classico around the corner, down two blocks past Tiananmen Square, and up the north side of the Summer Palace, where they entered a generic looking corporate building. *Nothing unusual about it,* Classico thought. They took the elevator to the fourth floor and entered the student gallery, leaving the door open. Painted scrolls made of silk and rice paper were stacked from floor to ceiling in the 16 by 16-foot, square room. Copies or slight variations of ancient motifs were perfectly rendered in tempera: the Dragon, the Empress, wild angry cats, Chinese mountains, or the ubiquitous green camphor tree foliage,

"I cannot believe they taught you this at the university," he said to the young man, thinking he was wasting his talent on these cliched motifs.

"What do you think?" The young student asked hesitantly.

Classico felt enormous responsibility to validate this young man's future. He did not want to crush his enthusiasm with the truth.

"Well, young man, they are beautifully rendered," he said inspecting the paint application for hints of reproductions: Ben Day dots for offset prints, continuous tone for ink jet prints, or pixels for digital prints. He found nothing but painted gouache surfaces. "But why are you painting classical themes? Why haven't you been creative? You have so much ability to paint this realistically. You must do something different."

The young man's faced suddenly drooped with sadness; the light in his eyes disappeared as did the smile from his face.

"Now, please, don't be discouraged. I can tell you how to become a famous artist and make lots of money. First, people are just discovering Chinese Contemporary Art. We love it in the West. However, you must paint something that is different from anything you have ever seen before. Go to the library and find books of contemporary artists. Study how they used their imaginations to envision new ways of understanding life. Your work should investigate the world from a new experiential perspective—a unique way of decoding our humanity. Paint what you feel most strongly about. It could be your family history, your friends, your hobbies, any subject will do. You have the tools and talent just make it personal. After you have finished 10 or 15 pieces, find a gallery. It shouldn't be too difficult, good, new work is always in demand. Above all else, you must be persistent and not give up. You must believe in yourself," Classico said.

"Thank you, Sir," the young man said. "I will do as you tell me. Can you please, now buy a painting?"

"Oh dear. Well, son, I don't know, I'd rather wait to see your new work."

"I have so many bills from school; it would help so much," the artist pleaded.

"How much are they?" Classico inquired

"Very good price, 300 U.S. Dollars."

"No, I don't think so young man. Well, good luck with your work," Classico said, turning to leave.

"Please, wait," the young man called out. "What can you give me? I will take anything you offer. It would mean so much to me if you took my paintings to America."

Feeling put on the spot and not wanting to ruin the artist's hopes for a career, and, at the same time not wanting to take advantage of his poor financial situation with an insultingly low offer, Classico said, "Okay, fifty dollars."

"I say yes, because you are very special man. I thank you, but please take two."

"All right, two," he said, thinking he was doing his good deed for the day by helping out the newly arrived Chinese. It had only been a short time since they were able to earn money, and because the the young man had such good manners, Classico felt obliged to help foster good relations between the countries. He carefully perused the scrolls; the young man did not utter a sound. "Okay, young man, I'll take these two," he said pointing.

The artist took down the two paintings: a portrait of beautiful

Empress Wu Cox dressed in all her finery with pearl-studded hair and bodice, and an angry sabertooth tiger lunging and baring its teeth—indicative of Classico's feelings at times. Both were exquisitely rendered, and so finely painted that not a brush stroke was visible—only a fluid, undulating line, elegantly drawn, and rooted in ancient calligraphy. Classico was certain the young man could have a great future. With extreme care, the artist rolled his precious, irreplaceable paintings in tissue paper and slid them into a mailing tube for the journey to the U.S.

"I'll be interested to see your new work. You can send me jpegs of the images. Here is my card."

"Sheh shia," the young man said. He walked Classico to the elevator with a smile of gratitude that Classico thought was heartfelt.

Classico went back to the hotel to drop off the paintings. That familiar burst of energy he always felt after buying art buoyed him along as if he would begin dancing any moment.

Chapter 16

The Fire Plug Gallery

Alouisha glanced approvingly at her new image in the mirror. Brown and gold highlights fell softly into shoulder length curls that cascaded about her face with a slight tussled "just-left-my-lover" look. The new black draped and ruched crepe Prada suit emphasized her figure's sculptural proportions. Her long legs were endlessly elegant in her new Louboutin pumps with 5-inch heels and bright-red soles. The sexy shoes were cut low on top and revealed the new style—toe—décolletage.

"A so-very regnant fashion statement," pronounced the gay New York-trend-setting designers, who would never have to suffer the pain of wearing them for an evening. They cost $750.00 and everyone had them.

Racing from the powder room to answer the phone, her five-inch stilts caught in the floor grating causing her to stumble. She almost twisted her ankle, but managed to right herself by grabbing on to the edge of the desk.

"Hello, Classico Gallery. May I help y...? She stammered out of breath.

"It's only me," a familiar voice cut her off.

"Jason," she exclaimed. "How are you?"

"Great, I heard you were running a gallery on Fifth Avenue."

"Well, not exactly, it's more like tripping than running, but I am still working for the Gallery and it's great. Of course, I don't have as much time for my own paintings as I would like, but I'm making a lot of good contacts, and Mr. Classico is such a knowledgeable and kind man. He's just off to China for a week or two. And what about you? What are you up to? How is your painting coming along?" Her words spilled like cornflakes at breakfast; her nerves crisped without the milk of his soothing arms.

"I'll tell you when I see you," he said. "I miss you, baby."

Alouisha smiled, it was exactly what she wanted to hear.

"Me too," she said.

"How about tonight?" Jason asked. "There's a new artist, Mannix Linkx, opening at the Fire-Plug gallery in Chelsea. His work is supposed to be awesome—tough, but great. Everyone will be there; we shouldn't miss it."

"Jason, I thought we agreed to take a break for a while. We decided it would be for the best," she said.

"There's no harm in it," he said.

"We agreed to give each other six months apart to figure it all out. Then we'd talk about staying together. Remember?" she said, her heart not agreeing with her empty words.

"I know Ali, but it's been five months. Being without you is crazy."

"Sweetheart, I miss you too, but I want you to have a chance to date other people. Then, when we get back together, you won't be wondering twenty years from now, if you missed out on something. And I still have to get my financial life in order. I can't let you support me. It wouldn't be right."

Alouisha was emblematic of the twenty-first century woman whose reinvented feminist agenda was never to become financially dependent on a man, although her heart tugged in the opposite direction.

"Oh Baby, I wish you wouldn't worry about such things. You know the money doesn't matter to me; all that matters is you," Jason said. "Let's just go to the gallery tonight."

Jason was desperate to see the love of his life. For two years at Yale, they had spent every day together painting, loving, studying, and exploring their art and each other. The self-imposed punishment she had inflicted on their relationship was unbearable. He needed her in his life—now, every day, always. Being apart was not an option. He felt victimized by her litany of moral regulations that kept them apart. One day she would be successful, but in the meantime, he did not want to suffer without her.

Alouisha listened to Jason's soothing voice and looked out the window. Her gaze rested on the few tiny buds on the otherwise empty branches, which swayed in the breeze. She longed for spring when leaves would fill the window with green flowing motion speckled with sunlight and shadows. She glanced at the shoes Classico had insisted she buy despite her wishes. *They are so sexy, Jason would love seeing me in them.* An enigmatic smile lifted the corners of her mouth. She moistened her lips and tasted the freshly applied color. It was raspberry, Jason's favorite.

"Well, just this once, then we return to our plan—one more month, okay? I can meet you at six when I'm finished at work."

"Great," he said. Her face streamed happiness. She missed him so much, almost more than she could bear. Nonetheless, she had made a promise to herself that she intended to keep. If they were to be together, it would be on equal terms. Alouisha had no time for mistakes; she had seen too many growing up. He needed time to explore relationships with other people, and she loved him enough to give him that chance.

She was also excited to see the Mannix Linkx opening. Everyone knew the Fire-Plug Gallery's branding championed young artists. If an artist were given a show at Fire-Plug, he or she would be "in," branded and catapulted to international art stardom. It was every artist's dream to be taken on by the gallery, and Alouisha was no exception. *Maybe I'll have a chance to explain Sentient Art to Fire-Plug himself. If I look great tonight, I can get his attention and possibly interest him in coming to my studio.*

She organized the papers on Classico's desk for his return. It was almost time to leave, but she worried that he would be upset after reading the mail. She wished the mortgage company would stop calling every day, and the Hollywood celebrity would be patient about receiving his check, and Sinbad DeMande would stop asking for Classico's telephone number in China. She just wanted all of the urgent phone calls to stop. She needed a moment of peace to think about her own work.

I'm sure he'll take care of all this when he comes home. If it's all true, I could lose my job. I'm sure there are extenuating circumstances. It could just be an oversight.

Alouisha placed the worst news——the letter threatening a gallery foreclosure on the bottom of the grim stack of news. She placed the remaining letters in ascending order of urgency contingent on the amount he owed.

When she finished the task, she freshened up in the powder room. After reapplying her mascara and blush, she leaned forward to arrange the overflow, spilling from the unbuttoned top of her suit jacket. She felt chic and sexy in her new outfit and was grateful that Classico had insisted she buy it. *Maybe, sometimes, I can be too stubborn. He was right; it does make a difference.*

Moving closer to the mirror until the fog of her breath shaped a cloudy circle, she stared at herself. Her eyes shone brightly reflecting light like crumpled aluminum foil in the midday sun. She repeated the words her mother so often had told her: "You can do anything you set your mind to, Alouisha."

Because it was Hans's day off, she turned on the alarm and locked the iron gates on the front door and windows. Then she left the pristine, marbleized version of life in the gallery and headed toward the Lexington Avenue subway at 77th Street. Bubbling with anticipation, she descended the steps into the grim subway, and considered how quickly life can change in only a few minutes and a few city blocks.

Exiting the subway at 23rd street, Alouisha stopped at the corner nearest to the gallery and leaned against the wall to change from her flip-flops back into her Louboutins. Shoving the rubber shoes into her large Chloe handbag, she reapplied her lip-gloss, and entered the mob scene—the hip-happening event of the New York night.

The New York art cognoscenti all attended, having come to stake their claim in the invisible hierarchy of art world movers and shakers. Outside the front door of the gallery, limos and Hummers lined up making the street impassable; while inside, the testosterone fueled crowd revved with palpable excitement. By anyone's measure, it was a glam-slam night. Two-hundred coiffed, pouffed, and puffed posers were ready, like armadillos to leap to future footholds in a split second if an opportunity presented itself.

Everything about the edgy group was exaggerated. From their fake smiles to their furtive glances, never looking at the person to whom they were speaking, but always at the door for the next, better offer. Some men and most of the women wore globs of makeup. When their own skin was not sufficient, a spray-painted integument re-pigmented their faces and exposed arms. The older ones had no wrinkles or lines, but old damaged souls that peered out from behind their young, newly cut faces, juxtaposing decades of inner aging with their outer vanity. Then there were the cougars—women who dated younger men. Not to be confused with the older women, who had gentlemen companions or walkers always at their side. The cougars had sex; the walkers were treated to dinners and parties. The older men had their own social formula—the greater his wealth, the younger and more gorgeous was the eye candy on his arm.

"Alouisha," she heard her name being called and scanned the room for the familiar voice. Her heart leapt skyward when she saw him. The hollow spaces inside her, suddenly filled with the helium of all the beauty in life. How much she had missed the solace of his clear, wide, hazel eyes, which had never witnessed pain or misfortune. How she missed running her hands through his hair to smooth it away from his eyes. How handsome he looked in jeans and a black long-sleeved T-shirt that chiseled him perfectly until he bulged in all the right places—top and bottom. It did not matter what he wore; his neon charisma had enough voltage to overpower any outfit.

Jason stood a head taller than everyone else and easily bulldozed his way through the crowd. And like a land easement, the path cleared to his desired destination. She felt the heat of his energy approach; a jolt of longing coursed through her body. Their gaze found each other's. Then, his wind tunnel smile blew right through her heart, clearing away all reason and excuse. It was only meant to be a hug, but once their energies reconnected, all the quantum physics textbooks could not quantify their expanding cosmic fields, which found earthly expression in their lust for each other.

"Jason," she gasped and pulled away from the kiss that lasted too long. He stepped back to arms length and placed his hands on her shoulders to assess the latest version of his girlfriend, now a fashionista.

"Wow, Ali, you look amazing," he said. This elegant phase flattered her more than her Michael Jackson phase or chameleon hair-color phase, which changed from purple one semester, orange in the spring, back to pink and punk. He adored her transformations. "This style is a keeper. The best one yet," he said, always surprised by the many forms to which her current mood subscribed. Her character, however, remained unchanged. And to him, he would always trust his caring, creative, hot-goddess.

"I am so glad to see you," he said, taking her hand and flashing the smile that made her heart skip-rope. "Let's look at the art, and I want to introduce you to a few people."

Fifteen large canvases, six-feet wide by eight-feet tall hung on the gallery walls, depicting men and woman in various configurations of sexual bondage. Often hooded wearing leather masks, they engaged in bizarre interpretations of fellatio and sodomy. There were torn parts of flags collaged onto the work: American, Chinese, French, British, and North Korean. Handcuffed figures hung from medieval torture devices with their feet and arms chained behind their backs. Bodies were entwined with tightly pulled ropes that puffed and quilted their skin, until their blood suppurated. Butchered animal parts stuffed in their mouths, ironically referenced the enforced brutalities necessary to create a democracy with freedom of speech.

"His work is challenging, but his paint application is amazing," observed Jason.

"The paintings appear to be addressing issues of brutality and torture that individuals inflict on each other, not just soldiers," said Alouisha. "Linkx is probably referencing Guantanamo Bay."

"Yes, Gitmo is also a recurring theme in my new work. How can anyone ignore it? Torture is so anti-American. But looking at the larger picture, I think these pieces are suggesting that all of life is a battle, particularly relationships," added Jason, with a meaningful glance.

"But what about the dogs? What do you think they represent?" she asked. Answering before Jason could respond, "They must be allegorical, representing the angel as compared to man. Dogs are so devoted and give unconditional love," she said, trying not to respond emotionally to the shock element of the work as they were repeatedly taught at Yale. Being sentimental about art criticism was self-indulgent, leaving no space for objectivity. Instead, the credo was to understand the artist's thoughts about our world, culture and society, often by deciphering the metaphor. It must always be put into context.

"I think they are just shootin' the shit," a voice interjected. Alouisha turned to see who was talking. A flat-nosed person with a flat-top hair cut, wearing a diamond earring and a too small Peewee Herman plaid suit stood next to them. It was a woman, although Alouisha thought she could have been a man. She and Jason were secretly laughing.

"Whatever," Jason countered, diminishing the rude interjection, but mostly trying to keep a serious expression. He and Alouisha were used to being approached by strangers. Their height, their extraordinary looks and their electrically charged mutual love created a force field that was a magnet to others. Neither of them was even aware of their power.

"Oh, there's the Naked Cowboy," Pee Wee Herman said. No art opening was complete without him making an appearance. For years, he stood in his tighty-whitey briefs and cowboy hat on Broadway and 45th street playing guitar, hoping to become famous. Only the tourists paid him any attention.

"Haven't you heard, he's running for mayor against Bloomberg? It was in the paper last week," said a bare-breasted sixty year-old woman standing in earshot. She was listening in to their conversation, as if she were a part of it. Her long, white-haired, artist-husband nodded and said, "Yes, it's true."

This self-famed couple attended every art opening in New York, exposing her signature bare breasts like a microphone on loudspeaker shouting: "Look at me!" She was somewhat shocking the first few times she came on the scene in her twenties, but now at 60 plus, one could only look away quickly and with pity.

New York was filled with self-famers, people from all over the world who reinvented themselves into vivid caricatures of their imaginary alter egos. They simply wanted to be famous, and because they had no viable talent, they settled for being noticed. After many years of stoical perseverance, these two had become a trademarked part of the art scene.

"There is Kimberly," Pee Wee Herman said to Jason and Alouisha, waving her over. "Look, she's wearing her retro-Moschino blazer sewn from fabric copied from a Lichtenstein painting. I just love it," Pee Wee said. "I'll introduce you."

She was a UBS financial adviser by day and art advocate by night, often found trolling for new clients among the rich and famous. Gallery openings were especially fortuitous for her business.

Bouffant-haired twins dressed in Marilyn drag stepped in front of Pee Wee and gave Kimberly a hug.

"Hey, we didn't see you in Switzerland this year, at Art Basel, or the Venice Biennale last year; we missed you," one twin said.

"Yeah, I couldn't make it this year, the market crash and all, I have lost sixty percent of my business. My clients all left when their accounts tanked forty or fifty percent. My whole career is finished—my whole life is over. Most of my savings were in the company's stock options, which are down by eighty percent. I don't know what I am going to do," lamented Kimberly.

"Oh you poor thing," commiserated the Marilyn twins. "Let's have a drink; that will cheer you up."

"Come on, Jason," said Alouisha, pulling at his arm."Let's meet the gallery owner, Mr. Grant. My work would be perfect in this gallery, if I can just get him to my studio to see it. He seems to be someone who can really appreciate a new art form. Oh, there he is."

Alouisha spotted him surrounded by the masses packed three deep; she was not daunted. Standing near the outer line encircling Mr. Grant, she tried to catch his attention, all the while pushing slightly to find a little opening to squeeze through. The middle-aged man in front of her turned slightly to greet a friend, and Alouisha took her gap moment to reach the second line of defense. Her breasts rubbed up against him, unintentionally.

"Excuse me," she said looking at the man. When he saw her face, he smiled.

"Well hello, and whom do we have here?" he asked, trying to make a little space for her, extending his hand.

"Hello, I am Alouisha, and I am an artist from the MFA program at Yale."

"Very nice to meet you Alouisha, Jack Beknown. I am a collector, here is my card. And what kind of work do you do?"

"I'm a painter. I've created a new art form *Sentient Art,* it's about receiving information through our five senses and processing it with our sixth sense, intuition," she replied, giving her well-practiced elevator sound bite.

"Sounds intriguing, is there any place I can see your work?" he inquired, as he admired the overflow emerging from the unbuttoned part of her jacket.

"Do you collect contemporary?"

"Only the best artists," he said.

"Yes, I would be happy to show them to you."

"Can I call you to make an appointment?" he asked.

"Yes, of course," she said.

"Perhaps we could have lunch," he said smiling.

"That would be great," Alouisha said.

Just then, a space opened up in the densely packed concentric circles that surrounded the gallery director. Thin, agile and fast, Alouisha slid through the second line and pushed along with the tide until at last, she found herself standing face-to-face with Him. Out of breath and momentarily losing her cool, she began to blush. *Pull yourself together, this is no time to be nervous,* she reprimanded herself.

She extended her hand. "Hello, I am so glad to meet you, Mr. Grant. I am Alouisha Jones from the Yale graduate program. I am a painter, and I love your show," she said, chattering nervously.

Because she was so attractive and wearing her five-inch heels stood a head taller than most, he had already noticed her in the crowd. His polished, hyper-fastidious demeanor cloaked him in a thick layer of pulsating air, which kept his solidified inner calm from escaping. He looked as if his barber had personally interviewed each follicle of his perfectly sheared white hair.

"A truly gorgeous creature has stepped into my realm," he said, his voice having the timbre of an electronic synthesizer, which alluded to layers of spatial significance that elongated his perspective on art and life. "How do you do my dear, would you like to meet the artist?"

"Yes, I would like that very much."

"Mannix Linkx," he called, stepping aside, "I would like to introduce you to a colleague, Alouisha Jones."

Turning to greet the artist, Alouisha gasped. Her face blanched, and in a second, like a tube of alizarin crimson paint squeezed onto a white surface, she turned bright pink then dark rose. She felt the crowd closing in around her. The glaring lights suddenly hurt her eyes, and the din grew louder, clashing like brass symbols. Alouisha's only instinct was to run. Nevertheless, she stopped herself when she heard her grandmother's voice reminding her of the family legacy.

"Garner your courage, and always keep your grace and dignity ... as upright as a palm tree." She straightened her shoulders, swallowed hard, and said, "Hello," to her neighbor —the Chain Man Perpetrator.

Chapter 17

Where There is One, There are Many

Finally, Classico had an agreeable experience in Beijing, which made him feel more favorably disposed to the country. With a smug half smile that curled one side of his mouth and a stride in his walk, he had made up his mind to enjoy his last days in China. Perhaps he would take in some last minute sightseeing and a museum or two, but first, he had to drop off his purchases at the hotel.

"Good afternoon, Mr. Classico, I hope you are enjoying your stay with us," the receptionist said, handing him an envelope."

"Yes, thank you; it's a fascinating country," he said hurriedly tearing open the seal.

Tomorrow 10 a.m. Huang Show.

Classico glanced around the lobby, and feeling as though he were caught in a guilty act, he stuffed the note in his pocket. Tomorrow would be his day of reckoning and would determine the remainder of his psychological life. If he were to relinquish the painting, a dark cloud would forever hang hot and close around him, smothering his every attempt at joy. He would be subsumed by a living art hell, painted with remorse.

The chilly air and overcast skies were not conducive to a leisurely stroll, but he had to clear his head and rethink his strategy. He wandered the crowded streets, always remembering his wallet in his breast pocket. *The streets in Beijing are more crowded than Rockefeller Center during the Christmas tree lighting,* he thought. When the wind whipped his cheeks crimson, he pulled his collar tighter. A few blocks farther, he was caught in the afternoon onslaught of 17 million Beijing residents scurrying home after work. Their proximity buffered the gusts, and warmed the temperature slightly. Every sound, sight, and smell ramped his senses into overdrive, until he perceived the world as if for the first time, which made him feel like a kid again.

He entered one of the new super-shopping malls not far from his hotel; they all looked the same. Garish colors, signs, and lighting all screamed and competed for the attention of thousands of frantic shoppers, crushing toward the cash registers, eager to satiate their consumer appetites with their newly acquired purchasing power.

The mall sold mostly low-end merchandise and played low-brow music. Abrasive voices conflated the sensory jolts into a headache producing cacophony. A music store blasted the latest Electro-punk, impaling anyone in a five-block radius. *What do they think this is a disco?* Unable to coexist with the racket and recoiling from the cheap, neon-colored plastic toys and the endless piles of generic household goods, he tried for a hasty getaway. He neared the exit. The endless mall took a labyrinthine turn, which led to an art gallery at the far end of the long corridor packed with shoppers. *I may as well check out the art vernacular while I am here,* Classico thought.

Plowing his way through the roadblock of people, while keeping his hand over his breast pocket to protect his wallet, he entered the gallery. Suddenly, he stumbled backward as if he were slammed in the head with a baseball bat.

"Oh F..." he gasped, as his cheeks ignited turning shock-red, shame-red, then anger-red. Gradually, a deep purple flush crept up his face inch by inch. His emotions hurtled out of control, torrents of rage flooded his throbbing arteries. He grabbed hold of the receptionist's desk to steady himself.

"Can I help you Sir? Are you okay?" the middle-aged receptionist with chopsticks in her hair asked. "You want to sit down"? He clutched the back of the chair and fell into it like a sack of potatoes. His hand caught his forehead to plug his racing thoughts from violently erupting. He clenched his teeth and his fists.

"Here drink some water," said the woman handing him a glass.

He looked up at her and wanted to take the chopsticks from her hair and break them into pieces. In one surge, he jumped up, knocked the glass out of her hand and stormed out of the gallery, bulldozing his way through the teaming crowds.

He could not believe it—that son-of-a-bitch. The paintings were exact duplicates of the student's work he had just bought—and there were hundreds of them.

Chapter 18

Stinking, Rotten, Lousy

The next morning a seething Classico paced the hotel room and checked his Chairman Mao watch for the third time in the last five minutes. He finished his breakfast of steamed dumplings and congee, and dressed comfortably in khaki trousers with a Ralph Lauren polo shirt under a blue blazer. His luggage was packed. It was almost 10 a.m.

"That stinking rotten lousy no good bastard, I'd like to break his arms and legs; that skanky crook should be shot. What kind of country is this where everyone is trying to steal something or trick you, even the kids? He was a professional; I really fell for it. That's the last time these Chinese will outsmart me. I am through playing nice-guy-gentleman to these petty criminals. And that Huang character has overcharged me for the Picasso copies," Classico muttered.

"Apparently, there are thousands of brilliant copyists cloned in this country, probably straight from the Internet addict hospitals, and that's after they mass murder their dogs. I am not leaving the real Picasso here. The original is coming home with me. If they are perfect copies, as he promised, Huang won't be able to tell the difference anyway."

Classico opened the combination safe inside the cupboard. Slowly, he recounted the thick roll of U.S. dollars he had brought for emergencies and placed it in the money pouch hidden under his shirt and left the room.

He stepped off the elevator into the cold marble lobby, and felt the icy stare of the portraits of Chairman Mao that seemed to be watching his every move. *He knows what I am thinking and what I am about to do.* Checking his cash, he patted his chest one last time, took a deep breath, and with the large strides of a determined man, he stopped at the front desk.

"Please, have my luggage brought down to the lobby. I'll be checking out now." He glanced at the waiting black car that flanked the entrance of the circular driveway. The attendant stood erect at the open door as Classico approached.

"Enjoy your day, Sir," he said.

"Thank you, perhaps I will."

"Good Morning, Classico, how you today?" Huang Show said from the front seat of the car.

"Very well, thank you."

"You enjoy Beijing?"

"Oh yes, very much," he replied.

With politesse complete, he settled back into the hard leather seat for the long ride back to the art colony. For more than two hours, they hardly spoke. Both Huang Show and Classico were preoccupied with the consequences and subsequent rewards of their impending transaction. It was a rare and glorious blue-sky day; the smog had left for Hong Kong, and Huang Show was about to make an enormous profit at Classico's expense. Huang Show could hardly contain his supercilious enthusiasm; he stared straight ahead to hide evidence of a satisfied snicker that shellacked itself to his face. Meanwhile, Classico fiddled with his gold-chained monocle in the back seat and tried to appear nonchalant as he planned his next move. Occasionally, he glimpsed the taciturn driver's mottled face in the rearview mirror. A few times their eyes met and Classico would instantly look away for fear the driver might read his thoughts.

I can't let that son-of-a-bitch get the original. He must think Americans are stupid, a country too young and naive to know any better. I need only a moment for Huang Show to leave SoLow and me alone. I'll go slowly, stretching out our time together, examining all the paintings inch by inch, until an opportunity presents itself. If I examine them for two hours, surely Huang Show will step outside for a cigarette or some air or a bathroom visit. He must never know. He won't know it ever happened. My plan had better work; it's all up to SoLow. SoLow, Picasso's future and mine are in your gnarled hands. Classico wiped his forehead with his handkerchief; *I hope the copies are good.*

The industrial art compound was empty that day, and the noonday sun had bleached the warm incandescent colors of night into nondescript cement gray. Last week's Gangsta Rap concert was replaced by an eerie, abandoned silence. Classico descried the dusty pallor that encrusted the buildings and the shine on his shoes.

The three men walked in a grave, ceremonial unison reserved for funerals or coronations. Down the shadow glazed alleyways, through the winding corridors, until they reached the lone, anemic light bulb hanging from the wire, eking out its last wattage. The driver pushed open the iron-collaged door, when Huang Show broke the silence.

"You won't tell difference between real and copy. SoLow is best, no one ever tell difference.

Yeah, not even you! Classico thought. He glanced at the overstuffed driver, no more than three feet behind them, who kept the fumes of his inner furnace smoldering with killer intensity—the heat always within range. They entered the gallery filled with forged masterpieces.

Classico felt a chill course through him, as he inhaled the musty mix of oil paints, dirt floors, and damp ancient walls.

"I could sell these many times," he told Huang Show.

"These commissioned and sold. Sometimes owners want one for each home. Other times, they keep original in vault and hang copy, no one ever know," explained Huang Show.

"It is the same as paste jewelry; many of my clients keep their real jewels in the vault," Classico said, trying to engage Huang Show in conversation.

He followed Huang Show into the back studio where three identical Picassos hung on the wall. They were finished, and they were perfect.

SoLow stood in the center of the room, faced the paintings and bowed slightly. He understood that he had copied a masterpiece, and by creating three additional paintings, he had given Picasso triple honor and respect.

Classico studied the copies from a distance, absorbing their power and grandeur. His entire being percolated with the flame of inspiration, and seasoned with whiffs of ripe linseed oil, his enthusiasm overflowed with conviction. His full heart rekindled his faith in art and the masterly accomplishments of humankind. In that second, a stampeding garbage truck clamored through the alleyway, dispersing rocks, pebbles and Classico's reverie. The entire structure shook as if it were about to be leveled by a tank. Even his feet shuddered. He leaned on the worktable to regain his balance, cleared his throat, and glanced at Huang Show who seemed amused.

Withdrawing his magnifying monocle from his pocket, Classico moved closer to the paintings to examine the details, carefully comparing the original with the copies. His snakelike-eyes slithered inch by inch over the surfaces of the paintings, studying the texture and density of the applied paint. Then, he inspected every nuance of color: hue, chroma, and value—all were rendered with flawless brush strokes. No frozen areas tripped the viewer with stasis, which would indicate that a forger had lost his feeling, rhythm, or connection to a higher intelligence—elements that Classico always found present in a work of genius. The transparency and opacity of the half tones, probably the most difficult part to duplicate, had been executed precisely. Picasso's work was difficult to copy because the edges of his strokes had no formulaic conclusion. Instead, they remained rough, irregular, and open to chance allowing the creative process to ebb and flow. The outlines undulated gracefully like melting glaciers, whose shapes and movement flowed from universal sources; their existence relied on a connection to a higher power. No mere mortal could trespass into this Picasso realm. *No one has ever been truly successfully in duplicating them,* Classico thought, not until now.

Classico continued his scrutiny. His eyes traversed the surface searching microscopically for any misstep. His eyebrows moved closer to his hairline; the creases in his forehead deepened, and the whites of his eyes rounded in astonishment. The colors and aged patinas matched precisely, as did the type of Belgian linen canvas that Picasso had used. Classico turned the painting around to inspect its back. SoLow's extraordinary eye for detail even replicated the frayed edges of the canvas where it had been nailed to the wooden stretchers. A graphology expert could not detect a fault in the signature.

The mysterious hardening agent that SoLow mixed with the pigments accelerated its aging. Any forensics would attest to the painting's age as older than fifty years, the time needed to fully harden.

"Amazing, perfect technical skill and perfect chemistry," said Classico.

Infused with Picasso's energy, the paintings resonated with an authenticity that any connoisseur would validate.

Classico studied one painting for over an hour, attempting to wear down Huang Show's patience. He meticulously examined every square inch from every possible angle with a flashlight and a magnifying loop, bending and lifting the edges. Not one angle or surface inch was overlooked.

"Well, this one passes. I cannot tell it from the original," Classico said. *That's what I want Huang Show to think.*

"We do good job in China. Ready now?" Huang Show said. "Okay?" he said, shifting his weight back and forth from one foot to the other, crossing his arms over his chest, and glancing frequently at the ceiling and the door.

"Almost done," Classico replied. *When is he going to leave the room? It should be soon now.*

Waiting for orders from his boss, SoLow squatted quietly in the corner; his bony body folded like an accordion. Classico sized him up and tried to curry his favor, by glancing back and forth from the painting to SoLow, nodding to him every five or ten minutes.

Classico had a safeguard in place. Before he left the U.S., he had devised a back up plan, just in case of any eventuality. He drew a tiny, light gray speck with indelible ink on the lower back right corner. If anyone noticed it, which was doubtful, it would look like a speck of dust. It was all he needed to tell the paintings apart, in case they were indistinguishable from one another. "Perfection," exclaimed Classico, as he finished studying the second painting. "Mr. SoLow, congratulations. You are brilliant."

SoLow lowered his head in acknowledgment; unable to decipher the words, but understanding Classico's appreciation from his tone of voice.

"I know you be happy, SoLow expert. He wrap them now for travel," Huang Show said.

"Wait. I have one more to review," Classico said, moving in slow motion. *Don't you have to go to the bathroom or something?*

Just as SoLow was removing the last copy from the wall, a round of bullets shattered the stillness outside. SoLow and Classico fell to the floor and took cover behind the table that held the Picasso copies. Classico buried his head in his arms, and Huang Show in true gangster form pulled a gun from his pocket and rolled on the floor to the partially opened back door. He kicked it hard and barged out onto the street firing his weapon.

"Okay, now!" This is your chance—Classico ordered his screaming nerves. *"Now. Move!"* Then without losing another second, Classico jumped up, seized the unguarded moment and switched the paintings.

He fumbled with his shirt until he reached his money pouch. He extracted the roll of dollars, yanking it from its safe-haven and pressed a little less than $10,000 into SoLow's hand; the exact amount of dollars that could leave the U.S. without being declared to customs. Classico spoke in Mandarin, "for your retirement, don't tell, we switch paintings quick." Classico had taken two lessons with the hotel translator to learn those fateful words. He had practiced until he had perfected his diction.

The seconds passed. To Classico they existed outside of time, without measure. They could have been days or decades. There was no air, no breath; only vacant spaces, which hung like weighted lead, hovering over SoLow's answer. SoLow did not move; he just stared at the cash in his hand. Classico could not read him. Was SoLow stunned at the choice he was about to make, the gunfire, or the cash he had received?

Classico fixated on SoLow's arthritic hands that held the cash and its critical consequences. He searched SoLow's face for a reaction. His eyes appeared misted, glazed-over, gripped by some distant place, as if he were no longer present. All his life, SoLow had barely scraped by, working the fields, working for the party, trying to survive on so little. Things had gotten somewhat better since he worked for Huang Show, but now, because his arthritis was too painful, his work was finished.

Classico could feel SoLow's mangy breath on his face, as he stared into SoLow's eyes resolutely—silently ordering him to take the cash.

"Do it! SoLow, take it. You will be set for life. You can do this." He closed SoLow's fingers over the cash and pushed it toward him. The nanoseconds skidded away, greased with fear. The gunshots outside stopped. Any moment now, Hang Show would return. Classico's nerves felt like firecrackers, the frayed ends about to explode.

"Come on Solow, take it!" SoLow's eyes widened. He looked down at the cash nestled in his tree-trunk hands with fingers that would not straighten out. His eyes focused. The dollars were the color of leaves. He lifted his cloudy eyes toward Classico, and they lit up with recognition. In a nano-second, he stuffed the money into the pocket of his drawstring pants, and together, they straightened out the switched paintings.

"Hurry," Classico said. They had to be laid out exactly as they were before the shooting. Classico could not risk a skewed alignment; not an inch out of place, lest Huang Show would notice, and he would end up buried in this remote graveyard gallery forever. In one deft motion, with seconds left before Huang Show returned, SoLow placed the original on the bottom of the two copies that lay on the table, which he had just inspected. He positioned the second copy on the wall, replacing the original.

Huang Show entered the gallery with hurricane force. His frazzle spewed with the impact from the shooting, rattling his calm.

"Guard fired shots in air; scare away two men trying to break in car. No one hurt, nothing stolen. Many workers come from countryside these days, stealing too much," Huang Show said.

SoLow carefully rolled the paintings into a specially fitted mailing tube, keeping his head down in humble servant mode.

"I am glad there was no damage," Classico said, feigning concern and maintaining his composure.

"The driver will return you to the hotel. I will stay here with my new masterpiece. It good doing business with you, Classico. You must come and visit again soon."

"And you too, Huang Show. Thank you for the great work. Goodbye."

"Goodbye," Huang Show bowed slightly.

Classico left for the car with SoLow scuffling behind clutching the paintings in his arms. Classico placed the two forgeries and one original in the trunk of the waiting car.

Back in the studio, Huang Show admired his Picasso and felt fortunate that his perseverance, fearlessness, and hard work postulated from the year of the Ox had paid off so well. "This art business very good. Better than shoveling shit."

Chapter 19

Rehab at the Boom Boom Room

Mannix Linkx locked gaze with Alouisha. She wanted to look away—to run, but was unable to move, paralyzed by the revelation of his upstairs, chain-linked debauchery. The strange noises she heard each night from his moonlighting activities took on a new dimension, one she wished she did not envision. Now, there was no escaping the truth—he operated a think tank for depravation, a virtual ideas factory that he documented on canvas. Her face turned chalk white as images of severed animal parts stuffed in human mouths flashed before her. Iodine-tasting bile rose in her throat making her choke. The nocturnal depictions in his paintings grew more alarming with each cruel image that fast-forwarded through her memory.

After what seemed like five minutes or five years, Mannix nodded and released her from his mind-hold. Without a second thought for Mr. Grant, the Fire Plug Gallery, or Jason, she bolted toward the exit pushing her way through the crowd onto the street. The gruesome images burned into her memory, leaving an indelible black residue. Her heart throbbed in her throat. Silence engulfed her and shut out all sound, as if she swam underwater floating through dead animals and contorted human bodies engaged in sexual depravities. She ran down the street and only stopped when Jason grabbed her arm.

"Alouisha, what happened?" he cried out, holding her by the shoulders. "Baby, what is it?" he asked looking sternly into her eyes. She tried to pull away. He held her firmly. She shook her head from side to side in slow motion, unable to speak. Her emotions galloped too fast for the words to catch them into a sentence. Jason buried her in his arms hugging her tightly, until she calmed down.

"Those paintings," she blurted out. "They are real. Mannix Linkx, the artist, he's my neighbor. His apartment is above mine, and that's what he is doing every night. I can hear him dragging the chains across the floor. I saw the chains; he wears them. Oh!" she half cried, half wailed, covering her mouth to keep the horror out. "Those poor tortured animals and people in the paintings; it's hideous. It's like having a glass ceiling in my apartment, and I can see everything he's doing."

"You're saying Mannix's paintings are not just his imagination. They're reenactments? He's documenting his life?" not believing what he was hearing, and holding her at arms length with both hands on her shoulders. "I thought the paintings were beautifully rendered allegories. Now, I know they're not a fantasy. It's worse than I expected, and the implications are horrifying. This is not art; this is sick, maybe even criminal," Alouisha said.

"That's horrible," he said.

"And did you see the way he looked at me with those steely, pitchfork eyes?" Alouisha continued rubbing her forehead, unable to erase the egregious images from her mind. "I'm fully awake in the middle of a nightmare."

Jason pulled her closer to him. "It's going to be okay. We'll figure something out; I promise. Maybe I'll call the police tomorrow. One thing is certain, you can't live there any longer. You are staying at my loft tonight."

"I don't know," she said.

"You can think about it during dinner, and I'm not asking. We're going to the Standard Grill, and we won't have to worry about getting a reservation—not the way you look." Taking Alouisha's hand, they walked the few blocks to the Meatpacking District, which was adjacent and south of Chelsea.

"In the nineteenth century, this part of the city was filled with factories and warehouses, now it's the foodie's district with all the trendy restaurants," Jason said, trying to get her mind off the neighbor.

She glanced at his profile; the light from the street lamp outlined his features as if drawn with a yellow felt marker. His sandy blond hair blew in flyaway strands onto to his high forehead, then back off his face. Back again, up again, down again, flapping like the wings of a bird. He smiled at her, and all sunbursts paled by comparison. They walked in sync almost gliding. Their heartbeats connected with the source of all life.

"You are going to love the Standard Grill, and it's going to love you. It's the ground floor of the Standard Hotel near the new High Line Park. Wait until you see it. It used to be an elevated railway track built in the 1930s. Now it's repurposed into an outdoor art gallery and a landscaped park," he said.

Jason's enthusiasm was infectious, and she felt herself beginning to relax. "Can we go to the High Line and see the art after dinner?"

"After dinner, we're going to the Boom Boom Room, the club on the penthouse floor of the hotel. They won't let you in unless you are gorgeous, famous, or rich—luckily, we have two of the three tickets," he said, trying to make her laugh.

"We'll go to the High Line during the day."

It wasn't the hot tub in the middle of the dance floor that intrigued Jason the most, or the ravishing waitress-models professionally styled as 1940s movie stars, wearing mini, liquid-silk-panty-showing dresses, but it was the huge outdoor terrace with sweeping views of the Hudson River from the Statue of Liberty to the George Washington Bridge that made his adrenalin foam.

"I can't wait for you to see it. At night, other than you, there is nothing more gorgeous than to watch the cars speeding in the distance—their headlights curling like ribbons in the wind over George's suspension bridge," Jason said. Alouisha looked up at him through her thick eyelashes. He saw that her eyes were smiling.

When they arrived at the restaurant, the maître d' took one look at Alouisha and immediately showed them to a table near the front entrance to the garden. All eyes were upon them. A large maple tree grew from an opening in the middle of the restaurant. The surrounding floor still had the original 150-year-old cobblestones, which battled the roots of the tree trunk pushing through the cracks. Jason pulled the chair out for her to sit and buried his face in her hair, lingering a moment longer than necessary. Goosebumps and tingles careened through her body. The waiter appeared with the menus and dislodged their preoccupation with each other. Jason forced himself to disconnect from Alouisha and move to the other side of the table. They glanced at the chef's specials then back to each other.

"We'll have the tasting menu," Jason said to the waiter. Wines by the glass began at fifteen dollars for a judiciously poured four-ounce serving. Jason decided on a vintage bottle of French Cabernet.

Before he took his first sip, he reached for Alouisha's hand across the table, "Sweetheart, you can move back into my loft. We can paint and be together the way we did in school. You don't have to struggle to make ends meet and be scared of your neighbors. My grandfather left me a trust fund, so I can do whatever I choose, and I choose to be with you."

"Jason, you're always so good to me, but you know I've got to make it on my own. We've spent so much time together over the last two years, and I would not have missed a second, but we need to try to date other people and explore our separate lives? Right now, we both want it to be each other forever, but we need to give each other some space to be sure. Forever is a long time. I would never want you to feel as if you missed your chance to explore your options."

"I got it." He jerked his hand away as he would from a flame.

"Oh, Jason, don't be angry."

He wished she would give it up. Sipping his wine, he turned sideways in his chair preferring to sulk for a while, instead of being dissuaded by her beauty. He never wanted her to be out of his sight. Her eyes glinted in the candlelight like fourth of July sparklers. The lips he used to kiss all the time belonged to only him—so soft and warm—the very essence of divine. And when she smiled, she lit up like a Broadway marquee.

"It makes me crazy to think of you dating other men."

"I'm not," she said. "I just work during the day and paint at night, when Mr. Classico doesn't need me to join him for an art event."

Jason turned back to face her and smiled again. He took her hand.

She loved that he never stayed angry for long. *He has such a good disposition,* she thought, as a shot of warm love coursed through her body. They were staring into each other's eyes, when the waiter interrupted bringing the first course.

"The food is designer gourmet," Jason said jokingly, as he observed the tiny portions perfectly arranged in colorful graphic sculptures. "The chef must also be an architect. These aren't French fries, they're Lincoln-logs," he said.

"They're not Lincoln-logs, they're truffled Parmesan yams," Alouisha said laughing.

"Look, they're cut exactly into half-inch by four-inch rectangles and arranged like a log cabin filled with beet and frisee salad," he said. The roofed overlay was hormone-free, paper-thin, translucent slices of Parmesan cheese, which alternated with layers of aged Italian prosciutto. The vivid contrast of orange yams and green lettuce accentuated the magenta runoff wherever the Parmesan blotted the beet juice. Blood-colored, marbleized prosciutto, sluiced down the sides of the Lincoln log roof.

"It's the clock in Salvador Dali's painting, *Soft Time*," Alouisha said, noting the similar shapes.

"The prosciutto looks just like it," Jason agreed. Lastly, a sprig-tree of thyme planted on top of the creation completed the first course's landscape.

"The chef is also a gardener," Alouisha joked.

Alouisha adored Jason. She loved him so much that it was painful to be without him, but she refused to become his financial burden. It was a sure way to end a relationship; preferring instead, to be loved without obligation. Proud but sensitive to her blue-collar origins, she rejected taking handouts. She had come this far, working her way through school to supplement her scholarship. With unyielding faith in her work, she knew success was imminent.

"Ali, I'm not free unless I am with you, because all I do is think of you when we are apart. If you moved into my loft, I would be able to concentrate on my work and calm down. Remember how good we were—together?" he implored.

Alouisha's head spun from the hectic day's events, encouraged by the wine's increasing bouquet. She listened to Jason enrapt by his words, his essence, his electricity. Twirling the liquid slowly in a circle, she watched it rise up the sides of the glass, then drip in transparent halftones back down to the well. The light fragments splattered and floated, caught in the sea of red-velvet colors, or maybe it was a micro-galaxy of constellations. She sipped again, and at the finish, the texture of the tannins gently velcroed the roof of her mouth to her tongue.

"Mmm, delicious,"she said pausing. "Yes, I remember; how can I ever forget?"

All those sweat-drenched moments they had shared—spent and weakened—so enervated, they would remain in each other's arms, motionless—for hours. *Should I move in with him? He is probably right that we're better together and need to take care of one another,* she thought. *He's so handsome, talented, and smart.*

Picking up their forks, they inserted them into one shared "death by chocolate" piece of cake. The semi-liquid center gushed onto their tongues. Slowly, they savored the melting textures and exploding flavors, as they renewed and dissolved with each mouthful. Languishing in silent pleasure, he took her fork from her mouth and brought it to his parted lips, taking the melted sweetness inside his smile. Neither one of them would blink; their eyes burrowed deeply into each other's most intimate self.

Clasping both her hands from across the table, their fingers interlocked in quadruple prayer formation.

"You're never leaving me, I'll wait," he said.

"Mr. Classico returns tomorrow. He'll be so grateful for the good job I'm doing, that soon he'll offer me a show. Then I'll be able to support myself and be free to love you without strings." The words sounded shallow compared to what she felt.

"I hope you're right. You know I'm here for you, always. Finished?" he asked, getting up from the table and pulling out her chair. "Let's get out of here, I want to take you dancing."

To access the Boom Boom room on the penthouse floor of the Standard Hotel, they took the famous elevator wallpapered on four sides with a video installation by artist Marco Brambilla, titled *Civilization*. Images of Heaven juxtaposed with those of Hell, depicted euphoric celestial kingdoms, alternating with ravenous underworld orgies.

"It looks like a Roman party at Caligula's palace," Jason said. They both laughed and decided they preferred the heavenly sequences.

The elevator opened, releasing them from the "in your face" sensory overload.

"Hey Ali, you've got to see the bathrooms in this place," he said. He led her through a narrow, curved passageway, where twenty tall doors and the surrounding walls were finished in black-glittering marble. Each door opened to a separate room with a high-tech toilet and floor to ceiling glass windows that framed the spectacular view. The hotel staff maintained they were fitted with one-way glass, the neighbors said otherwise.

The music pulled them right in, onto the dance floor. Jason's arms encircled her waist and held on tightly. An old Donna Summer number fueled their heat. His hand found the bottom of her blouse and crawled up her back between the two silky bounds of skin and fabric. Her whole body shivered. They were crazy-glued together, and they could not separate the beat of the music from the rhythm of their hearts.

Hot and sweaty and sipping apple martinis, they felt no pain and stepped outside onto the terrace for a cool breeze. The clean, crisp air was invigorating, and the full-voltage moon doused them in splendor.

"You are so beautiful—magical even," he said as he held her face in his hands and kissed her. Blasto, rockets—that familiar electromagnetic wave combustion, which never let them keep their hands off each other seared through them.

"Let's get out of here."He grabbed her hand, and they left as fast as they could, pushing through the crowd into the elevator inferno and out onto the street where Jason hailed a cab. They could hardly contain themselves in the back seat, but since the driver kept watching them in the rearview mirror, Alouisha tried to maintain some comportment. But, Jason's hand had a mind of its own, and slowly crept up her thigh, inch by inch, rendering her helpless with longing. It felt too good to make him stop.

"I know you're not looking for a library card," she finally said to break his mood.

"Yes, Baby, I'm looking for the stacks," he laughed.

"Almost home, Jason," she said, pushing him away. With her resistance weakened to featherweight, she could not hold out much longer. Luckily, the taxi pulled to the curb.

By the time, the elevator arrived and they reached the loft, they were a thunderstorm of pulsating ions barely getting inside the door with their clothes on. Jason had stuffed her panties in his pocket; his bare chest glistened.

"God, I missed you so much."

Alouisha moaned, "You too, Baby."

Chapter 20

12-Step Program for Art Collectors

C lassico was seated in the first class cabin of China Air heading back to New York. He stayed awake watching the forward closet that stored the mailing tube containing the three Picassos. After wiping the perspiration from his forehead, he loosened his bow tie and sighed deeply, releasing the tension of the day from having spent it with Huang Show in the industrial art colony. He never wanted to see him again. His whole body shuddered, collapsing into a heavy, somnolent peace—a numbing emptiness that only could be the absence of fear. He felt like he had just emerged from the Black Sea and left his oxygen tank behind, along with the moral carnage he had encountered on his descent into the void.

Classico knew that it was not often one had a second chance in life after teetering on the cliff of fiscal disaster so profoundly. He vowed to be more careful in the future and not become carried away by another questionable art endeavor. The next time a painting lured him irresistibly and compelled him to own it regardless of his losing all financial restraint in the process, he would garner some self-control. The auction houses did not encourage moderation by generously offering several deferred payment strategies. Private entreaties with third-party guarantors assured a bottom-line hammer price that made buying and selling art at auction as safe and easy as owning triple A-rated bonds. The guarantor would also receive thirty to fifty per cent of the amount over the guaranteed price. Those clandestine arrangements were particularly efficacious for the "flippers," whose worst-case scenario would be to come out even. To Classico, the back-room dealings were as seductive as an unlimited debit card issued to him by the Federal Reserve itself. Long ago, he had come to understand that he was not like everyone else—he was unable to place a limit on acquiring beauty.

Maybe I should find a 12-step program for art collecting, he semi-chortled. At the very least, Classico would be able to repay a portion of his debt and actuate the Apogee Fund's exit strategy. Although resolving credit disputes would require some paper juggling, Classico felt confident that with three Picassos in his possession, he could satisfactorily settle his affairs. He would only have to come up with a new plan. Once again, he would climb to the top of his game. His hand tightened into a hardball fist and his lips rolled inward, "Yes," he said, underscoring his resolve. "I know what I must do."

Safely away from the Chinese Mafia, he fell into an exhausted sleep. Picasso paintings appeared hanging on a clothesline blowing in the fresh breeze. He saw a woman. Is that mother hanging the laundry? The paintings grew larger and larger until only three remained in his line of sight. Suddenly, he heard gun-shots. Someone was using the Picassos for target practice. A police officer stepped into the shooting range; the gunfire became louder. Startled, he opened his eyes. It was only the flight attendant announcing immigration policies over the raw atonal loud speaker.

Chapter 21

Jack-hammered

C lassico descended the Louis XIV wrought-iron and marble staircase that led from his apartment to the gallery below. The morning sunlight poured through the oculus, imbuing him with a radiance that matched his self-satisfied glow.

"Good morning, Hans."

"Welcome home, Sir," said Hans waiting at the bottom of the staircase for his employer.

"It is so good to be home," Classico said.

"Will you take breakfast now, Sir?" inquired Hans.

"Just coffee in my office, please."

"I trust your trip went well?" Hans asked.

"Very well, thank-you. And how have you been?" Before Hans

could answer, "And how is Alouisha? I have so much work to catch up on, Hans," he said as his mind raced in fast-forward almost giddy with disbelief that he made it home. *I am lucky that I returned alive, and I'm even luckier that I have the original Picasso,* he thought. *And Huang Show will never find out I switched the paintings, so I don't need to worry.*

"She was a pleasure and handled all the clients and the front desk professionally. I am sure you will be pleased," Hans said.

Alouisha opened the front door just as Classico reached the last stair.

"Oh, there she is. Good morning dear," he said, smiling back at the joyous energy field that preceded her. The fresh breeze from the open door accompanied her "breath-of-fresh-air" smile that fused with her own jet propulsion.

"Welcome home, Mr. Classico," she said, removing her coat, thinking he looked a bit tired. "You must be happy to be home after an exhausting flight."

"Indeed I am. How did everything go?"

"Great" she said, radiant from last night's lovemaking. An image of her and Jason wrapped in each other's arms and legs flashed before her in cinematic realism. She gushed a thousand-watt smile, recalling how noisy Jason had been last night.

Taking a step backward, Classico paused, looking surprised. "Alouisha, you look lovely in your Channel suit. Turn around and let me see. Oh, absolutely beautiful," he said mesmerized by her transformation. Just as he would admire a beautiful painting, he admired her beauty. Whatever form it took, Classico always pleasured in pulchritude. The next five-seconds stretched to ten minutes in Alouisha's head. She felt her cheeks scald from Classico's glaring attention.

"Oh sorry," he said when he realized he was staring. "I hope you are enjoying your new clothes."

"Yes, thank you so much. It was very kind of you. And how was China?" she asked deflecting his attention.

"It's a fascinating, exotic country of harsh contrasts. Ancient cultures are juxtaposed with the forefront of innovation in art and architecture. It is quite impressive," he said. "Well, you must have a lot to report. Let's not waste any time. Get your things and we'll work in the office," he said.

"Yes, Sir." Alouisha fetched her notebook and pen from her desk in the entrance foyer and followed him to the office. Sitting in front of his desk, she crossed her legs and tugged at her skirt in a vain attempt to cover her knees.

"I will need two period gilt frames circa 1930 to 1940. They should be similar in style to the empty frame in the back room, but the size must be exact. Please call the framer to check his inventory. Then call Blackwater, we need to hire a heavy-muscled security contractor, perhaps a war veteran who has recently returned from Iraq who would be well trained. We have too many valuable works on display to retain only a Pinkerton security guard." *And just in case one of my clients becomes a bit too demanding, I will be prepared.*

"Make an appointment with the accountant, schedule a meeting for the Apogee board members. It will be a luncheon served in the gallery. Call Café Boulud to cater it, whichever day I am available. Then call the bank to see if Mrs. Aristoteil's check has cleared, and we'll review the mail after you arrange the appointments. Can you handle all of this Alouisha?"

"Of course, Sir, right away. Your mail is on your desk." *There is a lot going on, but I can handle it. I wonder what he will do about the gallery foreclosure. I do not want to find another job. I wish I were not the bearer of the distressing news. I could be out of a job tomorrow,* she thought, imagining the worst-case scenario.

"Now are there any other pressing items?"

Alouisha gulped and conjured up her most sympathetic voice.

"Yes Sir, I am afraid the mortgage company has rejected your refinancing application, and the bank is threatening to foreclose on your property."

Classico knew this was coming and was ready with an answer.

"Not to worry my dear; it is simply an accounting error. They have miscalculated the amortization. Did they give a date?"

"No, Sir." *I cannot believe how calmly he is taking the grim news. He must have had a successful trip to China. Maybe it was simply a temporary liquidity problem after all,* she reasoned.

"Get them on the phone," he said in a low, gruff voice. Determined to remain in control and handle the situation smoothly, he gloatingly reminded himself that he possessed the original Picasso—and two identical copies.

"Yes, Sir." Just as she reached for the phone, it rang.

"Classico Gallery, How may I help you?"

"Yes dear, this is Sondra Aristoteil. Is Henry back from China? I simply must speak to him."

"Yes, Mrs. Aristoteil, he returned last night. I will see if he is available. Please, would you hold for a moment?"

"Darling, how are you?" Classico said, stretching the legato tempo of his words. "I have missed you."

"How sweet of you to say so. Henry darling, I must speak with you right away."

"Is there something wrong?" He heard the desperation in her voice.

"I am so sorry, but I will not be able to buy the Picasso. The entire stock market collapse has affected us terribly. Sinbad tried keeping the dreadful news from me, but since Bear Stearns' and AIG's stocks crashed last year, and they were two of our largest holdings; we are almost destitute. I cannot believe it. We are trying to raise some capital by selling our paintings at auction and the house in Southampton—the one that has been in our family for three generations. At this point, we are hoping to keep the Fifth Avenue apartment. Oh Henry, I do not know what will become of us," Sondra Aristoteil said.

The sound of her voice faded away, as if overpowered by an airplane during take off.

Classico jumped up from his chair, reeling from shock and unable to speak. He had been counting on that $50 million to settle his debts and pay the mortgage company, the art fund investors, the Hollywood client for the Picasso, and the painter for the twelfth layer of skim coating on the gallery walls.

His brain jangled like tossing marbles. He could not think. His hands trembled. The phone dropped to the floor. "Damn it. What am I going to do now?" Dropping into the chair, he leaned on the desk and cradled his head in his arms, shielding his face from the reality of imminent poverty and prison.

"Mr. Classico, Mr. Classico," Alouisha cried. "Are you okay? May I get you something?" Bending down to pick up the phone, "Hello? Hello? Mrs. Aristoteil are you still there?" The line went dead along with Classico's hope for the future.

In March of 2009, returning from their annual winter stay at Round Hill Jamaica, Sabrina and Sinbad DeMande's driver picked them up at the airport.

"Driver, would you please take Madison Avenue uptown?" Sabrina asked, eager to see the international designers' spring collections in the Flagship stores. Driving home after the theater, opera, or a visit with friends was Sabrina's favorite time to window-shop the latest fashions. She had been gone only since New Years, but the change was horrifying.

"Sinbad," she cried. "Wake up. Wake up. What has happened? Madison Avenue looks like a war zone," she said shaking his shoulder until he opened his eyes. "Every second store is dark and appears looted. It's an abandoned ghost town."

Three months ago, the festive storefronts had displayed luxurious Christmas fantasies that inspired the grandest self-indulgences. Sinbad rubbed his eyes in disbelief at what he saw before him—empty, ravaged stores. Sleep had blurred his vision. He rubbed his eyes again and sat up to peer out the car window. Piles of ripped, discarded signage and naked mannequins, some with broken or missing limbs, contorted into body-bag positions, portended the tragic end. Empty display cases, pushed and smashed against the walls, punished the excess and arrogance as if it were an act of revenge from the Wall Street sub—prime mortgage makers. The brilliantly lit widows of the past Christmas season were dark and shadowed, visible only by the dim streetlight's jaundiced cast.

"Oh Christ," he said, observing the spectral remains of former elegance. "It's the end of the free markets as we have known them." Sinbad knew the truth, the Wall Street juggernaut devoured everything in its path, strewing toxic grenades of paper that reconfigured financial securities and personal security. Madison Avenue, the high-end venue of consumerism, fell the fastest and hardest, only the detritus of greed littered the vacant stores.

"Only the Chase Manhattan banks have remained open," Sinbad gasped. Their prime real estate consumed every second corner on Madison Avenue. By buying up smaller banks, they engulfed neighborhoods with their influence and power. With the threat of a financial Armageddon, the remaining banks forced the government to adopt oligarchical agendas, which distributed bailouts to a few select banks with taxpayer's (TARP) money, while other companies were forced to shut down and fail.

Sinbad had been a recipient of the banking sector's largeness. Through his hedge fund, he had sold many bundled, sub-prime mortgages to the banks. They in turn resold them to money managers, stock traders, and institutional investors. There, they were repackaged with partially worthless derivatives; nonetheless, they still garnered triple A-ratings. Eventually, the sub-prime mortgages landed in Middle America's 401k plans. Now, virtually worthless, they sold yet again as bad debt or traded into CDOs, Credit Default Swaps, the insurance on insurance that cost a few cents on the dollar.

The sub-prime mortgage debacle pervaded all financial markets. Suddenly, all money supplies evaporated; all credit lines went dry, and Sinbad, like everyone else, needed his cash flow to keep all his doorbells ringing. Because he counted on the substantial profit from Classico's Apogee Art Fund, he was not terribly worried. Classico had sold many of the original paintings at a large profit, and the distributions were due soon. Sinbad congratulated himself at having diversified his investments with a substantial percentage in art. He put his arm around Sabrina and hugged her reassuringly.

"Well, I suppose we are lucky because this downturn will not be affecting us," he said. She sparkled at him adoringly and rested her head on his shoulder.

"Sinbad, you are the best husband anyone could have," she said.

"I am the lucky one," he said. He did not know the first domino was about to fall.

By 2009, a full-blown disaster mode hit New York at all levels. Everyone lost almost half his net worth, as the stock market continued its decline and real property prices plummeted. In 2008, three million homes were lost in foreclosure as the velocity accelerated from the previous year. Unemployment rose to 9.7%. Men were disproportionately affected when twenty percent more men than women lost their jobs—a "mancession," proclaimed *The New York Times*. Several theories explained this phenomenon: men were fired first because they received higher salaries than their female counterparts, and typically, their jobs in finance and construction were cyclically more sensitive. Because women traditionally worked in health care and education, fields less affected by recessions, they remained employed longer than men. Newspapers fired 60-year-old senior editors that had worked at the same paper for their entire careers, replacing them with recent graduate students of journalism who worked for resume prestige and small salaries.

The blogosphere and social media threatened to overtake print journalism; speculators predicted its obsolescence daily. Twitter went mainstream during the elections in Iran. Since journalists were banned from the country, it was the only news source able to report the election results.

With the world in upheaval, and the news growing more grim with each headline, Classico worried if he would ever sell another painting.

Until recently, the market for high-end pieces had held their value fairly well. But, by the beginning of 2009, the trophy art collectors were desperate to raise cash to cover the "shorts" in their parabolic hedge funds and the mortgages on their art. They flooded the auction houses with inventory, trying unsuccessfully to unload the high-end names bought during the height of the bubble. But, no one was buying art. Instead, everyone waited and watched the global financial meltdown reconfigure lives in tandem with the global warming reconfiguring our planet. The Arctic melt had reached all the way to Wall Street.

Shopping for designer clothes became politically incorrect. Everyone stopped shopping until Saks Fifth Avenue had the seventy-percent-off-retail-sale-of-the-century at the beginning of the spring season. Fights broke out in the shoe department over the Manolo Blahniks. The police supervised the shoe delirium and erected a maze of roped-off lines for crowd control. The ladies packed themselves five deep, as they waited for their turn in shoe nirvana—after all, it was a "mancession."

People were scared, particularly the trust-fund babies, who had never even thought about working. Suddenly, their conservatively managed portfolios, triple A-rated from stalwarts Standard and Poors, and Moody, with heavy positions in Blue chips like, GM, Ford, AIG, or Lehman Brothers, were now worth a dollar or two a share. With their millions gone, Suzaahnne Whitetoe, while lunching with Sabrina DeMande asked, "Do you really think we will have to get a job?"

"Good Morning, Classico Gallery. How may I help you?" Alouisha said. "Hello, Mr. DeMande, yes I will see if he is available. Would you be so kind to hold a moment?"

"Thank you," Sinbad said, his foot tapped like a metronome set to staccato.

"Hello, Sinbad, how are you?" inquired Classico.

"Very well, and you? How was your trip to China?"

"Sinbad, I must tell you, it was absolutely brilliant. The art, the architecture, the food, the exotica, all were splendid."

"You must tell us all about the art scene, over dinner. I understand it is fabulous. Maybe, this will be an incentive to start a second art fund with the profits from Apogee. We can call it the Fifth Avenue Double Appreciation Art Fund, with only contemporary Chinese works," Sinbad said.

"What a clever idea," Classico said, trying his best to sound optimistic. "Actually, Sinbad, I was going to call you today. I am scheduling the board meeting for early next week to finalize the details of our exit strategy. Does Friday lunch at the gallery work for you? Let's say 11:30," he said, purposely stalling a week to figure out his next move.

"I thought we could get together this week and run the numbers," Sinbad said, not yet agreeing to the time, hoping to expedite the cash disbursements. Classico took ownership of the silent pause and allowed it to gain weight with each noncommittal passing second. He knew the game; the first one to break the silence would lose. Finally, when the quiet strained to rubber-band breaking point, "Okay, I guess I can wait until next week," Sinbad said. "I'll look forward to seeing you Wednesday then. Goodbye."

"Goodbye."

Letting out a mountainous sigh, Classico composed himself. *If I do not keep my senses about me, I will never be able to extricate myself from the mess I have gotten into. There has to be some way...some way...some...*

He went upstairs to his private library where he kept his treasures: a ballerina pastel by Toulouse Lautrec, a sepia drawing by Rubens, and a graphite sketch by Van Gogh of peasants plowing the fields. Classico never tired of studying their nuanced lines and strokes. He never failed to become absorbed by the divine energy exuding from the works. The more he looked at a piece, the more he could feel the artist's emotions as if he were sitting beside him. Centuries later, the artist's breath of life still remained intact—his creative moment pulsating as vividly today as the day it was rendered. Classico felt closest to the artist's process through their drawings. If he concentrated hard enough, a portal would open to an alternate reality; one of pure beauty that traversed the centuries unimpeded by calendars and categories and far removed from all his worries.

He ran his fingers along the leather bound rows of books in the Georgian mahogany case. Fitted on four sides of the room, it formed a protective enclosure that made him feel safe. The arugula-green ceiling had gilded pilaster cartouches that glossed the decor. Built the same year as the limestone mansion in 1856, the shelves contained his lifetime collection of rare art books, catalogue raisonnes', auction catalogues, and exhibition catalogues. When he had time, he spent hours perusing the pages, savoring the four-color photographs of his favorite artists. If it rained, he would listen to his own Philharmonic concert pattering on the roof in allegro tempo.

Classico sighed, sinking into the down sofa and releasing a cloud of worries. He greedily ripped off the plastic wrapping on the new Goodrich's catalogue for the Modern and Post Modern sale. The freshly inked pages overpowered the slightly ripe odor of the musty books. He turned the pages, savoring each eye-popping image. His mind, like a road map, knew all their former locations and owners. At first, he only admired the color photographs, gently gliding his hands over the slick coated surface that felt cool to his touch and smoother than his most beautiful lover's skin. He could feel the love; he could feel the money.

Scanning the page more closely, he noticed the seller. *What? That Braque was bought at auction last year.* He checked the provenance; he was right. The dealer, his colleague, was about to do the unthinkable— "flip" the painting. *He must be desperate; this could severely damage the artist's estate and could negatively affect the entire art market,* Classico thought. He turned the pages picking up speed. The edges felt sharp. Faster and faster, he rifled through the glossy double-weighted pages in disbelief at the numbers. It must be a mistake; these estimates cannot be correct. *They're like the year 2000 when the tech bubble broke. They must be misprints, or else … .* The world stopped moving; not a bird sang, not a horn honked, not a tree branch brushed against the window. He slammed the catalogue shut and gasped, "We are in free fall."

He could not sell the Picasso in this market; it would be suicide. Surely, in a year or two, the prices would be back up, near or close to their previous highs. But, he could not wait. At these prices, he could not cover his obligations. He tried to slow down and think logically. It was useless, he was jackhammered by exhaustion and worry. Unable to concentrate, he threw the catalogue on the floor.

"Damn it. What the hell am I going to do now?"

Chapter 22

Back to China

Nightfall hung a dusty scrim, draping the sky in semi-darkness. The last vestiges of low daylight flickered like fireflies in their final seconds of glory before being extinguished by a greater eminence. Huang Show turned out the lights in his gallery; a slow satisfied smile rearranged the crevices on his haggard face. He threw his shoulders back and straightened his posture, thinking how far he had come from his homeless days. He understood that his entire life had led up to this moment of greatness. Now that he owned the original Picasso, his increased political capital would make it possible for him to rise in the Organization. Perhaps he could gain control of the larger geographical provinces, and not be confined by the invisible borders of the contemporary art world.

Meanwhile, SoLow hummed softly as he finished putting away his paints and brushes for the last time. His life's work was over, and he could hardly believe his good luck. The Year of the Rat's optimistic prophecy had come true. The large roll of American dollars in the pocket of his drawstring pants exuded a radiant heat. Because he could hardly contain his happiness, SoLow kept his gaze to the floor, hoping that Huang Show would not notice the gleam in his eyes when he followed him through the meandering passageway.

Huang Show opened the door to leave; they both stepped outside into the night. SoLow followed, dragging his scruffy feet in a slow, shuffling motion. His thoughts turned to the surprised look on his wife's face when he would place the roll of cash in her hand. Married for 62 years, they hardly experienced one day without a struggle for their survival. Maybe they would now move to an apartment with hot running water, and buy a foam mattress, so their bones would not hurt so much when they slept on the floor covered with hay and blankets.

On his way home, he would stop at the market and pick up her favorite duck web for dinner, a delicacy they had eaten only three times in their lives. It made the rice taste so good along with a steamed bun.

It was now pitch-dark outside, and SoLow, engrossed in his hungry thoughts, did not notice the jutting rock on the dirt path. When his slipper caught the edge, he went down hard. A burst of scream escaped from him. The sound of brittle, cracking vertebrae echoed inside his head like crumpling saran wrap. Quickly, he scanned the location of his fragmented bones, but could only detect the thick roll of bills sliding down his pant leg toward the ground. He grabbed for it, just as Huang Show turned around, but he was not fast enough.

"Are you okay?" he asked. "What happened?"

The pockmarked driver with a topographical map for a face appeared with a halogen flashlight that locked gaze with SoLow, blinding him for an eternal second or two.

"You need help, Mr. Show?" the driver asked.

Huang Show grabbed the flashlight, disengaging SoLow's targeted eyes. The bulky driver pulled the old artist up from under his arms. SoLow gasped in horror. He watched as the cash made its final descent into culpability—the flashlight tasered the bills, indelibly illuminating his destiny.

"What's this? What's this?" shouted Huang Show as he fisted the bills and furiously shook his clenched hand. "Where did you get it?" he screamed, suddenly erupting with fiery dragon intensity that punctured the black stillness, halting all nightcreatures' song.

"Tell me who gave it to you."

SoLow, still held up by the driver, could not speak; his words stuck in his throat like sawdust. The driver dropped him on the ground, and Huang Show kicked him hard in the shins, demanding an answer. A searing blast of pain shot through SoLow's wracked body. He shook and trembled like a chain saw, and when his pain fused with his fear, he passed out. The driver slapped his face until he regained consciousness. When he awoke, SoLow felt nothing, except pure adrenalin fright.

Huang Show kicked him again. "Tell me!" he screamed. He whipped out his stiletto knife and pointed it to SoLow's throat. SoLow writhed in the dirt and made burrowing motions, seeking unavailable protection. He stretched his neck as far away from the knife as possible; he was the condemned fowl in the restaurant windows. The metal felt cold against his skin and Huang Show's angry spittle sprayed his face.

"I don't know," SoLow sputtered."It happened so fast; the gunshots—you left—he put money in my pocket—he switched the paintings—two seconds. I don't know, I don't know," he cried.

"What!" Huang Show went blank, frozen in disbelief, then, the rage inside him ramped to explosive. Seconds passed; it seemed like days. SoLow's heart stopped— seared from the heat of Huang Show's anger—but his mind scrolled in fast-forward. He shut his eyes tightly; his book of life loomed before him. All the paintings he had ever copied were printed on the pages that turned furiously in the roiling wind. One by one, the pages ripped from the binding and blew through the clouds into the sky. When every page had disappeared and just the spine remained, it disintegrated into dust.

Then, in slow motion, Huang Show spoke in a sandpaper voice, sonorous with incredulity. "What are you telling me? I don't have Picasso?"

SoLow shut his eyes more tightly and balled up into a fetal position. "Answer me."

"Y..Y..Yes."

"That cow dung pig intestine. We're not finished."

The the bloodletting furies buried in the ancient wetted soils of massacred civilizations reappeared. Huang Show's pulsating veins and cauldron-vesseled skin could barely contain his boiling blood. His dam of lifetime warehoused-misery had burst. With a scorching cry, he stabbed SoLow in the hand. "You'll never paint again. You'll never paint again." And, with each word, he stabbed him again and again. "Never, never, never paint, never again."

"Finish the job." He ordered the driver and threw his knife to the ground. "Take them off!"

Chapter 23

Picasso and Blackwater

"Good Afternoon," Alouisha said, as she held the door to the gallery open to accommodate the size of two deliverymen and the framed Picasso. "Where do you want it?"

"Hold on a minute," she said."I will get Mr. Classico."

Classico shuffled through the pile of bills on his desk. Most were stamped in red on the top of the page, "Accounts Past Due." Sorting them required further action on which he was drawing a blank. Instead, he neatly rearranged the letters and waited for a blast of inspiration. He looked up when Alouisha knocked on his door.

"Mr. Classico, the framed Picasso is here."

"Yes," he said, leaping up from his chair.

Finally, six months later, the successful conclusion to his China trip: the Picasso framed and suited up for public viewing. Will it still resonate with authenticity alongside the other paintings and the period furnishings in the gallery? Hurriedly, he left his desk of bad news. He sprinted through the hallway, like a man about to be reunited with his long-lost love.

"Watch out, I don't want to scratch the frame," the moving man warned.

"Here, bring it here," Classico said pointing to his office. We'll just hang it directly on the wall." He led the men to his office, where two lone hooks waited for Picasso. Each hook could hold forty pounds, just enough support to anchor the painting and its heavy, albeit simple period frame. One man slid behind the painting, while the other held the bottom steady, angling it so the top rested against the wall. Alouisha watched the precise movements of both men, who clearly had a system in place. The man bent his knees to slip out from under the painting, while his partner slowly released the weighted bottom until it lay flush against the wall.

Classico stepped back to the opposite end of the room to view the finished product. This was the final test. Will it pass, away from its clandestine home where everything looked surreal without a measure of authenticity for comparison? Classico's heart thumped wildly, pumped with adrenaline as his expectations collided with his excitement at having completed this risky undertaking.

Engrossed in the painting's potency, he did not utter a word. He studied the undulating, fluid lines that conveyed Picasso's tactile sensuality. Classico's arms crossed his chest, his lips tightened, and the scruff of his neck tingled. He felt like a voyeur, watching Picasso and his lover; he was in bed with them, and this painting would give him salvation. With the original safely hidden upstairs, *this copy will pass every scrutiny. SoLow is amazing. It is so good, I probably can get an auction house to take it.*

Alouisha stood in the doorway, thrilled to be so intimate with the historic work she had studied in school. She smiled, there were no coincidences in life. She had written her midterm treatise on this painting: "Pablo Picasso—The Influence of Greek Mythology and the Feminist Polemic." She had never imagined that she would actually see the painting, since it was privately owned and not lent to museums. She had studied it only from photographs.

Her smile and her eyes both glistered like sequins. It was more beautiful than she could have imagined.

"It is perfect. It electrifies the space, with energy, history, and emotion," she exclaimed.

"Ah, Picasso power, it subsumes the room, the earth, and perhaps the centuries, as his breath of life pulsates in this moment of living," Classico said. They both loved putting words around the bubble of feelings that welled up inside them when they viewed great art. Although the words could never fully describe their reactions, they opened a small crevice to effuse their emotions.

"What a difference to see it in front of me than from seeing only the photographs. It is giving me goose bumps," she said hugging her waist and doing a slight dip-swirl.

"You gotta sign the paper, Mister," said the deliveryman, putting the receipt up to his face and handing him the pen.

"Oh, yes of course." He scribbled his name with his illegible, movie-star signature. "Thank you, Gentlemen. Hans will see you out," he said buzzing him on the intercom.

Of all the Picassos he had ever sold, collected, borrowed, consigned, or partly owned, this one was by far the most important. It was a pivotal work in the arc of the artist's career, and rarely had it been shown publicly. Classico knew its reappearance on the market would be a global art event.

Alouisha tried to read her employer's thoughts, but he gazed somewhere into the distance or into the future. *He's gone again, lost in Google-Earth mode; he could be anywhere, certainly not anywhere close to the red-stamped letters on his desk.*

Classico stood in silence before the art-world altar, consumed by its "wall power" that momentarily freed him from his mundane financial pressures. Picasso's legacy was all that mattered. From the inquisitive mind of the great master came a new-world order, fracturing a staid three-dimensional perspective and cracking open the cosmos to envision Cubism—a portal into the multi-dimensional universe. Classico's belief in the evolutionary powers of art was again reaffirmed.

Alouisha stood next to her employer, hoping his contagion would spread. She wanted to feel the same way about Picasso as he did. "It really is extraordinary," she said, hoping to catch a glimpse into his mind to see Picasso though his eyes.

"It will be the saddest day of my life when I have to part with this priceless masterpiece. When is Grigory Baronovich coming to collect it? I hope it is after the board meeting next Wednesday. If not, change the appointment. Our board members must have one last chance to have lunch with Picasso," he said.

"I haven't heard from Mr. Baronovich," she said.

"That is strange. According to our contract, if he does not pay in full, he will forfeit his one-million dollar deposit, and I will be free to sell it to someone else and perhaps for a higher price."

"Do you really think he would lose his deposit? That is a great deal of money," she said. Maybe this recession has affected the Russians too.

"One million dollars is nothing to a man worth twelve billion. He may have other urgent matters on his mind. Along with each billion dollars comes a billion dollars worth of problems and responsibilities," he said.

"I see," she said, wishing she could have such problems.

Maybe my luck has changed, he thought. "Perhaps he won't come at all," he said.

His thoughts revisited the original painting rolled up, still in the mailing tube under his bed. *What if I am caught? Why should it matter, if the copy and the original are identical? What difference will it make? It will not detract from the viewer's pleasure,* he thought trying to assuage a nano-flash of guilty remorse.

No one will ever know; no one will ever know, never know, never know, never, never, never. *Not even Huang Show,* he thought.

Alouisha waited for his next instruction, "Will that be all, Sir?"

"Oh, yes, thank you for your work today Alouisha, I will see you tomorrow."

"Goodnight, Mr. Classico." Hesitating a moment before she opened the door, she wanted to talk to him about her own painting, but when she turned around, he had already ascended back into his silent reverie—preoccupied and inaccessible. *He has so much feeling for Picasso; surely, if he spent some time looking at my paintings, which he keeps in storage, he would feel the same way,* she thought, walking out the door flinging her Chloe bag with a dash of aggression and a slash of attitude.

Classico sighed, "Oh, to be alone with Picasso."

The doorbell rang, jolting Classico back to earth. A tall, muscular, man in his early thirties dressed in black tugged at his crew neck, and waited for someone to open the door. Neither hoodlum, criminal, nor serviceman, his skintight attire revealed his physical attributes and eliminated the possibility of his being a military recruit, or a candidate for squat-team alert. His hair was buzz-cut to a quarter inch, and his severe, tough-guy demeanor held no trace of happiness. A remembered dark pain from witnessing atrocities sealed his opaque eyes; not a glimmer of light escaped from them. His emotions were held hostage by a relentless ache. Jack carried a concealed weapon.

Classico hired the new Blackwater security contractor to protect the gallery and its contents. This lightweight job would be a vacation in the Caribbean compared to his previous duties in Iraq. A former Green Beret, Jack missed the adrenalin high from combat and his salary, so he joined the Blackwater contractors. He was trained as a highly skilled mercenary, well paid to maintain secure situations in dangerous places.

Each time the Bush administration announced a new color-coded terror alert, it rendered the public more vulnerable, more afraid, and more dependent on the President's and the Pentagon's judgement.

After all, no one knew how to fight colors—except Blackwater, who cheerfully became indispensable for protecting corporations, wealthy individuals, and embassies. They had convinced the world their efficacy far exceeded the United States military, and therefore, no one was safe without their expertise. As the world grew more vulnerable with every terror threat or attack, Blackwater grew more powerful.

"Please come in," Classico said, shaking Jack's hand. "How was your trip? Jack had just flown in from Blackwater's headquarters, the high-tech training compound located in Virginia.

"It was fine, Sir," he replied standing at attention.

"And I presume the traffic was not too bad? This time of the day, a trip from LaGuardia can easily take an hour instead of 15 minutes."

"Yes, Sir," Jack replied.

Understanding that Jack was a man of few words, Classico stopped trying to engage him in conversation and instead led him inside for a tour the gallery. Jack had never visited an art gallery before, and only once, on a class trip in grammar school had he visited a museum.

"Do you like art?"Classico asked.

Not knowing how to respond to this personal question, he mumbled, "Yes, Sir." Classico expected his heels to click.

Classico needed an extra layer of security detail to sleep at night. Dealing with large sums of money and many formidable personalities— oligarchs, hedge-fund managers, bankers, each pressuring him and making demands, he had no choice but to hire a contractor—everyone had one these days. In 2006, the Pentagon gave an invitation only, multinational, corporate seminar to introduce Blackwater. At the bottom of each slide that flashed on the screen, it read: "Security the New Gold Rush."

"Come with me," Classico said, leading Jack through the rooms to his office. "Here is my prize Picasso. It is priceless and must be protected at all costs, as well as the other paintings. One never knows when there can be a burglary, an exploding bomb, or just a crazy person with a knife. You must stay alert, always. Do not allow unsuitable persons to enter the gallery, which includes almost anyone without an appointment, unless of course, Alouisha, whom you will meet tomorrow, gives the go ahead.

"Yes, Sir."

"And about your uniform, you will be fitted first thing in the morning with something appropriate for a Fifth Avenue doorman. No one should suspect you are a Blackwater contractor."

"Yes, Sir."

"You certainly are agreeable. Hans will show you to your room," Classico said.

"Thank you, Sir."

Chapter 24

Politically Correct Flooring, Art, and Politics

J ason's 5,000 square foot loft was in a renaissance revival warehouse built in 1896 and renovated in the current vernacular of contemporary cool. The 12-foot ceilings and 10 large windows on two sides, provided a perfect space for an artist's inspiration to soar—north light by day and sunsets over the Hudson River at dusk.

He was working at his easel in a heightened state of concentration, when Alouisha gusted into the Tribeca loft accompanied by her invisible entourage—a trail of sparkling energy. "Jason, hi, I am here," she said, throwing her handbag on the sofa and kicking off her shoes.

"Hi, Sweetheart," he said, breaking out his fuel-injected smile.

Standing next to the window, the diffused late daylight rimmed his body with a golden outline. "Wow, you look like a Vermeer painting ," she said.

Walking toward him in bare feet, she stopped two inches from making physical contact, and searched his eyes for some residual glimmer of last night's sweat lodge. Trying not to paint her clothing, Jason held his brushes at arms length. When their glimmers connected, they burst out laughing. He pulled her close with a kiss that conjured up last night's heat.

"Later," she said suppressing a giggle and disentangling herself. "I'm going to have a Coke. Want one?"

"No thanks."

On her way to the kitchen, she walked through streaks of light pouring into the room from the floor-to-ceiling mullioned windows that strewed the floor with x-shaped patterns. Jason looked up from his work; his gaze followed her image. The saturated backlight erased the outlines of her body, blurring them until she seemed to float like feathers awash in the luster of infra-red film. She was aglow now, and the moving light silhouetted her, drawing wispy emissions like the edges of a solar eclipse. Last night still clung about him, resonating in every pore and wrapping him in a warm, moist blanket of memories. Now, she had stepped back into his daydream.

Alouisha opened the Sub-zero in Jason's high-tech kitchen and moved last night's container of Chinese food to reach the Cokes in the back. Admiring the shinning black granite counter tops, she slid her hand across them. The surface felt as it appeared, cold and slick. A polyurethane gloss finish sealed the requisite cherry-wood cabinets, distorting her reflection like the Coney Island fun-house mirrors. She remembered her family's splintery kitchen cabinets in Jamaica, which wobbled and often fell off, only to be replaced by a piece of flowery fabric.

"Hey Baby, what are you doing? I think I'll have that Coke after all," Jason said entering the kitchen to see Ali making faces at her reflections.

"Why does every apartment development in New York have the

same cherry kitchen and bathroom cabinets?" she asked, her hands still slithering along the irresistibly sleek counters.

"Well, it obvious, there must be an invisible color-coordinator who strictly enforces design protocol," he said jokingly.

"And their rules are as iron clad as a prison guard, enforcing acceptable behavior," she said laughing.

"And any deviations would condemn the apartment dweller to an eternity of bad taste experienced in solitary confinement, or even worse, social ostracism," Jason replied.

"Only in New York is it necessary for flooring to be politically correct," Alouisha laughed admiring the pale color of the environmentally friendly bamboo wood. She wondered if linoleum had a similar caveat in the 1950s. As she left the kitchen, her body rubbed up against his.

"Wait, I want to see what you are working on. You're still into your Gitmo painting?"

She flopped onto the sofa opposite his easel with her can of Coke and studied the six-foot painting.

"Yes, I've got to do something about the horrible situation."

"I love that you combine expressionist forms with torn newspaper articles about torture," she said.

"Bush has got to end the inhumane treatment of the prisoners at Guantanamo. Detaining men like animals in four-foot by eight-foot cages under the broiling Caribbean sun without court hearings is undemocratic and barbaric. Some of the accused terrorists are only teenagers plucked from the sidewalks outside their homes, with no understanding of anything except getting their next meal," he said pacing and flailing his arms.

"It is terrible. There has to be a better solution than rendition," Alouisha said.

"By re-contextualizing this information, maybe I can bring some awareness of the captives who are innocent," he said.

"You will, I am sure," Alouisha said, appreciating his strong opinions on politics, foreign affairs, and his passion for justice. She loved his inclination to have both his paintings and his flooring engage in dialogues about current events.

"And how was your day?" he asked.

"What a day I had. I think Mr. Classico is losing it. He seems really pressured, and he wants me to go to Southampton with him this weekend to help sell a painting to some hedge-fund guy. I'll never have a show at this rate, and frankly, I am sick of being a receptionist. But, I guess I am lucky to have a job."

"Again? Why can't he sell his own paintings?" Jason asked, in an annoyed tone.

"I feel sorry for him, and I am glad to be able to help. He has so many problems. The art auctions are in fire-sale mode. Everything is either half-price, or remains unsold. Major pieces are not even reaching their low reserves at auction. This financial meltdown is affecting everyone; art is simply not a priority when so many are losing their homes."

"This is not a good time for anyone," Jason said. "No one is buying anything. People are just trying to survive."

"Yeah, they're all trying to sell their collections to salvage their homes, and with prices plummeting, many homes are worth less than their mortgages. It seems as if the whole world is just one big paper mistake, and there never was any real money, only credit," she said.

"The cities are loaded with huge, empty banks, which essentially are warehouses for paper— loans, debts, and mortgage obligations. The entire financial system in this country is predicated on lies—there is no real money," Jason added.

"The banks and the one percent are vacuuming the sub-prime mortgage rooftops off of middle-America's homes and redistributing the proceeds into their own backyards and back-pockets," Alouisha added.

"The only remaining cash was sent in pallets to Iraq for the security contractors," he said.

"Remember the article we read in the Times about the $500 million cash found packed in a carton that left Iraq on an airplane? No one claimed responsibility for its origin or its destination. Well, I searched for a follow-up article, some explanation; but it was never mentioned again," she said.

"There is not much we can do about it except take care of ourselves," he said, searching her eyes and gently brushing a curl off her forehead. He could feel her sweet breath on his face and hugged her mightily. My family is smart; they have invested in prison security and railroads, two industries that will never have a recession."

"We do not have to worry, and I love you Ali."

"I love you too," she said. Small piles of clothing dropped like footprints marking a path to the bedroom. Jason left his unfinished painting to bask in the last moments of sinking light.

Chapter 25

The Art Collector from Hong Kong

The morning sun slashed through the quarter-inch slit at the bottom of the blinds. With laser precision, the light pierced through Classico's closed eyes, disrupting his REM dream state. Startled by the insistent morning invasion that forced him back into the present tense, he gasped. Suddenly he was caught in a choke-hold of his own primal fear. His sense of well being, his security, his career, his home and gallery were all on the threshold of extinction. The 800-count Pratesi sheets offered no comfort this morning. Usually, he would ball into a fetal position, arrange the four down-filled pillows in a fortress-like surround, pull his Hungarian comforter to his chin, then float in its fluffy cloud of protection. Barely touching his skin, it would encase his body heat, forming a warm cocoon enclosure. In this consoling dreamless state, he would linger in suspended time.

Today, however, his mind raced toward thoughts of his demise. He could almost hear the handcuffs clank shut, and see the police load the paintings onto a truck. The humiliation whipped and burned as the police took him away in front of the television cameras. Pulling the covers over his head, he wished the darkness would make it all disappear.

Tomorrow is the board meeting. I have to devise a schedule for their expected disbursements. I'll have to come up with a good story. I am so screwed. Why doesn't Grigory Baronovich call? I need to know his plan, so I can move ahead with the sale of the Picasso and find another buyer. Most importantly, I must remain calm and think clearly.

Classico sat up on the side of his bed and ran his hands through his hair. I shall imagine this is a mathematical equation, and I shall draw a diagram charting the polynomial rational inequalities. This way I will remove my emotions from a dire situation that has serious consequences. I'll start with a list.

Clients	Painting	Status	Asking Price	Projected Net Profit	Extraordinary Items
Hollywood celebrity	Picasso	Consignment	$50Million	20% $10 Million	On loan in traveling exhibit
Grigory Baronovich	Picasso	Received deposit $1M	$40M	$8M	Sold 2009 undervalued in bad market
Aristoteil	Picasso	Offer withdrawn	$50M	($10M)	Loss
Apogee Art Fund	21 post modern classic contemporary	Sold (ROI) return on investment due	Negotiable $60-90M	*Spent none	Reconfigure numbers
Three half-shares	Lichtenstein	Sold $24M $8M each			Refund one share

Hans knocked on the bedroom door.

"Good morning Sir, your breakfast. It is almost 9:00 a.m.. You slept in, Sir. You must be very tired," Hans said.

"Oh, yes—please—uh—please come in," said Classico, suddenly distracted from his analysis.

"Thank you, Hans." He placed a tray of steaming coffee, hot milk, toast, and his favorite Marmite on the bedside table.

"May I get you anything else, Sir?"

"No thank you, that will be all."

Just then, the intercom rang. "Yes, what is it, Jack?" said Classico, sounding annoyed.

"Sir, there is a woman here who wants to buy a Picasso."

"What are you talking about?"

"Well, she is asking for you and has a message about a show."

"What is her name?"

"She says she is from Hong Kong—a Ms. Peggy Lee."

"Well, tell her to make an appointment. We don't take walk-ins," Classico said.

"Sir, she says she is here only for two days for the winter auctions, and she was told you have access to the best Picasso," Jack said.

"Where is Alouisha? He looked at his watch. "Tell her to come back later."

"No, Sir, she cannot," Jack said.

"Well then, tell her to come back in half an hour." He gulped his coffee, took a bite of toast and threw off the covers.

"I'll prepare your clothes," Hans said as Classico headed toward the shower.

"Maybe I'll get lucky and sell her a painting," he said gurgling through the waterfall shower. It was not the first time Chinese art collectors had come to his gallery looking for a Picasso or a Warhol. In Hong Kong, the two artists were so popular that if they ran for Mayor posthumously, they would still win," Classico said wrapping himself in a towel.

"Fortunes are being made as we speak. Dealers buy Picasso and Warhol in the U.S. and sell them at auction in Hong Kong. So far, it's been a foolproof formula for large art profits," Classico said, as Hans helped him into his clothes and tied his bow tie. "Wish me luck," he said.

In precisely one-half hour, he heard the doorbell ring a short Chopin crescendo. "Yes, yes, coming," he said, opening the door. "Good Morning Ms. Lee, won't you please come in."

The exquisite Hong Kong beauty was flawlessly dressed and tailored to perfection, from her hand sewn invisible stitching to her hairstyle that ordered every strand to obey. Bejeweled and carrying a Balenciaga handbag, she exuded a precious quality borne of her newly acquired wealth—so prevalent in her country. Jack went inside for a moment as Classico turned on his charm, and led Ms. Lee into the vestibule. *My international reputation attracts the highest caliber of people to the gallery,* he thought.

The front door was half an inch from being shut when suddenly, it was shoved open and two ninja-looking men pounced on Classico throwing him to the floor. Ms. Lee disappeared into the crowded street. Before Jack had time to intervene, the men arm-locked Classico at the point of a stiletto with the steel blade depressing the skin on his neck, a nano measure from piercing the surface. He became cement still and held his breath. The stench of their sweat and their sewer breath sickened Classico. But the fear stabbed like a drill press running up and down his spine when he saw the hatred in their twisted faces and their anger black as hell.

"What do you want?" Instead of an answer, he received a swift kick in the stomach. He doubled over. *This can't be happening to me.* He imagined his body floating upwards as he watched the assault from above. One more kick and he was back inside his pain.

"Please, what do you want? Ow, my arms," he cried out, squirming like a dying snake, as they pinned him to the floor with their boot heels.

"Where is real Picasso? Huang Show want."

"Huang Show? He sent you?"

Another kick in his back, "That's from Huang Show."

"No, don't." Classico screamed at Jack, who was about to lunge at the attackers while the point of the knife still depressed the skin on Classico's throat. Jack recoiled, and steamed in his doorman-straight suit, barely able to contain his exploding mercenary training.

"Where?" they demanded.

"Oh my God. The real Picasso—in China with Huang Show."

They twisted his arms behind his back and pulled them over his head, "Say when to stop."

"Yes, yes, please stop. The original, it is with Huang Show." They kicked him again and twisted his arms almost pulling them out of their sockets.

Jack stood motionless, not daring to draw his gun with the knife so close to Classico's throat. He could see the first drop of blood dribble from the contact point of the stiletto. Jack waited for a millisecond of an opening to attack; it always came. But in the meantime, his new doorman uniform provided the perfect disguise. They would never suspect he was a trained mercenary.

Classico knew his time was up. "Okay. Okay," he cried pleading. "Stop, stop it! Let go of me, I'll show you where it is. It's in the other room, over there, over there," he screamed.

They released Classico, and in that moment, Jack jumped on top of the Chinese assailants, gripping them first in a choke hold, then banging their heads together—a little trick he learned at boot camp along with his martial arts training. One was kneed in the back, while he somersaulted the other man, smashing him to the floor. Jack was twice as big as they were and twice as strong, but his life was not on the line like the Chinese Mafia on a mission with direct orders from the homeland director.

"Get the original painting back to China. Do whatever it takes," Huang had ordered.

Classico shook, his sweat turned to ice on his body as he slithered across the floor toward the corner of the room, shrinking from the horror.

Just minutes away from the gallery, Alouisha hummed a tune on this beautiful morning and climbed the steps to the entrance. She anticipated another busy day working on interesting art projects and trying to finalize some sales. Surely, he slept well last night and worked out his problem with Mrs. Aristoteil. Everyone has small meltdowns; it happens to all of us at some time.

She walked-skipped with happiness from memories of last night. She and Jason had slept wrapped together, bound by one shared syncopated breath. His exhale was her inhale. He had held her close all night, and when their wave particles commingled and they felt as one...They left their gently resting bodies on earth, and flew translucently through the starlit universe and they became *Liquid Soul* [4]. That would be the title of her next painting.

Liquid Soul[5]   oil on canvas 32"x32"

5. To view Alouisha's paintings in color, go to www.RochelleOhrstrom.com

Jack was not in sight and the door was slightly ajar. Sensing something was up, she pushed it open, gingerly.

"Good Morning," she said, announcing her arrival with a singsong lilt in her voice. Just then, one of the Chinese assailants pinned to the floor by Jack's bulging biceps, bit Jack's leg, and broke the skin like a rabid dog. Jack flinched slightly, barely releasing his grip as his anger hurtled to killer ferocity. In that slackened second, the assailant whisked out his stiletto, stabbed Jack and ripped through his thigh. Blood spurted, but Jack was tough and fast. He drew his gun, as the two attackers rolled to the door and crashed into Alouisha, taking her down.

"You die, Picasso live in China. Real one back to China," they shouted, ducking the bullets, using Alouisha as their human shield. Jack stopped shooting; they ran outside. Alouisha's eyes darted around the room, trying to make sense of what had just happened. The blood still gushed from Jack's leg onto the marble floor. Classico slumped in the corner of the room into a pile of beaten-down misery. Jack hobbled to the door, but the assailants had disappeared onto the streets.

"Jack, Jack are you okay?" Classico frantically asked. "Alouisha call an ambulance, quick."

"Sir, I have called the police and an ambulance; they are on their way," Hans said from the top of the staircase.

"What happened? Who were those people?" Alouisha asked shaking. Grabbing a towel from the powder room, she tied a makeshift tourniquet around Jack's leg to stop the bleeding.

"It's okay," he said wincing from pain, but too proud to admit it hurt.

"Who were they? Why were they here?" she implored.

Classico shivering from fear and the draft from the opened door, tried to regain his composure.

"They wanted to steal the Picasso. They said something about the organization and China. Are you okay Alouisha?"

"Yes, I'm okay," she said, sitting down to catch her breath. "Are you?" She had never before witnessed a violent attack, much less a stabbing.

With each passing second, the sound of the sirens became louder and more insistent. She pulled the curtain aside and peered out the window. The weather had changed. The gray clouds hovered, casting gloom on the empty trees devoid of life or movement. She straightened her skirt and pulled the bottom of her jacket to smooth out the creases. Some of Jack's blood had stained her skirt.

Classico's mistakes closed in around him, shrinking his few remaining options. He was lucky this time, but he knew it was not over. Huang Show had contacted the Chinatown branch of the Mafia to retrieve the painting. Little had Classico suspected that Huang's influence reached this far. He thought his window of culpability had passed, and he was home free.

The medics arrived and Jack pushed the stretcher away, insisting on limping painfully to the ambulance.

"Damn," he cursed and muttered a trail of expletives.

"Damn those Chinese bastards, those skanky midget slimers. How could I let them get away?" he berated himself. "Ow, damn it," he said, wincing with pain and embarrassment, as he hobbled through the door.

The medics brought the stretcher to Classico. He pushed them away angrily. "No, I'm not going to the hospital. I'm only bruised." He watched in a daze as the splattered blood meandered along the white marble flooring and formed an abstract expressionist composition, like a Jackson Pollock painting.

Chapter 26

The Police Invasion

Still slumped in the corner, Classico stared at the floor mesmerized by the bloodstains that formed changing shapes with every glance. Suddenly, three police officers burst into the entrance foyer, sucked the air from the room, and replaced it with a force field of dire intention. Classico shuddered, shocked by the maelstrom of ferocious energy.

"Police, Police," they shouted. "Everyone freeze."

Startled from his stupor, Classico made an effort to stand up, but grimaced with pain and crumpled back down.

"Are you wounded?" asked Officer Brody, a young African American with a stern expression on his face. Classico looked up at the strange man and watched his lips move, but like a silent film in slow motion, he heard no sound escape from the officer's mouth.

"Do you need to go to the hospital? Are you wounded?" the officer repeated.

Classico blinked and remaining unfocused, he tried to register the words.

"No, no, I think I'm okay," he stammered. "No, I mean yes, I'm okay, thank you. Nothing is broken; I am only bruised," he said, wishfully thinking. He refused to spend the night in a hospital and be consigned to extreme vulnerability with strange medics prodding and poking him all night. To make matters worse, he could no longer afford a private room or a nurse. *No, the hospital is not an option,* he thought.

Officer Brody helped him up from the floor and over to the green brocade sofa in the sitting room. Classico grimaced from the ache in his stomach. He sank into the down cushions; his expectations followed in tandem. His short, labored breath excluded sufficient inhalation to release a tension-filled sigh. The torn collar on his jacket dangled from a few threads. Ponderously, he examined the stained Sulka handkerchief he had held to his neck at the knife's point of contact. "Just a pin prick," he said. "It's nothing." Officer Brody looked closely and agreed.

"You sure are lucky you weren't hurt badly, "Brody said. "We'll get those bastards. Have any idea who they are?"

Suddenly, Classico remembered the horrified look on Alouisha's face when the two men threw her to the floor.

"Is Alouisha all right? Alouisha, Alouisha, are you?" He stopped, unable to breath; he gasped for air. Looking up toward the far wall, where another Picasso portrait hung—a deranged face with three eyeballs jutting in divergent directions, starred down at him in mocking horror. He shuddered again as the sirens outside screamed their red-light warnings and rattled whatever remained of his inner resolve.

"Take it easy, Sir; you're gonna be okay," said Officer Brody when he noticed him twitch.

Alouisha stood nearby in the hallway trying to fight back the tears that welled up in her eyes, which nonetheless, rolled down her cheeks and stained the bodice of her silk Chloe blouse—irrevocably. She had kept her composure, remaining calm and in control, until the police stormed in with the severity of terrorist combatants. Two more officers appeared with their weapons drawn. They ran through the galleries and upstairs through the house, crouching in attack mode. They searched every room, behind every heavily lined silken curtain, and every festooned and ormolued closet door, screaming,

"Police, Police."

Classico did not move, but everything around him accelerated into a spinning blur. In a state of shock and denial, he was unable to comprehend that an attempted robbery had just taken place. His only concern was the police invasion disrupting the calm, orderly atmosphere of the gallery. There were too many people; he wanted them all to leave. *They are going to rip the curtains and destroy the furniture if they continue ransacking the house this way.*

"Show yourself—Police," they shouted. Classico wanted to say they had fled, but he could not get the words out.

"Can you tell me what happened here?" asked Detective Fulgenzi, apprising the bloodstained floors in a Fifth Avenue palace and two expensively dressed victims, one in shocked silence and the other in tears.

"They ran out. Two Chinese men dressed in black with dragons on their leather jackets—on the back," Alouisha blurted out. "They wanted the Picasso, something about sending it to China. I think Jack, the security contractor, shot one of them after they stabbed him. Mr. Classico, are you okay?" She stopped rambling when she saw him on the sofa bent over the side arm, cradling his head in his elbow.

"Yes, yes," he replied.

"Well," said the officer. "You'll both need to come down to headquarters for questioning. The police will guard the gallery tonight. Alouisha is there someone I can call for you?"

"I'll be okay," she said. *There is no need to bother Jason. He's probably in the middle of his painting,* she thought.

"No, thank you," she said. She yearned to be back at her easel, calm and in control immersed in the healing effects of her colors. Her place of perfect peace, where her creative energies coalesced, incubated, and explored the infinite possibilities. And she wanted Jason to be there with her.

Classico sat on the edge of the sofa lost in thought. He clasped his hands between his opened legs; his head bent down, and his shoulders sagged in abject surrender. He knew he had gone over the edge; things would never be the same again. Not for him or for Alouisha.

Hans appeared noticeably unshaken, save a slight dew that moistened his temples and a slightly askew bow tie. He carried a tray with tea and biscuits to Classico.

"Sir, have some tea, it will make you feel better," Hans said.

Classico sat up straight and looked into the eyes of his trusted butler, grateful for his phlegmatic disposition and the daily ritual he offered to soothe the unnerving incident. Having Hans in his life had been a great comfort.

"Thank you, Hans," he said, squeezing the lemon into the hot brew. The fresh citrus fragrance mixed with steam accessed his composure. Then, his thoughts splintered; shards of stinging anxiety stabbed him as viscously as the assailant's stiletto. *What am I going to do? I am in over my head. The board meeting is tomorrow; it will have to be canceled. After the attempted robbery appears in the newspapers, the press coverage will trigger an investigation into the Chinese's motive for stealing the Picasso. The details will focus on my trip to China. Eventually, Grigory Baronovich will hear about it and realize there is more than one Picasso, as will the Chinese Mafia and the Apogee Art Fund. Everyone will demand their money be returned, and I will be facing a lengthy litigation, prison, and poverty. Maybe I should have stayed in Nebraska. A farmer or a factory worker has to be better than a prison inmate. Why did I ever let things get so out of control?* "Damn it. I am so screwed," he blurted out.

"Get the blood samples over to the lab. We'll run a DNA test and see if we can match it in our data base," Detective Fulgenzi told Angela Ramirez, who had just arrived from the police forensic division. Officer Ramirez was a middle-aged overweight woman with close-cropped hair wearing an ill-fitted pantsuit. She had long ago given up the fem game to attract a man. Feeling the Picasso staring at her, she looked into the wayward asymmetrical eyes of the portrait on the wall. She was certain the woman in the portrait had been badly treated by her lover.

"Yes, Sir, right away," Ramirez replied.

"Sounds like we're dealing with the Triads from Chinatown," Officer Brody said. "They are some bad actors and always wear dragon emblems to proudly claim their victories."

"Since when did they get into art? They usually stick to heroin, extortion, gambling, or sex trafficking," said Ramirez.

"Those jerks are getting too full of themselves. Last week we found the body parts of a downtown shopkeeper in a cardboard box left at a bus stop. It was probably there for a couple of weeks, judging from the condition of the decomposed body. We recognized the victim by the sweater. Apparently, the shop owner did not want to pay rent to two different landlords," Fulgenzi said, standing with his arms crossed over his chest, watching the forensic team take their samples.

Detective O'Reilly from the art fraud division arrived.

"Sorry, I took so long. I was finishing up another case. So what do we have here?" he asked, opening his notebook. "So far its just assault and battery. They didn't take anything right?"

"Right," Fulgenzi said.

"And the victims? Was anyone hurt?" O'Reilly asked. "So let me understand, they wanted to steal the Picasso?"

Officer Fulgenzi filled him in on the details. Detective O'Reilly began taking notes and explained:

"Lately art theft has become more common than a good old-fashioned bank robbery. Because art is the most effective method for money laundering, it is extremely popular with the international drug cartels. A drug lord can hire an art consultant to bid at auction, and the house's nondisclosure privileges preclude them from revealing the winning bidder. The painting can be shipped to Switzerland to avoid taxes; it can be paid for with a secret bank account; then shipped to another undisclosed location, and sold again for cash—probably to a Russian oligarch, a member of the Qatari Royal Family or more recently to a Chinese or Indian billionaire—never to surface again from the hidden recesses of the Middle Eastern and Asian palaces," O'Reilly explained.

Classico straightened up and reverted to automatic pilot upon hearing him mention Russian oligarchs and Chinese billionaires. He stood up and cleared his throat in a feeble attempt to regain his voice, and assert his authority.

"Often stolen art goes underground and is not seen again for several generations. Only after the great grandchildren no longer know it is stolen, does it sometimes resurface at auction," Classico said.

"Black market art, including forgeries is a multibillion-dollar business," O'Reilly said, walking to the front door accompanied by Classico.

"The art world is currently in the midst of a sea change. The new Louvre and Guggenheim Museums, which are under construction in Abu Dhabi have unlimited acquisition funds, giving them the ability to out-bid every institution in Europe or the United States," Classico said, as a shot of pain traversed his leg to his stomach.

"So what you're saying is that all the good art, the masterpieces, will end up in the Middle East and Asia?" Ramirez asked, looking around at the paintings, then at Classico. She lifted her head to the source of the diffused afternoon light that spilled onto Classico from the oculus overhead, giving him deep dark shadows under his eyes.

"Nowadays, a police officer needs to have a degree in art history," Officer Brody muttered. *These rich people; what a pain in the ass,* he thought.

"Why don't you both get some rest? Tomorrow we'll see you at the station," Detective Fulgenzi said, stepping into the vestibule. Alouisha's gaze rested on his gold badge that glinted in unison with the golden cartouche carved into the front door.

"I'll have the police stand guard in the front and back of the house, Mr. Classico. You'll be safe. Fulgenzi turned to Alouisha, "The patrol officer will take you home."

"Thank you Detective, I am very grateful," Classico said as he leaned on the wrought-iron handrail trying to counteract the weight of his body and his emotions. On a good day, he would run up the stairs without losing his breath. Today, however, he could barely lift his legs. He pulled himself up the stairs, entered his damask, upholstered and curtained bedroom and bent down at the edge of his bed. He inserted his arm through the matching burgundy bed-skirt, then crouching lower to lengthen his reach, he felt it and grasped his truest devotion, the most meaningful thing in his life; the reason he risked everything— his reputation, his bank account, and his safety. Acquiring it had taken so many years of strategic planning. No, he could not allow it to slip away into the black hole of the great art void, sequestered in the Middle East or Asia for generations or for all of eternity. No, this was his rightful reward for his devotion to Picasso. He alone deserved it more than anyone, and he alone was qualified to cherish and accept the responsibility of caretaker for this world treasure for the remainder of his life. He unrolled the painting carefully and laid it on the bed. He threw off his torn, sullied jacket and unzipped his trousers. They fell to the floor.

Chapter 27

The Obligation

Classico awoke with a start. The ballistic rain pounded the traffic; taxis braked hard splashing passersby with dirt sprayed from the puddles. Angry horns blasted their revenge, as baritone-belching buses lurched forward ignoring the red lights. The forcible beasts disregarded the lesser vehicular creatures that crossed their paths. The rainstorm amplified the city racket, and unified the strident cadence with a common underlying score. Classico pulled the covers over his head, until the sounds receded into a single white-noise entity. Searching for respite from yesterday's ordeal, he entered the deepest recess of his sub conscious and returned to his childhood in Beatrice, Nebraska.

In 1965, nine-year-old Henry Classico sat at the Formica kitchen table covered with a blue-and-white checkered tablecloth with red cherry sprigs in each corner. Mother looked so pretty as she stood at the stove cooking his favorite breakfast wearing an apron that matched both the tablecloth and the curtains. The bright morning sun filtered through the window onto the flower boxes, which blocked some of the light, casting flower patterns on the table. He poured sugar onto his shiny white Melmac plate and tilted it to watch the shadows crawl like ants. The birds sang their morning joy perched on the apple tree outside the kitchen window.

Dad had left early for work that day, which suited Classico just fine, because then, he had mother all to himself.

"Sweetheart, which art books did you like best in the school library?" Mother asked, placing the fluffy French toast on his plate. Henry picked it up with his fork and waved it in the air. The steam floated upward toward his face. The cinnamon smelled so delicious; the whole house smelled like Christmas.

"I liked so many pictures, Mommy, especially the Pic, pic ... pic, you know, the one who makes the funny ladies with eyes all over their heads and arms—the way I feel when I get off the roller coaster, all jumbly and jittery."

She tussled his hair and kissed his forehead.

"Oh, you must mean Picasso dear, the same artist whose poster is hanging in the living room. You know, he is the greatest artist that has ever lived. Maybe one day, when you grow up and become rich and famous, you will own one. The best boy in the world should have the best art. Now finish your breakfast and hurry to school." Henry gulped the rest of his orange juice.

Before Classico had a chance to kiss his mother goodbye, the doorbell rang, hauling him back into real time. "Oh no, it wasn't just a nightmare, yesterday's ordeal did happen."

"Ow." He tried to turn over, but his bruises hurt preventing his escape into another dream. He pulled the covers more tightly around his body to prolong the last vestiges of comfort from his formerly charmed life. His body ached, and each stab of pain retold yesterday's events. Classico winced as he got out of bed and went to the mirror. Lifting his pajama shirt, he examined his black and blue marks, touching them gently.

"Ouch," he cried. "Thank goodness nothing was broken."

Now, at least I'll have more time to find some cash to reimburse the investors, he thought, rustling through his closet. He dressed and took the small elevator downstairs to his office.

At 10 a.m. Alouisha busily sorted papers at her desk, and organized the morning's mail. Her usual sunny disposition always lifted his spirits—this morning it was missing.

"Good morning, Mr. Classico."

"Good morning, Alouisha. How are you feeling today?"

"I am okay," she said not looking up from her work. She bit her lower lip and kept her eyes fixed on her desk, not wanting her employer to see the anxious look in her eyes. She wanted him to think she was stoic and could handle a crisis well. "And you?" she asked.

"I'm a little sore, but I'll survive. Did you sleep well?"

"Yes," she replied.

Jason had comforted her all during the night, although he had insisted repeatedly that quitting her job was crucial.

"I can't quit the first time things get tough," she had told him. Alouisha was used to tough; her life had never been easy growing up in Jamaica. A good day for Alouisha meant Mom had enough food for her five brothers and sisters.

Classico leaned on the edge of her desk.

"Alouisha, I am so sorry about yesterday, and that you had to be involved in this horrible assault. I promise I will make it up to you. Are you sure you are okay?"

She looked up at his face; the creases between his bushy brows had formed an inverted V and his eyes were narrowed to slits. His apprehension triggered her sympathetic nature, and her words spilled nervously.

"You don't have to worry, Sir, I am fine. I did get a good night's sleep. Are we going to the police station today? Have you heard from Jack? We should go to the hospital and see him. I suppose he will be all right."

She paused for a moment; her pen tapped the desk like an SOS signal, unconsciously crying for help. Her pent up curiosity, now mixed with fear and a tinge of suspicion, erupted in a full force onslaught of questions.

"Mr. Classico, I don't understand why the Chinese tried to steal the painting. Are they connected to the China trip in some way? Didn't you bring Picasso with you to sell? Did they change their minds about buying it? Is that why you brought it back?" Although she was aware that her curiosity had crossed the picket line, she demanded answers. She needed to know the truth. *Besides*, she thought, *I have a right to know, I am involved.*

Classico grabbed her tapping hand.

"My dear, that is enough. I will save the answers for the police station. I'll give them all the details. Would you please call the board members and cancel the meeting scheduled for tomorrow? Tell them, we had an attempted robbery yesterday, and the less said the better. They'll have plenty of opportunity to read about it in the newspapers.

"Certainly, Sir, no problem," she replied. *When this blows over, he will owe me—big time,* she thought.

Still clasping her hand, he lifted her chin with his free hand, until their gazes met on the same playing field. His eyes rounded and peered through her protective curtain of a few loose tendrils that fell in front of her eyes. "And thank you, Alouisha," he said in a low molasses voice. "I will not forget your loyalty when I most needed it."

Alouisha felt that his earnest commitment was warm and trusting. They were a team now. She nodded as if she understood.

"Good," he said. "Everything will be fine."

Classico walked down the marble hallway to his office followed by an invisible cloud of emptiness that ricocheted off the cold walls and floors, buffering him from all consolation.

Alouisha listened to the echo recede. The gallery became quiet again and she heard only rustling papers and the low grumble of traffic somewhere in the distance.

Chapter 28

Sinbad and Sabrina DeMande

"Darling, what time do you think you'll be home tónight?" Sabrina DeMande asked, stretching into wakefulness from atop her memory foam mattress covered in the finest 1000-count Egyptian cotton. The lace-embroidered sheets on her 200 year-old Georgian carved four-poster bed were swaged and curtained in mauve brocade to match the upholstered walls and window dressings. She kept the curtains opened during the night, so the second thing she would see in the morning after waking up in Sinbad's arms, was the beautiful light shimmering over the central park reservoir. This morning, however, their cuddling time was cut short.

"Sweetheart, I need to get to the office early today to finish up some paper work for the Apogee board meeting scheduled for 11 a.m., and I have the accountants to deal with first. They are preparing the final numbers from the sale of several major paintings, so they can authorize payments from Apogee. With any luck, we'll realize a sizable profit," Sinbad said, thinking the timing could not be better.

No one had any cash these days. Banks had stopped issuing loans, no mortgages were underwritten, all cash had evaporated. He could not bring himself to tell Sabrina of their impending bankruptcy, but maybe he would not have to. The board members had agreed, during confidential meetings conducted without Classico, that they would vote to dismantle the fund. Sinbad anticipated his share of the profit would be sufficient to cover his debts.

"Art, as an asset class, is a good diversification for our portfolio because it has kept its value better than all other investments. The housing and stock market have both crashed, but art appears to be holding steady, at least the good pieces, the ones Classico has chosen," Sinbad said.

"Oh darling, we'll have to celebrate. I have such an intelligent and handsome husband." She watched his six-foot-two reflection in the cheval mirror as he reviewed himself; his blue eyes shone with approval. He pulled down his white French cuffs until they were long enough to peek out from the sleeves of his English custom-tailored suit. He passed the comb through his thick black wavy hair, and flattened it down with his free hand. They both silently agreed he was very attractive.

"I won't be late; I promise. What's on the schedule this evening?"

"Tonight is the 347th Franco Zeffirelli production of *La Boheme* at the Metropolitan Opera and he is being honored. Angela Gheorghu is Mimi and Ramon Vargas plays Rodolfo. You cannot ask for a better cast. It will be divine, I promise you," she added as she rolled over, glancing at herself in the mirror.

"Will Levine be conducting?" Sinbad asked.

"I am afraid not, but Chaslin is fabulous. The tickets have been sold out for months," Sabrina said.

"It is hard to imagine that in this economy, the house is full with an average ticket price of $1,000," Sinbad said.

"It just proves that not everyone is broke, and afterwards, there is a small dinner dance on the promenade. I will have your dinner jacket laid out for you, my angel. If you prefer, we can skip the cocktails, so it won't be too long an evening," she said yawning.

She stretched her arms above her head, and Sinbad watched as her breasts rose to the occasion, only barely concealed by a thin layer of hand-embroidered mauve charmeuse that matched the upholstered walls perfectly. He smiled; her long blond hair cascaded to the tip of her nipples, reminding him of last night's kisses after she forgave him.

"I love you," he said, leaning over to kiss the top of her forehead on his way out the door.

Sabrina languished in bed a few more minutes, savoring her husbands renewed good spirits.

She leapt out of bed, threw off the covers, and stood at the window to breathe in the beauty of the day. She sat on the window seat with her arms wrapped around her legs, her head resting on her knees, while she thought about her charmed life.

Unable to contain her joy, she considered becoming religious, maybe even Evangelical, to provide a venue in which to be grateful for her good fortune. A few years ago, she was not so lucky. Her former husband, to whom she was married for fourteen years, began having an affair with his 22 year-old secretary. They divorced, and she bore the ugly scars of hurt, pain, as well as reduced income and diminished social status. The Judge awarded her six years of alimony and the coop apartment. If she remarried, it would be sold and the profits split with her ex.

Previously, she had worked in investment banking, methodically climbing the corporate ladder and enjoying her paychecks and bonuses. Her former husband persuaded her to stop working and start a family. Unfortunately, the babies never came, and the love they had was not sufficient to sustain them through this critical juncture—soon after, the affair began.

At forty-five years old, her employment prospects were grim. The new college graduates, willing to work an 18-hour day, were well versed in the latest technologies to navigate and arbitrage the trading platforms. Her job choices were limited to low wages at the entrepots, Goodrich's and Conway's. Sabrina's housekeeper earned more, twenty dollars an hour. A job would not even cover the maintenance on her co-op apartment.

She needed a new financial plan, and her only possibility was marriage.

Eventually, she met Sinbad during an intermission at Carnegie Hall; they began dating and fell madly in love. Everything had become a fairy tale of happiness, until lately, when he angered so quickly for no apparent reason, snapping at her sharply with volatile outbursts.

Last night during a quiet candlelight dinner at home, they chatted gaily as Mozart's Opus 20 played softly in the room. She moved the grilled Baby artichokes around on her plate; her eyes fixed on the lines of butter that formed in droplets on the glossy surface. "Sinbad, about the summer house, I thought we should hire a decorator to change the mildewed fabrics on the furniture and the curtains in Breeze Song before the season begins. Being on the ocean, everything is ruined by the dampness. It has to be reupholstered every few years, otherwise we'll have mold."

"Leave the damn fabrics alone. I like the house the way it is," he said shouting. "And don't you dare hire another decorator!"

"Okay, I won't," she said, recoiling as if her hand touched boiling water. Seared by his unexpected mood swing, she burst into tears, jumped up, and threw her starched linen napkin on the dinner table; the chair screeched as it grated against the limestone floor.

"Don't speak to me that way. You don't need to shout. It was only about upholstery."

Reaching for her arm, he stopped her from leaving the table. "I am sorry, darling, I don't know what has gotten into me." Still stinging, she pulled away from his unyielding grip, but his wrench was made of steel and did not budge.

"Let me go," she cried, knowing she just needed a moment alone.

"Sweetheart," he pleaded, releasing his grip. She turned and left, slamming the door behind her.

Sinbad gritted his teeth and hissed, releasing his steamy bad temper.

"Damn it. What have I done?" *Maybe I should tell her we are about to lose Breeze Song. The bankers are calling in all my loans and will not give me another penny. I hate to disappoint her with the bad news. Besides, Classico has the cash. We will be receiving the checks any day now. I just need to wait a few more days.*

This morning, all was forgotten after many promises, apologies and great sex. Sinbad was at the elevator about to leave, when his house manager brought him the phone.

"Hello, Mr. DeMande, this is Alouisha from Classico Gallery. How are you today?" she inquired trying to detect an intonation in his voice that might reveal his knowledge of the attempted robbery and assault. She hated having to be the one to break the news to Mr. DeMande, but Classico had asked her, and she could not say no to him. He was still in pain and had so much on his mind. The story appeared on the front page of the Metro section of the *New York Times*, just as Classico had predicted.

"I am very well, thank you," he said.

I guess he hasn't read today's paper, she thought.

"I am so sorry to have to tell you this, Mr. DeMande; the board meeting has been postponed until further notice. We had an attempted robbery and assault, and the police will be questioning us today. Mr. Classico will have to go to police headquarters," Alouisha said.

"What? What happened?" he said trying to hide his panic.

"Sir, I am not at liberty to discuss the incident, but you can read about it in the newspapers. You can be assured, they did not get the Picasso," she told him.

"Picasso! You still have the Picasso? I thought he sold it six months ago to the Chinese." Sinbad's baritone anger resounded with the coloratura of death, frightening Alouisha and reminding her of the Triads when they threw her to the floor. Her turquoise eyes opened wide and turned dark blue. Words stuck in her throat, corked and glued as images of the assault flickered before her. The ground trembled.

"I...I...I...am sorry Mr. DeMande, you are mistaken. It was not the Chinese; it was the Russian, Mr. Grigory Baronovich. But, he has only given us a deposit and we have not heard back from him. I am sorry, Sir. I have to go to Police headquarters now. I'll be in touch shortly. Goodbye." She slammed the phone down, closed her eyes and rubbed her forehead and the back of her neck.

Sinbad's heart halted, as did all movement, sound, time, and feeling. The life-altering millisecond hit him like a kiloton explosion. His plan for economic survival shattered, thrusting him into crisis-mode. He could not take a breath. The Picasso was not sold.

He dropped the phone to the floor and his heart beat wildly. He staggered to the bathroom, turned on the faucet and doused his burning face with cold water.

"That bastard, that lying bastard. He's going to pay. I'll squeeze every cent out of him, even if he has to sleep on the street. He held on to the sink to support his buckling knees; he felt sick, the knot in his stomach wrenched. Disgusted by the stranger in the mirror he looked away. He did not recognize the image of the ruined man.

Sinbad dried his face, and pulled himself together to review his options. Classico had not sold the Picasso and obviously did not have the cash. The market was dreadful, frozen in suspended animation. A few bottom-feeders had surfaced for the half-priced fire-sales. The auctions were not an option for the Apogee Art Fund; the loss would be too great. He had to raise some cash immediately or else his life would implode. What could he tell Sabrina? He wanted to keep that smile on her face forever.

Furiously fumbling with the *New York Times,* he turned to the front page of the Metro section—"Picasso Theft Thwarted at Classico Gallery. Chinese Mafia, the Triads, broke into ... . He threw the paper down and grabbed his coat and briefcase.

"Oh crap," he cried out, pushing the button for the elevator. "We have no other choice, but to go to auction, and we have to sell every damn painting in that gallery, no matter what the price."

Chapter 29

Classico's Game, Lost and Found

After returning home from police headquarters, Classico felt satisfied that the investigation did not warrant further questioning. On reflection, he thought his well-crafted answers saved him from increasingly dire circumstances. His emotions, dulled by the grimy station experience, gave him pause from all of his business anxiety. He needed a bath and a nap.

"Good afternoon, Sir," Hans said as he opened the door and took his coat.

"Good afternoon," Classico replied. "Has anyone been to see me today?"

"No, Sir, just the guards outside have been here. Will you have some lunch?"

"No, Hans, please draw my bath. I'll be up shortly, after I check the mail." Sitting down to his desk, the words, "IMMEDIATE ATTENTION REQUIRED" glared in bright red letters stamped across the envelope. He picked up the silver letter opener, which ablaze with reflections, accentuated the dagger-like point with a burst of light. He glimpsed at the distorted image of his face on the shiny surface that dared him to consider an alternative use for the potential weapon. And, just for a second, he hesitated. Then, his intended purpose prevailed, and he opened the letter from the Bank of New York.

Mr. Henry Classico,
1 East 79 Street
New York, N.Y. 10065

Dear Sir:

We regret to inform you that you have defaulted on your mortgage payments. As such, according to our agreement, a copy of which is attached, foreclosure proceedings on One East Seventy-Ninth Street are about to commence ...

Classico broke into a cold sweat, and his temples throbbed as if they wanted to escape. Dropping his head into his waiting hands, his elbows disappeared into the pile of papers on his gold ormolu and walnut *secretaire*. He crumpled the letter into a ball, and threw the makeshift grenade with all the force he could muster against the closed door.

Although he may not be caught with the forgeries, he still had to pay Hollywood, the Apogee board, the remaining shareholders, and reimburse one share of the Lichtenstein. If the bank repossessed the gallery, it would force the sale of the remaining paintings with legal claim to collect the proceeds. The ignominy would be unbearably humiliating. They could not imprison Classico for defaulting on a mortgage, but he would be prosecuted if the investors and consignors were not reimbursed.

His arms fell on the desktop; he buried his head in his hands, as the papers and mail slid to the floor floating sideways, back and forth like ships at sea. He wanted to disappear into deep blackness.

Hans knocked on the door and entered the office.

"Is there something I can do to help?" he asked, seeing his employer so distraught.

"No, thank you. It is nothing, I'm just tired."

"Your bath is ready, Sir."

The ringing phone startled Classico, hurtling him back into professional mode.

"Hello, Classico speaking."

"Have you or have you not sold the Picasso?" Sinbad demanded, his loud voice crusty over the speakerphone.

Classico cleared his throat and sat straight up.

"Ah, Sinbad, how are you?"

"Cut the crap Classico. Where is the Picasso? You told me that you sold it to the Chinese, and now they are trying to steal it?"

"Well, it's a bit more complicated than that. I can explain."

"You'll do more than explain. You had better have the cash, or I will personally strangle you," Sinbad said.

"Take it easy, Sinbad, you'll get your cash. There is just a slight delay," Classico said unconvincingly as he tried to imagine a plot scenario to assuage Sinbad's temper. "The deal with the Chinese did not go through, so I sold it to Baronovich, the Russian oligarch for his new museum in St. Petersberg. He gave me a deposit, but I haven't heard from him since we signed the contract. He has to pay the balance soon or he forfeits his deposit. In the meantime, as a backup plan"— *here I go*— "I have negotiated a favorable deal with Goodrich's for their important spring sale at a reduced commission." Classico paused; his eyeballs rounded as big as tennis balls. He did not blink; he dare not breathe. There was no reply. *Is he buying it?* "Their guaranteed reserve price is five million more than Conway's," he continued.

Sinbad paced the floor of his office. He could not believe what he was hearing; there was no cash! He grabbed his golf club from the corner of the room and pounded the sofa, although he really wanted to smash it into Classico's head.

"Why didn't you tell me this before?"

"Calm down, Sinbad. They are giving us the cover of the catalogue," Classico optimistically envisioned, his voice raising an octave with the high note at the end of the sentence. He waited a few silent seconds for Sinbad's response, but all he heard was a repeated muffled thumping sound, like a hard ball being caught in a catcher's mitt.

Classico's voice dropped down to normal pitch, and he continued, "Goodrich's spring sale, as you know, is the most highly regarded and includes only the best works. This Picasso will be the cornerstone of the auction. In addition, they are certain they will be able to pre-sell it."

"How soon?" Sinbad perked up at the mention of a reduced timeline.

"Goodrich's is configuring their marketing strategy as we speak. This is not an ordinary auction, but a global event heard around the world. They are sending the Picasso around the world by private jet for it to be previewed by the great collectors," Classico explained. By this time, his voice had regained a semblance of authority that exuded confidence; he almost believed the fabrication.

"I see," Sinbad said.

"The foreseeable sale price could reach two or three times the high estimate. A painting of this caliber never comes up for auction. Never. This is a once in a century occurrence. This painting is the Holy Grail of modern art, and they'll all be clamoring to own the sacred prize," he assured Sinbad. "Their marketing plan will bring all the competition out of the closet, from the museums to the important private collections—so they have told me. Apparently, the Abu Dhabi Louvre is interested. This sale will create a baseline for the modernist western movement in the Middle East," Classico said, as he glanced from the Picasso to the boiserie ceiling.

"It is possible then, that we could make a killing," Sinbad said. Suddenly, escaping financial ruin had a viable future.

"With some luck, and a few of the auctioneer's chandelier bids, he could run the price through the roof," Classico said.

"Now, I just need enough cash to get through the next few months. Unfortunately, there is none left in the fund—but it's only temporary." He could not tell Sinbad that Goodrich's had also cut off his line of credit.

"Where is it?" Sinbad asked.

"It's been spent," Classico said begrudgingly.

"On what?"

"There were expenses," Classico said.

"You'd better find it," Sinbad ordered. "Where is all the cash from the previous sales? I'm getting a forensic accountant to look at the books. If he finds any discrepancies, you'll pay, I assure you."

"You will get your money," Classico said trying to sound confident and in charge.

"You're damn right I'll get my money," Sinbad said and hung up the phone.

"Damn, I have to give it up," Classico said slamming his fist onto the desk. The thought of parting with Picasso jabbed the pit of his stomach, twisting it into a steel knot. *I cannot allow it to slip out of my life, leaving me to wallow in remorse—alone without Picasso. No, I can't envision life without it. Picasso's inner life force is imbued with the collective energies and attention of everyone who has ever looked upon it in awe; the same way a solar panel receives power from the sun. It cannot be sent to some remote part of the globe, never to be seen again.* I cannot let that happen. He rested his chin in his hand; a faraway look came over him.

"Maybe, I do not have to sell it after all," he said.

Classico's third chance to right his predicament presented itself, and again he felt conflicted. The neural connections of his frontal cortex argued the moral imperative, back and forth with the dendrites and synapse's of his amygdala, engaging the combatants in a treacherous repartee. A full-blown anxiety attack ensued that exhausted any chance of a resolution. He paced the floor. With his head and shoulders stooped, he gazed intently at the grout separating the large slabs of marble, as if the answers were hidden in between the lines.

Chapter 30

The Kindness of Drag Queens

"That will be all for today, Alouisha, thanks for coming down," said Detective O'Reilly at police headquarters. "Can I get you a ride home?"

"No, thank you, I'll be okay; I'll just jump on the subway. Well, good luck, Sir, I hope you find them," she said, gathering her things while the police officer helped her with her jacket. She left the precinct, pushing open the heavy steel doors. It felt good to be outdoors in the sunshine and fresh air.

The long day of questioning was over, and she had told them everything she knew about China and the Picasso; somehow, it did not make sense. Why had Classico taken the painting to China and then brought it back? The purpose of his trip was to buy Chinese contemporary art, which was understandable, given that it was the hottest contemporary market; but he returned home with only the same Picasso. Was he unable to find a buyer? And how did the Triads here know he had it? she wondered. *Well, I'm sure the police will figure everything out.*

Alouisha wanted to be at home painting and forget all the mysteries and violent memories. She grabbed her sack-of-a-handbag and hoisted it onto her shoulder. Clutching it tightly against her body, she descended into the subterranean transport.

When she arrived home, she used the edge of her jacket to open the front door. It was only four o'clock but the night creatures were already staking their turf on the stairwells. She saw the usual group of cross dressers, clothed in Salvation Army thrift-shop-chic, reconfigured to imitate 1940s movie stars. They probably engaged, as usual, in drug dealing and sex peddling, but, somehow, the scene no longer frightened her.

Lately, their graphic equivalents found their way into her newest series of paintings.

"Hey, pretty girl," said a Dorothy look-a-like wearing ruby slippers, ponytails, and a white apron with a ruffled border.

"How's our two-shoes-goody-goody today?" She asked affectionately, as she batted her heavily coaled eyelids and stepped out from under the stairwell.

"Oh hi," she said, only slightly startled, mostly because the dim hallway's flitting shadows reconfigured the images of its denizens into eerie specters. "I'm okay," she said. They had become used to her also, and hardly teased her anymore. Instead, they were more like a neighborhood watch group, even looking after her at times.

"I put your mail outside your door. I didn't want those nasty hoes to get it," Dorothy said, twirling her finger pointing upwards and spinning her body in a semi-pirouette—her voluptuousness followed.

"Thanks," Alouisha said nodding and holding her nose." Can you please close the garbage closet?" She asked the Loretta Young wannabe, who stood nearby smoking a joint, waiting for her next John.

She nailed Loretta with a perfect mix of precious and sexy, Alouisha thought slightly amused.

Recently, when she reminded them to keep the door shut, they obliged without a snide comment or an attitude. *I wish they would stop smoking marijuana; the hallway reeks. I can get stoned just walking up the stairs. And why doesn't the landlord fix the lock on the front door? What's wrong with him anyway? Well, I'm out of here very soon. Mr. Classico has got to give me a show. He cannot keep the three paintings he bought from me in storage forever.*

Running up the four flights was all the exercise she had lately. She stopped on the landing and looked up at the stained-glass vaulted skylight glommed with decades of residue. The faint incoming light cast acrid washes of color, which soured into toxic blight-yellow, tarnishing all who passed through its illumination. She imagined life in the house in mid-nineteenth century, when it was home to the archbishop. Humming the Bob Dylan classic, "The Times They are a Changing," she rummaged in her handbag for keys and unlocked the door.

Inside the apartment, Alouisha took off her black Prada pantsuit and silk blouse and hung them carefully in her makeshift closet: a rod hidden behind a curtain in the corner of the room. After changing into an old T-shirt and splattered jeans, she fastened her hair away from her face and opened the window to take a deep breath. The cold air blasted her with freshness and the clamor of gridlock ricocheting off concrete. It amplified the perpetual grumble of the hard, cold surfaces of the streets, which had no absorbing reprieve. The turpentine and pigment vapors that thickened the indoor air dispersed outside.

After pouring clean turpentine into the small metal tin cups fastened to her palette, she carefully added the exact proportion of Damar varnish to the paint. The luscious consistency now would glide sensuously over the canvas.

She was ready to complete her work in progress — the *Androgyny Series*[6].

Androgyny One[6]   on canvas 3'x4'

The subject, a four-hundred-year old cotton tree, ensnared its polymorphous trunk randomly with looped, braided, and zigzagged branches. They interlocked and twisted into voluptuous forms that echoed Alouisha's tactile feelings. She could feel their heat; she could feel her heat, as she imagined they had become petrified during a wild orgiastic encounter. She envisioned the organic parallels between man and nature with every brush stroke—both breathing the same air and engaging in the same earthly mating rituals. She was certain the strong silent trees, rooted in the centuries, spoke tacitly of their wisdom collected over time.

Taking a brush-full of burnt sienna, she slathered it on the palette with snapping motions to find the right consistency. Needing to add

6 To view Alouisha's paintings in color, go to www.RochelleOhrstrom.com

more transparency to the colors, she dipped the brush into the Damar varnish and unscrewed the bottle of turpentine. The colors had to look and feel perfect, and perfect always had a distinct sensation.

Suddenly, a loud commotion erupted on the stairs followed by a stampede and a heart-stopping crash. Fear ripped through her, ransacking her nerves; her terror alert rose to red measured by the flush of her face.

She tiptoed to the door, pressed her ear against it, and listened to the sinister thunder approaching. Then it stopped as abruptly as it began. She didn't know what to do. "Oh my God, *someone could be shot or killed." Should I call the police? Someone might be hurt.* She had to do something. The silence, fraught with foreboding, weighed more heavily with each passing moment. She held her breath afraid to move or utter a sound. She huddled against the door on the floor with her arms wrapped around her knees. The fumes from the open can of turpentine smelled stronger and more noxious by the minute. She dared not move the five feet needed to reach the cap, lest the floor would creak and reveal her presence. Torn between opening the door or staying safely inside and calling the police, she counted the seconds, straining to hear the faintest sound. The dead silence oozed dread. *There is no way I am going to spend another day at the police station.* Eliminating that option, she listened for footsteps.

Ten minutes passed—not a sound. Whatever the disturbance, it was gone. Gingerly, she unlocked the door. The second she removed the bolt the door rammed open, shoving her to the floor. Two men barged in wearing the same jackets emblazoned with the Triad's fire dragon insignia. Alouisha screamed a piercing mix of terror, shock, and panic. The two Triads picked her up and threw her on the bed. They tied her hands over her head and fastened them to the sides of the nearby easel. Kicking and screaming, she tried to break free.

"Shut up," one of the men said, slapping her head.

"Pretty face," the other said, as his grin studded with broken yellow teeth magnified his evil glare. Using his knife, he traced an outline, light as a feather and not drawing blood, across her cheek.

"Oh my God!" she cried. "Please, please what do you want?"

"Picasso, where is Picasso? The original, where is it?" he shouted and slapped her again. Alouisha trembled and sobbed.

"It's in the gallery, hanging in the back room." The taller of the two men ripped off her T-shirt, exposing her naked breasts.

"Why should we just kill her when we can fuck her first. She is too ripe to waste," he said to his partner in Chinese. He tore at her clothes, and like a rabid dog foaming at the mouth, he wrenched the waist of her jeans down to her knees. The stench of his spraying sweat nauseated Alouisha, and she began to gag. When he unzipped his pants and exposed his stiff intention, she started to dry-heave.

Meanwhile upstairs, Mannix Linkx, was awakened from his daytime sleep schedule, having been up all night painting and indulging his more venal pastimes. When he heard Alouisha scream, he threw the leftover sushi on the floor, clearing some room to get out of bed. He found his reverse periscope, a spying device he was proud of having invented some time ago, laying under a pile of old Hustler magazines. He placed it in the quarter-inch-wide hole that he had drilled through in his floor to Alouisha's ceiling. He had decided that an artist and a voyeur were similar vocations; they both relied on observation. Spying on Alouisha kept his art fertile, thereby exonerating him from any residual guilt. Long ago, he had given up contextualizing his behavior against a moral framework, preferring instead, to focus on his art and his immediate appetites. He looked through the eyepiece; the scene below instantly sobered him.

"What the fuck!" He grabbed his sledgehammer and ran to the stairwell shouting, "Hurry, hurry, grab a weapon and get the hell up here. The fucking Chinese, they're killing the girl."

The drag queens, the S&M-ers, the male prostitutes, and the drug dealers all stopped whatever they were doing and rallied. They opened the door to the garbage room and released a stink bomb, but it was not a deterrent. The slinkily dressed, high-heeled Jane Mansfield rummaged through the trash and found an old broomstick. Boa-boy wearing a pink voile tutu and green feather boa snatched the tops of the garbage cans, and visualized smashing someone's head in, or at the very least, using it as a shield.

"Move over Pocahontas, let me in there, let me in there, move over," demanded a big-bosomed woman with a five o'clock shadow and a pair of Dorothy ruby-red pumps. She found a broken whiskey bottle to add to the stockpile of weapons. The S&M-er with the swiftness of a Samurai's sword, whipped out his belt, studded with sharp nail heads. The drug dealer had a missing front tooth, a diamond earring, and a big Jell-O belly, which was barely covered by a sleeveless wife-beater T-shirt stretched to transparent over his mound of wobbly flesh. Bending down, he reached with his gorilla-hairy arms and yanked the carved mahogany balustrade from the handrail. Now, he too was armed. The colorful army of sexual misfits raced up the four flights brandishing their weapons, united by their determination to rescue the girl.

Hearing the onrush, the second Triad, who waited his turn with Alouisha, leapt to the open door, ran into the hallway and began shooting. At the same moment, Mannix, hanging over the upper stairwell, threw his sledgehammer at the attacker, striking his shoulder. The wounded man crumpled to the floor howling with pain, shouting Mandarin expletives.

Inside, his partner, distracted by the screams, halted his assault only inches from the targeted violation and moved the knife away from Alouisha's face. She took her gap-moment and delivered a swift kick to the attempted rapist's most vulnerable pair. He bent over in anguish and pulled up his pants. Just as he was about to retaliate and cut her with his knife, he heard more shots. The wounded Triad had managed to fire a few rounds, one of the shots grazed ruby-slippered Dorothy in the arm.

"Ow...wow! Son-of-a-bitch," she cried clutching her arm, still waving the broken whiskey bottle. In that minute, fueled by her wounded rage, she rammed the jagged broken glass into the assailant's face, grabbed the opened bottle of turpentine and poured it on the Triad's wound. The bloodied mess that remained of his features contorted with agony and disbelief, making his eyes appear to have unfastened from their sockets. He passed out.

The drug dealer swinging the mahogany balustrade stormed the room and became a shooting target for the surviving Chinese. He ducked, but caught one in the leg, just as he swung his heavy wooden piece at the Triad; the assailant stumbled and lost his balance. During that split second, Mannix knocked the gun out of his hand and smashed his head with the sledgehammer. The tutu-boa-boy laid the metal garbage lids on top of the floored Triad. She jumped on him until his limbs stopped flailing, pulverizing his bones and extinguishing his life. His macerated flesh, broken ribs, and vertebrae swam in a stew of blood pooling in the entrance to Alouisha's apartment.

Doris Day gasped when she saw Alouisha shaking and sobbing, still tied to the easel.

"Oh you poor darling," she said as she covered her naked, shivering body with her twin set cardigan and wrapped her in the bed quilt. The Pocahontas-look-a-like untied her hands, while Mannix finished off the remaining Triad with one last blow to the head. Alouisha fainted when she heard the sound of crushing skull. Loretta Young put her arm around Alouisha's shoulders and gently stroked her hair.

"Alouisha, Alouisha, Alouisha," she softly called her name trying to bring her around. "Wake up, wake up," she said caressing her cheeks gently, until a few minutes had passed and Alouisha opened her eyes and looked around. Her body jolted, fear flooded every sense, she trembled without pause.

Two enormous breasts covered in a flowered cotton dress, thick red-smeared lips, and coal-rimmed eyes as dark and smudged as New York City summer soot, loomed above her. Syrupy perfume mixed with marijuana and sweat saturated her neighbor's clothing. From somewhere in the distance, Alouisha heard a voice calling her name. Blinking and trying to focus, but still groggy, bewildered by the plethora of humanity inhabiting her apartment, she was unable to make sense of her surroundings: hairy muscle men, big-bellies, pink tutus, men wearing pearls and feather boas. The acrid odor of gunfire clung to her skin.

With her senses scraped raw, the three dimensional room flattened into a surrealist moment. The gaudy group became the foreground of the paintings that leaned against the walls of the studio. The paintings had been caught in the line of fire, and now were splattered with the assailant's blood. She squeezed her eyes shut.

"Don't be afraid darling," Loretta said, still stroking her hair and forehead. "It's all over now. You are going to be okay. They didn't hurt you; we got here just in time. It's going to be all right."

"Jason, Jason, I want Jason." She buried her head in Loretta's bosom and sobbed another round. Loretta held Alouisha in her arms, rocking and talking softly until she only whimpered.

"What's his number?" Mannix asked.

"212-717-6666," she whispered.

Everyone began talking at once.

"Are they dead?"

"Did we kill them?"

"We gotta get outta here."

"Should we call the police? They'll take us down for questioning," Dorothy said.

"And we'll all end up back in the slammer, where they'll rip me a new one," the drug dealer said.

"Let's get outta of here now and then call the police," Loretta added.

"Someone has to stay with her. I'll get thrown back in the can for violating my probation," the male prostitute said.

"Me too," said the boa-boy in the pink tutu. She tried to move her arm, but winced with pain. "I'm not allowed to perform violent acts."

"I'll stay here and take care of her until Jason comes," Mannix offered.

"I don't ever want to go to headquarters again," Doris Day said. "They are so mean to me, those macho police bastards."

"I need to get to a doctor and get this bullet outta me," the big-bellied drug dealer said.

"Let's get out of here, now," Ruby slippers, shouted.

Suddenly, they heard the downstairs door smashed open. Thundering boots and booming voices ricocheted throughout the hallways. The footsteps pounded the stairwell—louder, closer. Everyone froze, iced with fear.

"They sent backups," the large, muscle-man shouted.

Mannix seized the gun from the dead body. Pink tutu jumped out of the fourth-floor window onto the rooftop of the adjacent two-story apartments, preferring to risk a broken leg than another Triad attack. Mannix crouched behind the door clasping his sledgehammer positioned for combat. And Jane, loosening the front of her sequined bodice, gripped the iron bolt and pushed the door closed. The stampede came louder and closer, threatening annihilation, as they raced to the fourth floor landing. The only movement in the room was the beads of sweat running down the faces and armpits of Alouisha's defenders. She felt the walls close in around her. The stench of death and blood, spiced the air.

"Police, Police, freeze."

The words punctured the tension like a balloon expelling air; everyone sighed in unison; relieved it was not the Triad's back up team. For the beleaguered group of misfits gathered in Alouisha's studio, their relief quickly turned to dread.

"Don't anyone move," ordered the officer, his gun drawn as he surveyed the room: two dead bodies lying in puddles of blood, surrounded by transgender cross dressers and other strangely costumed souls who were not dressed for a stroll in the park.

"Alouisha. Oh no, it's Alouisha," Officer Fulgenzi said when he saw her wrapped in a blanket, trembling and crying.

"Are you okay? Are you hurt?" Fulgenzi asked. She couldn't speak, but a new wave of tears flowed down her cheeks.

"They didn't have time to hurt her officer," Mannix said. "We got here just in time. She is just shaken and scared. They roughed her up pretty bad."

"Okay everyone out in the hallway, we're taking you all downtown for questioning. Don't touch anything," the officer ordered as his colleagues checked the bodies to see if they were still alive.

"Alouisha, take a few minutes to gather your things, you cannot stay here. Officer Ramirez will help you." The officers stepped outside into the hallway, while Officer Angela Valdez helped her up.

Unexpectedly, old, gray Dick, from O'Reilly's Bar and Grill appeared at the top of the stairwell, sucking air in clipped staccato breath from the four-flight climb. Luckily, he had been outside across the street, had heard the gunshots, and called the police.

"What's goin on?" he asked, looking around the room.

"Oh, the Chinese Mafia? They're worse than the Italians. Is the girl awride?" he asked. He prided himself on his role as self-elected neighborhood watch-man. "Someone has ta take care of things around here," he told the police.

"Where are my clothes? Where are my clothes? Give me my clothes," Alouisha cried.

"I am afraid there is not much left to them," Officer Ramirez said, noticing her ripped jeans and shirt on the floor.

"Where are your other jeans?" Getting up, Alouisha stared at the blood on her floor and on her paintings. She rushed to the bathroom and retched, expelling the horror of the day.

"Oh my God. Oh my God," was all she could say.

The next morning Alouisha lay safely in bed, wrapped in Jason's arms. Snuggling more deeply into his loving embrace, she floated on the hilltop of her dreams and tried not to look down toward the ravine of horror scattered with Picassos, death, and art galleries.

Jason watched her beautiful face in repose, as he tenderly soaked in every nuance of her breathing: every eyelash flutter, every swell of her chest, every quiver of her mouth. He felt so saddened by her ordeal. He did not understand why someone would want to harm her, or why the pure light of her soul had to be marred by that rotten filthy assault. He could not fathom how this could have happened to her. It was Classico they were after.

They had just gotten back together, and everything had been going so well—until the police called.

"My beautiful sweetheart held at gunpoint, stripped naked, nearly raped, and then, having to witnessing two violent murders. It's not fair; you don't deserve this," he whispered, lightly brushing her hair from her face.

He pulled her closer to him, vowing to protect her always. Her body trembled in response. With each breath, she released some fear and lessened the emotional pain.

Chapter 31

At the Precinct

"Stop right there in front of the station." The meter read $6.90, and Classico handed the Pakistani driver a ten-dollar bill. "Keep the change," he said not wishing to engage in any physical exchange with anyone who reeked of street-cart gyros and onions. He opened the door and inhaled the fresh air. He brushed away any foul odors that surely permeated the fibers of his clothing during the ten-minute ride from his office.

I am not looking forward to this. With his gaze cast downward, he entered the Sixty-Eighth Street precinct, downtrodden as if he were harnessed to a wagon filled with rocks. He emptied his pockets, removed his coat, and walked through the metal detector.

"My name is ..."

"Over there," the guard said, cutting him off before he could introduce himself. The middle-aged, Hispanic man pointed Classico to an old wooden bench; the same model found in railroad stations intentionally designed to be uncomfortable lest a homeless person requisition it for a bed. Classico sat and waited with the other unhappy souls who would rather be anywhere than here.

The harshly lit fluorescent room cast a green pallor, stark as a Dan Flavin light sculpture. His head tilted slightly, and his fingers held his forehead. He gazed up at the formerly white-tiled checker-board walls, which had random missing squares stained with variations of yellow and brown grime. They reminded Classico of old rotting teeth.

His shallow breathing tempered the smell of dirty ashtrays; he did not dare to inhale deeply. He cringed inwardly from the foul surroundings. By ingesting the degraded atmosphere, he surely would risk permanent damage to his sensitivities. Preserving the pristine lifestyle he had created—one occupied with beauty, culture, cleanliness, and intelligence—had required carefully selected exposure to people, experiences, and locations. When he returned home, he would take a long, hot bath to remove any physical or emotional residue of this ordeal.

He sat where he was told and wished he had earplugs. The police continued shouting orders at the victims, assailants and witnesses, which kept everyone agitated and on high alert. Classico's skin prickled from the harshness of it all. The metallic noises reverberated off every hard, non-upholstered surface and were amplified by the jarring loud speakers. He winced each time the high-pitched articulation of clanking handcuffs locked and released.

Half an hour later, Alouisha arrived clutching Jason's arm, wearing jeans and his oversized sweater. He wore a similar outfit.

Classico cringed from seeing Alouisha so pale and shaken—her normal joy extinguished. All light had disappeared from her eyes; her smile was upside down, and her confident breezy manner had been blown away like dead leaves in autumn. *Those Chinese bastards did not have to involve her. She is a young, innocent woman.* "Damn those Chinese bastards," he said shaking his head, walking toward them.

"My dear Alouisha, I am so sorry about last night. Please, if there is anything I can do, anything at all, please let me know." *Are they blaming me?* he wondered. He searched Jason's face for a hint of judgment, incrimination or any telling detail from which he could glean a measure of her thoughts about his culpability. The tall, good-looking, young man had compassionate blue eyes that revealed no information about Alouisha's mental state. She appeared unresponsive. Classico extended his hand, "I am so sorry," he said.

"Yeah, me too," replied Jason, sizing up her employer, who looked to be somewhat of a dandy and a little too precious to be trusted.

"How are you feeling?" Classico asked her softly.

Alouisha blushed and turned away from him, not wanting to answer Classico or for him to see her like this. She whispered to Jason, "Why can't he go away, why can't all of this go away?" Jason felt her tense up and squeezed her shoulders, pulling her closer to him. She buried her face in his chest to relieve the scraping feeling in her stomach that made her feel sick.

"It's okay … it's going to be okay." Jason understood that in her fragile state her emotions stung more than her slapped face. Scared and humiliated, most of her healing would not be physical. Her neighbors had intercepted the rape and had risked violating their probations to rescue her. She was sorry; she could not be of much help to them now. It hurt so badly.

The harsh noises echoed in the room with poor acoustics. The piercing pitch scraped like chalk on the school blackboard. With each shouting person that entered the area, she flinched, and her inner resolve shattered into smaller pieces. Finding an empty corner near the overflowing trash bin, she huddled closely to Jason, and as far away from Classico as possible.

"Good morning, thanks for coming," said Officer Brody.

"Alouisha Jones, we need you to come with us for some questioning."

He turned to Jason, "Don't worry, we'll take very good care of her. Mr. Classico, you can go with Detective O'Reilly."

"Follow me." He led her through the dim hallway into a back office with bars on a window that faced a light-deprived courtyard. When he sat down, the utilitarian 1950's chair groaned with tones of metal fatigue. He motioned for Alouisha to sit in the matching chair, next to Detective Fulgenzi. She took her seat, the metal felt cold and hard and the room smelled like dirty socks.

"You remember Detective Fulgenzi?"

Glancing up she barely nodded, "Yes, hello."

"How are you doing, Alouisha? That was a frightening ordeal they put you through last night. You're a lucky woman because your neighbors were there to help you. It's about time they did something good for the neighborhood," Fulgenzi said.

"What in the world is a nice girl like you doing living in that crap house? Is that your boyfriend outside?" asked the Detective, blurting out too many questions, too quickly for her timorous emotional state.

"I'm so sorry you were victimized by those brutes. They're a nasty group and have caused a lot of trouble recently. At least they didn't harm you physically, only slapped you around a bit, and emotional scars can heal," he said. "You don't have to worry, I promise, we will apprehend whoever's behind this and put them away for a long time. We're here to help you," Detective Fulgenzi said.

"Yes," she replied softly, barely speaking above a whisper.

"What are you doing living in Hell's Kitchen all alone?" he asked.

"I ... I ... w ... wa ... was trying to support myself, while I painted, and it was cheap and only temporary. I thought Mr. Classico was going to give me a gallery show."

"Those were all your paintings?" Officer Brody inquired?

"Yes, Sir, I am an artist."

"And you work for Classico Gallery during the day?"

"Yes, Sir."

"And how long have you worked there?" he asked.

"I graduated from Yale in June, 2008, and I began working for Mr. Classico that November," she said. "It's been more than a year—a year and four months."

"During that time, what do you remember about Classico's dealings with the Chinese?" Fulgenzi asked. "Just relax, Alouisha, take your time."

She bit her lip and clutched the long sleeves of her sweater into a ball, stretching them longer to cover her trembling hands. She felt the penetrating cold from the metal armrests and tasted the rusty brine color of the walls.

"Alouisha," Fulgenzi said in his lowest voice. "I need you to remember every detail you can about the two incidents. First, is there anything else you remember about the assault at the gallery that you might want to add to your previous testimony?"

She swallowed hard, the words stuck in her throat. "No ... no ... I told had you everything."

"Well then, let's begin with yesterday afternoon, when you returned home from work," he said.

Classico's sweat glands went into over drive, and his heart pounded to the top of his throat, until his Adam's apple looked as though it were about to hatch. Focusing his attention inward, he canvassed his physiology for any remaining drop of sangfroid he previously possessed to prevent his hand made John Lobb shoes from fleeing out the door. He remembered feeling this fainthearted only once before, when the neighborhood bullies tied him to a tree and threw a bag of spiders on him. They punished him cruelly, simply because he missed third-base during softball practice. With trepidation suitable for a walk to the gallows, he followed O'Reilly down the long corridor. The distance between himself and the interrogation room shortened, as did the rope around his neck.

They are going to ask me why the Chinese wanted the Picasso and how they knew about it. What can I tell them? Usually, they prefer drugs, weapons, and sex trafficking. I'll ask them their opinion about the latest global money-laundering vehicle. Do they think it is art? Then, I'll subtly mention that the Russians and Middle Eastern Sheiks have unlimited funds and are increasing the demand for art. I'll let them think that money-laundering art in the Middle East is their idea.

"So, Mr. Classico, please tell us everything about your connections with China and the Picasso. We need to figure out how much back up is involved here. If we can expect another attack," Detective O'Reilly said.

Here goes nothing, Classico thought. *It is now or never.* He straightened his tie and his posture sitting tall as possible, he coughed and began.

"Well, this past winter I traveled to China to explore the Beijing art scene because global demand for Chinese contemporary is voracious. Then, I had an idea. Recently, I sold an important Picasso to the Russian oligarch, Grigory Baronovich for the modern art museum in St. Petersburg. I loved this Picasso so much that I could not bear never to see it again. So, I decided to commission a copy for my own enjoyment, and since China has the best copyists in the world, I took it there to be reproduced. Huang Show, my contact, liked it so much he wanted to keep the real one. Of course, I refused to sell it to him, having already promised it to Grigory Baronovich and had received his deposit." Classico calmly relayed the tale with earnest portrayal, and hoped his face was not glowing too much.

Two hours later, the detectives concluded the questioning, satisfied with the geography of facts in his story.

"That will be all for now, Mr. Classico. We appreciate your coming here today. In the meantime, we'll keep the security guards at your gallery, and get intelligence on the case. We have a few inside men downtown. Above all else, we do not want this to escalate. They can get pretty vicious as you have seen, particularly, when one of theirs gets killed," he said, showing him to the door.

"We'll be in touch," O'Reilly said.

"Thank you for your good efforts. I hope you find them," Classico said holding a bursting sigh from escaping his lungs. He felt their eyes staring at his back as if they were taking an x-ray of his veracity. *Slowly, slowly,* he ordered himself, and with every ounce of discipline he could summon, he did not bolt out the door to escape this dreadful experience.

Four doors down the hall from Classico's interrogation room, Alouisha finished recounting the assault to the officer and detectives. Sometimes their words fell away behind a veil of grayness, and she could no longer hear them. Sometimes the words came through a megaphone hurting her ears, and the screech of it all sent darts of coldness down her spine. Then the whispers came, falling softly as snow, only then, could she respond to the kindness in Officer Fulgenzi's eyes.

"Alouisha, please try to remember anything the assailants may have said about the painting or about China. Anything at all can be helpful," Detective Fulgenzi said in his most sympathetic voice.

"Mr. Classico went to China with one painting and returned with two. I think it was two. I'm not sure. He sold one to a Chinese client named Huang Show. Two men attacked me. No, I do not know if they were the same men that broke into the gallery last August, although they wore the same jackets with dragons on the back. They asked me where the original Picasso was located. It was hard to understand them because of their accents; I don't think they speak much English. I told them the Picasso hung in the back room at the gallery. Then, they slapped me and tied me to the easel," she said, as her chest heaved and a new round of rainforest tears fell.

An hour had passed, and her skin felt cold and clammy; her lips were parched. First, she would sweat, and then become cold. Feeling as if she might have a fever, she pulled her knees up on the chair and hugged them closely.

Another officer, whom she had not previously met, blustered into the room. The large, brutish man had a bulbous nose and crew cut hair accompanied by a static energy that couldn't escape, causing him to sweat. Officer Lopez was in charge of the rape unit.

"How are we doing in here?" he asked, seizing up Alouisha. He rifled through his papers, reviewing the facts before he began the questioning. Alouisha watched his stomach heave with each breath he took, as if life itself were an arduous task. Upon seeing Alouisha curled up in a ball on the chair, he expelled a large bag of a windy sigh and looked upward at the ceiling through his heavy eyelids. This was Officer Lopez's fourth case of the day. He tapped his foot in annoyance, crossed his arms over his chest, and loomed over Alouisha.

"Let's get this over with," he said losing his patience. "Did you experience penetration?" he blurted out. "Did they both touch you at the same time?" She hugged her knees tighter.

"So, did it hurt or did it feel good? Did you perform oral sex? Did they ejaculate on you or inside you?"

She could not answer; she pulled the sweater up over her head to shield herself from this invasion into the sacred part of herself. It was like a second attempted rape, this time it was to her dignity. The questioning shocked her as much as the incident itself, and made her wonder whose side the officer was on. She had heard about the aftermath for rape victims and the brutish methods the police used for questioning. It was common knowledge the police often blamed the victims, thinking they were in some way responsible by provocation. However, Alouisha could not believe this was happening to her; she was watching someone else's bad movie. The three large men overwhelmed the room with girth, sullying the atmosphere with harsh severity. Alouisha rose from her victim's seat and reached hurriedly for the exit, only to be blocked by the guard.

"I'm done! Where is Jason? Jason?" she called. "Let me out of here."

"Okay, Alouisha, take it easy. I think you have had enough for today," Detective Fulgenzi intervened. "Here, here is the number of a social worker whose specialty is trauma victims. She can help you get through this. Call Jason in," he told the police officer standing outside the door.

Chapter 32

Power Water and Goat Heads

A t eleven a.m., the morning after Alouisha's second visit to police headquarters, she lay in bed groaning in a labored sleep. Her suffering could not find refuge in Jason's arms or in her dreams. All during the night, he had held her tightly, soothing the whimpering cries that had surfaced from the tangle of violent dreams. He sat at the edge of the bed, watching her struggle in her sleep. She gripped the pillow urgently in a life or death hold. Even when she was consumed by utter sadness, her beauty mesmerized him. Gently not to wake her, he stroked her forehead and hair, tracing the structure of her face over high cheekbones and across the transverse of her brows. When he reached her mouth, his thumb parted her lips, and he bent down until he felt her breath on his lips. She stirred; her eyelids flickered but did not open. The wind of her sigh warmed his cheek and comforted him. He would do anything to protect her—anything.

Jason had left her for a few minutes, just as she began easing into wakefulness. The choir of morning birds sang in the trees outside the window. She stretched and listened to the rain hosing down the leaves, pelting the windows in polyphonic tones. It reminded her of the rain hammering the tin roof of her home in Jamaica and how cozy she would feel lingering in bed, listening to the September monsoon. She reached across the bed for Jason; the empty pillow was cold and dented. Suddenly, an arrowhead straight from Hades blasted through her morning sweetness, refueling the horror of yesterday's ordeal.

"Jason, Jason," she called.

"Coming Ali. Just a minute, I'm right here in the kitchen, getting your tea."

"Good morning, my angel," he said, attempting to sound cheerful although his solemn tone prevailed. He leaned over to kiss her; then, he pulled back an inch or so, just far enough to search her face for a sign of resolution. Any slight inkling of healing would mean so much to him. Their eyes delved deeply into each other's thoughts. They did not need words.

Jason played her favorite band on his iPhone, the Black Eyed Peas. The docking station was programmed to wireless digital speakers that rocked the loft. Alouisha sipped the tea; the liquid's flat surface sloshed in her unsteady hand, creating waves and ripples. Jason did not know what to do. Should he try to cheer her up and risk ignoring her feelings? Should he minimize the impact of the ordeal? Should he talk about it and validate her feelings? Surely, rehashing the incident would not be helpful. He only wanted her to be well again; to be her irrepressible self, brimming with spunk and determination, on her life's mission to paint her sentient world. He did not have to dwell on a course of action.

With tears running down her cheeks, "I can never go back there again and face all those people, even though they risked their own lives to help me." A flashback of the stiletto pointing at her throat, and the two ghouls tearing at her clothes had embedded itself like a branding iron into her anguished psyche. She wailed in raw agony, and her body shook all over. Then, still shivering from the gruesome memory, she pulled the covers over her head. The darkness engulfed her but did not release the terrible fear. Instead, it simmered and festered—made pungent with humiliation. She wanted yesterday erased, but the brutal thoughts came in torrents—an open floodgate, carrying the detritus of shattered emotions.

Frightened about her future safety and utterly ashamed to have been stripped naked in front of the neighbors, she felt disgraced. "What if their friends come back to kill me?" she said. Jason gathered her up in his arms and held her firmly, but with heart felt tenderness, "It's going to be all right. I promise. I will make sure no one ever hurts you again. Those bastards will never come near you again. You are safe here with me ... always. I love you, Sweetheart," he said gazing into her eyes with the endless loyalty of first love.

"Finish your tea while it is still hot. Why don't you stay in bed today and rest, I'll take care of everything." Putting her arms around his neck, she pulled him close to her not wanting to let him go—not now, not ever.

This de facto mode for cohabitation was not Jason's ideal venue for a romantic commitment. It should have been an intentional decision, which they chose together because living apart was unbearable. But, he was certain that his devotion to Alouisha could withstand comparison with every historic legend of love. Together, their energies commingled into a force field, which sent streamers of golden light that speckled their perimeter.

She bunched the pillow to her stomach; her knees rose toward her chest. "It feels as if the inside of my stomach is being scrubbed with steel wool," she said, in short whispering gasps, so softly, he barely heard her.

"Sweetheart, here, take a Xanax, it will make you relax."

He stayed with her until she lay back down, closed her eyes, and loosened her grip on the pillow and his arm. The doctor-prescribed sedatives seemed to be taking effect and she slipped into a peaceful sleep. Gently, he untangled himself from her grasp and tucked the blanket around her.

He sat at the edge of the bed transfixed by her sleeping innocence unable to fathom the brutal attack she had endured. How could anyone want to destroy something so beautiful? She was a rare treasure in this world, someone without a dark side, who treated all people with kindness and consideration. Taking her limp hand in his, he sat with her all morning, just watching her breathe; occasionally, her eyes flickered or twitched. The longer he watched her sleep, the more his emotions began flipping out of control. He wanted to cry. He wanted to kill. He wanted revenge.

Something was not right. Mr. Classico's lukewarm response to this tragedy was not acceptable. There was something else going on, and Jason was determined to find the truth.

A week had passed, and Jason watched her improve slowly. Yesterday the doctor had visited and suggested they take a walk in Central Park.

"A little fresh air will be good for her," he said.

"That'll be great, Doctor. I'll take her outside the minute she's ready to get out of bed," Jason said.

"Try to make it soon," he said with urgency in his voice.

Months had passed and Alouisha showed no signs of a recovery. Her days were spent staring out the window at some far away place, then she would retreat back to her bed and hide under the covers. Even on a sunny day, her expression was bleak. Jason, unable to make her happy, felt helpless and spiraled into his own depression. His paintings changed tone, and now, rendered with dark haunting images, they bemoaned his broken joy.

Alouisha continued languishing in bed, working through her sadness. Still half asleep, her thoughts drifted onto the full-blown sails of her childhood dreams. The breeze blew in from the open window, and the emotional grunge that stuck to her expanding energy field disseminated to the dark matter. She left the earthbound pull of encrusted horrors, and emerged wrapped in the protective fabric of the universe. Stirring and stretching, she released the macabre thoughts that clung to her every waking moment, and soon, felt lighter leaving them all behind— if only she could return to Jamaica. Instead of clouds of marijuana fragrance permeating the night, she smelled the sea and tasted its salt on her tongue, in her food, and in her chewing gum. The constant ruckus from the street dealers and boom boxes morphed into a celestial love sonnet, as the distance between her and the wretched cacophony grew wider. She imagined swimming far out into the ocean, where the vast sea and the sky became one, and she had only to surrender to the vanishing horizon to be embraced by father infinity—her own father she had never known.

Her thoughts turned to her great, great, grandmother who lived to be 110 years old, and whom she missed so much. If anyone asked grandmother, "How are you today?" Her stock answer was, "My eyes are dark, and my hearing is lazy, but I can still touch my toes." Alouisha had those words written on the rock in front of the wooden cross on the mountaintop grave in the backyard of grandmother's cabin, which was constructed of wood and coconut palm fronds.

Alouisha remembered her grandmother's funeral—a joyous grateful-to-God celebration. All her relatives, who included most of Hopewell Parrish, climbed the mountain until the clouds were at eye level. The peace, pure air, and jungle colors created a true paradise— one that easily accessed Godliness. She smelled the goat heads cooking over bonfires in ten-gallon metal pots, which simmered into "power water," a Jamaican delicacy infused with promise of increased potency.

Alouisha entered grandmother's one room cabin. She ran her hands over the walls   papered with photographs of the many generations of grandchildren who lived in descending order of birth down the side of the mountain and visited often. Grandmother was never alone, always surrounded by loved ones and great natural beauty. Taking the measure of a happy fulfilled life, Alouisha thought grandmother might be the winner.

She lifted her face to the afternoon sun; its heat melted her sorrow. She slowly got up from her bed and went to her easel. The canvas glared insistently, daring her to take control of nothingness—of whiteness—to reclaim her power. First, she subdued the stark gessoed emptiness with a gray wash, lessening the aggressive pure white. It brought her closer to a tonal reality, one that matched her emotions. Picking up a 1 1/2" horsehair brush, she dipped it into a mixture of turpentine, Stand oil, and Dammar varnish. Then, blending the slithering mixture with burnt sienna, she smoothed out the consistency until it was translucent. The brush bent, snapped, and grabbed hold of the mixture, finding its own rhythm. The delicious smell of oil paint wafted through the loft; it was as ripe with yearning as baking bread promised to an empty stomach. Placing the creamy oil pigments on the virgin canvas drenched the process in sensuality. The colors slid smoothly into a permeating repose, stopping only when Alouisha lifted her brush to complete the saturation. Her technique signaled the beginning of a journey into a metaphysical adventure where colors, shapes, and feelings were the only vocabulary. Previously invisible, intuitive content unfolded each time the brush pressed the canvas, translating and transforming it at will ... her will ... her rules ... her feelings ... her heart.

Suddenly, the front door slammed shut and wrenched her from her dream.

Chapter 33

The Attribution

Fifty-five year old Regina Bookman wore the latest black, Prada pantsuit made of stretchable, water and crease resistant, techno fabric, which shaped the ruching on the front and back of the bodice into a medieval warrior breastplate. Although she had no intentions of going into battle, her much-coveted job, as a top Goodrich's modern art specialist for the past twenty-five years, inevitably brought her into the line of fire. The auction house depended on her discerning, unforgiving eye for detecting forgeries. Thus far, she stood her ground deflecting negative innuendos, rumors, and art world scandals that could have taken down a lesser mortal. Her credentials, born of a Ph.D in art history from Columbia University, and her reputation for impeccable connoisseurship had fortified her position as an eminent modernist-painting authenticator. Her talent prevailed and boasted an unblemished record of accuracy— no lawsuits contesting her attributions were ever filed after a sale.

Featuring the Picasso from Classico gallery in the upcoming spring sale would complete Bookman's art world coronation on a global platform. The confluence of events that brought this painting to market could only occur once in a lifetime. When Wall Street's sub prime-mortgage debacle led to an urgent need to raise cash, this seismic moment in the history of the modern art world emerged—and Regina Bookman intended to take all the credit.

Her success, however, came at a price; after years of hard work and sacrifice on the job, she never had found time for a private life. Having worked her way up the corporate ladder for all her adult years, Regina had long ago given up sentimental or emotional ties to anything or anyone that could impede her scrupulously planned future. All her feelings had been compartmentalized and left curbside like a collection of recyclables from the last trash removal of her broken heart. Now, marketing, branding, and authenticating art for Goodrich's filled her empty spaces with "busyness," the de facto activity pursued by so many to help them remain disconnected from their feelings.

If she accepted the Picasso, a global marketing strategy would be put into play. Today that would be the topic discussed in her class.

Regina Bookman sat at her desk in the Goodrich's classroom reviewing auction documents. The interns enrolled in the History of Modern and Contemporary Art program eagerly waited for their lesson to begin. Regina Bookman rose from her desk.

"Good afternoon. Today we will explore the many steps involved in bringing a major Picasso to market for the spring sale," she said. The hum and rustle of the students settling down quieted instantly. "Auctioning a work of this caliber on the secondary market has its fiduciary advantages. It could be pre-sold to a museum, a collector, or a hedge fund, giving them terms of payment configured into an art mortgage or a price guarantee. If a consortium wanted to buy it, like the group that acquired Damien Hirst's diamond skull, the competition would become fierce, sending the bidding to the high estimate and over," Regina said.

"Prior to the sale, we will create a global media frenzy. The Picasso will be marketed and branded on a scale never before seen. It will be sent to Europe, Asia, and the Mideast by private jet to be viewed by select clients at lavish receptions and dinners. The evening auction will be the most coveted invitation in the country," she said, pausing to embrace the moment. Her slender body swayed to form an s-curve, as her elbow pointed upward and her hand revisited the tight, low knot at the nape of her neck to check for unruly strands of hair.

For the past two days, Regina and her assistants had scrutinized every detail of the Picasso that Classico had delivered last week. She codified an extensive checklist to vet artworks, which created a new threshold for unforgiving authentications. First, Regina studied the enclosed documents of provenance along with a forensic examiner. Then, using an especially high-powered magnifying glass, she analyzed the brushstrokes, comparing Picasso's penmanship of line with other works by the master. Her team studied the half tones, the edges of the shapes, consistency of tonalities, the chemical properties of the pigment, its application, and its ensuing surface textures. A graphologist gave a second opinion on Picasso's signature and a dendrochronologist determined the wooden frame's origin. Unfortunately, the x-ray and infrared investigation did not expose any under-painting that would have offered an intimate glimpse into Picasso's creative process. A transparent viewing was a rare experience in art circles—the exclusive domain of the art elite. If a connoisseur had privileged access to an artist's first strokes and first thoughts on canvas, a new level of interpretation and scholarship could be ascribed to the artist and his work.

"Usually some under-painting is evident," she continued to explain to her interns. However, its absence is inconclusive, and therefore, not regarded as evidential." Having vetted every aspect thoroughly, she was still somewhat hesitant to give the Picasso an A-plus and a sales contract.

Regina Bookman insisted on perfection in every category; her reputation depended on accuracy. The moment the press releases delivered her edict, the news would reverberate globally. Classico needed only to sign the contract to propel Regina's arrival to the pinnacle of art status—the sacred sphere where the market makers, Classico, Gagosian and Saatchi reside. Once they contracted a new artist, the price of his work doubled, then tripled; the power of their art brand was invincible. Regina's seal of approval like the British Monarchy's coat of arms would never be second guessed.

Regina gazed out the window lengthening her line of sight. She allowed herself a minute of daydreaming reverie to softly focus on a distant horizon. The wind blew the budding trees below as they shook and trembled, as if anticipating the excitement ahead. Blue skies patched the traveling gray clouds, and an incandescent rim of copper sunlight outlined the spire of the Chrysler building.

She tapped her Mont Blanc pen on the desk, envisioning herself as an honored guest of Sheiks, Heads of State, and museum directors worldwide, who would invite her to their palaces and country estates. At her convenience and dependent on her schedule, they would send private jets to New York to fetch her when they needed authentications, or simply an attractive, well-connected woman at their dinner party. Every important world collection would require her imprimatur before a purchase or sale. Catching herself in the daydream, her thoughts revisited her desk and the manila folder containing the unsigned contract for Picasso.

"One final criterion for a thorough evaluation remains—the Digital Art Analysis," she explained to the Goodrich's students. "This new field of authentication using computer imaging is impressive. However, it has not yet been proven 100 percent effective in the United States." Her eyes sparkled, and the icy shell that encased her emotions, warmed from the heat of her enthusiasm.

"First the painting is scanned into the computer and reduced to a black and white image. Then, perhaps six small sections are enlarged to close-up views. The computer creates algorithms that find patterns in the brush strokes, often relying on contrast for a numerical value. Then, a statistical portrait is created where the largest number indicates the highest contrast. The directions of the brush strokes are then analyzed from six different angles. At that point, one can assign a numerical value to the overlapping, excessive strokes commonly found in forgeries. This fascinating new field of digital forensics was invented in the Netherlands. It has had tremendous success and will continue to pioneer the future of authentication," she said.

Because it was unusual that no underpainting appeared during the infrared light test, Regina Bookman would have liked to have a digital analysis of the Picasso. But a slight gnawing in the back of her mind gave her second thoughts, generating some suspicion—nothing decisive, just a fleeting thought. In this terrible economy, no one's reputation or career could withstand the painting to be discredited—not Classico's, not Goodrich's, and certainly not Regina's. She would be disenfranchised, returned to the anonymous life of a regional specialist or a file-cabinet researcher, and her international power-base cut to nothing.

Classico's reputation would be impugned, and the entire art world would suffer the consequences from undermining the trust and assumption explicit in authentications. At this time, the art market and the economy were too fragile to absorb derogatory information about a painting of this caliber. Besides, the integrity of the most reputable dealer had never been an issue. Goodrich's needed this Picasso for the cornerstone of the auction to draw in other important works. What else could they put on the cover of the catalogue? No, she could not chance a digital art analysis. Although this method was the only procedure that did not rely on subjective opinions, she invoked the same logic used by the Museum of Contemporary Art when they chose not to use this definitive technique. "Algorithms are still under development," they had announced, secretly horrified at the thought of opening a Pandora's box of possible forgeries.

"Bookman here," she said, picking up the phone. "Please send him in. Class is dismissed," she announced, revisiting the precision of her tightly knotted bun. Fumbling through her purse, she found her mirror, reapplied her lipstick and checked her teeth. Her stone fortress, perfection in all that she did, provided protection and guarded her reputation.

Classico followed the young blond assistant through the sleek corridors to the back offices of Goodrich's—the rooms where susurrant arrangements were plotted and promised. These sacred hallowed halls, the sanctuaries of greed, provided the perfect caucus for unbridled capitalism to flourish. It was here that Classico's lust for culture and art conjoined into one entity of pure covetousness. During a great sale, he would prickle from an overload of oxytocin and vasopressin (chemicals produced from the body's reaction to love and shopping,) which kept Classico dazzling with confidence.

He continued down the minimalist white hallway, obsessing about his entire future that depended on this meeting. Like a mantra, he silently repeated his affirmations, "Yes, I can do this. Yes, I can do this."

Overhearing someone chanting, his concentration wandered to the source. The foreigner's sonorous voice echoed down the hallway in that familiar, overly projected tone used for calling overseas. Classico glanced inside the partially opened door to the private salesroom. Two trays lined with black velvet lay on the table containing piles of enormous gemstones set in platinum: emeralds, rubies, sapphires, and diamonds. A man dressed in traditional Saudi *dishdasha* held the telephone in one hand and a jewel in his other hand. Every few seconds, he bowed deferentially and recited his mantra: "Yes, Your Majesty, Yes, Your Majesty."

Classico turned the corner, and Regina walked toward him.

"Henry, how good to see you. Please come in," she said as she shook his hand firmly, acknowledging their commitment and shared good fortune.

"It is so good to see you, Regina. You are beautiful as always," Classico said clutching her hand and depositing a warm kiss on her cheek. Her hand felt cold; his hand felt clammy. She offered him a seat on the leather sofa near the window. Scanning the scene overlooking Rockefeller Center, two lone ice skaters danced in the rink that had not yet closed for the season. The usual hordes of tourists hijacked the streets, going nowhere, just looking. He thought of the great bronze sculpture of Atlas at the entrance to Rockefeller Center holding up the world and its problems. Classico knew just how Atlas felt— genuflecting to St. Patrick's Cathedral, as he genuflected to Regina Bookman.

The official purpose of today's meeting was to negotiate final terms of the sale and to collaborate on marketing strategy—if she chose to accept the painting. Of course, its attribution was not in question because Goodrich's assumed its authenticity when offered by the highly regarded Classico Gallery. However, normal procedure required vetting, and Classico knew she would have meticulously examined its every aspect. The final analysis was hers alone; her validation eclipsed all others and would determine his fate.

As he sat down, his belly rioted like jumping beans shaken over a fire. But, Classico remained outwardly calm and in control, while he inwardly struggled with his spiking nerves. His face glistened, almost breaking into a dreaded sweat.

It was not often in his life, not since his childhood, that he relinquished his power to another person. After leaving that hellhole in the dust bowl of the Great Plains, he made a solemn vow—never to allow anyone to control his future. Unfortunately, one woman's opinion would foretell the remainder of his life. *It is ironic*, he thought, *how one sentence in an entire lifetime can be responsible for 60 to 100 million dollars ... or nothing.* Those fateful words would deliver a passport to "the good life" or behind prison bars.

Without thinking, he removed his magnifying monocle from his waistband pocket. His fingers glided over the familiar gold chain, hanging limp without direction. The round shape fit so comfortably in his palm. He needed just one last chance to make everything right.

Classico watched Regina rifling through the papers on her desk.

Her erect posture echoed her formidable position at Goodrich's. Unconsciously, he straightened his shoulders and mirrored her authority. She looked up from her paperwork. Her gray eyes glinted like the tips of metal spears, as if she had the single-minded purpose to bore through his layers of defense to detect any sign of duplicity that could dismantle the integrity of the painting. Classico inwardly cringed, but his outward appearance remained immutable. He evoked his outstanding reputation: if ever any indication of malfeasance were to surface, he would be forthcoming.

"Henry, if we put Picasso on the cover of the catalogue, I truly believe all the buried cash will come out of the closets. Anyone who has any left is keeping it hidden, probably offshore much like many of the large corporations," she said, flicking her pen in the air.

"Yes," Classico said refocusing, buoyed by the positive response to Picasso. "Halliburton opened its corporate headquarters in tax-free Dubai to escape the IRS. Their greed contributed to America's high unemployment rate." *How clever they are to reduce their expenses,* Classico thought.

"How does a vice president of the United States sit by allowing his former company to behave so unpatriotically?" Regina asked, leaning on her elbow moving closer to Classico until he could identify the gold and diamond watch that peeked below her silk cuff as vintage Cartier.

"It's appalling," Classico said, stroking his chain as if they were Greek worry beads.

"One does not wish to be politically incorrect and spend large sums on nonessential goods, while so many people are losing their homes. This Picasso, however, is too important to pass up," she said.

"The new Wall Street billionaires, the recipients of the sub-prime mortgage revenues, will be unable to resist owning a high-profile trophy painting of this caliber," Classico said.

"Correct, and if it is bought though their hedge funds or corporations, it will become a huge tax deduction, saving them millions," she said.

"Why shouldn't corporations buy art instead of giving the revenues to the government, who would spend it on pork, wars, or weapons? It makes sense," he said.

"After they enjoy it for a few years, they can donate it to a museum to receive a lifetime of tax incentives, as well as becoming a trustee or chairman of a prestigious museum," Regina said.

"Isn't it extraordinary that hedge fund CEO's are now running our museums? There was a time when a museum's chairperson required a Ph.D in art history," Classico said.

"Great art is always a brilliant investment and one must continue to diversify one's portfolio. Don't you agree, Henry?" she asked.

"Uh, yes, yes," he said trying to remain present and engaged in the conversation. "Of course you are right, Regina. Aren't you always? That is how it has been until the graveyard art sales of last year. Let's hope it is over and 2009 is not repeated," said Classico.

"The upcoming 2010 spring sale will be unprecedented and will determine the future health of the art market for the next ten or twenty years," she said.

Is she just pacifying me or does she suspect something? She is the best. If anyone can detect a forgery, it is she. But, I still have not signed the contract. She still has not agreed to take it.

Classico quit searching for nuances in her facial expressions that might reveal any suspicions. Her emotional distancing made it impossible to garner a sense of her feelings or thoughts. Normally he read people easily, but Regina's chilly facade was inscrutable. There is no way in, he thought.

Regina slowly, methodically circled the desk to the front and leaned back on it, folding her arms across her chest. She towered over Classico who sat three feet away. His blood pressure reached a crescendo; he felt the beads of sweat breaking into puddles, and making his shirt stick to his back.

Then came those crucial words— "Well, Henry, we are thrilled to have the Picasso. It will be an extraordinary day in the history of the auction block. Not even an economy as dismal as this one will diminish the outcome of this extraordinary sale," Regina said, shaking his hand.

Trying to absorb the great news, he subdued the deep sigh that wanted to be released from the depths of his soul. A state of hyper-reality engulfed his senses with a brightly colored euphoria transmitted in high definition. The roses on the windowsill doused the room with perfume; the honking horns became a percussion ensemble; the leather sofa beneath him felt smooth and yielding; and the highly polished mahogany floor sparkled with bits and pieces of light fragments. The world became sweet again, as did the taste in his mouth.

Regina's distant words flooded back to Classico in decipherable sound bites. The painting had passed scrutiny from the highest echelons. His thoughts galloped—the story he had invented for Sinbad was now fact. Everything he had risked was paying off. He stifled the smile that wanted to stretch across his face like a Yue Minjun portrait— he was already spending the proceeds from the sale. *Damn, that SoLow is good.*

Chapter 34

A Cauterized Future

D uring the past winter, 2010, the financial markets had continued to annihilate the global economies, and Classico had no hopes left of salvaging the fund. The banks that had received federal bailout money refused to issue loans. Unemployment reached nine percent (40 percent for black males) and home foreclosures accelerated. Middle America remained helpless, as the Republicans fought with renewed hostilities to defend Wall Street's $100 million bonuses that the CEOs paid themselves with taxpayers's TARP money. The art markets were slower to fall, but eventually, by the end of 2009, they followed the uncertainty and crashed just as hard. A major Jeff Koons sculpture did not receive one bid at auction.

Sinbad slammed the phone and grabbed his coat from the mirrored closet, which reflected the view from his 35th-floor office on Madison Avenue and 58th Street. He stormed past his secretary. "Hold all calls," he said in a razor blade voice. Sinbad was in a rotten mood, and regretted not having paid more attention to the Apogee Art Fund's financials. Classico had buried the fund's accounting details under his perpetual optimism for the art market's profit potential. He alone knew the formula for holding a $3 million painting and reselling it, two years later for $8 million at auction. Undoubtedly, art profitability outperformed all others asset classes—until the bubble burst. Sinbad, like the other investors, had not asked too many questions. They all wanted to own helium-filled shares in the art market, and were grateful when Classico offered them positions in his private equity fund. His impeccable reputation branded the Apogee Art Fund as visionary, exclusive, and a rock-solid investment — second-guessing seemed unnecessary.

Growling and grumbling, Sinbad pushed through the crowded streets of New York in bully-pedestrian-mode. With angry pistons engaged, this indigenous form of transport required a large ego, which exuded serious intentions that implied an emergency. When properly worked, people stepped aside and allowed him to pass.

Now, I will have to hire a forensic accountant, and they will charge upwards of $800 an hour. I cannot afford another major outlay like that right now, and my hedge fund is down the toilet, he ruminated. The SEC had begun an investigation into worthless derivatives, and even if Sinbad could prove he was not in collusion, the legal bills alone would destroy him.

"I trusted that son of a bitch. I should have been suspicious when he moved into the new gallery. Get out of my way," he said, not slowing down for anyone, continuing to mutter under his breath.

Three years ago, they were lunching at 21 and Classico had been excited to tell Sinbad about a lead he had on a rare Lichtenstein war painting. "I just found out from a reliable source that the owners are getting divorced. I have been coveting that painting for sometime; and now, I might just convince them to sell it to me, discreetly of course. It would be a great addition to the fund."

"Good work, Classico. Your talent for finding new acquisitions is impressive," Sinbad had said.

"Yes, I have a great network of informants ... I mean close friends. The three Ds never fail to provide new inventory," Classico had said and sipped his glass of Meursault. He leaned back into the chair expanding his chest. Then, he leaned over the table toward Sinbad and, in his most discreet voice, barely above a whisper, "Sinbad, assembling this world-class collection has been a privilege and a joy for me. Now, it is necessary for the paintings to have a proper home and proper branding. They are unrivaled in connoisseurship and exclusivity, which increases their value and creates a model for future acquisitions. I have outgrown the gallery on Broadway and have bought a fabulous Beaux Art mansion on 79th street. It will be a perfect venue for the paintings. It is a "win-win" situation, and as a bonus to the investors, we would rotate the paintings to enjoy at home, like a lending library," Classico had explained. Sinbad listened to the plan; his eyes glistened with admiration and visions of profits.

How will I ever tell Sabrina? She has no idea of our impending catastrophe. Classico had better return my $20 million investment, or I will destroy him. Somehow, I'll get it back.

He climbed the limestone steps to the gallery, "Tell Classico, DeMande is here," he said to the Blackwater security guard who had replaced Jack.

"Do you have an appointment?" he asked.

"No, but I own this gallery, and I want to see him now," he said, thinking that Classico owed him so much money that he could sue for possession.

The guard pressed the intercom, "Sir, there is a Mr. DeMande here to see you. He says he owns the gallery. Should I let him in?"

Classico stood up from his desk and straightened his tie. Frantically, he assessed his alternatives. His choices flashed before him in a split second download. Mentally, he Googled the equation and scanned the hard drive of his brain more deeply. It was grim. Squinting from painful indecision, he tried to locate his lost courage.

These Wall Street bigwigs can get tough if they do not get their own way. They employ various types for a variety of circumstances, not all of which are white-collar jobs.

Outside on the steps, Sinbad's fuse was getting shorter by the minute. The iron-gated door was not opening. He refused to allow his anger to be harnessed by this brute. He needed to vent and look Classico directly in the eye to hear the truth. Furtively and repeatedly, he glanced left then right. His left foot tapped danced to the rhythm of his pulsating temper. Finally, he stepped in front of the guard, "Classico, open the door NOW," he shouted into the intercom.

Unable to stall Sinbad any longer, "Ah, yes, a ... please send Mr. DeMande in."

Classico walked to the foyer with his hand extended. Sinbad ignored it, and with a disgusted look on his face, passed him briskly and headed toward the office, dumping his coat on Hans' outstretched arm. Classico followed Sinbad.

"I am glad you came. We have a lot to discuss before our board meeting. How have you been?" Classico asked. Before Sinbad could answer, "Hans, please, offer Mr. DeMande something to drink. Would you like to join me in some old single-malt scotch?"

"Classico, I did not come here to be entertained," Sinbad said.

"Of course, Sinbad, please sit down. I want to review the details of the auction with you."

"Listen, you slimy bastard," he stood up and approached Classico gesturing combatively with a clenched fist. With expanding bravado, Sinbad loomed over Classico and watched him recoil. The former gallery giant cringed and sank more deeply into the sofa dragged by the magnet of guilt and fear. Classico continued to squirm; Sinbad began to laugh.

"The coward's out of the bag," he said mockingly. "Where is the cash from the sale of the Picasso, you sold to the Russians? It's time for some answers, and for some cash. Stop screwing around," Sinbad said.

Classico sighed, and sat upright. Hans entered the room just in time to save Classico from further humiliation. He carried a silver Georgian tray with Baccarat crystal glassware, which rested on delicate Irish-linen doilies. A tiny oblong sliver dish held English biscuits. Sinbad relaxed his emotional grip on Classico's neck.

"Sir, do you care for ice?" Hans asked.

"No thank you, Hans," said Classico, tugging at his strangling collar. "Sinbad, please sit down, and we can discuss this. I promise you the numbers are there. When we sell the Picasso at auction, the first round of investors will receive their return on equity. Perhaps this was not the original plan for the exit strategy. I personally would have waited until June for Art Basel in Switzerland. The art fairs bring in the last-chance collectors who are caught up in the buying frenzy. They will buy anything by an artist they missed at auction because they know it will never again be available on the secondary market—not in their lifetime, if ever. A similar work often sells at a fifty-per cent premium over the last auction price. However, having said that, I have negotiated an excellent contract with Goodrich's, which the lawyers are drawing up now," he paused to clear his throat. "It is to be approved, of course, by our board of directors."

"And exactly what are the terms?" Sinbad asked.

"Well, here are the bullet points," Classico said, rummaging through the piles on his desk.

"First, we are featured on the cover and have the best selling position on page twenty-seven, and they've waived the fee for placement and photography. There has been a scientific study to corroborate the psychological advantages of various placements. Apparently, the second painting in the catalogue by the same artist will fetch a higher price. The unsuccessful bidder, suffering from buyer's remorse, will leap at a second chance."

"Yes, Yes, go on," Sinbad said.

Classico again cleared his throat, and glanced at Sinbad to see his reaction. If Sinbad thought that he alone made the final decision about the financing, even though Classico's litany of pros and cons influenced his choice, then, perhaps Classico could restore Sinbad's confidence in him while stalling. Classico had to persuade him not to take the guarantee.

"Secondly, they waived the consignor fee and will rebate part of the buyer's premium. The exact figures depend on the guarantor, who agrees to pay a set price for the painting even though it may not sell or reach the reserve price. A guarantor, however, would lower our profit by 5 to 25 percent. Alternatively, Goodrich's offered a loan on the future amount of the guaranteed sale. This option would further reduce our profit. The auctioneer will simply state, "someone with financial interests may be bidding."

"Personally Sinbad, I would recommend passing on the guarantor. This seminal work by Picasso represents a great moment in art history. Goodrich's has offered an outstanding marketing plan. They will transport the Picasso by private jet all over the world, delivering it to homes, palaces, offices, and museums of the interested parties to view alongside their private collections. Goodrich's foreign and regional offices will host exclusive receptions for the potential buyers."

Classico looked sternly into Sinbad's eyes. "Sinbad, I cannot overemphasize the importance of this sale. The health of the global art market for the next decade will depend on it," he said, conjuring up all the earnestness he could muster.

Rivulets of perspiration dampened the collar of his bespoke shirt. His liability included reimbursing the full cost basis of the collection, not only a portion of the profits. The twenty-five paintings Classico presumably bought for the fund, hung in the gallery on consignment. In a moment of desperation, he used them to collateralize loans—money he spent.

"Interesting," replied Sinbad. He motioned to Hans for a refill. Relinquishing some of his hubris, he sank into the silk upholstery and listened with skepticism. "This had better not be another of your spurious perorations of hope and optimism," Sinbad said.

Sinbad had long ago given up Christian attributes of faith and trust, replacing them with Wall Street derivatives and sub-prime mortgages. However, when he heard, "immediate access to funds" he relaxed and allowed the aged single-malt's efficacy to take hold.

"Goodrich's also provided sales records, trend charts, projections, and previous auction results for Picasso. They are all in the file, right here," he said handing the statistics to Sinbad. He bowed slightly with one hand behind his back, invoking the same period of politesse as his furniture—the court of Louis XIV. His social capital needed a hoist after the humiliating reprimand he received earlier. Sinbad snatched the file from Classico's hand. Still not proffering respect, he squeezed his eyebrows together to concentrate.

"So, as you can see, there is no risk involved. It would be foolish of us to give away an additional five to twenty percent profit when it is unnecessary, when we have such a sure thing," Classico said.

"I understand your point of view. We will vote at the board meeting."

"But, Sinbad, you are the Chairman and have far more financial expertise in these matters than the others. Surely, you can influence them with your decision."

"I will get back to you after I spend some time reviewing the numbers. Also, I will need access to your account receivables, all your books, Classico, on the table," Sinbad demanded.

Classico gulped the remainder of his scotch. It was unlikely Goodrich's would extend additional loans to him. Once the mortgage, guarantor, and insurance departments compared notes and realized the extent of his borrowing, they would not give him another cent.

This is starting to feel like buying a house without a down payment, he thought, recalling how he spent all the millions.

Enhancing the collection took precedence over everything else, he reminded himself. The $800,000 Southampton summer rental was staged for entertaining, requiring eight full-time indoor staff to manage the *compound: two chef's, four maids, two-to-four in wait staff, and Hans. Two full time gardeners to keep the tennis court, pool house, guest house, grounds, and flowers beautiful for my attractive, rich, art-collecting guests, whom I adored and treated splendidly. The countless dinner parties and luncheons introduced important artists, collectors, museum directors, and curators. Everyone loved my parties. The CEOs and hedge fund Wall Street types wanted to diversify into cultural assets and gorgeous women; they all received invitations to mingle with both. I branded the collection. I spared no expense. The proliferation of beauty and art was all that mattered. My collectors expected the best from me: the best chef, the best champagne, and the best paintings. Addicted and intoxicated, I could not stop spending.*

Sinbad's distant words echoed from the long corridor of his memory. "Now, for the next item on your surreptitious agenda, what happened to Grigory Baronovich's million-dollar deposit?" Sinbad asked.

Outside, a fire truck hurtling in emergency mode, blasted its siren and punctured Classico's preoccupation. The marble floors amplified the ear splitting dissonance as the mind-numbing racket of car horns remained unrelenting; the clamor collided with whatever was left of his sanity.

"He did give me a deposit, and I tried to contact him repeatedly," Classico blurted out. "But I have not heard back yet." *Anyway its been spent,* he thought.

"That is strange. You expect me to believe that he walked away from one-million dollars?"

"Maybe it is only small change in his bottomless pocket, or perhaps they poisoned him. You know how medieval the Russians can be. But, not to worry, the purchase order clearly states in small print that the balance of $39 million is to be paid in full or the deposit is forfeited."

"And if he shows up with the cash, we are screwed. You sold it to him for forty-million dollars, and the auction house will guarantee fifty-five. Is that what you are telling me?" Sinbad's left foot turned metronome, underscoring the end of his patience. Classico bolted up from the desk.

"Yes, it is. But, at this late date, he probably won't show at all."

Sinbad grasped the large yellow envelope on the table, containing the remaining files from Goodrich's. Suddenly, his eyes glazed over oozing with hatred, fully aware of the magnitude of the looming disaster. Shouting with all the breath his bursting lungs contained, "You, you stupid moron. If you think you are going to get away with this ... you ... you had better come up with the cash for the investors or I am going to the police, and you will rot in jail. You have one week."

Classico grabbed his arm, "Sinbad, please, we can fix this." Sinbad jerked his arm away in disgust and slammed out the door.

"Wait, wait," Classico cried out. His skin turned white. "What have I done?" With his life energy force deactivated, expunged from his miserable, hurting soul, he fell into a limp pile onto the sofa, unrecognizable as the former art world titan. Irrevocably exposed, he shuddered from the enormity of his situation and its impending consequences. He felt trapped in a bare white room lit with hundreds of fluorescent tubes—stark and cold without shadows. There was no place to hide. Sinbad would get his cash or his revenge—of that Classico was certain.

He crossed his hands over his head to keep the truth from crushing him. The Napoleonic clock ticked louder, or maybe it was his pulse. His head fell to his knees. "It's over," he cried.

Chapter 35

Peanut Butter and Jelly

J ason opened the front door and bent to pick up the mail. Because he was preoccupied with Ali, he did not open the envelopes as usual but placed them on the kitchen table next to the hot sauce and jam. Alouisha showed very little sign of improvement. He paced the loft, the distance from his waiting canvas to the door of the bedroom. His thoughts were rabid; he thought of nothing except Alouisha's recovery and finding the missing pieces to the incident—the Chinese's motive and Classico's culpability.

Every five or ten minutes, he checked on her and listened to the low moans that kept escaping from her anguished dreams. Jason wondered how much longer the torment would continue. He bit his upper lip, gritted his teeth, and paced some more, faster this time.

Then, he grabbed the chin-up bar fastened to the top of the door-frame and did a quick twenty-five. His arm muscles bulged—first ten, then twenty, faster and stronger as he tried to burn off his anger. Suddenly, he dropped to the floor and clutched his stomach. The knots of tension roped tighter into a jabbing pain he could not ignore. Sick with worry and anxiety, he had forgotten to eat since yesterday or maybe it was two days ago. He could not remember. His emotions jumped up and down like a pogo stick, not giving him a moment's peace. After a few minutes the pain subsided. Although it was still morning, he went to the kitchen and grabbed a beer; he needed to chill. He popped the top on the edge of the table and fell into the chair. His long legs sprawled halfway across the kitchen floor; then an avalanche of sadness blanketed him. His raw emotions collided into one heap of numbing misery, but he could not cry. His head fell into his arms stretched out on the table. "When will she be well again?" he asked himself repeatedly. He could not stand seeing her like this. It hurt too much.

He missed their morning jogs in Central Park, particularly in spring when their bodies ran in sync with all the glory of the season and each other. She ran as gracefully as a gazelle, while he sprinted along beside her. They inhaled the beauty and freshness of these pheromone-exuding outings and later it transitioned into tender waiting embraces.

He particularly missed the summertime when she wore her short-shorts and sleeveless tees. He envisioned her exquisite, naked body curving through her damp clothing, as it clung to private places. He recalled their wet, sweaty, lovemaking—sometimes so primordial and urgent, like a pack of hungry wolves devouring fresh kill.

Jason missed the autumn, when falling colors cluttered their jogging path. The trees, however, remained strong and essential, divested of excess and stripped to their essence. It reminded him to simplify their relationship and stay focused on the heat and strength of their love.

Perhaps he missed the winter most of all. The snow fell on their faces and melted from the warm kisses they randomly exchanged when they could not contain their joy. They overflowed with affection, as the sky released its whiteness, silencing anything not derived from pure thought and substance. "Maybe, it is God erasing all evil," Alouisha had said. In those moments, they remained the only lovers in the world. The crisp, clean air brushed against their cheeks and enhanced the presence of everything divine.

Sitting at the kitchen table, Jason opened another beer and ripped open a few pieces of mail. Mostly junk, he crumpled them for shooting practice and hooped them into the trash. He noticed the large white envelope from Goodrich's. Usually he wrenched the plastic covering off the subscriptions to the Goodrich's and Conway's catalogues with gusto, impatient for the latest news in the contemporary art scene. He flung it on the floor and gulped his beer instead. His whole body collapsed on the table dropping the empty bottle to the floor next to the catalogue. He picked it up. All the color drained from his face. Stuck in suspended horror, he sucked in the air with staccato breath, until his lungs nearly exploded. It was impossible, there had to be some mistake. He could not believe what he saw before him. On the front cover of the Goodrich's catalogue appearing in four-color-glossy-glory was Classico's Picasso— the same painting responsible for almost getting Alouisha killed.

It felt like he had been punched in the face. Because Picasso was the impetus for the attempted murder, Jason thought it contemptible to award it high honors and elevate it to prominence on the world stage. Killed by a Picasso—killed for a Picasso, the difference was a small preposition. It was wrong. He hurled the insidious catalogue onto the bamboo floor. The Picasso incident was under investigation, and all transactions should be frozen as criminal evidence. His anger obliterated all reason into a ubiquitous mass, disseminating blame like scattered seeds on everything relevant to the terrible ordeal.

Alouisha had not dressed, left her bed, or communicated in any meaningful way. She wallowed in torpor beneath the sheets, as if her life were ebbing away. The doctor had prescribed patience and rest. Last night, however, the terrible nightmares did not return. The heaviness that shackled her to the bed was somehow lifting. "Jason, Jason," she murmured and stretched.

"I'm right here sweetheart."

"What time is it?" she yawned.

"It's 9:30. Good morning, Angel. How are you feeling?"

"Better, I guess."

"You slept like a baby, all cooing and stuff. You look much better. Your color has come back. Sweetheart, let's have a good breakfast; I'll make your favorite banana, coconut johnnycakes. Then maybe we can go for a run around the reservoir. If you feel up to it, of course."

"I'm not sure."

"The doctor thinks some fresh air would be good for you."

"I don't know, Jason. Maybe tomorrow."

He took both her hands and with an outpouring of total love, "Sweetheart, think of the cherry trees spreading their glorious pink blossoms, bursting with springtime renewal. Remember how we loved to watch the wind gently blowing the branches bare, and the cascades of pink petals scattering everywhere—everywhere the children laughed and played—sticking in their hair, on their clothing, and in their peanut butter and jelly sandwiches that the nannies carefully zipped into plastic baggies," he said, knowing Ali was always inspired by beauty.

Later in the day, the playgrounds would empty and the five o'clock shafts of April light would cast halos around those walking home. A back-lit radiance would silhouette the passersby walking through the golden twilight. For a few moments, they would glow as if selected by some otherworldly deity to join the cosmic elite. The shadows did not conceal a person's features in darkness, but instead, outlined the shapes with rims of incandescence. If Jason could bring Alouisha to the park to soak in the light and be surrounded by the profound beauty of nascent spring, he knew she would feel better.

"Why don't you get dressed? You'll feel so much better, please, you can do it," he said.

Opening the drawer, he pulled out two shirts. "Here I bought you the latest high-tech gear. State of the art, X-Static fabric t-shirt and jogging pants made of breathable micro-fiber, which wicks away moisture and regulates body temperature. And, if that is not enough to get you up and running, it's your favorite color, apple green. How cool is this? These shirts rock," he said jumping up on the bed waving the shirts like flags in a parade, and dancing to a silent samba beat. He tried his best to make her laugh. She smiled, the first one since the attack and Jason's heart leapt. Her inner light broke through the trauma that held it hostage, and, like a victim freed from her kidnapper—she was back.

"Oh, Jason," she beckoned to him with outstretched arms. She had returned from a long treacherous voyage.

"Baby, you're home. I love you so much."

Intense and desperate, their lovemaking pummeled the stored up hurtful emotions, bringing them first to the surface, then shattered into oblivion. Furtive and redemptive, they detonated the raw aching misery from their souls and memories with one profound explosion.

Chapter 36

The Exit Strategy

I t was three p.m., a week had passed since Sinbad had visited Classico. Unable to eat or sleep and devoid of options, Classico paced his upstairs rooms, wringing his hands. Yesterday, the bank ordered him to evacuate the premises in thirty days. Bereft of hope and utterly derailed, his involuted posture cradled his shattered emotions. The shots of scotch offered no reprieve, and the thin stripes on his pajamas forewarned of his future behind bars. Images flashed before him being physically removed from his home, foreclosed by the bank, then litigated and indicted in art fraud. Agitated and distraught, an unrelenting panic attack shook him to his core.

He slumped on the side of his bed near the Picasso, feeling utterly helpless. Anticipating the return of the Chinese, he feared for his life, his sanity, and his paintings. If the Chinese Mafia did not kill him first, most likely, he would be arrested for theft and fraudulent operations of the Apogee Art Fund—Sinbad would see to that. Classico envisioned the New York Post featuring him on the front page as he was hauled away. The title would read: Ponzi and Picasso.

I meant to buy paintings with the proceeds from the new investors, but I had to pay bills—just a small amount at first; the cash slipped away like moonlight through my fingers. Then, I needed larger chunks, which disappeared like calving glaciers into the bottomless ocean. I alternated paying invoices and mortgages for a while, but I was caught on empty in this terrible economy. He stared at the ice-cubes in the glass of scotch that jiggled in response to his twitching hand.

His final humiliation would be his inability to afford bail. The unbearable pressure closed in on all sides as he imagined his future squeezed out like a discarded tube of toothpaste. "What can I do?" he lamented, stretching his neck to relieve the tightness. His gaze fell on his uneaten breakfast. The toast was old and dry, the coffee cold, and the butter had melted amorphously out of its perfectly square shape. *I can't just cave and let everything crumble. I've worked too hard. There has to be a way out.*

Ruefully aware of the grave consequences of his predicament, yet powerless to rectify them, and with nothing left to lose, he switched gears and devised a new exit strategy—to leave the country.

He hated the prospect of leaving his beloved New York, his friends, his extraordinary life of cultural extravaganzas, his self-indulgent quests for more exalted levels of beauty and art, and all the sex with beautiful women a man could ever want.

"But what choice do I have?" he asked himself. He trembled, horrified at the thought of the alternatives. Making a fist with his right hand, he punched his left cupped hand repeatedly. The impact of his decision did not lessen its psychological grip. *No, prison is not an option. The inmates would crucify me: torture, rape, extinguish cigarettes on my arms, and the beatings—no, I don't think that would suit me very well.*

Tearing up and wrenching with sadness at his bleak future, his heart split into fragments as he ruminated over his losses. *How I will miss my early morning walks down Fifth Avenue, my barber, my manicurist at the Waldorf Astoria, and luncheons with clients at the Four Seasons. The maitre'd always gives me the best table up front near the pool, where I can see and be seen by everyone. I don't know how I can survive without Hans. I will send for him the moment I am settled. I have no other choice.*

For the third time that day, Classico said, "Hans, please check that all the curtains are drawn, the alarms are set, the doors and windows are locked, and the security guard maintains high alert."

"Yes, Sir," said Hans.

"And then please pack my bags, I will be going on a trip abroad."

Classico wiped the perspiration from his forehead and neck and took the stairs to the parlor floor. He entered the library, pushed the heavy curtain aside, and reached under and behind the lowest bookshelf for the button to release a hidden wall. The massive walnut deterrent slowly creaked its rusty dialogue and slid open to reveal a Mosler cast-iron safe from 1920. His unsteady hands shook from nervousness, rattling his patience, and making it difficult to dial the combination correctly. The turns had to stop in precise alignment. One increment too far, a sixteenth of an inch past the number, and he would have to begin again.

After several failed attempts the bolt moved, unlocking his past and accessing some hope for his future. The dark interior sequestered years of secrets, lost dreams, and escape money. The real numbers for the art sales were hermetically sealed in this clandestine womb of heavy iron. He had recorded all of Classico Gallery's transactions with scrupulous accuracy in this set of ledgers. He affectionately used the moniker "Wishful Thinking" for the second set of books—the set he kept in his office for Sinbad. Luckily, he took his mother's advice and saved for a rainy day, and just possibly, he had enough cash to start over, albeit, modestly. He pulled the rubber bands off the envelopes, greedily ripping them open with the fervency of a bank-robber. He counted the one hundred dollar bills. Each envelope contained exactly $9,999.00 dollars:

the amount of a withdrawal that would fly under the IRS radar. Tightly clutching the green tickets for his escape, he felt a surge of energy, as the certitude of impending incarceration began to fade.

With each bill he counted, his posture straightened, until he stood tall again. Reaching further into the recesses of the unlit pigeonholed-shelves, he desperately groped for more envelopes. He strained toward the far corner of the safe, hoping to excavate one more envelope, but the back wall was out of range. Fumbling around the bookshelves, he found a flashlight and climbed onto a step-stool. By maneuvering his shoulder partially into the opening, he was finally able to reach the back. He felt a crumpled protrusion and pulled gently. One remaining envelope emerged from the bowels of the cavernous safe, where it had been stuck between the shelf and the back-wall. The corner tore slightly when Classico released it from entrapment. Yellowed and stained from oxidation, the aged parchment was redolent with historic significance. It crinkled from dryness and from the brittle creases that crosshatched the partially translucent document. He held the precious paper up to the light and then slowly removed the letter from the envelope. Taking a deep breath, he released a buried sigh, hydroplaning the tension and worry to a distant shore. He held on to the moment, wanting the jolt from the heavens to last—to be embedded in a place so deep inside him that it would never escape.

He could not believe his luck—or maybe he could. Classico never believed in his failures. On the contrary, he always nurtured his accretive successes; they felt so justified, so right, like hitting the sweet spot in tennis.

Although the cursive inked words had faded into a pale opalescence, Classico still sensed the vitality of Picasso's signature. He imagined Picasso's sorrow upon signing away ownership of the painting of the woman he loved. After examining the French stamp dated 1932, he turned the envelope over, revealing a broken wax-embossed seal. Herein lay the missing document of provenance for the painting that Picasso sold to his dealer in Paris, France. The bill of sale, written in Picasso's hand, read:

"Artist, painter, Picasso has sold one
123.6cm x 152.6cm painting to Rosenfeld Gallery for
the sum of 179,000 francs."

Picasso had drawn a small sketch of the painting in the bottom right-hand corner. The second document read:

"Picasso, artist, painter has received the sum of
179,000 francs for oil painting, 123.6cm x 152.6."

Classico had searched for the receipts for months. Because it had been caught in the dark crevice, he had given it up for lost. Fortunately, he had persuaded Goodrich's to overlook this one missing detail needed to complete the package of historical documentation. He did, however, present Bookman with the last owner's bill of sale from mid-century, which satisfied her requirements. *It was difficult to always provide every piece of paper for every transaction,* he rationalized.

Like a crank turning two rusty wheels with spiked outer-edges, engaging in symbiotic rotation, the noisy clatter of Classico's brain greased into overdrive, and he again took the wrong dirt road. *I do not have to give this document to Goodrich's. At this time, there is nothing stopping me from keeping it. They believe it is lost. With this document, I can sell … .* Suddenly, he heard Hans coming up the stairs. His steps sounded urgent.

"One minute, Hans." Hastily, he stuffed the cash back into the safe, turned the bolt and listened with visceral satisfaction to the sonorous click. He placed the precious documents carefully inside a thick, ancient volume of Palladium Architecture and returned it to the bookshelf.

"Sir, there are three Russian visitors who insist on seeing you immediately. One man said that he has come for his painting, and I do not think he will take no for an answer."

"Damn it!" *Why did they have to show up now?* "Tell them, I will be down shortly." He looked at the clock, "Damn it." They had only one day remaining before the down payment was forfeited. *Why did they have to come the now? I can't withdraw the painting from Goodrich's; we are under contract. And besides, they have used their marketing magic to raise the price precipitously. Possibly Baronovich will let me return his deposit with interest—after the auction.*

"Sir, I will lay out your clothing."

Classico looked down at his attire, startled to realize he had not dressed in two days and still wore the same pajamas. He touched his face, and felt the stubble of forgetfulness and grief.

"Are you okay, Sir? Can I help you dress."

"No, Hans," he replied, trying to pull himself together. "Offer them some vodka and chat them up. I'll be down soon."

Classico stepped into the shower. The water was comforting and restorative, reviving his spirit and clearing his mind. He held his face up to the shower head, and wished to remain in that dark floating space where pain never entered. The water cascaded around him creating meandering tributaries of soapy streams and bubbles, covering his nakedness, caressing him with warm tenderness. He could almost imagine that someone cared for him. Drying vigorously with a bath sheet of Egyptian Pima cotton, he burnished away his sentimental thoughts—now was not the time. He was ready to meet the Russians—and he had plan.

Chapter 37

The Oligarch's Arrival

H e was a large, stocky man who wore his chin tucked into his neck and pulled back into the corpulent folds of his face, making him resemble an egret before lunging for its prey. Grigory Baronovich stared at the Cezanne in the front room of Classico Gallery. With lips shut tightly, the grim, straight lines of his mouth drew parallels to his thick-forested eyebrows. His small ears lay flat against his silver hair, and a dark-mole on the left side of his upper lip gave him a snide look from a distance. Faberge-blue eyes distracted one from noticing that he grunted constantly. Tough and intimidating, he reeked of billions, and the power that exuded from him filled the gallery.

In the chaos of post-communist Russia, sixty-two newly minted billionaire oligarchs emerged, and Grigory Baronovich was the "real deal." Because money bought them love, but not refinement, culture, or pedigree, they amassed excellent art collections to gain social status. All the Hermes, Chanel, or Yves Saint Laurent handbags, all the Cartier jewelry his wife and mistress bought, or his Tiffany diamond cufflinks and matching ring, or his double-breasted blazer with double rows of twenty-four carat gold buttons embossed with a recently created family crest—together they all did not compare with the prestige of owning a Picasso.

"How do you do, Mr. Baronovich?" Classico inquired, descending the grand staircase with an elegant, graceful flourish meant to impress the visitor. "You are admiring Cezanne's most notable work of his middle period. Only a true master could capture that fleeting moment of reflection portrayed in the young man's face, as if had just received important news and was running to tell his friends. The colors and the brushstrokes are exquisite. Don't you agree?"

"Yes, I do. It is quite beautiful," he replied in a rolling pebbled accent.

Classico stopped on the last step of the staircase, stunned for an instant; his art conversation halted. Two Russian bodyguards, brutish, thickset and hardened, flanked the front door, wearing their frightful intentions like a prison guard at a Stalin Gulag. Positioned on either side of the replacement contractor from Blackwater, the three men jockeyed for their turf. Their burly hands, like shields, hung low and crossed in front. They permeated the atmosphere with the solemnity of life-and-death urgency, ready to be activated in a split second. Their well-cut, off-the-rack black suits did not conceal the intractable grim nature of their mission. Standing motionless in a state of heightened awareness, they awaited a cryptically nuanced instruction from their oligarch; a lifted eyebrow could potentially trigger their kill-function.

Classico ordered himself to continue, "Please, Mr. Baronovich, join me in the sitting room. The boys can remain in the vestibule with my doorman. I didn't think I was going to hear from you again. I have tried repeatedly to contact you," Classico said.

"Is that why my Picasso is on the cover of Goodrich's catalogue?"

"Oh, I can explain that, Sir," Classico said.

His eyes burrowed ruthlessly into Classico, cutting him off and exposing his vulnerability.

"I am not going to buy my Picasso at auction and pay a premium. We had a deal and you'd better get it back, or you won't ever see another painting again." Baronovich was astounded by Classico's response. No one in his country would ever answer him back. Was this runt of a man about to give him an explanation?

"You are a small portion of caviar that deserves to be crushed like the eggs," he said. Still locking gaze with Classico, he filled the moment with a palpable tension. Classico, bullied into silence, held his ground.

"I don't do explanations," Grigory Baronovich said, his garbled baritone voice navigated to freedom from the deep folds of his chin.

Classico loosened his collar, pausing for a moment to focus his thoughts. "But, Sir, surely you are a man who can appreciate a well-orchestrated arrangement, and I have a great one for you."

"You'd better get me back the Picasso."

"I can offer you more favorable terms than our previous agreement."

"Now you are beginning to understand."

"Well, Mr. Baronovich, this ... uh ... arrangement, has to be done in the strictest confidence. I assure you that you will be very satisfied. Can we agree to keep it between ourselves?"

"This better be good."

"May I offer you another vodka?"

"Yes, a double, no ice this time."

Classico poured him the drink and formulated a new plan. Downing it in one gulp, Grigory Baronovich's head jerked like an old car ignition backfiring.

"Please, Mr. Baronovich, come with me." Classico led him to his back office where the second copy hung.

"What the hell is this? Listen, you sac of merde, I am about to stuff you in a burlap bag and throw you into the East River. Or do you prefer the boys to turn you into gray borscht soup? Instead of beets, we use blood. We make the same color."

"Wait a minute, calm down. You are looking at the real Picasso, and I have the papers to prove it. Furthermore, due to our confidentiality agreement, you are going to save ten-million dollars on the purchase. You can take the painting to Russia and it will be safe."

"There is, however, one small problem, as you can imagine, since it is on the cover of the Goodrich's catalogue. Discretion is foremost, a quality I am sure you have cultivated to perfection. The Goodrich's Picasso will most likely end up in the Middle East, maybe Saudi Arabia or Dubai. The Burj Khalifa in Dubai, as you know, is the tallest building in the world. Surely, some eager Bedouins have extra wall space that needs to be covered, or perhaps it will find its way to a remote Sultan's palace, or acquired by a money-laundering operation. Once it has left this country, it will not surface again for generations," Classico said.

Classico counted on Baronovich's comfort zone with forgeries. It was well known in art circles that forgeries comprised 40 percent of Russian art collections and the Russians looked the other way.

Classico waited for the oligarch's reaction. Baronovich's pupils dilated as he glared at the painting. Was the vodka taking effect or was he responding to Picasso? Classico held the silence, not daring to speak first. *Is he going to buy the painting and my story?* Classico's thoughts returned to the original Picasso, safely hidden upstairs; his heart thumped wildly.

Extracting the morsels of his former self-confidence, he envisioned his spine as a steel rod sustaining his strength and conviction. *Those thugs outside are ready to extinguish me if Baronovich so much as raises his pinky. I hope they do it painlessly. If I cannot keep Picasso—well then—nothing else matters.*

Baronovich turned around, his eyes bore into Classico's, drilling for the truth with unmentioned threats. "You expect me to believe this ersatz story?" he asked.

"Mr. Baronovich, please, I have the original bill of sale written by Picasso's dealer in Paris, dated 1932. Goodrich's only has a later document de' provenance, from the mid-century sale. Give me a moment, I will bring it to you."

"Oh, hi fellows, excuse me." He squeezed through the massive bulks now flanking the door outside his office. They bellowed something in sandpaper Russian to Baronovich. The guards took a quick survey, and readied themselves for action with the slightest provocation. Baronovich nodded his command for retreat back to sentry position.

He spoke in Russian, half to himself and half to the guards. "How do I know if he is telling the truth without a Russian art specialist?" he said to the bulks not expecting an answer. He would not dare defraud me. He is aware of the consequences. It must be the real Picasso; only a fool would try to deceive me."

Baronovich sat down and unbuttoned his family crest. His shirt buttons pulled taut and gapped at his stomach, testifying on behalf of too many blinis with sour cream.

Staring at the painting, he thought of his long road to success; how it had not been easy and was often ugly. He never intended to murder those who would not step down, or who presented obstacles to his conglomerate's growth. Unfortunately, if they were too stubborn the hostile takeovers required extreme measures. Now, it was time he changed course and rebranded the company. He would follow Altria, the American tobacco conglomerate's philanthropic role model and sponsor museums and cultural events. If they could successfully change their reputation from killing to culture, he would do the same in Russia. He needed to find some grace in life, and this Picasso would be greatly appreciated by the Russian people.

Unable to unlock his gaze from the painting, he felt subsumed by this icon of art history. Picasso's passion and vision had entered the realm of timeless creation that belonged to eternity, and the oligarch's Russian soul wanted access.

Upstairs in his study, Classico removed one of the documents de' provenance from the parchment envelope and placed the bill of sale written in Picasso's hand, back into the old leather book. Baronovich would receive the bill of sale from the Parisian dealer that transferred the ownership title, stipulating the purchase price, size, and date. Classico alone knew the existence of the second letter, and he intended to keep it that way for as long as possible.

To most people, what does it matter which painting is authentic if they are identical? If two paintings look exactly alike, can someone receive more pleasure from having paid a higher price than its counterpart? What defines intrinsic value? Is it branding by the auction house? Classico ruminated trying to assuage his guilty conscience. Rummaging through his files, he found a large black velvet folder with a grosgrain ribbon closure. "Ah perfect," he said, placing the letters carefully between the covers. He heard Hans' footsteps approaching, "Yes, Hans, I am coming. Wish me luck."

"I see you are enjoying the painting," Classico said, *and the vodka,* he thought. "It is quite an extraordinary work. Many believe it is the cornerstone of his career, the height of his love interests. Oh, how I will miss it," he said raising one hand to his heart. "Having it in my possession has given me unspeakable joy. Well, never-mind, I have been fortunate to have it for this past year. Now it is your turn to have the honor of guardianship of this great treasure of the twentieth century. As the years pass and the decades continue, the painting will gain significance. Someday, people will come to understand that great art belongs to all mankind, unhampered by geographic ownership. America had its turn, so has France, now it will have a new home and be honored and revered Russian style."

"I will tell you a little secret," said Classico, placing his forefinger in front of his mouth. "It is good for the painting to be appreciated by a new audience." He waved his arm in half circle for emphasis. "The power of a masterpiece is the sum total of all those who have ever marveled at it and received and returned its energy. Like a giant scissors cutting a postage-stamp sized moment from the sky and pasting it on the wall of eternity, Picasso's existence is glued onto the collective memory of our planet. A true masterpiece disengages itself from disappearing unnoticed into fleeting time by alternately becoming a repository for human emotion. With each viewer's reaction, a painting acquires more power and significance."

Classico turned slightly to see the expression on his client's face. *Is he convinced that he cannot live without it?*

"And look at the fluidity of line, he is making love to the canvas and his lover simultaneously, a veritable ménage a' trois. Fueled by a pervasive, universal inspiration, the organic symmetry is found only in visual expressions from the divine."

"Cut the crap, let's see the documents."

Slowly, with solemnity suitable for the drum roll of a royal ceremony, Classico placed the folder on his desk. Then, gesturing like a conductor wielding his baton, he untied the grosgrain ribbon and held the document up to the light. The translucent parchment glowed in the sunlight pooling in its creases and wrinkles. The envelope transformed into a reliquary containing the sacrosanct history of Picasso.

Baronovich examined it closely. The left side of his mouth lifted slightly, which Classico thought might be a smile. Otherwise, his expression remained inscrutable.

Clutching the velvet casing, Baronovich became aware of a mystical essence imbued in the brittle letter; it resonated with authenticity. He felt the texture of Picasso's DNA permeate his pores, and he knew from the depth of his Russian viscera that it was authentic; the same way Tolstoy knew the soul of Anna Karenina and Ivan Ilyich, or Chekhov knew the soul of Uncle Vanya. Baronovich's deeply brooding Russian sensitivity had found truth and validation for his yearning soul.

"Art always has been a great source of comfort to the Russian people after the many wars we endured, and the millions of sons we lost though bloodshed and starvation. We never returned any of the German art the Nazi's stored in our country during World War II. No, we kept it in partial payment for the devastation inflicted on our families. It is little compensation, but we carry on and the art gives us some solace," Baronovich said.

Classico was astonished at the change in Baronovich. His acrimonious tone and facial expression softened. His steely posture relaxed. *He is a human being underneath that surly attitude. Picasso never stops surprising me with the effect his work has on people.*

"I understand how you must feel, Mr. Baronovich. This painting will bring your country much gratification."

"You have a deal, Classico. I'll pay you half now and the remainder on delivery. My jet will be leaving from Westchester airport tomorrow at nine p.m. . "Have it there no later than six."

"Yes Sir, with pleasure," Classico said, offering him a firm handshake to seal the transaction. Although Picasso was a done deal, Classico was not yet finished.

Chapter 38

Flesh Tones

`

Two days had passed since Alouisha's smile had surfaced. Yesterday, she and Jason went for a five-mile jog around Central Park. During the run, they sweated away the horror that congealed onto their every thought, and supplanted it with the soothing cloud of a pheromone high. Together, they took the cure.

Sitting at the breakfast table, she in an oversized white terrycloth robe, and he in a T-shirt and plaid boxers, Alouisha poured milk into a bowl of mini Wheat Chex and spread boysenberry jam on her English muffin. The kitchen had that morning toasty smell. Music by the Black Eyed Peas spilled onto their day, and the light glinted on the rim of her glass, as the dust mites frenzied in front of the windows.

"You were right," she told Jason. "I feel so much better after our run in the fresh air and seeing the spring colors. The cherry blossoms are incredibly beautiful, and I love the waterfall we found hidden near 110th Street; what a surprise, I didn't know it was there. I am just so lucky to be alive. Those horrible men, they didn't really hurt me, just roughed me up and scared me to death. They were so disgusting and filthy. Has Mr. Classico called?"

"No, I haven't heard from him. Don't even think about going back to work at the gallery. It's too dangerous. The Triads could attack again at any time. I am sure they have plenty more back ups," Jason said.

"I have to get my paintings back, even if they are blood splattered. Can we go back to the apartment today?"

"I'll call the station and see about getting access. They can't keep your studio barricaded with orange tape forever. I'll have Classico pay for the wrapping, movers, and insurance and have them sent here. That's the least he can do. You can have the North wall for your work, and I'll take the south wall. A 5,000 square foot space is large enough for us to open our own gallery right here. What do you think?"

"I think you are my angel." Rising from the table, she gave Jason a hug, and he pulled her down onto his lap. His hand entered the folds of her robe searching for his happiness. Feeling the electromagnetic waves begging for attention, she sighed deeply and absorbed the voltaic essence of the man she loved. The robe fell from her bare shoulders, and when Jason buried his head between her pink voluptuousness, her body quivered, anticipating his continued exploration of the littoral geography of her southernmost regions. He drank from the snow-capped mountains, but his thirst was not quenched. Compelled by forces beyond personal topography, he continued his journey, slowly following the soft, yielding terrain, melting and warming from the spring rains to the final drenched destination.

Suddenly, the breakfast crashed to the floor, and she whimpered again like a hungry puppy, and pulled him up from a squatting to a sardine position. Mightily engaged in linear formation, the hardness of the table paled by comparison. His large, sensitive hands held her firmly by the small of her back, pressing her ever more closely to him. He could almost encircle her entire waist when she took a deep breath.

"Baby, I love you so much. You are my perfect mixture of burnt sienna, alizarin crimson, and titanium white. I want to do a finger painting on your body using those colors. I want to feel the sculptural forms of your naked artistry."

"But Jason, this time can you use water based paint so it won't be so difficult to remove? Remember how long it took to scrub off last time?"

"And remember how fabulous it looked?" he said. "I have an idea, let's first coat our bodies with lanolin-based cream and then use acrylic mixed with gel medium. The colors will glide and slither before they set, allowing time for translucent layers to coalesce, while they resonate from our tactile feelings."

"You love that slippery, gliding, gooey, stuff," she said.

"Listen Ali, I've got it. First, we squeeze the tubes of paint in lines on each other's bodies. Then we lie on a large canvas, lets say, ten-feet by fourteen-feet and by having sex the colors will naturally blend into a true-love painting. We can create an entire series called, Flesh Tones, a documentation of the fingerprints and footprints of love," he said. His hands traced her sculptural forms, which were as elegantly proportioned as Jean Arp's *Torse Des Pyrenees* and a lot warmer than marble.

"Jason," she feebly admonished, grabbing his maneuvering hands. "The art world will go crazy for the paintings because they'll need the back-story to figure out the process. When the painting's significance is eventually understood, when they do 'get it,' they will be willing to pay the price to solve the mystery. We will have a new art form, an updated version of *Action Painting* for the twenty-first century. We will use a "neo," to name it, a … a let's see … "

"I know, we'll call it, *Neo-Action*," he said.

"That's very cool. I love it. We can be an art team like Christo and Jeanne-Claude or the Starn Twins. That's my brilliant boyfriend, always thinking of great new ideas. Come on, let's have a shower and get dressed," she said.

Jason's new high-tech shower equipment had five shower-heads with varying pressures and angles. Embedded in green glass-tiled walls and strategically positioned, they would strike their targets perfectly. The fifth and the largest, the head affixed to the ceiling was the Amazon forest's monsoon equivalent. Large infrared numerals easily selected a desired temperature, and the brushed stainless-steel fittings, levers, and buttons, kept the water pressure constant and sprayed them from all angles.

They took turns slathering each other with the foaming, frothy soap, until they slithered like tropical chameleons. The hot rain massaged and pummeled them into submissive ecstasy.

Jason grabbed the towel off the warmer and wrapped Alouisha in its white coziness. He put another heated towel around his waist. She watched as the droplets of water on his chest attached to his hair follicles and glistened in the morning light. Her sea colored eyes gleamed incandescently with turquoise happiness. *God, he is so gorgeous*, she thought, smiling and looking into his eyes with utter love as he rubbed her dry.

"Whoops. There you go again," she said laughing. "Hey, wait a minute. I want to go to the gallery today and collect my things before the bank takes possession. They are about to begin foreclosure proceedings."

"No Ali, it is out of the question; you cannot go back. It is too dangerous. You never know when those monsters might show up again, and this time they might get lucky and not miss. After suffering two terrible incidents, don't try for a third."

"But my journal is still there, over a year's worth of notes, research, and contacts. Please come with me this afternoon. The Blackwater contractor will be standing guard. We'll be safe, I promise," she said, looking deeply into his eyes not blinking, accessing that innermost place where the truth of their love held firm.

"It is impossible for me to say no to you. Okay, let's get dressed and get this over."

Throwing her arms around him, she hugged him tightly and urgently. "Thank you, Sweetheart, you're the best, and we'll paint later."

Chapter 39

The Caryatids

*J*ason and Alouisha raced down the stairs to the subway, when they heard the beastly grumble approaching the station. They squeezed through the closing doors just in time to safely gather the loose ends of their clothing inside, away from the vicious jaws of the steel-crushing doors. A little out of breath and laughing at their victory, Alouisha nudged Jason with her elbow. With a slight head-jerk, her eyes directed him toward an advertisement for a plastic surgeon, who specialized in male breast reductions, complete with illustrated descriptions of this embarrassing malady.

"I have never heard of such a thing. Do men really care about this?" she asked.

"Not unless he needs a bra," Jason said. They both laughed.

They exited the train at 77th Street near Lenox Hill Hospital, where the underground station was black washed in grime.

"It is incomprehensible that the MTA could be one billion dollars in debt and never allocate one cent for cleaning the station's floors or walls. The grime grows thicker each year, just like their budget deficit." Jason stopped before impugning the subway restrooms, although he thought about it. No one dared enter them, except crack heads or prostitutes or more often, men used them to find other men.

"Look Jason," Alouisha said as she passed the Tasti D-Lite, "They have my favorite flavors today, acacia berry pomegranate and cake batter." Jason took her hand, and pulled her in the opposite direction, navigating through the crowds.

"Come on, Ali, this is not a time for ice cream," he said pulling her along while being bumped and pushed by the crowd.

The streets intersecting at the subway station amplified the stewed cacophony roiling from the crowd that hurried in every direction. "Watch it," he said as the taxis viciously zigzagged like stray arrows shooting through the streets. Competing for the next fare became a near death experience.

"What did you say?" she shouted over the ambulance sirens that punctured any semblance of tranquility and underscored one's temporary residency in life. Ubiquitous hip-hop music played bass to the trebled ear-shattering discord.

They walked toward the gallery without speaking, heading west across Park and Madison Avenues, then north to 78th Street. The cement islands in the middle of Park Avenue had furiously blooming tulips and cherry trees, which shed pink cascades of petals into the blue sky. Because there were no buses or music on Park Avenue, they now could hear each other talk.

"I will never get use to the extreme change of neighborhoods from walking just one block around a corner. I never know what to expect from this city," Alouisha said. She thought of her walks in Jamaica alongside the ocean that delineated her space from the rest of the world.

"What you always can expect is a surprise; it's New York magic," Jason said and smiled.

She wondered if she would ever become entirely comfortable living in New York. Could she assimilate to the random city patterns that were so far removed from the natural rhythms of nature and her childhood. She missed tasting the sea with every breath, and the constant comfort of breaking waves that permeated every aspect of life, pummeling all into submission to the mighty sea. She had taken it all for granted, until she left Jamaica and realized her emptiness that was raw and needy— then she met Jason. She watched the wind blow through his hair, and double-stepped to catch up, contented to walk in rhythm with his unfurling energy. The corners of her mouth traveled upward, and her smile expanded like a cosmic field.

Three blocks farther, they arrived at the gallery. No guard appeared giving them pause.

"Is something wrong? What should we do?" she asked stepping backward and clutching Jason's hand tightly. "Call the police?"

"Let's ring the bell and see who answers," Jason said. They walked up the steps hesitantly, hoping they made the right decision.

"Who is it?" answered an unfamiliar voice with a southern accent.

"Alouisha and Jason, I am Mr. Classico's receptionist, and I have come to collect my things."

"Just a minute," he said.

They stood and watched as the wrought-iron gate opened slowly, majestically, drawn by invisible hands.

"The gate needs a Beethoven symphony to realize its full cinematic potential," Jason said to ease the tension. The new Blackwater contractor opened the door and sized them up, assessing their potential for violence. He allowed them entry into the marble vestibule.

"I am Alouisha," she said. He nodded and said nothing.

"Hi man, how are you doing?" Jason asked trying to create a level playing field.

"Good. Mr. Classico is in a meeting. Hans will take your coats."

"Oh, that's okay. We are not staying long. I just came to clean out my desk," Alouisha said."

"Go ahead Ali, I will wait right here," Jason said.

When she noticed the two men who flanked the doorway of Mr. Classico's office, a chill cut through her body stopping her deadbolt. Looking like two stone caryatids holding up the Acropolis in Athens; they did not move or breath. She turned to read Jason's expression to be sure his eyes matched his words, they did.

"Take your time sweetheart." He was grateful to have a few minutes alone with Blackwater to see what he could find out.

She conjured up some attitude, threw her shoulders back, held her head high, and walked past the Russian guards down the corridor to her desk. "Good afternoon," she said.

"I see why you were not outside," Jason said to Blackwater, acknowledging the two bodyguards who had kill written all over them. Their unspoken threats were clear. You have visitors from ... where?"

"I think they said something about Russia," he said.

"Oh, I see. What do you think they are doing here?"

"Probably buying a picture," he said.

"It must be hard to choose; there are so many beautiful works in this gallery. Do you have a favorite?" Jason asked.

"No, not really. I don't know much about art," he said.

"I wonder which one they like the best?" Jason said.

"I think I heard them mention Picasso."

"Well, that's too bad, because the Picasso is on the cover of the Goodrich's catalogue and it has gone to auction." Blackwater moved both his feet hip width apart and crossed his arms over his chest.

"Hmm," he replied, nodding his head with a brief upward motion, signaling the end of the conversation.

"I'm going to look at the paintings in the other room," he said to Blackwater. When he walked past the Russian sentinels, they stared right through him. Although their eyes were devoid of emotion, they seared with intensity and probed far too deeply into his comfort zone.

Their invasive gaze that attempted to dismantle his confidence infected the room with insidious power—a rotten, menacing, foreboding, power that scourged all beauty in life and art. He wanted to get out of there ... now.

He continued down the hallway to the galleries, stopping at his favorite American masters nineteenth-century *Luminist* school of art. "Ah, behold the magnificence," he said, allowing himself to become mesmerized by the shimmering light brilliantly captured in the American landscape.

In a few minutes, he heard Alouisha's footsteps on the marble flooring, which brought him back to earth. She gently slipped her hand into his. Sharing these art-filled moments of reverie with Jason was like making love without sex. Awed by the exquisite beauty of the landscapes and aware of the extraordinary talent required to render them in perfect photo-realism, they let the feelings percolate through their bodies.

"They are so amazing, really a miracle if you think about it. I can still feel the same joy the artist experienced so many years ago, as if there were no time separating us from his act of creation," she said.

"Beauty transcends time, the centuries and all of mankind's iniquities. It is so disappointing that art today has little resemblance to nineteenth-century artistic values. Now, a successful contemporary artist's main concern is marketing and branding his work at auction. Sometimes it can be so discouraging because talent and craft count for very little," Jason said.

"All I want to do is paint, I don't want to be branded like cattle going to the slaughter house," she said.

"We can talk about this later, let's get out of here. Did you get all your things?"

"Yes, I just want to say good-bye to Mr. Classico."

"Maybe the suits will let you enter. There must be something big going on inside," Jason said.

He glanced sideways at Blackwater and then at the Russians. They all stood statue-still, vigilantly securing their positions, and no one relinquished an inch of control. Are these guys for real? Jason whispered. Hubris infused the air.

"Excuse me," she said to the guards, knocking on the door. "It's Alouisha, Mr. Classico," raising her voice to be sure he heard her through the thick door.

Classico's eyebrows almost reached his hairline. "Damn it," he muttered. *What is she doing here now? The Picasso is in plain sight,* he thought.

"Alouisha, I am busy now," he said. "Damn it, Damn it." "Don't open the door," he shouted to Baronovich who stood near it while finalizing his delivery arrangements and admiring his new purchase.

"What did you say?" he replied, aghast at Classico's direct order. Are you telling me what to do? Do you really want me to shred you like the cabbage in my soup?" He grunted, then his chin jolted upward, and he opened the door. "Well, hello," he said in his most charming voice. "What fortunate circumstance brings this beautiful young woman to my acquaintance?"

"I am here to see Mr. Classico. I hope I am not disturbing you. I just came to say goodbye," she said.

"Not at all. We are just finishing up a small transaction. Please come in. It would be my pleasure," said the oligarch.

"Thank you, Sir."

Classico faced the wall, his head leaned into the bend of his raised elbow.

"Good afternoon Mr. Cla"... she stopped in mid sentence when she saw the painting. "Another Picasso? It's not possible," she shouted. She looked at Classico, and then to the Russian, searching their faces for an explanation. Classico averted her eyes, his gaze drifted sideways, then to the floor.

Ten thousand acupuncture needles pierced the surface of his skin at once, and did not stop, until he felt like dry ice—numbed and smoking. His cover was blown, irreversibly; there were no excuses left. Fully exposed by unfortunate timing, this was a nightmare gone viral. It was unstoppable. *What can I tell her?* He loosened his collar and dug his fingers into his wrinkled forehead foraging for a remote solution.

The Russian said nothing, but his smirk told it all. He was enjoying the unfolding drama.

Unable to move, cemented with horror to the marble floor, Alouisha's mind raced through a thousand possibilities to the irrefutable finish line of startling implications. *He is a fraud dealing in forgeries. He lied to me all this time. I thought he was a hero; I believed in him.* Then, as if doused with a bucket of iced reality, a more horrible truth dumped its bitter wrath upon her. "Oh my God!" she cried out. Gasping sharply, her hand slapped her open mouth and remained glued to it. She could not inhale another breath of his hideous scheme. In a suspended state of time and place, she did not move. No sounds, no breath, nothing reached inside. Her eyes were round as snowballs, frozen in disbelief. She could not disengage them from the Picasso. Finally, after what seemed like forever with the room rippling and waving in silent slow motion—all movement and blur halted. The edges of the Picasso were sharply focused now. She heard the ice cubes clank in the Russian's glass in response to his snort-grunt emissions. She noticed the thinning spot on the back of Classico's head as he continued to face the wall. The pit of her stomach wrenched—assaulted by the truth, it sickened her and blighted the innocence of her past.

"That's why the Chinese tried to kill me. It was your fault entirely. And poor Jack, still unable to walk. You are responsible for all of this," she shouted at Classico.

He grabbed her arm pleading, "Alouisha, Alouisha, please I can explain. You must calm down. This is not as it appears," he said making a final attempt to change her mind and the staggering consequences. Alouisha could bring criminal charges against him, second degree attempted manslaughter.

I cannot let her ruin this deal. I wish she would shut up. I must find a way to stop her.

She wrestled her arm loose and pulled away from him. "Jason,

Jason." They both ran out the door onto the street and kept running.

Classico turned his composure dial to cool and turned to Baronovich.

"Oh well, she does have a tendency to get dramatic at times. But, there is no need to worry, she's just a kid; she will get over it. The Chinese roughed her up a bit, but she is okay, and Jack, the former guard, well, that's his job."

"We all have our problems," Baronovich said unfazed. He placed the document de' provenance under his arm and tried not to gloat. He was more than pleased with this arrangement that saved him ten million dollars on the purchase price, and as an extra bonus, a branded copy was being offered at auction and highlighted on the cover of the catalogue. The global prominence garnered from the sale offered more status than he ever had thought possible.

"I am glad you understand," Classico said.

"The only stipulation is to keep the purchase quiet until after the sale," Classico reminded him. "Details of the buyer are never revealed to the press, only the price is public knowledge. Therefore, when the Picasso re-emerges in Russia, it will be uncontested, and its assimilation will be seamless. The copy will probably find its way to the Middle East where it will be among similar compatriots. According to recent statistics, copies comprised thirty-eight percent of the contemporary art residing in Asia and the Middle East," said Classico. He did not mention Russia in the forgery equation; however, every international art dealer was aware of the magnitude of fraudulent art in Russia's holdings. It surpassed all other countries.

"Very well," Baronovich said, shaking Classico's hand.

"It has been a pleasure doing business with you, Sir. The most coveted modern painting on this planet will have its home in Russia," Classico said. "Congratulations."

Chapter 40

Weighing the Alternatives

very few blocks, Jason and Alouisha turned to see if anyone was following them—the Russians, Blackwater, perhaps the Chinese, or the NYPD questioning their involvement. They ran for their lives, away from the insidious betrayal that threatened to engulf their innocence by collusion. The lies and deceit struck at the very core of their primal beliefs—of all they considered good and true.

Alouisha had idolized her employer, believing he championed the art world, unselfishly, tirelessly, raising the standards of high culture to new levels of artistic expression and connoisseurship. She wished she had not opened the door. She did not want to bear witness to Classico's heinous crime, one that tore the truth from virtue and cast an evil net that ensnared anything of beauty that fell into its trap.

"Maybe all his paintings are copies," Alouisha said as they ran through Central Park.

"He's got quite a racquet going," Jason said.

Alouisha's world became muted as though a can of indelible paint had been poured over her, gray-washing the bright colors of her joy with deceit and betrayal. Unwittingly, she had participated in his scheme by trusting his every apocryphal word.

They ran and ran to Central Park West, then headed downtown through the theater district, past the Port Authority and Lincoln Tunnel where the air thickened with car exhaust, and onto the colorful streets of the Chelsea art galleries to the West Gay Village, and finally gasping for breath, they arrived home. Jason unlocked the door just as the phone rang.

"Don't answer it," he said.

"You have reached the Jason Biggs studio, I am in a color session. Please leave a message." E-sharp-extended ddddd ... bleep.

"Alouisha, this is Mr. Classico, please Alouisha, I want to talk to you. I want to explain what happened, and I promise I can make it up to you. I never wanted to put you in harm's way. Things got out of control. How could I ever have known there was a Chinese Mafia stealing Picassos? Please pick up the phone, we can make this right," click...F-sharp-dddd ... bleep.

They dropped their things on the floor and collapsed on the sofa in a heaping mass of exhaustion. Their minds spun, trying to make sense of what happened. The brutal truth slammed them with a staggering blow. The police had searched for answers in the wrong direction.

"When is this nightmare going to be over?" Alouisha said pulling her knees up to her face. The horror she endured returned in full force as she grasped the extent of Classico's deception. She was a pawn in his fraudulent dealings—no more than a front-desk face, an enabler. He never intended to give her a show; he just led her to believe that once he settled his affairs, he would jump-start her career. All his specious intentions about morality, quests for beauty and culture were simply profiteering expeditions in conceit and ultimately diversions. How often had she heard his favorite panegyric—"The evolution of the human race through art?" All his credibility vanished the instant she saw the second Picasso.

"We have to go to the police," she said.

"Wait a minute, let's think this through," Jason said.

"What is there to think about? The forged Picasso is at Goodrich's about to go to auction."

"If that's true, what did he sell to the Russian, the copy or the original? And how do we know there are not more? Jason said.

"Wait a minute. You could be right. When he returned from China, he asked me to order three antique frames, all the same size. He told me to take the measurements from the Picasso on file. I didn't think about it at the time; I had too many other things going on," she said. "What should we do? We can't let him get away with this."

"No, Ali, not after what he has put you through. That bastard, I'm going to kill that pompous asshole." He got up from the sofa and threw the books on the side table at the door.

"Wait a minute, Jason, take it easy. Let's go to the police and let them deal with this," she said.

"Do you really want to spend the next week uptown at police headquarters being interrogated by the detectives and the art fraud department. We would be involved in a horrible litigation. Think of it; we would be key witnesses in a high-profile trial, and we would never have any privacy again," he said. "And the trial could last for years."

"But aren't we somehow liable for withholding evidence, when we know there is an ongoing criminal investigation? And besides, we can't allow him to walk away free, he'll continue ripping people off. People like him are destroying the fabric and ethics of the art world. We can't simply become silent witnesses and do nothing," she said.

"Perhaps we can talk to Goodrich's instead of the police. Surely, they've been confronted with similar circumstances on occasion and will know how to deal with it properly. They have the most at risk," Jason said.

"I could do the decent thing and speak to Classico first. I do not want to be responsible for sending someone to prison," she said.

"That would be tough to live with Ali," he said. "But he deserves prison; he hurt you, and deliberately put you in harm's way. It would serve him right," Jason said feeling his anger returning.

Alouisha put her arms around him to calm him down. Then, in a final attempt to retain a modicum of hope and optimism, Alouisha said: "It is possible that he has an explanation. There could be extenuating circumstances," she said, not yet ready to relinquish all her childhood optimism and believe the world is truly cruel. She could not understand the scope of greed or criminal intent, not having had any personal experience with it. It simply did not exist in her emotional makeup. She sat quietly, hugging her knees to her chest, weighing the various courses of action."I'm not going back there again," she said.

"I'll go," he said. "We have to find out the truth." He sat next to her on the sofa, placed one arm around her shoulder drawing her closely. Her head relaxed on his collarbone and settled upon her familiar spot. With his free hand, he traced the outline of her lips, willing them to smile, and they did. "But first, do you feel like painting—*Flesh Tones?*"

Chapter 41

Inside the Giant Jewel Box

C lassico was in green money heaven. "Yes, Yes," he cheered strutting around the room, his arms stretched overhead, punching an invisible portal into the circle of winners. "I've done it. He's bought it."

"Sir?" Hans said, overhearing his employer's jocular outburst.

"The Russians certainly live up to their reputation in art circles for having eccentric business practices," Classico said.

Baronovich showed no concern for the questionable number of copies in existence. *It did not faze him in the least. Is it possible the Russians care only about the collective perception of reality, and not about a painting's integrity?* Classico thought.

"Indeed, Sir. Would you still like your bags packed?" Hans inquired.

"Yes, please, although I may have to postpone my trip for a short time," he said, his eyebrows raised and lowered briefly with emphasis.

If Classico suddenly needed to flee, he would be prepared. With only one week remaining until the auction, he would juggle the details and loose ends of his financial exploits keeping everything carefully in motion and under strict supervision, at least until next week. If nothing else unforeseen occurred, he could pay off the investors with the proceeds from the Baronovich sale. His mind sprinted to the finish line, the day of the auction.

The police should have the Triads under control by now. I can pay down the mortgage tomorrow, and reimburse one of the Lichtenstein shareholders, apologizing profusely for the misunderstanding. That will be an enormous relief. The only problem remaining is Alouisha and Jason. I must persuade them not to go to the police. If only Alouisha would answer her phone, I could make her understand. I could make it up to her some way. Wait a minute, I have an idea, he thought.

"Very well, Sir," Hans said.

"Oh, yes, thank you Hans," Classico had forgotten he was in the room. "I need to get back to work now. The art transport company will be here shortly to crate the Picasso, and I must call the bank to stop the foreclosure proceedings. These temporary liquidity problems can become so annoying at times."

"I am sorry, Sir," Hans said as he left the room.

Jason saw the guard when he turned the corner on 79th street. "Oh, not him again," he said under his breath. "Hey man, what's happening? Is Classico in? I need to talk to him."

Blackwater crossed his arms in front of his chest and did not respond. "Yes, I know we left in a hurry, but she was upset. Please tell Mr. Classico I am here. I am sure he will want to see me."

"Excuse me, Sir, Jason is here to see you," said Blackwater, buzzing the intercom.

"Oh great," Classico said. *They are finally coming to their senses.* He straightened his tie, the papers on his desk, and glanced briefly in the mirror before going to greet Jason in the foyer.

"I am so glad to see you Jason, please come in. Is Alouisha okay?"

"She's hanging in there."

"Please, let's go to my office," he said, leading him down the corridor. Jason followed Classico past the smiling Cezanne, past John Singer Sargent's *Boating Party* dappled with lake light, and past the oculus effusing a veiled glow that beamed onto Jason, which he was certain rearranged his molecules, enhancing his artistic vision. He passed the silken-lined curtains acoustically insisting on hushed tones. He continued down the hallway through pools of refracted light, like misty spotted dreamscapes in an impressionist painting. By the time they reached the office, the posh surroundings had Jason feeling diminished by its awesome beauty, quiet, and high boiserie-gilded ceilings. He was locked in a giant jewel box where it was too warm to be wearing a sweater. He wanted to remove it, but that would be too awkward. His neck felt damp; he began to sweat.

"Please, sit down."

"I'll stand, thank you." Jason tried to remain calm although he had jumping jacks in his stomach. He rooted himself firmly in position to inspect the Picasso that still hung on the wall and to make eye contact with Classico. Bolstering his bravado, he crossed his arms over his chest, and wondered which painting was the copy, the one in front of him or the one at Goodrich's.

He's going to give me a hard time, Classico noted indignantly, as he assessed his optimal approach for this encounter.

"Look, Mr. Classico, before we go to the police, I thought it was only fair to hear your side of the story. We do not want to be implicated in your fraudulent art schemes, nor do we want to withhold evidence in a criminal investigation," Jason said.

"Wait a minute now, please, Jason, sit down and let me explain." *This kid needs some convincing, some guidance perhaps. I need him to see my point of view. That shouldn't be too difficult.*

"What possible explanation is there for a forgery?" Jason asked, trying to maintain his position of offense. "This better be good, or I am out of here—directly to the police."

"Take it easy, Jason." Classico approached his grand desk, slowly as possible for additional time to concoct his plan. His thoughts weighed heavily in the battlefield of his mind. He sat tall as the window light spilled onto his shoulders, rimming his head in nimbus formation, and burnishing the gilded secretaire with golden specks. Jason anxiously waited for the potentially criminal, formerly esteemed art dealer to speak.

Classico cleared his throat, "Jason, we both love art, and we both want the best for Alouisha. We are a rare breed that have dedicated our lives to the pursuit of higher levels of consciousness through the creation, accumulation and investigation of art. Because it is not a mathematical formula, it involves feelings—subjective feeling—about beauty, interrelationships, and a unique understanding of how we view the world and our humanity. You, as an artist, are aware that it is extraordinarily difficult to navigate the nuances and complexities of the art markets with the many commercial aspects necessary to sustain our different needs. I have tried all my life to do the right thing," Classico sighed and paused. His eyes gazed upward, as if he remembered a distant time.

"You know Jason," he stood up for emphasis, and slowly walked the room—a pensive walk with eyes cast downward.

"I grew up in the Great Plains, in the small town of Beatrice, Nebraska. We did not have art, only hard work, blister-popping hard work. My only inspiration was survival and escaping the bullies at school. The day I discovered art on a school trip to a museum, the whole world came alive and resonated with hope and beauty. It gave me something to live for besides always hiding and being afraid. It gave me a lifetime of passion, upon which I have built all of this," he said arcing his arm in a semi-circle. He glanced sideways at Jason who seemed to be listening intently. *Is that compassion I see on his face?* Classico wondered.

"Unfortunately, I too, got caught in this bad economy and so many people depended on my liquidity." He peered at the rare Napoleonic clock on his desk that he could not resist buying when it came up for auction. It cost him over a year's worth of mortgage payments.

"Cash flow dried up—everywhere," he continued. "I am so terribly sorry that the Chinese hurt Alouisha. I never meant her to be involved. I never meant that to happen. You must believe me. Things got out of control. I originally wanted a copy of the Picasso for my own pleasure; I could not bear to part with it. Then, the bills piled up, and life's complications overwhelmed me. Putting Picasso up for auction became the only viable solution. However, since Baronovich had given me a deposit and I had not heard from him, I was trapped."

"You have to let me make it up to you. Everything can work out now. You must let this auction take place. The Russians are not particularly concerned with authenticity; they are to a point, but almost half of their modern art is forged. They seem to enjoy the copies just as much as the originals."

Jason almost began to feel sorry for Classico as he listened to his compelling storyline about his life of virtue devoted to the arts. Jason believed Classico's assertions that he never had dishonest intentions, but rather that he had fallen victim to the current economic crisis.

Classico's plan was to level the playing field and exonerate himself from this unfortunate situation. Would his critical observations about forgeries override his transgressions? He had addressed the eternal art riddle: If two identical paintings provided the same amount of pleasure to the viewer, why should it matter if one owned the copy or the original? What quantifies a painting's inherent value?

"I'll talk to Alouisha," Jason said, still not fully persuaded, but beginning to yield to Classico's line of reasoning.

"Jason, tell her that I want to make it up to her. Tell her, I want to exhibit her work—a one-woman show," he said.

"Really? Wow, that would be amazing."

"In the realms of art and love, we all need to help each other. We are the special people of the planet, chosen to cultivate higher levels of evolution. We are not investment bankers, glued to a computer all day. We are the poets, seeking inspiration and superior truth; we are doctors finding a new cure; the tennis players hitting the sweet spot and glimpsing perfection. We are like athletes winning the Olympic Gold ;or a sailor hoisting a sail fully powered by the wind, at one with the natural energies; or Tom Ford taking a bow on the runway during fashion week; a curator hanging her first show at the Whitney," Classico said.

"Okay. Got it, Classico," Jason said cutting him off. I'll be in touch." He left the room and most of his anger behind.

Chapter 42

Sentient Art Solace

Alouisha slumped on the sofa at the loft. Hugging her knees with her eyes glazed over, she appeared stuck on a distant planet. She ruminated about all she had endured: horror, betrayal, violence, and lies. She could not understand how she had misjudged Classico's character so completely and been oblivious to his illegal activities. She felt as though she had looked into a contaminated lake filled with industrial runoff, but had only noticed the beautiful play of light reflected on the toxic surface.

Each time Classico expounded on the interpretations of artistic metaphor, framed a work within its historical and cultural context, or spewed lengthy diatribes on the importance of enlarging the narrative of someone's collection, she had listened with awe and rapture to his self-serving words.

How could I have allowed myself to be so gullible and self-centered? I only thought about my painting career and Jason. When Classico returned from China without having bought a single Chinese contemporary painting, I should have known something was wrong. When he ordered three identical frames, or when the bank continued to threaten foreclosure—I should have known something was wrong. I thought only about colors and Jason. Feeling enormous regret for her oversight, she lay face down on the sofa with her head cradled in her arms. The sobs erupted from her bottomless mineshaft of sadness. *I am so lucky Jason is in my life; I could not get through this without him.*

After some time had passed, she stopped crying and went to the bathroom to wash her face and comb her hair. Her turquoise eyes blended with the redness of her tears and were violet now. With her emotions straining for release, she sought the waiting canvas.

She opened the window next to the easel. The breeze felt cool on her flushed cheeks, as it rollicked through the maple tree's budding leaves. With extreme sensitivity, the leaves seemed to tremble in response to every gusty whisper, as if they engaged in their own private dialogue— their interaction in-sourced from an intelligence in a parallel universe.

Whenever Alouisha felt particularly vulnerable or excessively sensitive, she gave her feelings full reign in her painting. She found comfort in knowing that she could access multi-verses through her creative process. At times, she thought her artistic temperament was like a television commercial for prescription drugs: offering a panacea accompanied by an unforgiving list of harmful side effects. Her hyperactive sensitivity lacked an on-off switch, and was not confined only to creative acts. On the contrary, it kept her constantly alerted to alternate states of reality, which she drew upon in her signature art form.

Her highly tuned psychic abilities often connected her to another person's innermost feelings. Sadness in others triggered her compassion center and she would feel their sorrow. Often in the middle of a conversation, people repeated the exact words she was thinking. *Am I reading their minds, or am I imposing my thoughts onto theirs?* She often wondered.

Picking up her paintbrush, she studied the glaring white canvas. It dared her to begin. It dared her to expel the sadness and remorse, to heal her emotions with intuitive pursuits and to own the whiteness.

First, she slashed the pure linen canvas with large swashes of blood—red—a female red, one that depicted the cycles of a life-giving force; not a male red, the color of war injuries and death. Then she manipulated the cerulean blue to add depth to a big sky perspective. The seeping edges of the sky soaked into the red areas, blending it into holy purple, which she expunged immediately. Then, she skimmed a glazed overlay of hopeful yellow, and immediately killed it with black, turning it into vengeful, mud-green. She wanted to lose herself in the slathered color fields, and allow the detritus of her emotions to exit her mind the same way the paint pushed out of the tube.

She noticed that each color felt unique to the touch, as if each emitted a distinct electromagnetic field—a type of sensory projection. She wondered if she imagined this visceral response, or had she discovered a new interpretation of color physics. Continuing her investigation, she placed the tubes of yellow, red, blue, and black paint into a small container and lay four sheets of heavy rag paper on the worktable. Putting on a black sleeping mask, she closed her eyes making sure no light entered her self-imposed blackout. In total darkness she shook the container to rearrange the tubes of paint and picked a color.

She squeezed the tube onto the first piece of paper, folded it and spread the paint as in a Rorschach test. She then unfolded and flattened it. Holding her palms over the saturated paper, she concentrated on feeling the color. Certain it was yellow, she could sense its warmth like a vivid canopy of radiance. She wrote down, "number one, left side, yellow." Repeating the process with each remaining color, she recorded the results of each sensory experience. The blue felt rich and embracing like the sea. The black grasped and pulled; an empty hole siphoning energy, a greedy energy that extracted something essential. The red felt vibrant and strong. She could sense its power pulsating with energy.

The four tubes of empty paint lay scattered across the table. She pulled off her blindfold to see the results."I knew it!" she cried out in delight. "I have created an entirely new modality of perceiving color through sensory experience." She had named each color correctly. The experiment was a success.

Her next step in the investigation of sensory color brought her closer to understanding quantum theory. Physics accessed multi-verses and parallel universes—the Many-Worlds theory, by using equations to codify random patterns into predictable statistics. It reduced the guess-work from probabilities. With Alouisha's hyper-sensitivity, she could feel the wave particles emanating from the colors. If she could convey this critical exploration through a multidimensional color experience, it would elevate perceptions and ultimately humanity. She paced the room immersed in thought. The answer came in a sudden flash. It required a larger, fully absorbent color experience, perhaps a full-body color exposure.

She grabbed her sketchpad and designed four black boxes that would be large enough for a person to stand inside. Each box would be fitted with rows of fluorescent tubular lighting covered in red, blue, and yellow gel cells. The fourth box, without gels, would be lit with unforgiving white fluorescent. She sketched the slip-on sleeves that provided the vivid color illumination. "Great, it's a post-modern dialogue referencing Dan Flavin's light sculptures," she said aloud, feeling excited and happy for the first time in months.

The plan was to blindfold people and lead them individually into each primary color theater. Once inside, they would be subsumed by yellow, red, blue or white, and instructed to identify the color using their intuition. Alouisha was certain that people would eventually get it right. Some would feel it faster than others. But, once they were aware of this dormant, innate sentient ability, it would develop quickly.

"Hi, Sweetheart, I'm home,"Jason said, unlocking the door. Alouisha sat on the floor, lost in thought, surrounded by pages torn from her sketchbook. He assumed she was in one of her transcendent states talking to colors. Slowly and quietly, not to break her concentration, he walked over to her and gently put his arms on her shoulders. She stood up to receive his hug, his love, and his energy. Being in so open and vulnerable a creative space, she let her love fall freely into his heart. As their electricities connected and melded with a thousand other parallel universes, they became part of the divine. Uplifted by the torque of their love, they could float off the earth together. But, now was not the time; Jason was hungry. Rather than joining her in float mode, he placed his arms around her waist, and with the deft motion of turning an imaginary crank, he reeled his flying kite back to earth. She always laughed when he did that. He understood her so well.

"What are you working on?" he asked.

"Oh, just an experiment to see if I can identify the colors by the way they feel. Do you want to try it? I interpreted them all correctly," she said.

"I'll blindfold you, and you simply concentrate on each color and name it. Of course, I will mix up their order. Want to try?" she asked again.

"I will, later, when four of my five senses are not overpowered by one.

"Is lust one of the five senses?" she asked.

"No, I guess not," he laughed, "although it should be. I know hunger is one. Is there anything to eat?"

"Later, I can't wait another moment. What did he say? Tell me," she insisted.

"Well, it is not as bad as it appears. Classico did not have malicious intentions. He is so sorry for your attack, and desperately wants to make it up to you. He talked about the difficulty of a life dedicated to pursuing art and culture, and that we, as kindred spirits having the same mission, need to support one another. Because he loved the Picasso so much and could not bring himself to part with it, he had it copied in China for his eyes only. He said he was a victim caught in the bad economy, and he became desperate to save the collection. Afterwards, when the Apogee shareholders demanded their cash, it forced him to consign the painting to Goodrich's." Jason repeated Classico's words, slowly, cautiously, not wanting to upset Alouisha.

"What?" she said, incredulously.

"Wait, this story gets better. When Baronovich showed up at the last moment, demanding his painting—that's when things things got ugly. He could have been killed at any moment by the Russians or be imprisoned by fraud."

"Jason, those are excuses for criminal behavior. What are you saying? He is a cheat and a liar and deserves to be imprisoned. How can you listen to his ideological rhetoric when his only intention was commercial profit." She implored him to understand the absurdity of his logic.

"Sweetheart, you are probably right. He was so persuasive that I started to feel sorry for him. He was pathetic, talking about his terrible childhood and how he found redemption only through art. But he wanted me to tell you something ..."

"What can he possibly say? Another excuse? I don't think so." She stood warrior-strong with her arms akimbo, waiting. Resurrecting all the moral fortitude her ancestors needed for their daily survival, she silently dared him to disagree.

"He wants to give you a one-woman exhibition."

Chapter 43

The Invitation

Classico strolled through the downstairs galleries admiring his paintings and finding comfort in the permanence of their unending beauty. He could be suffocating from the pressures of his crumbling life, but regardless of his misfortunes, the paintings offered him steadfast beauty like his mother's unconditional love. The collection never wavered from its mission to access higher levels of culture and intelligence. Reassured that his purpose was noble, their beauty assuaged any lingering guilt he may have accumulated. The very act of ingesting their timeless splendor rekindled his self-righteousness. "What I do, I do for art," he often repeated.

A fresh rain pelted the windows in baritone and plinked in soprano.

The soothing rhythm was an antidote to stress and underscored the beauty of the paintings. He closed his eyes, savoring the wet symphony. Classico pulled the curtain aside and looked out onto the street. The pedestrians struggled with the winds that turned their umbrellas inside out. The vise in his head began to un-clamp, loosening the tension with Baronovich's departure and Jason's visit. A sanguine outlook for the future had replaced imminent jail time.

With a little encouragement and a little drama, Classico felt he had convinced Jason that his altruistic intentions were for the advancement of art and culture, and not for personal gain. Now, he needed Alouisha to have compassion for a situation that had gotten out of control, which he blamed on the recession. He needed her to believe that he never meant her to be harmed. *If she can just loosen her moral corset and let me make her famous; it's not a bad exchange. I'll call her later, after she has some time to think about my offer. Threatening to go to the police ... She has to grow up sometime and to realize the world is more complex than cartoon figures on the back of cereal boxes saving the world. We each must do what we can in our own way,* he waxed philosophical.

He stepped away from the window, drew the curtain and returned to his desk with renewed confidence. Hans appeared with a letter on a silver tray. "Sir, this has just arrived by hand."

"Thank-you Hans," he said taking note of the engraved linen envelope from Goodrich's, which was certainly an invitation and not a bill. "Well, I have never received an engraved bill," he said chuckling.

"Your distinguished presence is requested ... ," he read out loud. "Ah ha. Here is the champagne and caviar reception given for the wealthiest clients and their best friends to entice them to bid on the Picasso and create a buzz. Well done Goodrich's," Classico exclaimed.

"Congratulations Sir. Will that be all?" Hans inquired.

"Yes, of course. Thank-you." Without missing a beat, Classico continued: "New York's 'A' list, the glitterati, will attend—bejeweled, coutured and oh, so lovely," Classico grinned, imagining his future reverie.

To qualify for the price of admission, one had to be an UHNW (ultra high net worth) individual or to have had fifteen minutes of fame. *Oh yes,* he reminded himself. *There is an additional criterion for admission if one is not an UHNW—young, beautiful, and/or a pedigree will always guarantee an invitation. Alouisha must come to the art gala and promote her work, as she had previously planned.*

I must pull myself together; I cannot afford to miss this one. My board members will all be at the reception taking the measure of my optimism. By acting with unflinching confidence, I will convince them the 55-million-dollar high estimate is as good as a "done deal." It will be my Academy Award night. I can do it, he assured himself straightening his bow tie in the mirror.

He closed his office for the evening and headed toward his private quarters, stopping one more time in the far gallery to admire the nineteenth century Hudson River School paintings. Just one more dose of their grandeur would relieve his constant ache for beauty. Just once more, he would sacrifice himself to the alter of luminous light, to receive a veritable art communion dipped in incandescence. Suddenly, his face turned hot and red.

"Damn," he said out loud. I still have to sell these paintings which were bought with Apogee funds." *Well, I'll deal with them later—after the Picasso auction. Surely, I can interest the new Louvre Museum in Abu Dhabi. I know, I'll suggest the similarities between the rapid Westward expansion of nineteenth-century America, and the rapid cultural and economic expansion of twenty-first century Abu Dhabi—both bearing witness to the endless possibilities of mankind.*

A wistful look slid across his face, as he thought about losing the paintings that he so loved. Never again would their proximity resonate with an historical dialogue. Together, their collective energies and light-filled virtuosity inspired boundless optimism. A cloud of sadness engulfed him. "Goodbye, Bierstadt, goodbye Moran, goodbye Inness. I will miss you my friends."

Chapter 44

Brand Baby Brand

“**J**ason look, here's the invitation to the Goodrich's gala for next week's auction," Alouisha said. " I had our names included on the guest list."

Alouisha opened the cream-colored linen envelope and removed the folded card, which felt thick and soft as a blotter. The tissue paper insert fluttered to the floor, caught in a breeze from the open window. She studied the light-play that speckled across the engraved gold letters. Jason took the invitation from her hand.

"Ali, we've got to do this."

The determined look in his eyes collapsed into misted affection when he saw her reaction. Her mouth tightened, and her bottom lip disappeared under her grimacing bite. Alouisha never wanted to see her former employer again, and certainly not support him by attending the reception. Jason sensing her apprehension, pulled her close. Their noses barely touched; they said nothing, but listened instead to each other's thoughts. Jason spoke first. "This is too important a networking opportunity for us to pass up."

Alouisha pulled back, "I can't. I feel so betrayed by him," she said shaking her head. The pit of her stomach lurched with remembrance.

"Ali, you have got to keep your feelings for the canvas, not for marketing. There are other important art dealers besides Classico. They will all be at the Picasso gala. We are lucky we received an invitation. This is the hottest art ticket on the planet, and we could not ask for a better networking opportunity. The art world is small; just ignore Classico. We will always be running into him."

"Not if he goes to jail where he belongs," she said.

"You need to toughen up Ali. There will always be Classicos in the world," he said.

He gave her a hug and held her tightly. "Baby, come on, you can do it. We'll do it together."

Arguably, they worked hard and had sacrificed more secure professions in pursuit of their artistic dreams. Their careers required a twenty-four-seven commitment that did not offer reliable monetary compensation. The Yale Master of Fine Arts program had warned them repeatedly that the odds were against them for becoming famous artists—a necessity equated to earning a living from art. Their fellow Yalies would earn large paychecks in corporate professions, while they continued struggling to make ends meet.

Belief in their work, however, kept them undeterred. A good portion of Yale's curriculum had focused on marketing and branding one's work. "I know I cannot simply stay at home painting in a vacuum,"she said.

"It's not an option," he said, "not after we have worked so hard." She finally relented when Jason persuaded her to act professionally and put her feelings aside.

The Lincoln Town Car arrived at the South side of Rockefeller Center and stopped in front of Goodrich's. The doorman helped Classico from the car as he scanned the crowd of people congregating on the wide sidewalk. His heart raced anticipating the electrical combustion detonating from the bling-dripping crowd with their millions to spend on art. As much as he hated to admit it, his nerves jittered and ratcheted up his pulse rate. All the guests displayed mantles of self-importance—afraid of becoming diminished if they relinquished one self-congratulatory thought for being among the invited or for being fabulous. By focusing all their attention on themselves, their orbit would remain intact, not diluted by thoughts of others. They sourced their own self-intoxicating gravitational pull that stoked the transient solar system of revolving society.

Whoosh … kiss, whoosh … darling, whoosh … air kiss, two sides, sparkle … sparkle, emit some light … ignite, air kiss only … please germs, germs… it's all love darling, divine, divine, truly divine. Murmuring the evening mantras, Classico managed to pass through the gauntlet of searingly beautiful twenty-something-year-old hostesses dressed in the latest, skimpy mini-dresses. Their thick hair swooped into loose curls and looked disheveled, as though they had just returned from a lust-filled encounter. The wait-staff, positioned in military formation, wore black tie and offered fluted champagne ammunition that would keep the guests authenticity well guarded.

Classico inhaled the voltaic exhilaration that infused the atmosphere in the large marbled entrance hall. The air was densely charged, as if an army of photographers had just fired their strobes in unison. This private event, however, insisted the paparazzi remain on the street outside.

Classico maneuvered through the well-heeled crowd. He was buoyed along the crest of a wave toward the prize—the holy grail of art. On the far wall of the main gallery, displayed alone in the large space, Picasso reigned and towered over its supplicants. Its heraldic presence caused a hushed moment to overcome each guest as they passed it. The precisely arranged lighting did not spill onto the wall; instead, it aligned perfectly, stopping at the edges of the canvas. It gave the Picasso an other worldly, inner glow that added to its mystique and its hammer price.

Suddenly, the magnitude of the sale and the consequences it would incur hit Classico like the strike of a military drone. Selling Picasso was no longer a white-bread problem—shuffling papers, and inventing excuses. No longer was it a future event planned for an unspecific time. Now, he could smell the millions and taste the green. A stab of fear shot through him as he came face-to-face with the gravity of his deed. There were only a few days until the auction, after which, the truth of Picasso's legitimacy would remain buried forever. Until that time, a multitude of unforeseen events could dismantle his plan. Condemnatory names appeared on an endless video loop in his thoughts: Alouisha, Jason, Huang Show, Sinbad DeMande, Baronovich, or the Police. Any one of them could cause his imminent demise.

"It does look fabulous," Mrs. Aristotelian said, startling him back from his turbulent worries. She smiled, knowing she caught him off guard; she stepped closer. The silken fabric of her dress felt comforting on his cold hand as he put it around her waist and drew her toward him.

"Darling, how are you? So good to see you." Two air—kisses later, "You look exquisite." he said, stepping back a bit to admire her. "Is it Oscar or Carolina? The nude-colored chiffon is perfect for your skin tones. Not many women can wear that color, but on you, it is brilliant."

"Well, thank you, and we will also thank Oscar. This is all too exciting for words. The Picasso should fetch a hefty sum. They are saying that Sheik Mohammad of Abu Dhabi is interested."

"I have heard some Chinese industrialists are going to bid," interrupted Sinbad DeMande. He shook Classic's hand and patted him on the back.

"Hello, Sinbad," Classico said, not looking at him directly, but seizing him up to take the measure of his mood. He still felt the sting of humiliation from Sinbad's temper tantrum. *He really should learn to behave himself,* thought Classico.

Along with Picasso, Classico was the center of attention, and tonight he would take control and make sure Sinbad knew it.

"It would be a shame for the painting to leave this country. It has been well marketed to the hedge-fund players; perhaps one of them will be the successful bidder," Classico said, turning his back to Sinbad.

"Dear Sabrina, don't you look lovely this evening," he said in his most sonorous, ocean-sounding tone, offering the obligatory cheek to cheek. *If ever the term "dripping with diamonds" applied, it would be this moment; or perhaps the term was invented specifically for her,* thought Classico. The twenty-four-and-a-half carat yellow diamond ring offset her heavily encrusted chandelier earrings, which reflected the full spectrum of colors from her Eternity diamond necklace.

She would look stunning even without the jewels. *It does not surprise me that Sinbad is hard up for cash. She is wearing it all. I am glad that I don't have the expense of a wife. He should sell some of her jewelry.* Classico's eyes flitted from face to face, scanning the crowd that encircled him. Everyone offered his and her congratulations for bringing the work to auction. This sale reinforced his reputation as the preeminent art dealer of modernism in the twenty-first century—and tonight—he was the rock star.

Because Alouisha and Jason wore their best evening clothes, they splurged on a taxi instead of taking the usual subway to Goodrich's. As they exited the cab, all eyes were upon them. Alouisha was a head-turner; no one could pass her without being startled by her radiance. It left them curious for a more intimate knowledge of whom she may be. People stared without reserve, searching her face for some detail that might unlock her mystery. Over six-feet tall in heels and wearing a size four, her tightly fitted, purple sateen dress made the clouds thunder in sunshine, crocuses burst in late winter, and foghorns sound on a blue sky-day—and she did not wear jewelry or underwear. Jason took her hand, and they entered the great hall where a host checked their names on the guest list.

The concentration of millionaires and billionaires per square foot was unrivaled. "It doesn't look like there is, or ever has been, a recession in this town," Jason said, trying to absorb all the stimuli at once. "Come on, let's find Picasso," he said taking her hand.

Hundreds of glasses clinked with cocktail happiness that played wind-chime music. The laughter blended the tones into a melodious mix that buoyed them along.

"It's awesome," Alouisha said, standing mesmerized by the Picasso and its presentation as a sacred enshrinement.

"Do you think this is the real one?" she whispered.

"Better not discuss that now, but it looks good, doesn't it?" He asked, not certain he was convinced.

As if a telepathic apparition suddenly appeared out of thin air, "Yes, it's the good one," the voice said.

Startled, they quickly turned to "in-your-face" Classico. She started to walk away, but he grabbed her by the wrist—gently at first.

"Please, please, Alouisha, you must let me explain."

"She does not want to talk to you," Jason said stepping between them.

Classico held his ground. "Tomorrow, I would like to bring Mr. Veridian from the Gray Cube to see your work. He has asked me to recommend a talented emerging artist. I am sure when he sees your work, he will be interested in giving you a show," *especially since I helped him poach several top artists for his new gallery in Chelsea.* "Please give it some thought, you can tell me your decision tomorrow. In the meantime, allow me to introduce you to the director. He is just standing over there."

She hesitated, knowing every artist in New York coveted this opportunity for an introduction from Classico. It made no sense to refuse. Unable to say "no," and unable to make eye contact with Classico, Jason intervened, taking her hand and pulling her along.

"We have got to do this. This is your chance," he whispered in her ear.

She bit her lips and yanked her hand away from Jason's grasp. "No, I don't want to," she said trying to regain her authority. But Classico was too quick.

"Alouisha, it would give me great pleasure to introduce you to Vincent Veridian of the Gray Cube. Vincent, this is Alouisha, the talented and gifted artist, whom I mentioned to you, and her friend Jason, who is also an accomplished artist."

Veridian was sleek, slick, and terribly good-looking, with a well-honed bone structure that had been cultivated through the centuries by his Scottish lineage. Groomed to perfection with every dark brown hair in place, he wore his forty-six years like a well-earned medal—proud and entitled. His silk ascot configured precisely into folds around his neck and matched his teal-blue eyes.

"Alouisha," he said, smoothing the legato tempo of his voice, like waves of the rolling surf, until it blended with the infinite grains of sand, "It is indeed an honor to meet you."

He took one look at her, and she became silhouetted while everything else in the room dissolved into a diaphanous wall of white. Every painting, forced smile and conversation evaporated like steam through an open window, until it all disappeared and no longer mattered. Nothing in the room existed for him but her beauty. His gaze burrowed deeply through the maze of protective doorways that led to her heart center, where the nakedness of her emotions found form.

Feeling embarrassed by his attempt to invade her private domain, she blushed alizarin-crimson pink. Jason squirmed and postured with bravado, uncomfortable with this new acquaintance's reaction to his girlfriend. Classico, however, could not have been more pleased. He stood next to Alouisha and Veridian, focusing his full attention on their exchange to expedite the bond that he hoped would grow between them.

Classico had arranged this meeting to sway her opinion of him and reconsider her moral imperative.

"It is nice to meet you too," she said removing her hand from

Veridian's grip, and lowering her gaze to the floor. She wanted to flee but was incapable of being rude.

"I look forward to seeing your Sentient paintings. I have been told they are quite interesting."

"Thank you," she replied, afraid to look up at his face and risk turning pink again.

Jason, stepped in to save her from this unpleasant encounter and asserted his territorial prerogative.

"It was very nice to see you, Mr. Veridian, but we have to be leaving now. We will be in touch," he said, taking her arm and leading her across the room.

A few paces away, he ripped into Veridian. "What a pompous jerk. It is unbelievable that these jokers are the market-makers for art, and we have to kiss up to them to have our work shown. Whenever he takes on a new artist, the price of their work doubles and their future success is assured," Jason said.

"Sure, as long as the artists don't disagree with him. I've heard he pressures them like crazy to produce until all connections with their creative center is lost, and they become artistic automatons. Well, I won't do it. I don't want to be part of his stable," Alouisha said.

"They don't deserve you," he said, pulling her closer. We will figure something out … the right thing."

They strolled hand-in-hand through the galleries, taking in the collection of paintings and people. They stopped to look at Vik Muniz's photograph of Rodin rendered in sugar; at Wayne Thiebaud's, *Brie with Cherry,* painting; and a 20" by 24" oil-on-canvas by Gerhard Richter with its high estimate at $2,500,000—the top price for a living artist.

"His work is overrated, but brilliantly branded; don't you think so?" Alouisha asked.

"I agree," Jason said. "Particularly, when compared to our work, which has substance, history, and context," he said, only half jokingly.

"I cannot understand why the art world is so crazy about his blurry portraits," she said.

"They are better than his recent abstract expressionist period, which as a second-generation abstract artist, shows little or no inventiveness, except that he scrapes away his top-coat with a metal car fender. I did that in kindergarten with crayons. We covered bright swashes of color with black crayon and scraped it off until the under colors showed through," said Jason.

"And his colors are so garish," she said."

As much as they loved engaging in conversations about visual art syntaxes to understand its effect on contemporary art, they thought their own visual dialogues were far more cutting-edge than those on display. Nonetheless, the very thrill of seeing these works come onto the secondary market after years in private collections, excited Alouisha and Jason. It fortified their commitment to art and each other.

"Come on Ali, let's 'work the room' and see who we can meet. Remember painting is only half of our occupation; we've gotta 'brand baby brand,'" he said half-jokingly but also in earnest. They moved into the next room, and like two gazelles radiating grace and beauty, their spatial expansion preceded their arrival, creating a quantum-unified-force-field. All heads turned in their direction.

The evening continued with the nuclear excitement billowing into ever-larger clouds of accolades uplifted by the combustible triumvirate of art, money, and sexual possibilities. Nonetheless, beyond the marrow of those cultural enthusiasms, the quixotic questions remained: What drove artists to create? What compelled their engagement in silent visual conversation with each other? What connected artists to other dimensions in the universe? What inspired their further investigations, and ultimately to share their findings visually? Maybe, it was the hot adrenaline that tickled the inside of their brain that urged a response—and they did—just because it was too much fun not to.

Chapter 45

The Delivery

Alouisha slept late the next morning. She had opened her eyes earlier, but her gauzy head prompted her to remain horizontal. The champagne she had last night at Goodrich's continued bubble dancing behind her eyes. A distant noise tore through her sleep and she lunged for the phone.

"Oh, my paintings, they're being delivered today. I almost forgot," she said, getting out of bed.

Jason had arranged with Classico to have them sent from the crime scene, at the gallery's expense. She pulled on her jeans, while dashing to the ringing house phone. Her body jerked like a jalopy racing down a potholed dirt road. Sucking in her breath to tuck in her shirt, she fumbled for the phone.

"The White Glove movers are here with a delivery," said the Hall Captain at the front desk.

"Please send them up," she said.

Peering through the glass peephole of the front door, she identified the moving men and unfastened the two locks: one deadbolt, a pick-proof cylinder, and finally the safety chain.

"Good morning, please come in."

"Where would you like these, Miss?"

"Over there, please," she said, pointing to the far wall.

Noticing the cadence in Alouisha's voice, the Jamaican man broke into a grin and a Jamaican Patois dialect—that mellifluous sound of river rocks being smoothed by running waters triggered her longing for home. One syllable melded into the next, omitting unnecessary vowels and consonants, until the separate words became indistinguishable. The distilled, condensed, English syntax contained reinvented phrases derived from Jamaican folklore and held meaning only for Jamaicans.

The Jamaican mover tried to warn Alouisha of the blood splattered all over her paintings.

"Irie, mon, oh how they show so," he said, as he removed them from the cardboard boxes. (Translated: Take it easy; stay cool, because they are looking very bad ... meaning good.)

Alouisha anticipated the defaced paintings, but not her reaction when she pulled off the remaining bubble wrap. The vicious bloodletting had coagulated on the surface of the paintings. It stung, hit hard, and flooded her interior spaces with a violent scream that quashed all sense of safety. Then with a swift stab of pain the horror resurfaced and forced her to revisit the terrible ordeal. Her hands muffled her mouth; her body recoiled backward, but her eyes could not disengage from the bloody mess. An image of the naked ghouls flashed before her. She gagged and staggered toward the floor.

The Jamaican man caught her arm, "Irie mon," he said again, trying to calm her. When she heard those words, the safe, carefree feelings of her childhood flashed before her, and she realized how distant they had become.

"I warned you Lady. These are tough."

She swallowed hard, placed her hand on her throat, and took a deep breath.

"I can handle it," she said sucking in the air and puffing up her cheeks. Slowly she exhaled … pausing … sighing, replacing the fear with renewed determination.

"What's a little blood? I can mix the exact color with alizarin crimson and burnt sienna," she said, feigning callousness. She would not allow this desecration to ruin her years of work. Alouisha viewed each painting as iconic and irreplaceable. Each depicted a major creative consequence that she extracted from the curvature of the space-time continuum. Each was cut from the patchwork of ephemeral eternity. Standing with her arms crossed over her chest, her analytical eye surveyed the work as she tried to incorporate the additional layer of color into a meaningful concept. After a while, her gaze wandered to the sky; her unfocused vision hinted at distant thoughts. Perhaps she traveled to another galaxy to confer with her quantum physics doppelganger—perhaps to get some advice. Her eyes gleamed, "I know," she said excitedly, they are a new interpretation of *Sentient Art.*"

"They look like they need a bath and a disinfectant to me," the Jamaican said. "It'll probably wash off."

"No, you don't understand, my work is about experiencing art through our five senses, and the sixth sense is for intuition. Therefore, when we turn off our minds and our egos, we receive information from our sixth sense. Only then can we experience life in quantum inflationary dimensions accessed through our feelings."

"I still think ya ought to get some Lysol," the Jamaican said, shaking his head and collecting the torn bubble wrap.

"Since body fluids are an accepted art medium, crossing a new threshold, another layer of meaning is added to the work. By exposing the paintings to a dimension of real pain, they are repurposed into a new syntax."

"If ya have pain, ya should get some aspirin," he said, stuffing the wrappings into a trash bag. The popping bubble wrap sounded like ricocheting bullets; they punctuated Alouisha's art-speak.

"I never did understand modern art. Well, you take care now; we gotta be goin to the next job. It's not supposed to have any violence, just baby furniture. Irie, Mon," the man said.

"Bye," she said, seeing them to the door.

A few minutes later, Jason arrived home from his morning run.

"Hi Sweetheart," he said, bending to kiss her. I let you sleep in this morning; you deserve it after last night. You were the most beautiful woman there. All those men were hitting on you; luckily, I was there to protect you," Jason said. She smiled, remembering all the attention she had received.

The telephone rang and voice mail picked up.

"This is Mr. Classico. Alouisha are you in? Mr. Veridian and I, we would like to stop by your studio and see your work. Would that be okay? Let's say 4 p.m.?"

"Alouisha, pick up the phone; let them come. Do it sweetheart," Jason said.

Alouisha moved to the far end of the room, as far away from the telephone as possible, shaking her head and her eyes widening.

"Alouisha are you there? Please call me."

"Hello, Mr. Classico, this is Jason. Yes, you can both visit this afternoon. Yes, we will see you at 4 p.m."

"Thank you, Jason, we'll see you then," Classico said and hung up.

Making a chinning-bar motion with clenched fists, Jason jerked his arms in a downward thrust, shouting, "Yes. Yes."

"Jason, what did you do?" Alouisha asked frantically searching his eyes for an answer.

"Look Ali, we cannot ignore this opportunity. It may be a once—in—a—lifetime chance. Let's just let them see our work, and we'll make all the decisions later. We can just listen to what they have to say."

"I cannot do it, Jason."

"You don't have to be here. I'll show them everything. Okay?" he said in a pleading tone. Alouisha lowered her gaze to avoid his eyes. She said nothing, her silence more eloquent than words.

"We still have plenty of time before the auction to make a final decision. Let's just go with this for now. Please Ali, for me, for us."

First one tear crawled down her buttery cheek, then two more at a faster rate. Trying to hold back, she whimpered. The wet glistening drops of overwhelming sadness cascaded to her lips and chin. How could she allow her pure creations, truly gifts from the universe, to be infected by Classico and Veridian's greed, dishonesty, and ultimately fraud?

"Nothing good will ever come from associating with them. This is not the plan I had for becoming a successful artist," she said.

Taking her in his arms Jason lifted her face to his, and with a gentleness that only comes from heartfelt love, he kissed away her tears. Alouisha pushed him away, torn between yielding to his physical influence or upholding her violated principles.

"Leave me alone. How can you give in to that crook? I'm finished with Classico and anyone involved with him. He's going to jail, just wait and see," she said.

"Well, maybe arranging a show for you will be his last good effort before they put him away. Let them come here today and just talk. We'll decide what to do later. I still need to find out, which painting is the original. I'll need some more time with him to figure out what's going on. Where do you think he has the third one stashed? Alouisha remained silent.

"Okay sweetheart?" Jason cajoled.

"No, it's not okay. I don't want them near my work,"she said stamping her foot.

"You know, Ali, it is ironic that as artists we are scrupulously honest in our work ethic and have chosen a profession filled with rogues. It is almost comical. You have to laugh; you must see the humor in it."

"No, I don't."

"Come on, sweetheart, you know how much I love you, and I will never let you be hurt again. It will be okay, I promise," he said.

With her gaze cast downward, he kissed her lips, her cheeks, and her eyes; everywhere with short light wispy breaths, until her smile broke free from disappointment.

"Okay?" he asked.

"I don't know," she said almost inaudibly, still reluctant to relinquish her position and marginalize her convictions.

Suddenly, Jason froze; he stood as motionless as a fossilized Pompeian stalled in action. After several moments, he wrenched his head trying to dislodge the startling, frightful truth that lay before him. He saw the bloodied paintings. The monstrous ordeal that crucified the canvases confronted him with the force of an AK-47.

Alouisha's beautifully painted landscapes with nudes, her former sensuous responses to nature, were now slathered with death. Jason felt sick when he saw the vicious, swaths of blood spurting onto her sentient world. He swallowed hard and pulled himself together. He needed to be strong for her.

"Ali, are you okay having them here? You don't have to look at them; we can put them in storage."

"I know they are disgusting, but they are real. Now they have become powerful commentaries on violence referencing woman's issues, a dynamic tension that was not there before—creation and extinction."

"I can see your point," he said, wanting to be supportive. "If you can handle it, so can I. Let's get our work organized, they'll be here this afternoon."

Chapter 46

The Studio Visit

Classico was in Classico heaven … almost. Because Jason and Alouisha agreed to his and Veridian's visit, he assumed they would be discrete about the delicate situation, and would be willing to discuss a future exhibition of her work instead. Classico simply had to keep Jason and Alouisha away from Goodrich's until the auction was over. Short of a kidnapping, the promise of a show should sufficiently dissuade them from indulging their scruples, Classico was certain.

Vincent Veridian owed Classico, and now was the time to call in the favor. But first, Veridian had to be convinced that she was the latest art-world sensation, and only needed to be branded to reach six-figure sales. That should not be difficult.

"Hans, please get my coat, and call Veridian and tell him I'm leaving now to pick him up. I'm going downtown to Alouisha's studio, and please hold all calls and visitors."

The security guard hailed a taxi and waited, holding the door open as Classico descended the limestone steps to the street below.

It is only a week until the auction. I can promise them everything. All the kids really want is to be famous. The smart ones go to a good school to learn the ground rules, the dialogue, the art speak, whatever; then, they bore me with all that morality crap. Fundamentally, it is only about money, and to be successful, one needs to be charming and create relationships. Whether you are a shoe salesman at Bergdorf's, a car dealer, a real estate agent, or the President of the United States, one needs charm and charisma. Perhaps that is the true foundation of democracy, because nothing gets done without it, he concluded with a smirk.

"There is one stop along the way, driver," he said, giving him Veridian's address in Chelsea.

Veridian was waiting at the door of the gallery on West 22nd Street dressed in essential gallerist attire: black blazer, black rib-hugging collarless t-shirt, and black straight-leg trousers. His affectation was part Hollywood, part Chelsea, perfectly groomed and dripping with "cool"—and he knew it. Because he was in a state of perpetual self-promotion, his smooth and elegant manners were sometimes feigned, but mostly he appeared august.

"I am glad you will have the opportunity to see her work," Classico said.

"She is working in conceptual modalities; something about drawing parallels to quantum physics. I was very impressed when she explained it. I think she could be the next Damien Hirst; she investigates cosmic dimensionality as he does, but I will, of course, leave that to your judgment. You have the great contemporary eye, the vision and the discernment to find great talent, as you have repeatedly proven," Classico understood that flattery always got results.

"You are too kind," Veridian replied. I am always looking for new talent with an equally good disposition to accompany it. The artists in my gallery are not only required to have enormous talent, but must also be able to handle the media and their evolving public personas. I cannot have emotional prima donnas who check their feeling thermostat before any decision is made. They must be equipped to follow the program, and at times, it can be difficult."

Being a successful and famous artist means living in the public eye. One's privacy is compromised; one's soul is on view to the entire world and available for sale, which is often demeaning to the artist. It is not an easy profession," Veridian said.

"In addition, once the curators start their scholarly investigations, knowledge of the artist's sex life becomes public fodder. The curators always feel entitled to discuss an artist's sexual proclivities under the guise that it influenced his work. I am always amused by their lack of boundaries—everything is fair play," Classico said chuckling.

"Considering the astronomical prices received at auction in 2007 and the first half of 2008, the stakes have never been higher. Earning six or seven figures as an artist, requires commitments to ideologies as well as emotions," Veridian said.

"And a lot of discipline," Classico added.

"That's fifteen dollars and sixty-five cents," the driver said, as they pulled up in front of the 1900 Thread Building, replete with gargoyles and pilasters. Veridian noted the minimalist sculpture in the lobby, which long ago lost touch with "art-world-speak" that could have explained its metaphorical significance.

Alouisha and Jason had been painting and had just finished scrubbing the sticky remains of acrylic paint off their bodies. The lanolin base-coat was easy to remove. Their latest "Flesh Tones" canvas lay on the floor, almost dry enough to hang on the wall. Together and naked, they stared in amazement at their creation. The half tones and glazing, like a slow-moving glacier suffused with coruscating light, undulated and flowed into nuanced shapes that echoed their actions from moments before.

"It's gorgeous," she said.

"You're gorgeous," he said, as they both stood transfixed by their creation—dumbfounded at the power of art and love.

The house phone rang, jolting them back to earth. "You have two visitors, Mr ... "

"Yes, please ask them to wait a minute, I'll call you right back," Jason said, and turned to Ali. "Quick, put on your clothes," he said, pulling on his jeans, scrambling to the bedroom to find a clean shirt. Alouisha grabbed the crumpled outfit from the floor that Jason had practically torn off her a short time ago. She pulled the large canvas over to the empty wall, and lifted it to the hook. Jason pulled the other side up and fastened it.

"There, it's fabulous," she said, bending over at her waist allowing her hair to fall forward. She ran her fingers through it with scrubbing motions, fluffed it and swung it, like a pony flicking its tail. Then, she straightened her shoulders and was ready. "Okay let's do this."

"You are the best," Jason said as he picked up the phone. "Please send them up."

Chapter 47

An Arrogant Piece of Work

G raffiti-like clouds lashed the tormented sky with crosshatched wisps that formed patches of darkness. Refracted light entered the large picture windows of the loft, and skimmed the surfaces of Alouisha's paintings giving them an ethereal glow.

Classico and Veridian's arrival zapped the warmth of their love nest with a lethal shot of acrid realism.

"Good afternoon, Alouisha and Jason. It's a bit blustery out there today," Classico said, as he made small talk and took the lead to keep the situation under his control. He glanced around the loft; they both were radiant in the sex-drenched atmosphere, which held the invisible bonds that connected them securely fastened. Classico could smell the fresh paint and the recent sex. Alouisha and Jason both gushed, as they tried to appear normal and not laugh.

"Alouisha, I am so glad to see you again," Veridian said, as he approached her and took her hand. As before, he stared too deeply into her eyes and probed straight to her vulnerability. He wanted to know everything about her.

"Nice to see you too," she said, pulling her hand away from his grasp. *What's with this guy? He gives me the creeps, and he looks at me like a lecherous jerk, she thought. Just because he's so good looking, it doesn't mean that he has to come on so strong.*

"Would you like something to drink?" Jason asked, purposefully severing Veridian's concentration, but wishing it were his head instead.

"No, thank you. Alouisha, please show me your work," he said. Veridian had seen it all: cow dung paintings, pornography, garbage enclosed in Plexiglas, used tampons, dead animal carcasses hanging in the Lever Brothers Building, and the Cremaster Cycles, which filled the Guggenheim Museum with tons of Vaseline that imitated body secretions. They replaced traditional mediums, and professed the "newest-latest-greatest," but, after a while, they all blurred into the same vulgar, attention-getting effect as carnival barkers. Nevertheless, when Veridian saw Alouisha's bloodied paintings, he felt as if he were held upside down from a flying helicopter, and all his preconceived notions about art were shaken and emptied from him.

The paintings delivered a wallop. They forced the viewer to acknowledge her post-structural syntax, the juxtaposition between violence and sentient body landscapes. The resulting conflict created scathing tension.

Alouisha's work forever changed the view of self-perception, when one wore the 3-D lens of her meta-narratives. There was nothing sentimental, superfluous, or gratuitous about the subject—women and violence.

Gripped by intrigue, Veridian continued staring at the paintings. Jason and Alouisha joined him and stood on either side. They entered into his silent realm of cognition to experience his reaction to the work. In this way, they were seeing it again for the first time. Alouisha smiled enigmatically, secretly acknowledging the exquisite mystery of art—the expansion of another person's thoughts with insights and sensations that redirected one's perceptions.

Classico broke the silent reverie in which the three were engaged. "The work is difficult, but brilliant. Alouisha chose not to have the canvases cleaned, but to view the violence as integral to the work by adding a layer of real-time."

"An excellent decision. Their power exists on many levels. There is a strong possibility I can take you on as the new emerging artist, Alouisha," Veridian said, turning to meet her eyes. Then, releasing his gaze, his eyes traveled south and lingered on her breasts. "Why don't we have lunch and discuss this further? Let's say Friday, at Cipriani's, the day after the auction."

Alouisha glanced at Jason for some guidance. His eyes rolled to the ceiling. Disgusted and impatient, he finally relented giving her a nod, imperceptible to anyone but her.

She tried desperately to separate her emotions from the business of art marketing. The two-sided argument in her head battled her ethical boundaries. She wanted no involvement with Veridian or any other unscrupulous person who would compromise her values. Her work had been motivated and conceived from pure intellectual curiosity; Veridian's only motivation was profit and sex.

Would associating with him adversely affect my future work? If Classico and Gray Cube galleries are two of the best in the world, I can only imagine what the others must be like. If I don't sell my work, I may as well consider it a hobby, she thought.

The light from the window had shifted and dimmed. It no longer illumined the paintings with an inner glow. A favorite quote from Carl Jung popped into her head: "Your vision will become clear only when you look into your heart. Who looks outside, dreams. Who looks inside, awakes."

"So, It's Friday lunch. Let's say one o'clock at Cipriani's," Veridian said, breaking into her thoughts.

"Well, y ... y ... yes, I guess so," she stammered.

"I'll have my assistant be in touch. We have a lot to discuss." He glanced at his watch. "I must be going now. Thank you for the visit," Veridian said.

"Mr. Veridian, we can show you more work," Jason said, with an earnest look on his face.

"I am sorry, not today, perhaps some other time. I have another appointment, and I must get uptown," he said walking to the door with Classico right behind him.

"Thank you both," said Classico. "Enjoy your evening."

Jason closed the door and sank into the sofa. He put his elbow on the armrest and cradled his head in his hand. "That was quick; I didn't have a chance to show him anything. He was interested only in your paintings and getting into your panties. What an arrogant piece of work he is."

"I'm sorry sweetheart," she said sitting next to him and giving him a big hug. "If he were truly interested in art, why wouldn't he want to see your work? And that Classico, what a pompous jerk. He did not even mention the forgery, as if I am just going to pretend I never saw it. What are we going to do?" she asked.

"We either call the police or Goodrich's and have him arrested. Unfortunately, I think that would backfire on us. The global repercussions would be staggering. They could go viral, spreading toxic suspicion exponentially to all art transactions," he said, as he stood up to feel in control again.

"Consider the possibilities. The entire international art market would be shaken if this fraud were exposed. Everyone is depending on the Picasso sale to reaffirm the future health of the art market. With the recession continuing, an art market recovery is, at best, fragile. If it got out that forgeries were involved, we would be responsible for pulling the cornerstone of the sale and inciting a further crash in the markets," he said.

Jason paced the room and stared at the floor deep in thought; occasionally he shook his head. "A collective guilt of mythic proportions would affect the art dealers worldwide, because they are all in collusion. When someone discredits a work, accusing it of being forged, they are sued for liable and dragged through the courts for years at a tremendous expense. When the paintings have multi-million dollar price tags, a million-dollar law-suit is not excessive to defend its credentials. You can imagine why there are so few authentication suits being litigated. When forgeries are suspected, people prefer to look the other way. There is simply too much money at stake. It has lost all sense of proportion to real life values," Jason continued.

"I do not want to have that much power. I didn't ask for this. All I want to do is paint without the politics," she said. "If we reveal the truth, we'll be shunned forever by the art world—vilified, like art pariahs. No one will ever want to show our work," she bemoaned.

"Or, we could be sued for defamation. Our lives would be miserable, our art-lives finished," Jason said.

"When a painting that hangs in someone's home is more valuable than the home itself, or when its hammer price could feed an entire starving nation, or build hospitals and schools in the third-world parts of the United States, something is seriously wrong," she said.

"Whether it is the emperor's-new-clothes syndrome, or a money laundering scheme that filters down to sketchy provenances, forgeries, or stolen art, it is still the 'long-necked' profession—everyone agrees to stretch the truth, ignore it and look the other way," he said. Jason stretched his neck and buried his face in her neck. Alouisha laughed.

"Jason this is serious. What are we going to do?"

"The government needs to intervene by updating art security and surveillance systems. I never thought I would be in support of bureaucratic agencies regulating art, but something like the Security and Exchange Commission that governs Wall Street would help," he said.

Other than fraud, galleries and museums need to reconsider terrorist threats and transform themselves into fortresses. Our art treasures are far too vulnerable to vandalism, look what happened to Iraq's Museum of Antiquities," she said.

"Or the Gardner Museum in Boston," he added. "Alouisha, you are right. I don't know what we should do. I don't know what we can do. I wish we had never met Classico," Jason said.

"This will compromise my work, my values, and my life. If I don't go to the police, I am withholding evidence during a criminal investigation. I could be complicit—guilty as Classico. How can I possibly accept a show under these circumstances from such a contemptible man?" she asked.

Imploringly, she searched Jason's face for an answer. He said nothing. Slowly he shook his head from side to side.

They both knew that their lives were about to be changed drastically, if she were to agree to the show and bring her work to the forefront. Her long sought after goal was in reach, but the stepping-stones pitted with sharp-edges and ankle-breaking crevices were ready to snag her the moment she stumbled.

They stared at each other, and with each passing moment, the gravity of their dilemma grew more haunting. There was no escaping the consequences of either choice.

Chapter 48

The Petrified Forest

So far so good, Classico thought, congratulating himself as he dressed in his finest Anderson and Sheppard bespoke suit for the big day. Like his close shave, things were going smoothly. At the Goodrich's reception, the Picasso had worked its magic on Sinbad's temper. It cooled him down enough to wait patiently for the auction results and his cash disbursement from the Apogee Art Fund. After having stood beneath the sacred art-world alter, Sinbad became a believer again ... anointed by the luminosity of the color green and by Classico's redemption from the wafer of attention and power.

With Sinbad's anger in retreat, Classico was freed from threats of criminal charges and certain financial ruin. He had paid the mortgage with the proceeds from the oligarch, and assured the angel investors of the imminent profits from the Goodrich's sale. Not having heard from Alouisha and Jason, he assumed they agreed to collaborate. No artist would pass up an opportunity with Gray Cube Gallery. By now, she must realize that everything in life comes with a price, and that we cannot all be pure souls.

Occasionally, Classico had a moment of nostalgia that overrode his speed dial, which lately had been set to greed. Sometimes, he would long for the days when connoisseurship took precedence over branding, and scholarship defined motives rather than a museum's box office receipts from a blockbuster show. Sometimes, he felt a twinge of guilt when an auctioneer ran up a hammer price with chandelier bids, or when endless back-room agreements guaranteed a favored client's reserve price— but not today. Today all would be resolved, and he would be back, ruling his art world fiefdom.

He hummed a little tune from his favorite childhood musical, Bye Bye Birdie: *Put on a happy face.*

Checking his posture in profile, he thrust his chest forward, pulled his shoulders back, patted himself on the chest and sighed. There, that's better. He held two Hermes ties to his face. One had small blue dolphins and lighthouses on a yellow background, and the other, the same blue print with a red background.

"Hans, which do you think looks better with my navy suit? Should I wear red, the power color or go with the yellow for a more subtle approach?"

"Sir, the red one suits, most definitely," Hans said. "Today is the highlight of your career, the culmination of all your hard work."

"Yes, I suppose you are right. The Picasso is the most expensive work I have ever placed at auction. Well, wish me luck."

"Good luck, Sir."

Classico's self-esteem meter launched into high gear as he glimpsed his future life when all would be right again in the world of Classico. He envisioned waking up each morning powerful and hard, without that constant gnawing feeling inside his stomach, like a carrot being grated. Soon this nightmare would be over. Because he wanted to get to Goodrich's early, before the first hammer fell at 7 p.m., he did not hire a car. It was faster to walk, and not get stuck in the 45-minute limousine pileup outside Goodrich's. Evening was almost upon him as he walked the twenty blocks to clear his head. His step was as springy as a trampoline; he had batteries in his shoes. Walking through the bristling, hectic, and wonderful streets of New York's Upper East Side, he reflected on his life. *After the sale, my image will be restored from having suffered Sinbad's verbal attacks, and my irregular undertakings will be obscured, cushioned within the context of profitability. Everyone loves a winner, no matter how he won.*

Tonight he was a contented man, because tomorrow he would again reside in his favorite neighborhood— Richistan, where the meritocratic society voted with accolades and dollar bills. He vowed never again to fall into such a dreadfully compromising position. *Never again will I grovel and placate to the investors—I will make them beg to be back in my fund.*

Classico continued his ruminations, reviewing his past and imagining his future. New York busyness animated every street. The continuous onslaught of images was dizzying, as if unlimited gigabytes of digital files stored in the cloud came crashing through cyberspace. Glamorous comings and goings of people of every description flattened into illusory four-color, glossy moments. The New York night pulsated with its own indigenous rhythms, many involving secret nocturnal contracts. The mysterious currents crossed the spheres of entertainment, dining, openings of every venue, or else sordid, shadowy solicitations.

Classico noted it all, breathing deeply to balance his energy with the fleeting, blurry objects that streaked in neon colors all around him. He felt the world spin with a centrifugal force that reaffirmed his ego, restoring it back to a condensed more powerful version of himself. He was the one static object at the center of it all—he and his life's commitment to art.

As he continued along Fifth Avenue, he reflected on his privileged life in New York and its endless source of entertainment and intrigue. *I could not live anywhere else.* He passed a group of monks protesting torture in Tibet. They dressed in sheeted robes belted with rope and held cardboard signs that read: "Stop Tibetan torture by the Chinese."

We all have our problems, Classico thought, as he walked past all thirteen of them. *They are crowding our streets unnecessarily. Why do they have to come here? No one cares about torture in Tibet. People are only interested in their strangeness. How did they get here anyway? New Yorkers care more about the torture from their credit card companies or telephone providers when they are placed on hold for hours.*

Farther down the avenue, near the Plaza Hotel, he passed the break-dancers blaring their boom boxes and performing feats of acrobatic marvels. Pumping out dance steps on their heads, on one hand, or kicking up their heels like bucking broncos, they were quick and fierce. The tourists loved the African American entertainers, and filled their lone sidewalk hat with loose change and dollar bills.

He passed the Bergdorf Goodman window displays—the soothsayer of fashion's future. Classico chuckled at the mannequins' narrative. The telekinetic-looking sorceresses were rigidly suspended in orgiastic positions and clothed in feathered, black underworld attire. They looked omniscient. *Perhaps they knew Picasso's hammer price.*

Finally, when he arrived at Goodrich's, his adrenalin spiked into high gear and gave him the energy of a twenty-one year old. He and his board members were given a private viewing room with one-way glass, upstairs, overlooking the auction proceedings. A white-gloved wait staff would serve the champagne and hors d'oeuvres from Le Cirque. Tonight, he reigned royal and with some luck, the Picasso would reach its high estimate, and they would drink the Dom Perignon in celebration.

The collectors, who had bought art from Goodrich's in the past, flew in from all over the world. The closer their seat was to the podium, the more costly was their previous acquisition. The regulars had the same place for each auction. Tonight's sale would be the defining moment for

2010. It would either jump-start the dormant art market or reinforce its demise. No one wanted to miss tonight's gladiatorial event—the witnessing of the vast sums of money being spent publicly or the art market's slaughter.

Friendships, born of mutual privilege, developed over the years between those seated next to one another. They basked in each other's glory and winning bids, and professed undying best-friend love to each other and to art. They were part of a rarefied group, not there by accident but by their superior intelligence and keen eye to judge a great work of art—or so they had convinced themselves. There existed no greater satisfaction than to see a painting by an artist whose work they owned sell for ten times more than they had paid several years back.

"I am so smart; I have just made ten million dollars," said the lucky collectors to their spouses, their mistresses, or to only themselves. Art profits elevated their mood better than any serotonin, and one dose over the high estimate lasted for weeks.

"Hello Classico, so good to see you," a colleague said, shaking his hand with gusto. Before he had a chance to respond, Edwina Mass appeared.

"Darling, we are all so excited," she said kissing him. Her perfume and powder encircled him in her misty aura, until he caught himself and regrouped his jangling emotions. People he hardly knew or only briefly had met, stuck out their hands intrusively and acted like close friends. He could not escape many of the handshakes.

Taking Edwina's arm, he walked through the gathering crowd, hardly able to navigate the throngs of acquaintances, art notables, and parvenus crushing alongside them. They sought his opinion about each painting on display and the future of the art market. Would Chinese contemporary hold its value? How did he acquire the Picasso? Will the markets ever return to 2007 levels? Finally, he stopped and turned to face them. He glowed with confidence, turbocharged by the outpouring of attention. The energy that rippled through his body ignited his testosterone and bestowed on him God-like powers. The flock listened intently.

"Tonight's sale will be recorded in the annals of art history as the most important sale of the twenty-first century—the pinnacle of the modern master's career. The entire global art market awaits the outcome, which will foretell art pricing for the next fifty years," Classico said, as a cloudy blend of whispered words, sighs, and gasps rose from the group. His electric charisma worked in overdrive, recharged by the prospect of all that money. The air was rich as syrup, and so thick with promise it could be spooned.

"But Mr. Classico, what impact will the recession have on tonight's sale?" Random people from the crowd fired questions. He raised his hand to silence them.

"We will soon see my friends, although I am very optimistic." Latching onto Edwina's arm more tightly, he turned, heading toward a less densely packed area.

"Hello Henry," said Morgan Carey the Chairman of Goodrich's America, as he approached bristling with anticipation. The elegant Chairman shook Classico's hand with strength and determination that solidified their mutual intention. Classico felt the heat emanating from the physical exchange of their quantum molecules. It charged the room like live electrical wires connecting.

"Edwina, darling," he kissed her gently on both cheeks. "I am so glad to see you both," he said hurriedly, as his orbit, crackling and sparking, gained velocity. "Well, its time to find our seats. Please follow me," Chairman Carey said.

While being escorted upstairs to the private viewing room, Classico spotted Alouisha and Jason admiring a painting by Robert Rauschenberg at the far corner of the gallery. He caught their attention and waved through the crowd. Not having heard from them or the police, he assumed they had agreed to his offer.

I knew they would see it from my point of view, he thought, as his chest expanded along with his confidence.

Alouisha's stomach fell to her knees. A shot of ice-cold anxiety coursed through her. "Don't look, there's Classico," she said, turning away from his gaze. "Please, God, don't let him come over here."

Unable to sleep, they had been awake all night, worrying about their responsibility to the police, to Goodrich's, and to art. But most importantly, they worried about maintaining their personal ethics if they did nothing. They had argued, cried, and parleyed the alternatives until the night sky turned morning pale.

"Would we have any morals left? Is it ethical to withhold crucial information from the police? Would we be able to live with the guilt? What kind of people are we to keep a secret so largely consequential that would affect an entire industry. Are we really weak-willed enablers who need to enroll in a twelve-step program?" Alouisha had said. And finally, the bottom-line question, "Do all successful artists have to sell out—exchanging principles for profits?"

"I hope not Ali," Jason said. "Eventually, I suppose we'll find the answers. In the meantime, we are stuck," he admitted. "Nevertheless, we don't want to miss this auction. Every art person of consequence will be there, and you know it would have been impossible to get tickets on our own," he said. Alouisha hit him with a pillow and stormed out of bed.

"Hey, come on," he implored. "Nothing is perfect. Our government sanctions sketchy policies such as Credit Default Swaps, TARP distributions filled with pork, bailouts to some and nothing for others, or CEO's being paid multi-million dollars bonuses with taxpayer's money. Yet we still want to be citizens, and be invited to the White House," he said, trying to persuade her to reduce her convictions, strengthen her profit motives, and attend the auction.

"I don't know if I can live with myself, if we don't tell the police. It's not right, Jason," she said.

"Sweetheart, you'll have your exhibition, and you'll become the next hot artist. You'll be able to support yourself with your work. It's everything you've ever wanted, and an opportunity like this may never happen again. Think of it this way, any guilty feelings you may have will be ameliorated by the satisfaction you will have from sharing your work with the public."

Jason's argument was good, but after discussing the ramifications, Alouisha was still not convinced. Neither of them sought the newly acquired power that had found its way to their doorstep. If they revealed the forgery, the repercussions would be staggering. They would reverberate exponentially around the world causing an art world earthquake, vilifying them and destroying their careers forever.

"How did this happen to me?" Alouisha could not let it go. "I feel as if I'm being drawn and quartered during an art execution."

"Ali, it will be okay. I promise," Jason said.

"Okay, we'll go to the auction. We'll see it firsthand and decide then, if we are going to take down the art world," she said.

Jason sighed and agreed.

They had standing room tickets in the rear behind a thick burgundy-velvet rope, which cordoned them off from the seated area reserved for paddle holders. Alouisha wiggled her way toward the front of the roped area for a better view. The world press, also roped off, stood nearby crowded together in steerage. They fidgeted constantly in the overheated, airless room impatient for the auction to begin, and ready to text the breaking news to their papers across the world.

"So much for appreciating the world press," Jason said, as he noticed how uncomfortable they appeared while suffering from proximity and jet lag. Jason calculated what percentage of the hammer price was directly attributed to the international press's auction coverage.

"It's surprising they are not treated as honored guests, or at the very least, given proper seats," he said. If it weren't for them, there would be very little art market buzz. They are the spin-doctors, not Damien Hirst with his little spin paintings. Why aren't they given more credit for strengthening the art market and adding value?" Jason expounded.

Alouisha squirmed and held firmly to her square footage of territorial domain. The watchful eye of the velvet gatekeepers kept them under strict surveillance. The future art careers of the young interns would be nonexistent if someone, not holding a paddle, were to slip out of the roped enclosure.

With the sacred transmutations—changing canvas into cash—about to begin, the dealers and collectors glinted more brilliantly than a night constellation. The room crackled like cold milk poured onto Rice Krispies.

"You have a great turnout," Classico told Morgan Carey, as they waited for the elevator.

"Everyone who could manage a ticket is here. What a mad house it has been. People called from all over the world asking for invitations and inventing extraordinary stories to gain access. They must think they will get rich by association—an osmosis of sorts. We needed a lot of vetting to separate substantial collectors from the dilettantes," said the Chairman.

"As always, you have done a brilliant job," Classico said.

"And thank you for allowing us to be your favored auction specialists. Let's find our seats. The sale is about to begin," Morgan Carey said.

They took the elevator to the second floor, stopping one last time at the top of the balcony to savor the stunning spectacle of guests who had traveled from all parts of the world, lured by the enduring power of art. They all clamored to find their seats.

This is the night; I can feel it. It will be great. Everything I have been through, will have been worth it after tonight's victory, Classico thought.

About to enter the private viewing room, he caught sight of Regina Bookman coming his way, escorted by her entourage of assistants and important collectors. Isadora Brioche chatted gaily to the men in the group. *Regina looked so attractive and vital,* he thought. Her self-confident bearing preceded her as she approached Classico to wish him luck. She too was awash in the glittering success of the evening, and was enjoying the lavish attention from so many attractive, rich people. Her tailgating entourage stayed in close range to feel the singe of fervor from the enormous quantities of cash soon to be spent.

"Henry, I am so glad to see you," she brush-kissed his cheek. She too was electrified and thrilled from the turnout. Just then, a man standing behind her who was talking to Isadora Brioche stepped to her side. "Henry, I'd like to introduce you to a friend of Isadora's and two of our most important new collectors from China, Mr. Huang Show and ..."

He did not hear the second name. Regina Bookman's voice trailed off into the dark matter—the black hole in the universe that sucked all life into the one-way abyss. Classico was deafened. The mute button on his remote control for social situations could not turn on the sound or turn off this horror film. The color drained from his face as a chill engulfed him. His body stiffened and like the trees in the Petrified Forest, he was without cover—defenseless and utterly exposed. One spark would destroy it all.

Chapter 49

The Auction

For major sales, Brandon Surge took the helm at the podium on Goodrich's stage. First, a strip of light broke through the slit in the dark velvet curtains. Then he appeared. His crusty static discharged like an electric probe. All exhales paused; unfinished sentences hung in mid-air.

His urgency defined the crucial nature of this sale and the future art markets worldwide. Would they recover from the plunging market of 2009? The dead year—the year art lost all footing, and prices slid faster than a sand dune in a desert storm. Many of the artists' careers followed; their work "burned" not by the sun, but by missing their reserve price. How many times since 2008 had Brandon Surge used the dreaded word—"passed?"

It had been expected. The stalwarts, AIG, Chrysler, and GM verged on bankruptcy, while America's entrepreneurial backbone trended toward extinction—the only products manufactured in America were financial documents. Why would anyone buy art when all real property was in free fall? The Democratic mindset reverted to survival mode— more spending by government.

Jason squeezed Alouisha's hand in a gesture of consolidation for their decision to attend the auction. Instead of returning his affection with her usual smile, she turned away from him toward the crowd. He did not know what she was about to do, and Alouisha was determined to keep it that way.

The tension rose in the hot room. The smell of unspent money triggered pheromone levels that rose to high alert. Bursting pallets of yet-to-be-spent cash, stuffed in pockets and purses around the room, wrestled for visibility. Alouisha could hear a shoelace being tied.

Then the gavel fell. That sweet plunk removed the keystone and freed the soon-to-be-cascading cash. Lot number one came on the block; the bidding began.

An electronic wall monitor converted bids into five different currencies simultaneously, mesmerizing Alouisha. The relentless onslaught of cash recorded in split-second intervals, erupted and punched nonstop like an electric stapler out of control. The avalanche of world currencies blasted through new price ceilings with each raised paddle. Numbers, fueled by unknown forces and faces, flew by with a median closing time of fifty-seconds.

Alouisha ripped the corners of the catalogue and counted three more pages to Picasso. She braced herself and rolled the torn pieces into small balls, flicking them on the floor. Her mind was made up. The harsh overhead lighting seemed spotlighted in her direction and glared unbearably. She raised her hand to shield her eyes, and shifted her weight from foot to foot. Suddenly, the crowd screamed wildly. The Giacometti bust sold for ten million dollars over the high estimate. A thunderous applause broke out, giving everyone an excuse to move. Rustling papers invaded the stillness.

"Why are they clapping so hard? This is not a curtain on Broadway or a winning touchdown. Why do people get so excited when someone spends a lot of money and Goodrich's profit margins increase? Don't they realize the artwork may never again be seen publicly for generations, if the purchaser chooses to stay anonymous?" Alouisha whispered.

"If art is the measure of passion for a culture, the stronger the reaction, the higher the sale price will be. Maybe, when someone bids up the price, they are expressing enthusiasm for free markets and democracy," Jason said, grinning and attempting to validate her opinion.

"I can see your point," she said.

Alouisha tried to keep calm by continuing one of their philosophical discussions, but to no avail. The F word kept rising in her throat. She glanced at the journalists; yes, they were close enough to hear. Inside her body, a ping-pong tournament played its final round. The Picasso moment came closer—faster—almost here. She had only to shout the F word and stop the sale; the journalists would take care of the rest.

She had not told Jason of her decision; she did not want to risk his persuading her otherwise. It was unnecessary to involve him in what she was about to do. They both did not need to be vilified by the art world. She alone would take responsibility for saying the word—the one word that would derail the sale and create global repercussions that would cost hundreds of millions of dollars in lost revenues.

Tomorrow her name would appear in newspapers throughout the world. She wished it could be under different circumstances, but no other options remained. Her conscience rattled like tin roofs in a hurricane and her heart thumped louder than an elephant's stampede. The terrible power she inadvertently acquired doused her with anguish; her insides felt like the bottom of a waterfall. Only two lots remained until the Picasso. Only two lots remained until the art world massacre. She would shout out the F word to the audience, loud enough for the press to hear, and loud enough to abort the auction. The hammer would remain suspended in mid-air. A sudden silence would engulf the room. Horrified, everyone would gasp in unison. Then, pandemonium would break loose, inciting full-blown chaos when Alouisha said the one word that would suck the air from the room—FORGERY.

Chapter 50

The F Word

Huang Show's gaze bore through Classico's armor of exhilaration. It penetrated as swiftly as a steel machete and instantly deflated Classico's confidence and his plan. The Classico urban myth peeled away in layers until he felt flayed—raw and exposed. Huang Show's imperious stare gripped Classico in a vise of tacit allegations—the irredeemable deed that needed vindication. His eyes widened as round as the full moon, and his blood surged like a mountain river in the spring.

Oh no, not now, not tonight; this can't be happening. What can I do? He scanned the hard drive of his mind for possible options to escape and delete the dreadful confrontation from his life and his memory.

Suddenly, Isadora Brioche sent Classico a divine ray of light transported by her smile and distributed by her quantum-energy field. Classico's plunging charisma reconnected with hers, and it pulled him back from collapsing into the free fall of incrimination.

"Oh, ... umm, how do you do, Mr. Show? So good to see you," he managed to utter the words.

Huang Show's steeled emotions offered scant acknowledgement; he nodded imperceptibly.

"Are you okay?" inquired Regina Bookman, noticing how pasty white he turned.

"Yes, very well thank you. It is just warm in here," he said, pulling on his collar. "You look divine tonight as always," he said, trying to appear normal and plan his next step.

If I could get out of here before Picasso goes on the block, I may have a chance. He won't try to kill me here, not in front of everyone. He'll probably wait until the sale is over and then take his shot. I've got to call Hans.

"Please, excuse me," he bowed slightly using Asian politesse. "I will be right back; I must phone a client."

He left the viewing room, found a quiet corner near the elevator, and turned to face the wall. "Hans, hello. I am in travel mode and will be leaving immediately for an urgent trip abroad. Please have my bags downstairs. I need you to get some envelopes from my safe. The combination is fastened to the underside of my top desk drawer. Open it according to the instructions you'll find with the combination, then remove the two large manila envelopes and the ledger book. I'll be home in ten minutes. Also, in the closet behind the dressing room, you'll find a mailing tube. Please have that in the foyer as well. Thank you, Hans." He paused as a wave of sadness fell upon him, knowing he may never see Hans again, or at the very least, not for a long time. He felt a tear well up, but he choked it back before it rolled to his mouth into a salty gumdrop. "You are a good man, Hans." Without saying goodbye, he hit call END.

He pushed his way through the crowded rooms down the staircase, out on to the street, and grabbed a taxi without waiting for the doorman's help.

That bastard Huang Show, why did he have to show up now? I thought I was finished with him. He's going to kill me if I stick around. I have to leave. There is no other choice. His heart jumped in his chest like a kid on a pogo stick. *Where can I go, where he won't find me?* He suddenly felt strangled and tugged at his collar. His head leaned against the window. It felt cool on his forehead; his hand covered his eyes. The darkness did not block his desperation.

"Where to mister?" the driver asked.

"Seventy-ninth and Fifth."

If I go to the police for protection, I'll need proof that Huang Show is connected to the Triads. Why else would Huang Show be implicated, and how would I know that he is trying to kill me, if he has not already made the attempt? If they take him in for questioning, he will shred my story into worthless scraps, reopening the previous investigation. And, because he is Regina's client, he will have credibility. Eventually, they will uncover the true motive for my China trip. I will be forced to disclose the whereabouts of the other copies. Eventually, Sinbad will get involved and testify that the Russian bought the Picasso.

His eyebrows almost reached his hairline; his eyes followed upwards as he bit his lower lip. *I am so screwed. I am facing jail or death. I would as soon die than to face the humiliation of prison.* "Damn it!" *What am I supposed to do? If I travel abroad, Huang Show will come after me and find me. I will always be looking over my shoulder. I can't live that way. If I stay and face the charges, they'll probably put me in a minimum-security prison; it can't be that bad.* He wiped his forehead and twirled his brow. *But, my art reputation will be excoriated forever. The disgrace would be unbearable.*

He smashed his fist into his opened hand, and tried to knock some sense into himself. *It's hopeless,* he concluded. *I may as well leave while I am still alive. I will be starting over. Damn, all those years I've spent digging myself out from the dirt fields of Beatrice, Nebraska. Everything was going so well. I almost had everything resolved. If only Huang Show hadn't turned up at the last moment.*

"Wait a minute," Classico blurted out.

"Which way now?" The driver turned to ask.

"No, not you driver." Classico's lips and fist tightened; his eyes lit up. *I still have the real Picasso and the bill of sales. This will be okay. I'll just stay away for a couple of years, until all is forgotten, and the other two Picasso's are safely enshrined in their owner's palaces away from the public's eye. Without the auction house's secret policies, I would never be able to sell it a third time and have a safe cover. Because Goodrich's is privately owned, they have no legal obligation to disclose the buyer's name, except under a court order. All the information regarding sales is strictly confidential, and that is the reason I chose Goodrich's over Conway's,* he reminded himself.

Hans can tell everyone that I am away on urgent business; Sinbad can make all the financial arrangements for the Apogee Art Fund. That's what I will do. Then, I'll stay undercover in Monte Carlo. Surely, I can find a way to change my identity and get in a witness protection program. Monaco is famous for harboring exiles ... I mean expatriates.

He pulled up to the front door of the gallery, past the Tibetan Monks protesting Chinese torture on the corner.

"They are always moving locations; don't they ever go home? Driver, we are going to Kennedy Airport. I am just collecting my bags; please keep the meter running."

"Good evening, Mr. Classico," said the security guard, opening the door of the taxi.

"Ah, yes, please get my bags and hurry. They're in the front hall." Impatiently, he got out of the taxi, stretched his legs and checked his watch; it was exactly 7:48 p.m.

The lot numbers flew faster than a hawk diving for his prey. Brandon Surge controlled the room with his iron-fisted intentions and a laser-sharp mind that corralled all thoughts to focus on the bidding. The entire room was enrapt as he seemed to draw, yet another bid, from thin air. Bidding for the Picasso began at $58 million, and the low estimate passed in 45 seconds; magically, he ratcheted up the tempo and the tension.

Jason squeezed Alouisha's hand encouraging her bravery, while acknowledging their guilty collusion. She remembered the first auction she attended with Mr. Classico, almost a year and a half ago. *Everything had changed since that day,* she thought, glancing at her designer pumps. She had been excited and hopeful about her new job, her career, and working with Mr. Classico. Her innocence had buoyed her along with a steadfast trust in the integrity of the art world, and her belief that talent took the highest honors. She winced when she thought of the blood-stained paintings. The ghoulish faces of the rapists flashed in her mind, causing the knot in her stomach to yank tautly like a swift kick. Lately, the images came less often. She wiped the beads of sweat from her temples with the back of her hand.

A year ago, she never would have imagined being in this room determined to take down the international art establishment. *How did this happen to me?* She asked herself one last time. Resurrecting her last drop of courage, Alouisha straightened her shoulders, thrust her chest forward, and took a deep breath. About to shout the F word, the microphone blared and cut her off.

"Do I hear $85 million?" The strident screech iced right through her, discharging a shiver of fear and crushing her resolve. The "word" stuck in her throat like a ball of cotton.

"Yes, over here, on the phone. Do I hear $88 million?" Brandon Surge implored. The audience held its breath. In utter astonishment, the oxygen-deprived attendees seemingly stuck in suspended animation, held still enough to hear the painting breath. Their eyes remained fixed on the monitor as the numbers careened out of control, flipping faster and faster, calculating the currencies with each new bid in two-million dollar increments. Two bidders remained, one in the audience and one on the phone. It was exactly 7:47 p.m..

For a few seconds, the bidding's momentum stalled. Brandon

Surge leaned in toward the audience; his elbow rested on the lectern. Appearing elastically elongated, he bent at the waist, and with his arms outstretched, he gesticulated into the air as if he were reeling in a new bid with an invisible line. He grasped and pulled in earnest. He tugged, encouraged, and beseeched the unseen bidders to forge ahead and distribute their millions. Then, wielding his authority by using eye contact as hardcore as a military deployment, he demanded—and received—yet, another bid.

A pause ... the weighted seconds hung heavy as sandbags. No one moved. If one thread of woven tension broke pattern, all weft and waft would crash and tangle making the bidding's further ascension unsustainable. Another bid came in from the telephone soldier—silence again. The only sound Alouisha heard was her beating heart.

Awe struck and stunned into silence, the audience was under the spell of the powerful cult leader of the international money machine; no one could breath. Alouisha opened her mouth, but the word did not come out. Her parched vocal cords denied emission, contradicting her intentions until she was about to burst. She could not override Brandon Surge's gripping hold on the house. His absolute control of the crowd rivaled that of any third-world leader whose artful intentions stimulated newly made fortunes, possibly straight from the money laundry.

"Do I hear $95 million? $95 million, that's $95 million," he said, the five raised an octave higher. The elegant crowd shouted and cheered as rambunctiously as if they were placing bets in a bar room brawl.

"Fair warning at 95 million dollars," said Brandon Surge. He paused, owning the seconds and used the silence as a weapon of intimation. No one dared breath or speak. He held the gavel—aggressively, threateningly, high in the air. The final blow would be fatal. When the rubber-band silence stretched thin, almost to breaking and could go no further ... .

It was exactly 7:49 p.m. Classico stepped out of the taxi to stretch his legs. On the corner nearest the gallery, one of the Tibetan Monks who protested torture by the Chinese, reached into his robe and pulled out a nine mm Beretta with a four-inch silencer attached. Classico took two in the back and crumpled to the floor. The guard, thinking Classico was having a heart attack, dropped the bags and ran to him.

The bogus monk approached, supposedly to offer help. But, as the guard bent to lift Classico, the monk plugged his head with a bullet. A second monk broke line and grabbed the mailing tube that contained the original Picasso.

It was exactly 7:49 p.m. at Goodrich's on May fourth 2010. The gavel slammed hard—underscoring the finality of the winning bid.

"On the telephone, sold, for 95 million dollars, Picasso's, *Marie Therese with Leaves and Bust*," Brandon Surge announced. And, with a full-body half twirl, he drew an upward arc with an invisible baton to punctuate this joyous moment.

It was the most expensive painting ever sold at auction. And where it will reside, no one in the Western world may ever know.

Author's Note

*"It is certain my conviction gains infinitely
the moment another soul will believe in it."*
-- Novalis

Throughout 2007, prices in the overheated global art markets hurtled past old benchmarks with each slam of the auctioneer's hammer. Newly minted hedge-fund billionaires competed for easily recognizable trophy pieces. Talented art consultants and dealers chose pivotal works in an artist's career that added scholarly depth to their clients growing collections. Others bought art to match the color of their sofas.

Sotheby's and Christie's combined art sales in 2007 totaled $2.7 billion. Unparalleled financial and visual rewards attracted a new group of players—the wealthy collectors from China, the ex-Soviet Republics, and the Gulf, who continued to drive prices through the stratosphere.

The twenty-first century witnessed a seismic shift in the global art markets. Qatar and Abu Dhabi, having unlimited resources from oil revenues, embarked on a bulk buying spree and snapped up the finest European and American artworks for the Qatar National Museum of Art and Abu Dhabi's new satellite museums, the Louvre and the Guggenheim.

The final fusion of art and commerce occurred in August 2007 when Damien Hirst, the mother of all branding masters, assembled a consortium of investors to buy his newest creation: a diamond-encrusted platinum skull from White Cube's Hoxton Square Gallery in London for fifty million pounds. International headlines reported that it was, "The highest price ever paid for a living artist's work." Pyramiding on the enormous publicity generated by the skull, Damien's global online empire hired 170 technicians to produce art, and a hundred-member sales force to sell art-branded T-shirts, books, posters, and skull-studded jeans.

Andreas Gursky's prescient and iconic photograph, *99 Cent II, Diptych* warned us of the encroaching banality inflicted by our consumer excesses. Every branded item on the grocery store shelves was blended into the same commonality—tiny, patterns of color waiting to be purchased. The view of Art Basel from the second floor of the Miami convention center has an eerie similarity.

In an ever-expanding quest to extend the boundaries of art to the periphery of "cutting-edge," a lurid mindset emerges, one that jars the senses like the florescent supermarket lights. It proclaims dead animals, vacuum cleaners, human excretions, used tampons, pornography, and body fluids all to be valid art mediums. The real talent, however, is to convince a dealer or curator that it is indeed art. One can only conclude:

The only "true-new" art form of the twenty-first century is— *MARKETING.*

About the Author

Rochelle Ohrstrom is a familiar figure in the New York art world in roles as diverse as artist, patron, and collector. Throughout her career, she has known many of its most fascinating figures. As a painter, she has had three works exhibited by *Lowry Simms*, the former contemporary curator of *The Metropolitan Museum of Art*. Her work has been collected by the Vassar and Syracuse Museums. When she was commissioned by *British Airways Concorde* to paint the experience of Super Sonic Flight, she flew in the cockpit for takeoff and landing. In the winters of 1976 through 1979, Rochelle was a guest artist of the Dominican Republic, where she painted many of the works featured in *Ponzi & Picasso*. As a collector, board member of museum committees, and major donor, she has spent time at the cutting-edge of art from Beijing to Tehran and Dubai. Ohrstrom was the first woman CEO of a nationally recognized advertising agency. She has also produced eight television shows and directed several commercials. When not traveling to places of extreme natural beauty, she resides and works in Manhattan. She has two adult children. *Ponzi & Picasso* is her first work of fiction. She is working on a sequel.